CONTENTS

Editorial Foreword   7

Acknowledgements   9

Thomas Hardy (1840–1928)
THE DISTRACTED PREACHER   11

Rudyard Kipling (1865–1936)
WILLIAM THE CONQUEROR   71

T. F. Powys (1875–1953)
THE BUCKET AND THE ROPE   105

E. M. Forster (1879–1970)
THE ROAD FROM COLONUS   113

James Joyce (1882–1941)
IVY DAY IN THE COMMITTEE ROOM   126

Virginia Woolf (1882–1941)
THE MARK ON THE WALL   142

D. H. Lawrence (1885–1930)
THE HORSE DEALER'S DAUGHTER   150

Katherine Mansfield (1888–1923)
FEUILLE D'ALBUM   168

Joyce Cary (1888–1957)
GOVERNMENT BABY   174

Robert Graves (1895–)
THE LOST CHINESE   194

V. S. Pritchett (1900–)
HANDSOME IS AS HANDSOME DOES   215

Graham Greene (1904–)
THE DESTRUCTORS   254

Angus Wilson (1913–)
AFTER THE SHOW   271

Muriel Spark (1918–   )
   YOU SHOULD HAVE SEEN THE MESS   301

Kingsley Amis (1922–   )
   INTERESTING THINGS   308

The Second Penguin Book
of
English Short Stories

EDITED BY
CHRISTOPHER DOLLEY

PENGUIN BOOKS

This selection first published by Penguin Books 1972

This selection copyright © Penguin Books Ltd, 1972
All rights reserved

Published by arrangement with the Penguin Group,
27 Wrights Lane, London W8 5TZ, England

Reprinted in the People's Republic of China
by the Foreign Languages Press 1989
in association with
the Chinese Literature Press and New World Press,
24 Baiwanzhuang Road, Beijing 100037, China

ISBN 7-119-00885-4/I·142

Not for sale outside the People's Republic of China

The Second Penguin Book of
English Short Stories
英国短篇小说精选（二）

本书第一版出版于 1972 年，前后已重印 15 次。编者在第一版前言中写道:《英国短篇小说精选（一）》出版后的五年中，有法国，意大利，美国等短篇小说集陆续问世，这表明短篇小说并没有衰退，而正欣欣向荣地发展。编者又说：本选集不仅编选英国已故作家的短篇小说最佳代表，而且力求向读者介绍更多的仍活跃在英国当今文坛上的名作家，包括格雷夫斯，普里特切特，格林，威尔逊，斯巴克和金斯莱·艾米斯等人。本书包括的 15 个短篇小说可代表这一文学品种的黄金时代。

外文出版社
中国文学出版社　出版
新世界出版社

EDITORIAL FOREWORD

IT is now five years since the first *Penguin Book of English Short Stories* appeared and during that time companion volumes containing French, Italian and American stories have appeared. Their publication has demonstrated that, far from continuing its supposed decline, the short story is enjoying a revival all the more encouraging when viewed against the gloom surrounding the future of the literary novel.

The first *Penguin Book of English Short Stories* set out to survey the history of the genre in its present form and inevitably the need for compression made the choice difficult. I am grateful therefore that this volume allows me to widen the range of authors representative of the best of English short story writing and at the same time to bring the selection forward in time so that it includes more writers who are still at the height of their powers.

C.D.

ACKNOWLEDGEMENTS

FOR permission to reprint the stories specified we are indebted to: the Trustees of the Hardy Estate, Macmillan & Co. Ltd and Macmillan Company of Canada for Thomas Hardy's 'The Distracted Preacher' from *Wessex Tales*;

Mrs George Bambridge and Macmillan & Co. Ltd for Rudyard Kipling's 'William the Conqueror' from *The Day's Work*;

Francis Powys Esq. and Chatto & Windus Ltd for T. F. Powys' 'The Bucket and the Rope' from *God's Eyes a' Twinkle*;

the Society of Authors on behalf of the Trustees of the Estate of E. M. Forster for 'The Road from Colonus' from E. M. Forster's *Collected Short Stories*;

the Executors of the James Joyce Estate and Jonathan Cape Ltd for James Joyce's 'Ivy Day in the Committee Room' from *Dubliners*;

the Literary Estate of Virginia Woolf and the Hogarth Press Ltd for Virginia Woolf's 'The Mark on the Wall' from *A Haunted House*;

Laurence Pollinger Ltd, the Estate of the late Mrs Frieda Lawrence and William Heinemann Ltd for D. H. Lawrence's 'The Horse Dealer's Daughter' from *The Complete Short Stories of D. H. Lawrence*;

the Society of Authors as the literary representative of the Estate of Katherine Mansfield for Katherine Mansfield's 'Feuille d'Album' from *Bliss and Other Stories*;

the Joyce Cary Estate for Joyce Cary's 'Government Baby' from *Spring Song and Other Stories*;

Robert Graves Esq. for his 'The Lost Chinese' from *The Collected Short Stories of Robert Graves*;

A. D. Peters & Co. and Chatto & Windus Ltd for V. S. Pritchett's 'Handsome Is As Handsome Does' from *The Saint and Other Stories*;

Graham Greene Esq. and William Heinemann Ltd for Graham Greene's 'The Destructors' from *Twenty-one Stories*;

Angus Wilson Esq. and Martin Secker & Warburg Ltd for Angus Wilson's 'After The Show' from *A Bit off the Map*;

Mrs Muriel Spark, Macmillan & Co. Ltd and J. B. Lippincott Company for Muriel Spark's 'You Should have Seen the Mess' from *The Go-away Bird and Other Stories*. Reprinted by permission

Thomas Hardy

THE DISTRACTED PREACHER

I · How his cold was cured

SOMETHING delayed the arrival of the Wesleyan minister, and a young man came temporarily in his stead. It was on the thirteenth of January 183– that Mr Stockdale, the young man in question, made his humble entry into the village, unknown, and almost unseen. But when those of the inhabitants who styled themselves of his connection became acquainted with him, they were rather pleased with the substitute than otherwise, though he had scarcely as yet acquired ballast of character sufficient to steady the consciences of the hundred-and-forty Methodists of pure blood who, at this time, lived in Nether-Moynton, and to give in addition supplementary support to the mixed race which went to church in the morning and chapel in the evening, or when there was a tea – as many as a hundred-and-ten people more, all told, and including the parish-clerk in the winter-time, when it was too dark for the vicar to observe who passed up the street at seven o'clock – which, to be just to him, he was never anxious to do.

It was owing to this overlapping of creeds that the celebrated population-puzzle arose among the denser gentry of the district around Nether-Moynton: how could it be that a parish containing fifteen score of strong full-grown Episcopalians, and nearly thirteen score of well-matured Dissenters, numbered barely two-and-twenty score adults in all?

The young man being personally interesting, those with whom he came in contact were content to waive for a while the graver question of his sufficiency. It is said that at this time of his life his eyes were affectionate, though without a ray of levity; that his hair was curly, and his figure tall; that he was, in short, a very lovable youth, who won upon his female hearers as soon as they saw and heard him, and caused them to say, 'Why didn't we know of this before he came, that we might have gi'ed him a warmer welcome!'

The fact was that, knowing him to be only provisionally selected, and expecting nothing remarkable in his person or doctrine, they and the rest of his flock in Nether-Moynton had felt almost as indifferent about his advent as if they had been the soundest churchgoing parishioners in the country, and he their true and appointed parson. Thus when Stockdale set foot in the place nobody had secured a lodging for him, and though his journey had given him a bad cold in the head he was forced to attend to that business himself. On inquiry he learnt that the only possible accommodation in the village would be found at the house of one Mrs Lizzy Newberry, at the upper end of the street.

It was a youth who gave this information, and Stockdale asked him who Mrs Newberry might be.

The boy said that she was a widow-woman, who had got no husband, because he was dead. Mr Newberry, he added, had been a well-to-do man enough, as the saying was, and a farmer; but he had gone off in a decline. As regarded Mrs Newberry's serious side, Stockdale gathered that she was one of the trimmers who went to church and chapel both.

'I'll go there,' said Stockdale, feeling that, in the absence of purely sectarian lodgings, he could do no better.

'She's a little particular, and won't hae gover'ment folks, or curates, or the pa'son's friends, or such like,' said the lad dubiously.

'Ah, that may be a promising sign: I'll call. Or no; just you go up and ask first if she can find room for me. I have to see one or two persons on another matter. You will find me down at the carrier's.'

In a quarter of an hour the lad came back, and said that Mrs Newberry would have no objection to accommodate him, whereupon Stockdale called at the house. It stood within a garden-hedge, and seemed to be roomy and comfortable. He saw an elderly woman, with whom he made arrangements to come the same night, since there was no inn in the place, and he wished to house himself as soon as possible; the village being a local centre from which he was to radiate at once to the different small chapels in the neighbourhood. He forthwith sent his luggage to Mrs Newberry's from the carrier's, where he had taken shelter, and in the evening walked up to his temporary home.

As he now lived there, Stockdale felt it unnecessary to knock at the door: and entering quietly he had the pleasure of hearing footsteps scudding away like mice into the back quarters. He advanced to the parlour, as the front room was called, though its stone floor was scarcely disguised by the carpet, which only overlaid the trodden areas, leaving sandy deserts under the furniture. But the room looked snug and cheerful. The firelight shone out brightly, trembling on the bulging mouldings of the table-legs, playing with brass knobs and handles, and lurking in great strength on the under surface of the chimney-piece. A deep arm-chair, covered with horsehair, and studded with a countless throng of brass nails, was pulled up on one side of the fireplace. The tea-things were on the table, the teapot cover was open, and a little handbell had been laid at that precise point towards which a person seated in the great chair might be expected instinctively to stretch his hand.

Stockdale sat down, not objecting to his experience of the room thus far, and began his residence by tinkling the bell. A little girl crept in at the summons, and made tea for him. Her name, she said, was Marther Sarer, and she lived out there, nodding towards the road and village generally. Before Stockdale had got far with his meal a tap sounded on the door behind him, and on his telling the inquirer to come in, a rustle of garments caused him to turn his head. He saw before him a fine and extremely well-made young woman, with dark hair, a wide, sensible, beautiful forehead, eyes that warmed him before he knew it, and a mouth that was in itself a picture to all appreciative souls.

'Can I get you anything else for tea?' she said, coming forward a step or two, an expression of liveliness on her features, and her hand waving the door by its edge.

'Nothing, thank you,' said Stockdale, thinking less of what he replied than of what might be her relation to the household.

'You are quite sure?' said the young woman, apparently aware that he had not considered his answer.

He conscientiously examined the tea-things, and found them all there. 'Quite sure, Miss Newberry,' he said.

'It is Mrs Newberry,' she said. 'Lizzy Newberry. I used to be Lizzy Simpkins.'

'O, I beg your pardon, Mrs Newberry.' And before he had occasion to say more she left the room.

Stockdale remained in some doubt till Martha Sarah came to clear the table. 'Whose house is this, my little woman?' said he.

'Mrs Lizzy Newberry's, sir.'

'Then Mrs Newberry is not the old lady I saw this afternoon?'

'No. That's Mrs Newberry's mother. It was Mrs Newberry who comed in to you just by now, because she wanted to see if you was good-looking.'

Later in the evening, when Stockdale was about to begin supper, she came again. 'I have come myself, Mr Stockdale,' she said. The minister stood up in acknowledgement of the honour. 'I am afraid little Marther might not make you understand. What will you have for supper? – there's cold rabbit, and there's a ham uncut.'

Stockdale said he could get on nicely with those viands, and supper was laid. He had no more than cut a slice when tap-tap came to the door again. The minister had already learnt that this particular rhythm in taps denoted the fingers of his enkindling landlady, and the doomed young fellow buried his first mouthful under a look of receptive blandness.

'We have a chicken in the house, Mr Stockdale – I quite forgot to mention it just now. Perhaps you would like Marther Sarer to bring it up?'

Stockdale had advanced far enough in the art of being a young man to say that he did not want the chicken, unless she brought it up herself: but when it was uttered he blushed at the daring gallantry of the speech, perhaps a shade too strong for a serious man and a minister. In three minutes the chicken appeared, but, to his great surprise, only in the hands of Martha Sarah. Stockdale was disappointed, which perhaps it was intended that he should be.

He had finished supper, and was not in the least anticipating Mrs Newberry again that night, when she tapped and entered as before. Stockdale's gratified look told that she had lost nothing by not appearing when expected. It happened that the cold in his head from which the young man suffered had increased with the approach of night, and before she had spoken he was seized with a violent fit of sneezing which he could not anyhow repress.

Mrs Newberry looked full of pity. 'Your cold is very bad tonight, Mr Stockdale.'

Stockdale replied that it was rather troublesome.

'And I've a good mind –' she added archly, looking at the cheerless glass of water on the table, which the abstemious minister was going to drink.

'Yes, Mrs Newberry?'

'I've a good mind that you should have something more likely to cure it than that cold stuff.'

'Well,' said Stockdale, looking down at the glass, 'as there is no inn here, and nothing better to be got in the village, of course it will do.'

To this she replied, 'There is something better, not far off, though not in the house. I really think you must try it, or you may be ill. Yes, Mr Stockdale, you shall.' She held up her finger, seeing that he was about to speak. 'Don't ask what it is; wait, and you shall see.'

Lizzy went away, and Stockdale waited in a pleasant mood. Presently she returned with her bonnet and cloak on, saying, 'I am so sorry, but you must help me to get it. Mother has gone to bed. Will you wrap yourself up, and come this way, and please bring that cup with you?'

Stockdale, a lonely young fellow, who had for weeks felt a great craving for somebody on whom to throw away superfluous interest, and even tenderness, was not sorry to join her; and followed his guide through the back door, across the garden, to the bottom, where the boundary was a wall. This wall was low, and beyond it Stockdale discerned in the night shades several grey headstones, and the outlines of the church roof and tower.

'It is easy to get up this way,' she said, stepping upon a bank which abutted on the wall; then putting her foot on the top of the stonework, and descending by a spring inside, where the ground was much higher, as is the manner of graveyards to be. Stockdale did the same, and followed her in the dusk across the irregular ground till they came to the tower door, which, when they had entered, she softly closed behind them.

'You can keep a secret?' she said, in a musical voice.

'Like an iron chest!' said he fervently.

Then from under her cloak she produced a small lighted lantern, which the minister had not noticed that she carried at all. The light showed them to be close to the singing-gallery stairs, under which lay a heap of lumber of all sorts, but consisting mostly of decayed framework, pews, panels, and pieces of flooring, that from time to time had been removed from their original fixings in the body of the edifice and replaced by new.

'Perhaps you will drag some of those boards aside?' she said, holding the lantern over her head to light him better. 'Or will you take the lantern while I move them?'

'I can manage it,' said the young man, and acting as she ordered, he uncovered, to his surprise, a row of little barrels bound with wood hoops, each barrel being about as large as the nave of a heavy waggon-wheel. When they were laid open Lizzy fixed her eyes on him, as if she wondered what he would say.

'You know what they are?' she asked, finding that he did not speak.

'Yes, barrels,' said Stockdale simply. He was an inland man, the son of highly respectable parents, and brought up with a single eye to the ministry; and the sight suggested nothing beyond the fact that such articles were there.

'You are quite right, they are barrels,' she said, in an

emphatic tone of candour that was not without a touch of irony.

Stockdale looked at her with an eye of sudden misgiving. 'Not smugglers' liquor?' he said.

'Yes,' said she. 'They are tubs of spirit that have accidentally floated over in the dark from France.'

In Nether-Moynton and its vicinity at this date people always smiled at the sort of sin called in the outside world illicit trading; and these little kegs of gin and brandy were as well known to the inhabitants as turnips. So that Stockdale's innocent ignorance, and his look of alarm when he guessed the sinister mystery, seemed to strike Lizzy first as ludicrous, and then as very awkward for the good impression that she wished to produce upon him.

'Smuggling is carried on here by some of the people,' she said in a gentle, apologetic voice. 'It has been their practice for generations, and they think it no harm. Now, will you roll out one of the tubs?'

'What to do with it?' said the minister.

'To draw a little from it to cure your cold,' she answered. 'It is so 'nation strong that it drives away that sort of thing in a jiffy. O, it is all right about our taking it. I may have what I like; the owner of the tubs says so. I ought to have had some in the house, and then I shouldn't ha' been put to this trouble; but I drink none myself, and so I often forget to keep it indoors.'

'You are allowed to help yourself, I suppose, that you may not inform where their hiding-place is?'

'Well, no; not that particularly; but I may take any if I want it. So help yourself.'

'I will, to oblige you, since you have a right to it,' murmured the minister; and though he was not quite satisfied with his part in the performance, he rolled one of the 'tubs' out from the corner into the middle of the tower floor. 'How do you wish me to get it out – with a gimlet, I suppose?'

'No, I'll show you,' said his interesting companion; and she held up with her other hand a shoemaker's awl and a hammer.

'You must never do these things with a gimlet, because the wood-dust gets in; and when the buyers pour out the brandy that would tell them that the tub had been broached. An awl makes no dust, and the hole nearly closes up again. Now tap one of the hoops forward.'

Stockdale took the hammer and did so.

'Now make the hole in the part that was covered by the hoop.'

He made the hole as directed. 'It won't run out,' he said.

'O yes it will,' said she. 'Take the tub between your knees, and squeeze the heads; and I'll hold the cup.'

Stockdale obeyed; and the pressure taking effect upon the tub, which seemed to be thin, the spirit spirted out in a stream. When the cup was full he ceased pressing, and the flow immediately stopped. 'Now we must fill up the keg with water,' said Lizzy, 'or it will cluck like forty hens when it is handled, and show that 'tis not full.'

'But they tell you you may take it?'

'Yes, the *smugglers*; but the *buyers* must not know that the smugglers have been kind to me at their expense.'

'I see,' said Stockdale doubtfully. 'I much question the honesty of this proceeding.'

By her direction he held the tub with the hole upwards, and while he went through the process of alternately pressing and ceasing to press, she produced a bottle of water, from which she took mouthfuls, conveying each to the keg by putting her pretty lips to the hole, where it was sucked in at each recovery of the cask from pressure. When it was again full he plugged the hole, knocked the hoop down to its place, and buried the tub in the lumber as before.

'Aren't the smugglers afraid that you will tell?' he asked, as they recrossed the churchyard.

'O no; they are not afraid of that. I couldn't do such a thing.'

'They have put you into a very awkward corner,' said Stockdale emphatically. 'You must, of course, as an honest person, sometimes feel that it is your duty to inform – really you must.'

'Well, I have never particularly felt it as a duty; and, besides, my first husband –' She stopped, and there was some confusion in her voice. Stockdale was so honest and unsophisticated that he did not at once discern why she paused: but at last he did perceive that the words were a slip, and that no woman would have uttered 'first husband' by accident unless she had thought pretty frequently of a second. He felt for her confusion, and allowed her time to recover and proceed. 'My husband,' she said, in a self-corrected tone, 'used to know of their doings, and so did my father, and kept the secret. I cannot inform, in fact, against anybody.'

'I see the hardness of it,' he continued, like a man who looked far into the moral of things. 'And it is very cruel that you should be tossed and tantalized between your memories and your conscience. I do hope, Mrs Newberry, that you will soon see your way out of this unpleasant position.'

'Well, I don't just now,' she murmured.

By this time they had passed over the wall and entered the house, where she brought him a glass and hot water, and left him to his own reflections. He looked after her vanishing form, asking himself whether he, as a respectable man, and a minister, and a shining light, even though as yet only of the halfpenny-candle sort, were quite justified in doing this thing. A sneeze settled the question; and he found that when the fiery liquor was lowered by the addition of twice or thrice the quantity of water, it was one of the prettiest cures for a cold in the head that he had ever known, particularly at this chilly time of year.

Stockdale sat in the deep chair about twenty minutes sipping and meditating, till he at length took warmer views of things, and longed for the morrow, when he would see Mrs Newberry again. He then felt that, though chronologically at a short distance, it would in an emotional sense be very long before tomorrow came, and walked restlessly round the room. His eye was attracted by a framed and glazed sampler in which a running ornament of fir-trees and peacocks surrounded the following pretty bit of sentiment:

Rose-leaves smell when roses thrive,
Here's my work while I'm alive;
Rose-leaves smell when shrunk and shed,
Here's my work when I am dead.

Lizzy Simpkins. Fear God. Honour the King.
Aged 11 years.

''Tis hers,' he said to himself. 'Heavens, how I like that name!'

Before he had done thinking that no other name from Abigail to Zenobia would have suited his young landlady so well, tap-tap came again upon the door; and the minister started as her face appeared yet another time, looking so disinterested that the most ingenious would have refrained from asserting that she had come to affect his feelings by her seductive eyes.

'Would you like a fire in your room, Mr Stockdale, on account of your cold?'

The minister, being still a little pricked in the conscience for countenancing her in watering the spirits, saw here a way to self-chastisement. 'No, I thank you,' he said firmly; 'it is not necessary. I have never been used to one in my life, and it would be giving way to luxury too far.'

'Then I won't insist,' she said, and disconcerted him by vanishing instantly.

Wondering if she was vexed by his refusal, he wished that he had chosen to have a fire, even though it should have scorched him out of bed and endangered his self-discipline for a dozen days. However, he consoled himself with what was in truth a rare consolation for a budding lover, that he was under the same roof with Lizzy; her guest, in fact, to take a poetical view of the term lodger; and that he would certainly see her on the morrow.

The morrow came, and Stockdale rose early, his cold quite gone. He had never in his life so longed for the breakfast hour as he did that day, and punctually at eight o'clock, after a short walk to reconnoitre the premises, he re-entered the door of his dwelling. Breakfast passed, and Martha Sarah attended, but nobody came voluntarily as on the night before to inquire if there were other wants which he had not mentioned, and which she would attempt to gratify. He was disappointed, and went out, hoping to see her at dinner. Dinner time came; he sat down to the meal, finished it, lingered on for a whole hour, although two new teachers were at that moment waiting at the chapel-door to speak to him by appointment. It was useless to wait longer, and he slowly went his way down the lane, cheered by the thought that, after all, he would see her in the evening, and perhaps engage again in the delightful tub-broaching in the neighbouring church tower, which proceeding he resolved to render more moral by steadfastly insisting that no water should be introduced to fill up, though the tub should cluck like all the hens in Christendom. But nothing could disguise the fact that it was a queer business; and his countenance fell when he thought how much more his mind was interested in that matter than in his serious duties.

However, compunction vanished with the decline of day. Night came, and his tea and supper; but no Lizzy Newberry, and no sweet temptations. At last the minister could bear it no longer, and said to his quaint little attendant, 'Where is Mrs Newberry today?' judiciously handing a penny as he spoke.

'She's busy,' said Martha.

'Anything serious happened?' he asked, handing another penny, and revealing yet additional pennies in the background.

'O no – nothing at all!' said she, with breathless confidence. 'Nothing ever happens to her. She's only biding upstairs in bed because 'tis her way sometimes.'

Being a young man of some honour he would not question further, and assuming that Lizzy must have a bad headache, or other slight ailment, in spite of what the girl had said, he went to bed dissatisfied, not even setting eyes on old Mrs Simpkins. 'I said last night that I should see her tomorrow,' he reflected; 'but that was not to be!'

Next day he had better fortune, or worse, meeting her at the foot of the stairs in the morning, and being favoured by a visit or two from her during the day – once for the purpose of making kindly inquiries about his comfort, as on the first evening, and at another time to place a bunch of winter violets on his table, with a promise to renew them when they drooped. On these occasions there was something in her smile which showed how conscious she was of the effect she produced, though it must be said that it was rather a humorous than a designing consciousness, and savoured more of pride than of vanity.

As for Stockdale, he clearly perceived that he possessed unlimited capacity for backsliding, and wished that tutelary saints were not denied to Dissenters. He set a watch upon his tongue and eyes for the space of one hour and a half, after which he found it was useless to struggle further, and gave himself up to the situation. 'The other minister will be here in a month,' he said to himself when sitting over the fire. 'Then I shall be off, and she will distract my mind no more! ... And then, shall I go on living by myself for ever? No; when my two years of probation are finished, I shall have a furnished house to live in, with a varnished door and a brass knocker; and I'll march straight back to her, and ask her flat, as soon as the last plate is on the dresser!'

Thus a titillating fortnight was passed by young Stockdale, during which time things proceeded much as such matters have done ever since the beginning of history. He saw the object of attachment several times one day, did not see her at all the next, met her when he least expected to do so, missed her when hints and signs as to where she should be at a given hour almost amounted to an appointment. This mild coquetry was perhaps fair enough under the circumstances of their being so closely lodged, and Stockdale put up with it as philosophically as he was able. Being in her own house she could, after vexing him or disappointing him of her presence, easily win him back by suddenly surrounding him with those little attentions which her position as his landlady put it in her power to bestow. When he had waited indoors half the day to see her, and on finding that she would not be seen, had gone off in a huff to the dreariest and dampest walk he could discover, she would restore equilibrium in the evening with 'Mr

Stockdale, I have fancied you must feel draught o' nights from your bedroom window, and so I have been putting up thicker curtains this afternoon while you were out'; or, 'I noticed that you sneezed twice again this morning, Mr Stockdale. Depend upon i t that cold is hanging about you yet; I am sure it is – I have thought of it continually; and you must let me make a posset for you.'

Sometimes in coming home he found his sitting-room rearranged, chairs placed where the table had stood, and the table ornamented with the few fresh flowers and leaves that could be obtained at this season, so as to add a novelty to the room. At times she would be standing on a chair outside the house, trying to nail up a branch of the monthly rose which the winter wind had blown down; and of course he stepped forward to assist her, when their hands got mixed in passing the shreds and nails. Thus they became friends again after a disagreement. She would utter on these occasions some pretty and deprecatory remark on the necessity of her troubling him anew; and he would straightway say that he would do a hundred times as much for her if she should so require.

2 · How he saw two other men

Matters being in this advanced state, Stockdale was rather surprised one cloudy evening, while sitting in his room, at hearing her speak in low tones of expostulation to some one at the door. It was nearly dark, but the shutters were not yet closed, nor the candles lighted; and Stockdale was tempted to stretch his head towards the window. He saw outside the door a young man in clothes of a whitish colour, and upon reflection judged their wearer to be the well-built and rather handsome miller who lived below. The miller's voice was alternately low and firm, and sometimes it reached the level of positive entreaty; but what the words were Stockdale could in no way hear.

Before the colloquy had ended, the minister's attention was

attracted by a second incident. Opposite Lizzy's home grew a clump of laurels, forming a thick and permanent shade. One of the laurel boughs now quivered against the light background of sky, and in a moment the head of a man peered out, and remained still. He seemed to be also much interested in the conversation at the door, and was plainly lingering there to watch and listen. Had Stockdale stood in any other relation to Lizzy than that of a lover, he might have gone out and investigated the meaning of this: but being as yet but an unprivileged ally, he did nothing more than stand up and show himself against the firelight, whereupon the listener disappeared, and Lizzy and the miller spoke in lower tones.

Stockdale was made so uneasy by the circumstance, that as soon as the miller was gone, he said, 'Mrs Newberry, are you aware that you were watched just now, and your conversation heard?'

'When?' she said.

'When you were talking to that miller. A man was looking from the laurel-tree as jealously as if he could have eaten you.'

She showed more concern than the trifling event seemed to demand, and he added, 'Perhaps you were talking of things you did not wish to be overheard?'

'I was talking only on business,' she said.

'Lizzy, be frank!' said the young man. 'If it was only on business, why should anybody wish to listen to you?'

She looked curiously at him. 'What else do you think it could be, then?'

'Well – the only talk between a young woman and man that is likely to amuse an eavesdropper.'

'Ah yes,' she said, smiling in spite of her preoccupation. 'Well, my cousin Owlett has spoken to me about matrimony, every now and then, that's true; but he was not speaking of it then. I wish he had been speaking of it, with all my heart. It would have been much less serious for me.'

'O Mrs Newberry!'

'It would. Not that I should ha' chimed in with him, of course. I wish it for other reasons. I am glad, Mr Stockdale, that you have told me of that listener. It is a timely warning, and I must see my cousin again.'

'But don't go away till I have spoken,' said the minister. 'I'll out with it at once, and make no more ado. Let it be Yes or No between us, Lizzy; please do!' And he held out his hand, in which she freely allowed her own to rest, but without speaking.

'You mean Yes by that?' he asked, after waiting a while.

'You may be my sweetheart, if you will.'

'Why not say at once you will wait for me until I have a house and can come back to marry you.'

'Because I am thinking – thinking of something else,' she said with embarrassment. 'It all comes upon me at once, and I must settle one thing at a time.'

'At any rate, dear Lizzy, you can assure me that the miller shall not be allowed to speak to you except on business? You have never directly encouraged him?'

She parried the question by saying, 'You see, he and his party have been in the habit of leaving things on my premises sometimes, and as I have not denied him, it makes him rather forward.'

'Things – what things?'

'Tubs – they are called Things here.'

'But why don't you deny him, my dear Lizzy?'

'I cannot well.'

'You are too timid. It is unfair of him to impose so upon you, and get your good name into danger by his smuggling tricks. Promise me that the next time he wants to leave his tubs here you will let me roll them into the street?'

She shook her head. 'I would not venture to offend the neighbours so much as that,' said she, 'or do anything that would be so likely to put poor Owlett into the hands of the Customs-men.'

Stockdale sighed, and said that he thought hers a mistaken generosity when it extended to assisting those who cheated the king of his dues. 'At any rate, you will let me make him keep his distance as your lover, and tell him flatly that you are not for him?'

'Please not, at present,' she said. 'I don't wish to offend my old neighbours. It is not only Mr Owlett who is concerned.'

'This is too bad,' said Stockdale impatiently.

'On my honour, I won't encourage him as my lover,' Lizzy answered earnestly. 'A reasonable man will be satisfied with that.'

'Well, so I am,' said Stockdale, his countenance clearing.

3 · The mysterious greatcoat

Stockdale now began to notice more particularly a feature in the life of his fair landlady which he had casually observed but scarcely ever thought of before. It was that she was markedly irregular in her hours of rising. For a week or two she would be tolerably punctual, reaching the ground-floor within a few minutes of half past seven. Then suddenly she would not be visible till twelve at noon, perhaps for three or four days in succession; and twice he had certain proof that she did not leave the room till half past three in the afternoon. The second time that this extreme lateness came under his notice was on a day when he had particularly wished to consult with her about his future movements; and he concluded, as he always had done, that she had a cold, headache, or other ailment, unless she had kept herself invisible to avoid meeting and talking to him, which he could hardly believe. The former supposition was disproved, however, by her innocently saying, some days later, when they were speaking on a question of health, that she had never had a moment's heaviness, headache, or illness of any kind since the previous January twelvemonth.

'I am glad to hear it,' said he. 'I thought quite otherwise.'

'What, do I look sickly?' she asked, turning up her face to show the impossibility of his gazing on it and holding such a belief for a moment.

'Not at all; I merely thought so from your being sometimes obliged to keep your room through the best part of the day.'

'O, as for that – it means nothing,' she murmured, with a look which some might have called cold, and which was the worst look that he liked to see upon her. 'It is pure sleepiness, Mr Stockdale.'

'Never!'

'It is, I tell you. When I stay in my room till half past three in the afternoon, you may always be sure that I slept soundly till three, or I shouldn't have stayed there.'

'It is dreadful,' said Stockdale, thinking of the disastrous effects of such indulgence upon the household of a minister, should it become a habit of everyday occurrence.

'But then,' she said, divining his good and prescient thoughts, 'it only happens when I stay awake all night. I don't go to sleep till five or six in the morning sometimes.'

'Ah, that's another matter,' said Stockdale. 'Sleeplessness to such an alarming extent is real illness. Have you spoken to a doctor?'

'O no – there is no need for doing that – it is all natural to me.' And she went away without further remark.

Stockdale might have waited a long time to know the real cause of her sleeplessness, had it not happened that one dark night he was sitting in his bedroom jotting down notes for a sermon, which occupied him perfunctorily for a considerable time after the other members of the household had retired. He did not get to bed till one o'clock. Before he had fallen asleep he heard a knocking at the front door, first rather timidly performed, and then louder. Nobody answered it, and the person knocked again. As the house still remained undisturbed, Stockdale got out of bed, went to his window, which overlooked the door, and opening it, asked who was there.

A young woman's voice replied that Susan Wallis was there, and that she had come to ask if Mrs Newberry could give her some mustard to make a plaster with, as her father was taken very ill on the chest.

The minister, having neither bell nor servant, was compelled to act in person. 'I will call Mrs Newberry,' he said. Partly dressing himself, he went along the passage and tapped at

Lizzy's door. She did not answer, and, thinking of her erratic habits in the matter of sleep, he thumped the door persistently, when he discovered, by its moving ajar under his knocking, that it had only been gently pushed to. As there was now a sufficient entry for the voice, he knocked no longer, but said in firm tones, 'Mrs Newberry, you are wanted.'

The room was quite silent; not a breathing, not a rustle, came from any part of it. Stockdale now sent a positive shout through the open space of the door: 'Mrs Newberry!' – still no answer, or movement of any kind within. Then he heard sounds from the opposite room, that of Lizzy's mother, as if she had been aroused by his uproar though Lizzy had not, and was dressing herself hastily. Stockdale softly closed the younger woman's door and went to the other, which was opened by Mrs Simpkins before he could reach it. She was in her ordinary clothes, and had a light in her hand.

'What's the person calling about?' she said in alarm.

Stockdale told the girl's errand, adding seriously, 'I cannot wake Mrs Newberry.'

'It is no matter,' said her mother. 'I can let the girl have what she wants as well as my daughter.' And she came out of the room and went downstairs.

Stockdale retired towards his own apartment, saying, however, to Mrs Simpkins from the landing, as if on second thoughts, 'I suppose there is nothing the matter with Mrs Newberry, that I could not wake her?'

'O no,' said the old lady hastily. 'Nothing at all.'

Still the minister was not satisfied. 'Will you go in and see?' he said. 'I should be much more at ease.'

Mrs Simpkins returned up the staircase, went to her daughter's room, and came out again almost instantly. 'There is nothing at all the matter with Lizzy,' she said; and descended again to attend to the applicant, who, having seen the light, had remained quiet during this interval.

Stockdale went into his room and lay down as before. He heard Lizzy's mother open the front door, admit the girl, and then the murmured discourse of both as they went to the store-cupboard for the medicament required. The girl

departed, the door was fastened, Mrs Simpkins came upstairs,
and the house was again in silence. Still the minister did not fall
asleep. He could not get rid of a singular suspicion, which was
all the more harassing in being, if true, the most unaccountable
thing within his experience. That Lizzy Newberry was in her
bedroom when he made such a clamour at the door he could
not possibly convince himself, notwithstanding that he had
heard her come upstairs at the usual time, go into her chamber,
and shut herself up in the usual way. Yet all reason was so
much against her being elsewhere, that he was constrained to
go back again to the unlikely theory of a heavy sleep, though
he had heard neither breath nor movement during a shouting
and knocking loud enough to rouse the Seven Sleepers.

Before coming to any positive conclusion he fell asleep
himself, and did not awake till day. He saw nothing of Mrs
Newberry in the morning, before he went out to meet the
rising sun, as he liked to do when the weather was fine; but as
this was by no means unusual, he took no notice of it. At
breakfast-time he knew that she was not far off by hearing her
in the kitchen, and though he saw nothing of her person, that
back apartment being rigorously closed against his eyes, she
seemed to be talking, ordering, and bustling about among the
pots and skimmers in so ordinary a manner, that there was no
reason for his wasting more time in fruitless surmise.

The minister suffered from these distractions, and his
extemporized sermons were not improved thereby. Already he
often said Romans for Corinthians in the pulpit, and gave
out hymns in strange cramped metres, that hitherto had
always been skipped, because the congregation could not
raise a tune to fit them. He fully resolved that as soon as his few
weeks of stay approached their end he would cut the matter
short, and commit himself by proposing a definite engagement, repenting at leisure if necessary.

With this end in view, he suggested to her on the evening
after her mysterious sleep that they should take a walk together just before dark, the latter part of the proposition being
introduced that they might return home unseen. She consented
to go; and away they went over a stile, to a shrouded footpath

suited for the occasion. But, in spite of attempts on both sides, they were unable to infuse much spirit into the ramble. She looked rather paler than usual, and sometimes turned her head away.

'Lizzy,' said Stockdale reproachfully, when they had walked in silence a long distance.

'Yes,' said she.

'You yawned – much my company is to you!' He put it in that way, but he was really wondering whether her yawn could possibly have more to do with physical weariness from the night before than mental weariness of that present moment. Lizzy apologized, and owned that she was rather tired, which gave him an opening for a direct question on the point; but his modesty would not allow him to put it to her; and he uncomfortably resolved to wait.

The month of February passed with alternations of mud and frost, rain and sleet, east winds and north-westerly gales. The hollow places in the ploughed fields showed themselves as pools of water, which had settled there from the higher levels, and had not yet found time to soak away. The birds began to get lively, and a single thrush came just before sunset each evening, and sang hopefully on the large elm-tree which stood nearest to Mrs Newberry's house. Cold blasts and brittle earth had given place to an oozing dampness more unpleasant in itself than frost; but it suggested coming spring, and its unpleasantness was of a bearable kind.

Stockdale had been going to bring about a practical understanding with Lizzy at least half a dozen times; but, what with the mystery of her apparent absence on the night of the neighbour's call, and her curious way of lying in bed at unaccountable times, he felt a check within him whenever he wanted to speak out. Thus they still lived on as indefinitely affianced lovers, each of whom hardly acknowledged the other's claim to the name of chosen one. Stockdale persuaded himself that his hesitation was owing to the postponement of the ordained minister's arrival, and the consequent delay in his own departure, which did away with all necessity for haste in his courtship; but perhaps it was only that his discretion was reasserting itself, and telling him that he had better get clearer ideas of Lizzy before arranging for the grand contract of his life with her. She, on her part, always seemed ready to be urged further on that question than he had hitherto attempted to go; but she was none the less independent, and to a degree which would have kept from flagging the passion of a far more mutable man.

On the evening of the first of March he went casually into his bedroom about dusk, and noticed lying on a chair a greatcoat, hat, and breeches. Having no recollection of leaving any clothes of his own in that spot, he went and examined them as well as he could in the twilight, and found that they did not belong to him. He paused for a moment to consider how they might have got there. He was the only man living in the house; and yet these were not his garments, unless he had made a mistake. No, they were not his. He called up Martha Sarah.

'How did these things come in my room?' he said, flinging the objectionable articles on the floor.

Martha said that Mrs Newberry had given them to her to brush, and that she had brought them up there thinking they must be Mr Stockdale's, as there was no other gentleman a-lodging there.

'Of course you did,' said Stockdale. 'Now take them down to your mis'ess, and say they are some clothes I have found here and know nothing about.'

As the door was left open he heard the conversation downstairs. 'How stupid!' said Mrs Newberry, in a tone of confusion. 'Why, Marther Sarer, I did not tell you to take 'em to Mr Stockdale's room?'

'I thought they must be his as they was so muddy,' said Martha humbly.

'You should have left 'em on the clothes-horse,' said the young mistress severely; and she came upstairs with the garments on her arm, quickly passed Stockdale's room, and threw them forcibly into a closet at the end of a passage. With this the incident ended, and the house was silent again.

There would have been nothing remarkable in finding such

clothes in a widow's house had they been clean; or moth-eaten, or creased, or mouldy from long lying by; but that they should be splashed with recent mud bothered Stockdale a good deal. When a young pastor is in the aspen stage of attachment, and open to agitation at the merest trifles, a really substantial incongruity of this complexion is a disturbing thing. However, nothing further occurred at that time; but he became watchful, and given to conjecture, and was unable to forget the circumstance.

One morning, on looking from his window, he saw Mrs Newberry herself brushing the tails of a long drab greatcoat, which, if he mistook not, was the very same garment as the one that adorned the chair of his room. It was densely splashed up to the hollow of the back with neighbouring Nether-Moynton mud, to judge by its colour, the spots being distinctly visible to him in the sunlight. The previous day or two having been wet, the inference was irresistible that the wearer had quite recently been walking some considerable distance about the lanes and fields. Stockdale opened the window and looked out, and Mrs Newberry turned her head. Her face became slowly red; she never had looked prettier, or more incomprehensible. He waved his hand affectionately, and said good-morning; she answered with embarrassment, having ceased her occupation on the instant that she saw him, and rolled up the coat half-cleaned.

Stockdale shut the window. Some simple explanation of her proceeding was doubtless within the bounds of possibility; but he himself could not think of one; and he wished that she had placed the matter beyond conjecture by voluntarily saying something about it there and then.

But, though Lizzy had not offered an explanation at the moment, the subject was brought forward by her at the next time of their meeting. She was chatting to him concerning some other event, and remarked that it happened about the time when she was dusting some old clothes that had belonged to her poor husband.

'You keep them clean out of respect to his memory?' said Stockdale tentatively.

'I air and dust them sometimes,' she said, with the most charming innocence in the world.

'Do dead men come out of their graves and walk in mud?' murmured the minister, in a cold sweat at the deception that she was practising.

'What did you say?' asked Lizzy.

'Nothing, nothing,' said he mournfully. 'Mere words – a phrase that will do for my sermon next Sunday.' It was too plain that Lizzy was unaware that he had seen fresh pedestrian splashes upon the skirts of the tell-tale overcoat, and that she imagined him to believe it had come direct from some chest or drawer.

The aspect of the case was now considerably darker. Stockdale was so much depressed by it that he did not challenge her explanation, or threaten to go off as a missionary to benighted islanders, or reproach her in any way whatever. He simply parted from her when she had done talking, and lived on in perplexity, till by degrees his natural manner became sad and constrained.

4 · At the time of the new moon

The following Thursday was changeable, damp, and gloomy; and the night threatened to be windy and unpleasant. Stockdale had gone away to Knollsea in the morning, to be present at some commemoration service there, and on his return he was met by the attractive Lizzy in the passage. Whether influenced by the tide of cheerfulness which had attended him that day, or by the drive through the open air, or whether from a natural disposition to let bygones alone, he allowed himself to be fascinated into forgetfulness of the greatcoat incident, and upon the whole passed a pleasant evening; not so much in her society as within sound of her voice, as she sat talking in the back parlour to her mother, till the latter went to bed. Shortly after this Mrs Newberry retired, and then Stockdale prepared to go upstairs himself. But before he left the room he remained standing by the dying embers awhile, thinking long of one thing and another; and was only aroused by the flickering of his candle in the socket as it suddenly declined and went out. Knowing that there were a tinder-box, matches, and another candle in his bedroom, he felt his way upstairs without a light. On reaching his chamber he laid his hand on every possible ledge and corner for the tinder-box, but for a long time in vain. Discovering it at length, Stockdale produced a spark and was kindling the brimstone, when he fancied that he heard a movement in the passage. He blew harder at the lint, the match flared up, and looking by aid of the blue light through the door, which had been standing open all this time, he was surprised to see a male figure vanishing round the top of the staircase with the evident intention of escaping unobserved. The personage wore the clothes which Lizzy had been brushing, and something in the outline and gait suggested to the minister that the wearer was Lizzy herself.

But he was not sure of this; and, greatly excited, Stockdale determined to investigate the mystery, and to adopt his own way for doing it. He blew out the match without lighting the candle, went into the passage, and proceeded on tiptoe towards Lizzy's room. A faint grey square of light in the direction of the chamber-window as he approached told him that the door was open, and at once suggested that the occupant was gone. He turned and brought down his fist upon the handrail of the staircase: 'It was she; in her late husband's coat and hat!'

Somewhat relieved to find that there was no intruder in the case, yet none the less surprised, the minister crept down the stairs, softly put on his boots, overcoat, and hat, and tried the front door. It was fastened as usual: he went to the back door, found this unlocked, and emerged into the garden. The night was mild and moonless, and rain had lately been falling, though for the present it had ceased. There was a sudden dropping from the trees and bushes every now and then, as each passing wind shook their boughs. Among these sounds Stockdale heard the faint fall of feet upon the road outside, and he guessed from the step that it was Lizzy's. He followed the sound, and, helped by the circumstance of the wind blowing from the direction in which the pedestrian moved, he got nearly close to her, and kept there, without risk of being overheard. While he thus followed her up the street or lane, as it might indifferently be called, there being more hedge than houses on either side, a figure came forward to her from one of the cottage doors. Lizzy stopped; the minister stepped upon the grass and stopped also.

'Is that Mrs Newberry?' said the man who had come out, whose voice Stockdale recognized as that of one of the most devout members of his congregation.

'It is,' said Lizzy.

'I be quite ready – I've been here this quarter-hour.'

'Ah, John,' said she, 'I have bad news; there is danger tonight for our venture.'

'And d'ye tell o't! I dreamed there might be.'

'Yes,' she said hurriedly; 'and you must go at once round to where the chaps are waiting, and tell them they will not be wanted till tomorrow night at the same time. I go to burn the lugger off.'

'I will,' he said; and instantly went off through a gate, Lizzy continuing her way.

On she tripped at a quickening pace till the lane turned into the turnpike-road, which she crossed, and got into the track for Ringsworth. Here she ascended the hill without the least hesitation, passed the lonely hamlet of Holworth, and went down the vale on the other side. Stockdale had never taken any extensive walks in this direction, but he was aware that if she persisted in her course much longer she would draw near to the coast, which was here between two and three miles distant from Nether-Moynton; and as it had been about a quarter past eleven o'clock when they set out, her intention seemed to be to reach the shore about midnight.

Lizzy soon ascended a small mound, which Stockdale at the same time adroitly skirted on the left; and a dull monotonous roar burst upon his ear. The hillock was about fifty yards from the top of the cliffs, and by day it apparently commanded a full view of the bay. There was light enough in the sky to show her disguised figure against it when she reached the top, where she paused, and afterwards sat down. Stockdale, not wishing on any account to alarm her at this moment, yet desirous of being near her, sank upon his hands and knees, crept a little higher up, and there stayed still.

The wind was chilly, the ground damp, and his position one in which he did not care to remain long. However, before he had decided to leave it, the young man heard voices behind him. What they signified he did not know; but, fearing that Lizzy was in danger, he was about to run forward and warn her that she might be seen, when she crept to the shelter of a little bush which maintained a precarious existence in that exposed spot; and her form was absorbed in its dark and stunted outline as if she had become part of it. She had evidently heard the men as well as he. They passed near him, talking in loud and careless tones, which could be heard above the uninterrupted washings of the sea, and which suggested that they were not engaged in any business at their own risk. This proved to be the fact: some of their words floated across to him, and caused him to forget at once the coldness of his situation.

'What's the vessel?'

'A lugger, about fifty tons.'

'From Cherbourg, I suppose?'

'Yes, 'a b'lieve.'

'But it don't all belong to Owlett?'

'O no. He's only got a share. There's another or two in it – a farmer and such like, but the names I don't know.'

The voices died away, and the heads and shoulders of the men diminished towards the cliff and dropped out of sight.

'My darling has been tempted to buy a share by that unbeliever Owlett,' groaned the minister, his honest affection for Lizzy having quickened to its intensest point during these moments of risk to her person and name. 'That's why she's here,' he said to himself. 'O it will be the ruin of her!'

His perturbation was interrupted by the sudden bursting out of a bright and increasing light from the spot where

Lizzy was in hiding. A few seconds later, and before it had reached the height of a blaze, he heard her rush past him down the hollow like a stone from a sling, in the direction of home. The light now flared high and wide, and showed its position clearly. She had kindled a bough of furze and stuck it into the bush under which she had been crouching; the wind fanned the flame, which crackled fiercely, and threatened to consume the bush as well as the bough. Stockdale paused just long enough to notice thus much, and then followed rapidly the route taken by the young woman. His intention was to overtake her, and reveal himself as a friend; but run as he would he could see nothing of her. Thus he flew across the open country about Holworth, twisting his legs and ankles in unexpected fissures and descents, till, on coming to the gate between the downs and the road, he was forced to pause to get breath. There was no audible movement either in front or behind him, and he now concluded that she had not outrun him, but that, hearing him at her heels, and believing him one of the excise party, she had hidden herself somewhere on the way, and let him pass by.

He went on at a more leisurely pace towards the village. On reaching the house he found his surmise to be correct, for the gate was on the latch, and the door unfastened, just as he had left them. Stockdale closed the door behind him, and waited silently in the passage. In about ten minutes he heard the same light footstep that he had heard in going out; it paused at the gate, which opened and shut softly, and then the door-latch was lifted, and Lizzy came in.

Stockdale went forward and said at once, 'Lizzy, don't be frightened. I have been waiting up for you.'

She started, though she had recognized the voice. 'It is Mr Stockdale, isn't it?' she said.

'Yes,' he answered, becoming angry now that she was safe indoors, and not alarmed. 'And a nice game I've found you out in tonight. You are in man's clothes, and I am ashamed of you!'

Lizzie could hardly find a voice to answer this unexpected reproach.

'I am only partly in man's clothes,' she faltered, shrinking back to the wall. 'It is only his greatcoat and hat and breeches that I've got on, which is no harm, as he was my own husband; and I do it only because a cloak blows about so, and you can't use your arms. I have got my own dress under just the same – it is only tucked in! Will you go away upstairs and let me pass? I didn't want you to see me at such a time as this!'

'But I have a right to see you! How do you think there can be anything between us now?' Lizzy was silent. 'You are a smuggler,' he continued sadly.

'I have only a share in the run,' she said.

'That makes no difference. Whatever did you engage in such a trade as that for, and keep it such a secret from me all this time?'

'I don't do it always. I only do it in winter-time when 'tis new moon.'

'Well, I suppose that's because it can't be done anywhen else. . . . You have regularly upset me, Lizzy.'

'I am sorry for that,' Lizzy meekly replied.

'Well now,' said he more tenderly, 'no harm is done as yet. Won't you for the sake of me give up this blamable and dangerous practice altogether?'

'I must do my best to save this run,' said she, getting rather husky in the throat. 'I don't want to give you up – you know that; but I don't want to lose my venture. I don't know what to do now! Why I have kept it so secret from you is that I was afraid you would be angry if you knew.'

'I should think so! I suppose if I had married you without finding this out you'd have gone on with it just the same?'

'I don't know. I did not think so far ahead. I only went tonight to burn the folks off, because we found that the preventive-men knew where the tubs were to be landed.'

'It is a pretty mess to be in altogether, is this,' said the distracted young minister. 'Well, what will you do now?'

Lizzy slowly nurmured the particulars of their plan, the chief of which were that they meant to try their luck at some other point of the shore the next night; that three landing-places were always agreed upon before the run was attempted with the understanding that, if the vessel was 'burnt off' from the first point, which was Ringsworth, as it had been by her tonight, the crew should attempt to make the second, which was Lulwind Cove, on the second night; and if there, too, danger threatened, they should on the third night try the third place, which was behind a headland further west.

'Suppose the officers hinder them landing there too?' he said, his attention to this interesting programme displacing for a moment his concern at her share in it.

'Then we shan't try anywhere else all this dark – that's what we call the time between moon and moon – and perhaps they'll string the tubs to a stray-line, and sink 'em a little-ways from shore, and take the bearings; and then when they have a chance they'll go to creep for 'em.'

'What's that?'

'O, they'll go out in a boat and drag a creeper – that's a grapnel – along the bottom till it catch hold of the stray-line.'

The minister stood thinking; and there was no sound within doors but the tick of the clock on the stairs, and the quick breathing of Lizzy, partly from her walk and partly from agitation, as she stood close to the wall, not in such complete darkness but that he could discern against its whitewashed surface the greatcoat, breeches, and broad hat which covered her.

'Lizzy, all this is very wrong,' he said. 'Don't you remember the lesson of the tribute-money? "Render unto Caesar the things that are Caesar's." Surely you have heard that read times enough in your growing up?'

'He's dead,' she pouted.

'But the spirit of the text is in force just the same.'

'My father did it, and so did my grandfather, and almost everybody in Nether-Moynton lives by it, and life would be so dull if it wasn't for that, that I should not care to live at all.'

'I am nothing to live for, of course,' he replied bitterly. 'You would not think it worth while to give up this wild business and live for me alone?'

'I have never looked at it like that.'

'And you won't promise and wait till I am ready?'

'I cannot give you my word tonight.' And, looking thoughtfully down, she gradually moved and moved away, going into the adjoining room, and closing the door between them. She remained there in the dark till he was tired of waiting, and had gone up to his own chamber.

Poor Stockdale was dreadfully depressed all the next day by the discoveries of the night before. Lizzy was unmistakably a fascinating young woman, but as a minister's wife she was hardly to be contemplated. 'If I had only stuck to father's little grocery business, instead of going in for the ministry, she would have suited me beautifully!' he said sadly, until he remembered that in that case he would never have come from his distant home to Nether-Moynton, and never have known her.

The estrangement between them was not complete, but it was sufficient to keep them out of each other's company. Once during the day he met her in the garden-path, and said, turning a reproachful eye upon her, 'Do you promise, Lizzy?' But she did not reply. The evening drew on, and he knew well enough that Lizzy would repeat her excursion at night – her half offended manner had shown that she had not the slightest intention of altering her plans at present. He did not wish to repeat his own share of the adventure; but, act as he would, his uneasiness on her account increased with the decline of day. Supposing that an accident should befall her, he would never forgive himself for not being there to help, much as he disliked the idea of seeming to countenance such unlawful escapades.

5 · How they went to Lulwind Cove

As he expected, she left the house at the same hour at night, this time passing his door without stealth, as if she knew very well that he would be watching, and were resolved to brave his displeasure. He was quite ready, opened the door quickly, and reached the back door almost as soon as she.

'Then you will go, Lizzy?' he said as he stood on the step beside her, who now again appeared as a little man with a face altogether unsuited to his clothes.

'I must,' she said, repressed by his stern manner.

'Then I shall go too,' said he.

'And I'm sure you will enjoy it!' she exclaimed in more buoyant tones. 'Everybody does who tries it.'

'God forbid that I should!' he said. 'But I must look after you.'

They opened the wicket and went up the road abreast of each other, but at some distance apart, scarcely a word passing between them. The evening was rather less favourable to smuggling enterprise than the last had been, the wind being lower, and the sky somewhat clear towards the north.

'It is rather lighter,' said Stockdale.

''Tis, unfortunately,' said she. 'But it is only from those few stars over there. The moon was new today at four o'clock, and I expected clouds. I hope we shall be able to do it this dark, for when we have to sink 'em for long it makes the stuff taste bleachy, and folks don't like it so well.'

Her course was different from that of the preceding night, branching off to the left over Lord's Barrow as soon as they had got out of the lane and crossed the highway. By the time they reached Shaldon Down, Stockdale, who had been in perplexed thought as to what he should say to her, decided that he would not attempt expostulation now, while she was excited by the adventure, but wait till it was over, and endeavour to keep her from such practices in future. It occurred to him once or twice, as they rambled on that should they be surprised by the Preventive-guard, his situation would be more awkward than hers, for it would be difficult to prove his true motive in coming to the spot; but the risk was a slight consideration beside his wish to be with her.

They now arrived at a ravine which lay on the outskirts of Shaldon, a village two miles on their way towards the point of the shore they sought. Lizzy broke the silence this time: 'I have to wait here to meet the carriers. I don't know if they have come yet. As I told you, we go to Lulwind Cove tonight, and it is two miles further than Ringsworth.'

It turned out that the men had already come; for while she spoke two or three dozen heads broke the line of the slope, and a company of them at once descended from the bushes where they had been lying in wait. These carriers were men whom Lizzy and other proprietors regularly employed to bring the tubs from the boat to a hiding-place inland. They were all young fellows of Nether-Moynton, Shaldon, and the neighbourhood, quiet and inoffensive persons, even though some held heavy sticks, who simply engaged to carry cargo for Lizzy and her cousin Owlett, as they would have engaged in any other labour for which they were fairly well paid.

At a word from her they closed in together. 'You had better take it now,' she said to them; and handed to each a packet. It contained six shillings, their remuneration for the night's undertaking, which was paid beforehand without reference to success or failure; but, besides this, they had the privilege of selling as agents when the run was successfully made. As soon as it was done, she said to them, 'The place is the old one, Dagger's Grave, near Lulwind Cove'; the men till that moment not having been told whither they were bound, for obvious reasons. 'Mr Owlett will meet you there,' added Lizzy. 'I shall follow behind, to see that we are not watched.'

The carriers went on, and Stockdale and Mrs Newberry followed at a distance of a stone's throw. 'What do these men do by day?' he said.

'Twelve or fourteen of them are labouring men. Some are brickmakers, some carpenters, some shoemakers, some thatchers. They are all known to me very well. Nine of 'em are of your own congregation.'

'I can't help that,' said Stockdale.

'O, I know you can't. I only told you. The others are more church-inclined, because they supply the pa'son with all the spirits he requires, and they don't wish to show unfriendliness to a customer.'

'How do you choose 'em?' said Stockdale.

'We choose 'em for their closeness, and because they are

strong and surefooted, and able to carry a heavy load a long way without being tired.'

Stockdale sighed as she enumerated each particular, for it proved how far involved in the business a woman must be who was so well acquainted with its conditions and needs. And yet he felt more tenderly towards her at this moment than he had felt all the foregoing day. Perhaps it was that her experienced manner and bold indifference stirred his admiration in spite of himself.

'Take my arm, Lizzy,' he murmured.

'I don't want it,' she said. 'Besides, we may never be to each other again what we once have been.'

'That depends upon you,' said he, and they went on again as before.

The hired carriers paced along over Shaldon Down with as little hesitation as if it had been day, avoiding the cart-way, and leaving the village of East Shaldon on the left, so as to reach the crest of the hill at a lonely trackless place not far from the ancient earthwork called Round Pound. A quarter-hour more of brisk walking brought them within sound of the sea, to the place called Dagger's Grave, not many hundred yards from Lulwind Cove. Here they paused, and Lizzy and Stockdale came up with them, when they went on together to the verge of the cliff. One of the men now produced an iron bar, which he drove firmly into the soil a yard from the edge, and attached to it a rope that he had uncoiled from his body. They all began to descend, partly stepping, partly sliding down the incline, as the rope slipped through their hands.

'You will not go to the bottom, Lizzy?' said Stockdale anxiously.

'No. I stay here to watch,' she said. 'Mr Owlett is down there.'

The men remained quite silent when they reached the shore; and the next thing audible to the two at the top was the dip of heavy oars, and the dashing of waves against a boat's bow. In a moment the keel gently touched the shingle, and Stockdale heard the footsteps of the thirty-six carriers running forwards over the pebbles towards the point of landing.

There was a sousing in the water as of a brood of ducks plunging in, showing that the men had not been particular about keeping their legs, or even their waists, dry from the brine: but it was impossible to see what they were doing, and in a few minutes the shingle was trampled again. The iron bar sustaining the rope, on which Stockdale's hand rested, began to swerve a little, and the carriers one by one appeared climbing up the sloping cliff, dripping audibly as they came, and sustaining themselves by the guide-rope. Each man on reaching the top was seen to be carrying a pair of tubs, one on his back and one on his chest, the two being slung together by cords passing round the chine hoops, and resting on the carrier's shoulders. Some of the stronger men carried three by putting an extra one on the top behind, but the customary load was a pair, these being quite weighty enough to give their bearer the sensation of having chest and backbone in contact after a walk of four or five miles.

'Where is Mr Owlett?' said Lizzy to one of them.

'He will not come up this way,' said the carrier. 'He's to bide on shore till we be safe off.' Then, without waiting for the rest, the foremost men plunged across the down; and, when the last had ascended, Lizzy pulled up the rope, wound it round her arm, wriggled the bar from the sod, and turned to follow the carriers.

'You are very anxious about Owlett's safety,' said the minister.

'Was there ever such a man!' said Lizzy. 'Why, isn't he my cousin?'

'Yes. Well, it is a bad night's work,' said Stockdale heavily. 'But I'll carry the bar and rope for you.'

'Thank God, the tubs have got so far all right,' said she.

Stockdale shook his head, and, taking the bar, walked by her side towards the downs; and the moan of the sea was heard no more.

'Is this what you meant the other day when you spoke of having business with Owlett?' the young man asked.

'This is it,' she replied. 'I never see him on any other matter.'

'A partnership of that kind with a young man is very odd.'

'It was begun by my father and his, who were brother-laws.'

Her companion could not blind himself to the fact that where tastes and pursuits were so akin as Lizzy's and Owlett's, and where risks were shared, as with them, in every undertaking, there would be a peculiar appropriateness in her answering Owlett's standing question on matrimony in the affirmative. This did not soothe Stockdale, its tendency being rather to stimulate in him an effort to make the pair as inappropriate as possible, and win her away from this nocturnal crew to correctness of conduct and a minister's parlour in some far-removed inland county.

They had been walking near enough to the file of carriers for Stockdale to perceive that, when they got into the road to the village, they split up into two companies of unequal size, each of which made off in a direction of its own. One company, the smaller of the two, went towards the church, and by the time that Lizzy and Stockdale reached their own house these men had scaled the churchyard wall, and were proceeding noiselessly over the grass within.

'I see that Mr Owlett has arranged for one batch to be put in the church again,' observed Lizzy. 'Do you remember my taking you there the first night you came?'

'Yes, of course,' said Stockdale. 'No wonder you had permission to broach the tubs – they were his, I suppose?'

'No, they were not – they were mine; I had permission from myself. The day after that they went several miles inland in a waggon-load of manure, and sold very well.'

At this moment the group of men who had made off to the left some time before began leaping one by one from the hedge opposite Lizzy's house, and the first man, who had no tubs upon his shoulders, came forward.

'Mrs Newberry, isn't it?' he said hastily.

'Yes, Jim,' said she. 'What's the matter?'

'I find that we can't put any in Badger's Clump tonight, Lizzy,' said Owlett. 'The place is watched. We must sling the apple-tree in the orchet if there's time. We can't put any more under the church lumber than I have sent on there, and my mixen hev already more in en than is safe.'

'Very well,' she said. 'Be quick about it – that's all. What can I do?'

'Nothing at all, please. Ah, it is the minister!– you two that can't do anything had better get indoors and not be zeed.'

While Owlett thus conversed, in a tone so full of contraband anxiety and so free from lover's jealousy, the men who followed him had been descending one by one from the hedge; and it unfortunately happened that when the hindmost took his leap, the cord slipped which sustained his tubs: the result was that both the kegs fell into the road, one of them being stove in by the blow.

''Od drown it all!' said Owlett, rushing back.

'It is worth a good deal, I suppose?' said Stockdale.

'O no – about two guineas and half to us now,' said Lizzy excitely. 'It isn't that – it is the smell! It is so blazing strong before it has been lowered by water, that it smells dreadfully when spilt in the road like that! I do hope Latimer won't pass by till it is gone off.'

Owlett and one or two others picked up the burst tub and began to scrape and trample over the spot, to disperse the liquor as much as possible; and then they all entered the gate of Owlett's orchard, which adjoined Lizzy's garden on the right. Stockdale did not care to follow them, for several on recognizing him had looked wonderingly at his presence, though they said nothing. Lizzy left his side and went to the bottom of the garden, looking over the hedge into the orchard, where the men could be dimly seen bustling about, and apparently hiding the tubs. All was done noiselessly, and without a light; and when it was over they dispersed in different directions, those who had taken their cargoes to the church having already gone off to their homes.

Lizzy returned to the garden-gate, over which Stockdale was still abstractedly leaning. 'It is all finished: I am going indoors now,' she said gently. 'I will leave the door ajar for you.'

'O no – you needn't,' said Stockdale; 'I am coming too.'

But before either of them had moved, the faint clatter of horses' hoofs broke upon the ear, and it seemed to come from the point where the track across the down joined the hard road.

'They are just too late!' cried Lizzy exultingly.

'Who?' said Stockdale.

'Latimer, the riding-officer, and some assistant of his. We had better go indoors.'

They entered the house and Lizzy bolted the door. 'Please don't get a light, Mr Stockdale,' she said.

'Of course I will not,' said he.

'I thought you might be on the side of the king,' said Lizzy, with faintest sarcasm.

'I am,' said Stockdale. 'But, Lizzy Newberry, I love you, and you know it perfectly well; and you ought to know, if you do not, what I have suffered in my conscience on your account these last few days!'

'I guess very well,' she said hurriedly. 'Yet I don't see why. Ah, you are better than I!'

The trotting of the horses seemed to have again died away, and the pair of listeners touched each other's fingers in the cold 'Good-night' of those whom something seriously divided. They were on the landing, but before they had taken three steps apart, the tramp of the horsemen suddenly revived, almost close to the house. Lizzy turned to the staircase window, opened the casement about an inch, and put her face close to the aperture. 'Yes, one of 'em is Latimer,' she whispered. 'He always rides a white horse. One would think it was the last colour for a man in that line.'

Stockdale looked, and saw the white shape of the animal as it passed by; but before the riders had gone another ten yards Latimer reined in his horse, and said something to his companion which neither Stockdale nor Lizzy could hear. Its drift was, however, soon made evident, for the other man stopped also; and sharply turning the horses' heads they cautiously retraced their steps. When they were again opposite Mrs Newberry's garden, Latimer dismounted, and the man on the dark horse did the same.

Lizzy and Stockdale, intently listening and observing the proceedings, naturally put their heads as close as possible to the slit formed by the slightly opened casement; and thus it occurred that at last their cheeks came positively into contact. They went on listening, as if they did not know of the singular incident which had happened to their faces, and the pressure of each to each rather increased than lessened with the lapse of time.

They could hear the Customs-men sniffing the air like hounds as they paced slowly along. When they reached the spot where the tub had burst, both stopped on the instant.

'Ay, ay, 'tis quite strong here,' said the second officer. 'Shall we knock at the door?'

'Well, no,' said Latimer. 'Maybe this is only a trick to put us off the scent. They wouldn't kick up this stink anywhere near their hiding-place. I have known such things before.'

'Anyhow, the things, or some of 'em, must have been brought this way,' said the other.

'Yes,' said Latimer musingly. 'Unless 'tis all done to tole us the wrong way. I have a mind that we go home for tonight without saying a word, and come the first thing in the morning with more hands. I know they have storages about here, but we can do nothing by this owl's light. We will look round the parish and see if everybody is in bed, John; and if all is quiet, we will do as I say.'

They went on, and the two inside the window could hear them passing leisurely through the whole village, the street of which curved round at the bottom and entered the turnpike road at another junction. This way the officers followed, and the amble of their horses died quite away.

'What will you do?' said Stockdale, withdrawing from his position.

She knew that he alluded to the coming search by the officers, to divert her attention from their own tender incident by the casement, which he wished to be passed over as a thing rather dreamt of than done. 'O, nothing,' she replied, with as much coolness as she could command under her disappointment at his manner. 'We often have such storms as this. You would not be frightened if you knew what fools they are. Fancy riding o' horseback through the place; of course they will hear and see nobody while they make that noise; but they are always afraid to get off, in case some of our fellows should burst out upon 'em, and tie them up to the gate-post, as they have done before now. Good-night, Mr Stockdale.'

She closed the window and went to her room, where a tear fell from her eyes; and that not because of the alertness of the riding-officers.

6 · The great search at Nether-Moynton

Stockdale was so excited by the events of the evening, and the dilemma that he was placed in between conscience and love, that he did not sleep, or even doze, but remained as broadly awake as at noonday. As soon as the grey light began to touch ever so faintly the whiter objects in his bedroom he arose, dressed himself and went downstairs into the road.

The village was already astir. Several of the carriers had heard the well-known canter of Latimer's horse while they were undressing in the dark that night, and had already communicated with each other and Owlett on the subject. The only doubt seemed to be about the safety of those tubs which had been left under the church gallery-stairs, and after a short discussion at the corner of the mill, it was agreed that these should be removed before it got lighter, and hidden in the middle of a double hedge bordering the adjoining field. However, before anything could be carried into effect, the footsteps of many men were heard coming down the lane from the highway.

'Damn it, here they be,' said Owlett, who, having already drawn the hatch and started his mill for the day, stood stolidly at the mill-door covered with flour, as if the interest of his whole soul was bound up in the shaking walls around him.

The two or three with whom he had been talking dispersed to their usual work, and when the Customs-officers, and the formidable body of men they had hired, reached the village cross, between the mill and Mrs Newberry's house, the village wore the natural aspect of a place beginning its morning labours.

'Now,' said Latimer to his associates, who numbered thirteen men in all, 'what I know is that the things are some-where in this here place. We have got the day before us, and 'tis hard if we can't light upon 'em and get 'em to Budmouth Custom-house before night. First we will try the fuel-houses, and then we'll work our way into the chimmers, and then to the ricks and stables, and so creep round. You have nothing but your noses to guide ye, mind, so use 'em today if you never did in your lives before.'

Then the search began. Owlett, during the early part, watched from his mill-window, Lizzy from the door of her house, with the greatest self-possession. A farmer down below, who also had a share in the run, rode about with one eye on his fields and the other on Latimer and his myrmidons, prepared to put them off the scent if he should be asked a question. Stockdale, who was no smuggler at all, felt more anxiety than the worst of them, and went about his studies with a heavy heart, coming frequently to the door to ask Lizzy some question or other on the consequences to her of the tubs being found.

'The consequences,' she said quietly, 'are simply that I shall lose 'em. As I have none in the house or garden, they can't touch me personally.'

'But you have some in the orchard?'

'Mr Owlett rents that of me, and he lends it to others. So it will be hard to say who puts any tubs there if they should be found.'

There was never such a tremendous sniffing known as that which took place in Nether-Moynton parish and its vicinity this day. All was done methodically, and mostly on hands and knees. At different hours of the day they had different plans. From daybreak to breakfast-time the officers used their sense of smell in a direct and straightforward manner only, pausing nowhere but at such places as the tubs might be supposed to be secreted in at that very moment, pending their removal on the following night. Among the places tested and examined were:

Hollow trees	Cupboards	Culverts
Potato-graves	Clock-cases	Hedgerows
Fuel-houses	Chimney-flues	Faggot-ricks
Bedrooms	Rainwater-butts	Haystacks
Apple-lofts	Pigsties	Coppers and ovens.

After breakfast they recommenced with renewed vigour, taking a new line; that is to say, directing their attention to clothes that might be supposed to have come in contact with the tubs in their removal from the shore, such garments being usually tainted with the spirit, owing to its oozing between the staves. They now sniffed at –

Smock-frocks	Smiths' and shoemakers'
Old shirts and waistcoats	aprons
Coats and hats	Knee-naps and hedging-
Breeches and leggings	gloves
Woman's shawls and	Tarpaulins
gowns	Market-cloaks
	Scarecrows.

And as soon as the mid-day meal was over, they pushed their search into places where the spirits might have been thrown away in alarm:

Horse-ponds	Mixens	Sinks in yards
Stable-drains	Wet ditches	Road-scrapings, and
Cinder-heaps	Cesspools	Back-door gutters.

But still these indefatigable Custom-house men discovered nothing more than the original tell-tale smell in the road opposite Lizzy's house, which even yet had not passed off.

'I'll tell ye what it is, men,' said Latimer, about three o'clock in the afternoon, 'we must begin over again. Find them tubs I will.'

The men, who had been hired for the day, looked at their

hands and knees, muddy with creeping on all fours so frequently, and rubbed their noses, as if they had almost had enough of it; for the quantity of bad air which had passed into each one's nostril had rendered it nearly as insensible as a flue. However, after a moment's hesitation, they prepared to start anew, except three, whose power of smell had quite succumbed under the excessive wear and tear of the day.

By this time not a male villager was to be seen in the parish. Owlett was not at his mill, the farmers were not in their fields, the parson was not in his garden, the smith had left his forge, and the wheelwright's shop was silent.

'Where the divil are the folk gone?' said Latimer, waking up to the fact of their absence, and looking round. 'I'll have 'em up for this! Why don't they come and help us? There's not a man about the place but the Methodist parson, and he's an old woman. I demand assistance in the king's name!'

'We must find the jineral public afore we can demand that,' said his lieutenant.

'Well, well, we shall do better without 'em,' said Latimer, who changed his moods at a moment's notice. 'But there's great cause of suspicion in this silence and this keeping out of sight, and I'll bear it in mind. Now we will go across to Owlett's orchard and see what we can find there.'

Stockdale, who heard this discussion from the garden-gate, over which he had been leaning, was rather alarmed, and thought it a mistake of the villagers to keep so completely out of the way. He himself, like the Preventives, had been wondering for the last half-hour what could have become of them. Some labourers were of necessity engaged in distant fields, but the master-workmen should have been at home; though one and all, after just showing themselves at their shops, had apparently gone off for the day. He went in to Lizzy, who sat at a back window sewing, and said, 'Lizzy, where are the men?'

Lizzy laughed. 'Where they mostly are when they're run so hard as this.' She cast her eyes to heaven. 'Up there,' she said.

Stockdale looked up. 'What — on the top of the church tower?' he asked, seeing the direction of her glance.

'Yes.'

'Well, I expect they will soon have to come down,' said he gravely. 'I have been listening to the officers, and they are going to search the orchard over again, and then every nook in the church.'

Lizzy looked alarmed for the first time. 'Will you go and tell our folk?' she said. 'They ought to be let know.' Seeing his conscience struggling within him like a boiling pot, she added, 'No, never mind, I'll go myself.'

She went out, descended the garden, and climbed over the churchyard wall at the same time that the preventive-men were ascending the road to the orchard. Stockdale could do no less than follow her. By the time that she reached the tower entrance he was at her side, and they entered together.

Nether-Moynton church-tower was, as in many villages, without a turret, and the only way to the top was by going up to the singers' gallery, and thence ascending by a ladder to a square trap-door in the floor of the bell-loft, above which a permanent ladder was fixed, passing through the bells to a hole in the roof. When Lizzy and Stockdale reached the gallery and looked up, nothing but the trap-door and the five holes for the bell-ropes appeared. The ladder was gone.

'There's no getting up,' said Stockdale.

'O yes, there is,' said she. 'There's an eye looking at us at this moment through a knot-hole in that trap-door.'

And as she spoke the trap opened, and the dark line of the ladder was seen descending against the white-washed wall. When it touched the bottom Lizzy dragged it to its place, and said, 'If you'll go up, I'll follow.'

The young man ascended, and presently found himself among consecrated bells for the first time in his life, nonconformity having been in the Stockdale blood for some generations. He eyed them uneasily, and looked round for Lizzy. Owlett stood here, holding the top of the ladder.

'What, be you really one of us?' said the miller.

'It seems so,' said Stockdale sadly.

'He's not,' said Lizzy, who overheard. 'He's neither for nor against us. He'll do us no harm.'

She stepped up beside them, and then they went on to the next stage, which, when they had clambered over the dusty bell-carriages, was of easy ascent, leading towards the hole through which the pale sky appeared, and into the open air. Owlett remained behind for a moment, to pull up the lower ladder.

'Keep down your heads,' said a voice, as soon as they set foot on the flat.

Stockdale here beheld all the missing parishioners, lying on their stomachs on the tower roof, except a few who, elevated on their hands and knees, were peeping through the embrasures of the parapet. Stockdale did the same, and saw the village lying like a map below him, over which moved the figures of the Customs-men, each foreshortened to a crab-like object, the crown of his hat forming a circular disc in the centre of him. Some of the men had turned their heads when the young preacher's figure arose among them.

'What, Mr Stockdale?' said Matt Grey, in a tone of surprise.

'I'd as lief that it hadn't been,' said Jim Clarke. 'If the pa'son should see him trespassing here in his tower, 'twould be none the better for we, seeing how 'a do hate chapel-members. He'd never buy a tub of us again, and he's as good a customer as we have got this side o' Warm'll.'

'Where is the pa'son?' said Lizzy.

'In his house, to be sure, that he mid see nothing of what's going on – where all good folks ought to be, and this young man likewise.'

'Well, he has brought some news,' said Lizzy. 'They are going to search the orchard and church; can we do anything if they should find?'

'Yes,' said her cousin Owlett. 'That's what we've been talking o', and we have settled our line. Well, be dazed!'

The exclamation was caused by his perceiving that some of the searchers, having got into the orchard, and begun stooping and creeping hither and thither, were pausing in the middle, where a tree smaller than the rest was growing. They drew closer, and bent lower than ever upon the ground.

'O, my tubs!' said Lizzy faintly, as she peered through the parapet at them.

'They have got 'em, 'a b'lieve,' said Owlett.

The interest in the movements of the officers was so keen that not a single eye was looking in any other direction; but at that moment a shout from the church beneath them attracted the attention of the smugglers, as it did also of the party in the orchard, who sprang to their feet and went towards the churchyard wall. At the same time those of the Government men who had entered the church unperceived by the smugglers cried aloud, 'Here be some of 'em at last.'

The smugglers remained in a blank silence, uncertain whether 'some of 'em' meant tubs or men; but again peeping cautiously over the edge of the tower they learnt that tubs were the things descried; and soon these fated articles were brought one by one into the middle of the churchyard from their hiding-place under the gallery-stairs.

'They are going to put 'em on Hinton's vault till they find the rest!' said Lizzy hopelessly. The Customs-men had, in fact, begun to pile up the tubs on a large stone slab which was fixed there; and when all were brought out from the tower, two or three of the men were left standing by them, the rest of the party again proceeding to the orchard.

The interest of the smugglers in the next manoeuvres of their enemies became painfully intense. Only about thirty tubs had been secreted in the lumber of the tower, but seventy were hidden in the orchard, making up all that they had brought ashore as yet, the remainder of the cargo having been tied to a sinker and dropped overboard for another night's operations. The Preventives, having re-entered the orchard, acted as if they were positive that here lay hidden the rest of the tubs, which they were determined to find before nightfall. They spread themselves out round the field, and advancing on all fours as before, went anew round every apple-tree in the enclosure. The young tree in the middle again led them to pause, and at length the whole company gathered there in a way which signified that a second chain of reasoning had led to the same results as the first.

When they had examined the sod hereabouts for some minutes, one of the men rose, ran to a disused part of the church where tools were kept, and returned with the sexton's pickaxe and shovel, with which they set to work.

'Are they really buried there?' said the minister, for the grass was so green and uninjured that it was difficult to believe it had been disturbed. The smugglers were too interested to reply, and presently they saw, to their chagrin, the officers stand several on each side of the tree; and, stooping and applying their hands to the soil, they bodily lifted the tree and the turf around it. The apple-tree now showed itself to be growing in a shallow box, with handles for lifting at each of the four sides. Under the site of the tree a square hole was revealed, and an officer went and looked down.

'It is all up now,' said Owlett quietly. 'And now all of ye get down before they notice we are here; and be ready for our next move. I had better bide here till dark, or they may take me on suspicion, as 'tis on my ground. I'll be with ye as soon as daylight begins to pink in.'

'And I?' said Lizzy.

'You please look to the linch-pins and screws; then go indoors and know nothing at all. The chaps will do the rest.'

The ladder was replaced, and all but Owlett descended, the men passing off one by one at the back of the church, and vanishing on their respective errands. Lizzy walked boldly along the street, followed closely by the minister.

'You are going indoors, Mrs Newberry?' he said.

She knew from the words 'Mrs Newberry' that the division between them had widened yet another degree.

'I am not going home,' she said. 'I have a little thing to do before I go in. Martha Sarah will get your tea.'

'O, I don't mean on that account,' said Stockdale. 'What *can* you have to do further in this unhallowed affair?'

'Only a little,' she said.

'What is that? I'll go with you.'

'No, I shall go by myself. Will you please go indoors? I shall be there in less than an hour.'

'You are not going to run any danger, Lizzy?' said the young man, his tenderness reasserting itself.

'None whatever – worth mentioning,' answered she, and went down towards the Cross.

Stockdale entered the garden-gate, and stood behind it looking on. The Preventive-men were still busy in the orchard, and at last he was tempted to enter and watch their proceedings. When he came closer he found that the secret cellar, of whose existence he had been totally unaware, was formed by timbers placed across from side to side about a foot under the ground, and grassed over.

The officers looked up at Stockdale's fair and downy countenance, and evidently thinking him above suspicion went on with their work again. As soon as all the tubs were taken out they began tearing up the turf, pulling out the timbers, and breaking in the sides, till the cellar was wholly dismantled and shapeless, the apple-tree lying with its roots high to the air. But the hole which had in its time held so much contraband merchandize was never completely filled up, either then or afterwards, a depression in the greensward marking the spot to this day.

7 · The walk to Warm'ell Cross and afterwards

As the goods had all to be carried to Budmouth that night, the next object of the Custom-house officers was to find horses and carts for the journey, and they went about the village for that purpose. Latimer strode hither and thither with a lump of chalk in his hand, marking broad-arrows so vigorously on every vehicle and set of harness that he came across, that it seemed as if he would chalk broad-arrows on the very hedges and roads. The owner of every conveyance so marked was bound to give it up for Government purposes. Stockdale, who had had enough of the scene, turned indoors thoughtful and depressed. Lizzy was already there, having come in at the back, though she had not yet taken off her bonnet. She looked tired, and her mood was not much brighter than his own. They had but little to say to each other; and the minister went away and attempted to read; but at this he could not succeed, and he shook the little bell for tea.

Lizzy herself brought in the tray, the girl having run off into the village during the afternoon, too full of excitement at the proceedings to remember her state of life. However, almost before the sad lovers had said anything to each other, Martha came in in a steaming state.

'O, there's such a stoor, Mrs Newberry and Mr Stockdale! The king's officers can't get the carts ready nohow at all! They pulled Thomas Artnell's, and William Rogers's, and Stephen Sprake's carts into the road, and off came the wheels, and down fell the carts; and they found there was no linch-pins in the arms; and then they tried Samuel Shane's waggon, and found that the screws were gone from he, and at last they looked at the dairyman's cart, and he's got none neither! They have gone now to the blacksmith's to get some made, but he's nowhere to be found!'

Stockdale looked at Lizzy, who blushed very slightly, and went out of the room, followed by Martha Sarah. But before they had got through the passage there was a rap at the front door, and Stockdale recognized Latimer's voice addressing Mrs Newberry, who had turned back.

'For God's sake, Mrs Newberry, have you seen Hardman the blacksmith up this way? If we could get hold of him, we'd e'en a'most drag him by the hair of his head to his anvil, where he ought to be.'

'He's an idle man, Mr Latimer,' said Lizzy archly. 'What do you want him for?'

'Why, there isn't a horse in the place that has got more than three shoes on, and some have only two. The waggon-wheels be without strakes, and there's no linch-pins to the carts. What with that, and the bother about every set of harness being out of order, we shan't be off before nightfall – upon my soul we shan't. 'Tis a rough lot, Mrs Newberry, that you've got about you here; but they'll play at this game once too often, mark my words they will! There's not a man in the parish that don't deserve to be whipped.'

It happened that Hardman was at that moment a little further up the lane, smoking his pipe behind a holly-bush. When Latimer had done speaking he went on in this direction, and Hardman, hearing the riding-officer's steps, found curiosity too strong for prudence. He peeped out from the bush at the very moment that Latimer's glance was on it. There was nothing left for him to do but to come forward with unconcern.

'I've been looking for you for the last hour!' said Latimer with a glare in his eye.

'Sorry to hear that,' said Hardman. 'I've been out for a stroll, to look for more hid tubs, to deliver 'em up to Gover'ment.'

'O yes, Hardman, we know it,' said Latimer, with withering sarcasm. 'We know that you'll deliver 'em up to Gover'ment. We know that all the parish is helping us, and have been all day! Now you please walk along with me down to your shop, and kindly let me hire ye in the king's name.'

They went down the lane together; and presently there resounded from the smithy the ring of a hammer not very briskly swung. However, the carts and horses were got into some sort of travelling condition, but it was not until after the clock had struck six, when the muddy roads were glistening under the horizontal light of the fading day. The smuggled tubs were soon packed into the vehicles, and Latimer, with three of his assistants, drove slowly out of the village in the direction of the port of Budmouth, some considerable number of miles distant, the other men of the Preventive-guard being left to watch for the remainder of the cargo, which they knew to have been sunk somewhere between Ringsworth and Lulwind Cove, and to unearth Owlett, the only person clearly implicated by the discovery of the cave.

Women and children stood at the doors as the carts, each chalked with the Government pitchfork, passed in the increasing twilight; and as they stood they looked at the confiscated property with a melancholy expression that told only too plainly the relation which they bore to the trade.

'Well, Lizzy,' said Stockdale, when the crackle of the wheels had nearly died away. 'This is a fit finish to your adventure. I am truly thankful that you have got off without suspicion, and the loss only of the liquor. Will you sit down and let me talk to you?'

'By and by,' she said. 'But I must go out now.'

'Not to that horrid shore again?' he said blankly.

'No, not there. I am only going to see the end of this day's business.'

He did not answer to this, and she moved towards the door slowly, as if waiting for him to say something more.

'You don't offer to come with me,' she added at last. 'I suppose that's because you hate me after all this!'

'Can you say it, Lizzy, when you know I only want to save you from such practices? Come with you! – of course I will, if it is only to take care of you. But why will you go out again?'

'Because I cannot rest indoors. Something is happening, and I must know what. Now, come!' And they went into the dusk together.

When they reached the turnpike-road she turned to the right, and he soon perceived that they were following the direction of the Preventive-men and their load. He had given her his arm, and every now and then she suddenly pulled it back, to signify that he was to halt a moment and listen. They had walked rather quickly along the first quarter of a mile, and on the second or third time of standing still she said, 'I hear them ahead – don't you?'

'Yes,' he said; 'I hear the wheels. But what of that?'

'I only want to know if they get clear away from the neighbourhood.'

'Ah,' said he, a light breaking upon him. 'Something desperate is to be attempted! – and now I remember there was not a man about the village when we left.'

'Hark!' she murmured. The noise of the cartwheels had stopped, and given place to another sort of sound.

''Tis a scuffle!' said Stockdale. 'There'll be murder! Lizzy, let go my arm; I am going on. On my conscience, I must not stay here and do nothing!'

'There'll be no murder, and not even a broken head,' she said. 'Our men are thirty to four of them: no harm will be done at all.'

'Then there *is* an attack!' exclaimed Stockdale; 'and you knew it was to be. Why should you side with men who break the laws like this?'

'Why should you side with men who take from country traders what they have honestly bought wi' their own money in France?' said she firmly.

'They are not honestly bought,' said he.

'They are,' she contradicted. 'I and Mr Owlett and the others paid thirty shillings for every one of the tubs before they were put on board at Cherbourg, and if a king who is nothing to us sends his people to steal our property, we have a right to steal it back again.'

Stockdale did not stop to argue the matter but went quickly in the direction of the noise, Lizzy keeping at his side. 'Don't you interfere, will you, dear Richard?' she said anxiously, as they drew near. 'Don't let us go any closer: 'tis at Warm'ell Cross where they are seizing 'em. You can do no good, and you may meet with a hard blow!'

'Let us see first what is going on,' he said. But before they had got much further the noise of the cartwheels began again; and Stockdale soon found that they were coming towards him. In another minute the three carts came up, and Stockdale and Lizzy stood in the ditch to let them pass.

Instead of being conducted by four men, as had happened when they went out of the village, the horses and carts were now accompanied by a body of from twenty to thirty, all of whom, as Stockdale perceived to his astonishment, had blackened faces. Among them walked six or eight huge female figures, whom, from their wide strides, Stockdale guessed to be men in disguise. As soon as the party discerned Lizzy and

her companion four or five fell back, and when the carts had
passed came close to the pair.

'There is no walking up this way for the present,' said one
of the gaunt women, who wore curls a foot long, dangling
down the sides of her face, in the fashion of the time. Stockdale recognized this lady's voice as Owlett's.

'Why not?' said Stockdale. 'This is the public highway.'

'Now look here, youngster,' said Owlett. 'O, 'tis the
Methodist parson! – what, and Mrs Newberry! Well, you'd
better not go up that way, Lizzy. They've all run off, and folks
have got their own again.'

The miller then hastened on and joined his comrades.
Stockdale and Lizzy also turned back. 'I wish all this hadn't
been forced upon us,' she said regretfully. 'But if those
Coast-men had got off with the tubs, half the people in the
parish would have been in want for the next month or two.'

Stockdale was not paying much attention to her words, and
he said, 'I don't think I can go back like this. Those four poor
Preventives may be murdered for all I know.'

'Murdered!' said Lizzy impatiently. 'We don't do murder
here.'

'Well, I shall go as far as Warm'ell Cross to see,' said
Stockdale decisively; and, without wishing her safe home or
anything else, the minister turned back. Lizzy stood looking
at him till his form was absorbed in the shades; and then, with
sadness, she went in the direction of Nether-Moynton.

The road was lonely, and after nightfall at this time of the
year there was often not a passer for hours. Stockdale pursued
his way without hearing a sound beyond that of his own
footsteps; and in due time he passed beneath the trees of the
plantation which surrounded the Warm'ell Cross-road.
Before he had reached the point of intersection he heard
voices from the thicket.

'Hoi-hoi-hoi! Help, help!'

The voices were not at all feeble or despairing but they
were unmistakably anxious. Stockdale had no weapon, and
before plunging into the pitchy darkness of the plantation he
pulled a stake from the hedge, to use in case of need. When he

got among the trees he shouted – 'What's the matter – where are you?'

'Here,' answered the voices: and, pushing through the brambles in that direction, he came near the objects of his search.

'Why don't you come forward?' said Stockdale.

'We be tied to the trees!'

'Who are you?'

'Poor Will Latimer the Customs-officer!' said one plaintively. 'Just come and cut these cords, there's a good man. We were afraid nobody would pass by tonight.'

Stockdale soon loosened them, upon which they stretched their limbs and stood at their ease.

'The rascals!' said Latimer, getting now into a rage, though he had seemed quite meek when Stockdale first came up. ''Tis the same set of fellows. I know they were Moynton chaps to a man.'

'But we can't swear to 'em,' said another. 'Not one of 'em spoke.'

'What are you going to do?' said Stockdale.

'I'd fain go back to Moynton, and have at 'em again!' said Latimer.

'So would we!' said his comrades.

'Fight till we die!' said Latimer.

'We will, we will!' said his men.

'But,' said Latimer, more frigidly, as they came out of the plantation, 'we don't *know* that these chaps with black faces were Moynton men? And proof is a hard thing.'

'So it is,' said the rest.

'And therefore we won't do nothing at all,' said Latimer, with complete dispassionateness. 'For my part, I'd sooner be them than we. The clitches of my arms are burning like fire from the cords those two strapping women tied round 'em. My opinion is, now I have had time to think o't, that you may serve your Gover'ment at too high a price. For these two nights and days I have not had an hour's rest; and, please God, here's for home-along.'

The other officers agreed heartily to this course; and, thanking Stockdale for his timely assistance, they parted from him at the Cross, taking themselves the western road, and Stockdale going back to Nether-Moynton.

During that walk the minister was lost in reverie of the most painful kind. As soon as he got into the house, and before entering his own rooms, he advanced to the door of the little back parlour in which Lizzy usually sat with her mother. He found her there alone. Stockdale went forward, and, like a man in a dream, looked down upon the table that stood between him and the young woman, who had her bonnet and cloak still on. As he did not speak, she looked up from her chair at him, with misgiving in her eye.

'Where are they gone?' he then said listlessly.

'Who? – I don't know. I have seen nothing of them since I came straight in here.'

'If your men can manage to get off with those tubs, it will be a great profit to you, I suppose?'

'A share will be mine, a share my cousin Owlett's, a share to each of the two farmers, and a share divided amongst the men who helped us.'

'And you still think,' he went on slowly, 'that you will not give this business up?'

Lizzy rose, and put her hand upon his shoulder. 'Don't ask that,' she whispered. 'You don't know what you're asking. I must tell you, though I meant not to do it. What I make by that trade is all I have to keep my mother and myself with.'

He was astonished. 'I did not dream of such a thing,' he said. 'I would rather have scraped the roads, had I been you. What is money compared with a clear conscience?'

'My conscience is clear. I know my mother, but the king I have never seen. His dues are nothing to me. But it is a great deal to me that my mother and I should live.'

'Marry me, and promise to give it up. I will keep your mother.'

'It is good of you,' she said, moved a little. 'Let me think of it by myself. I would rather not answer now.'

She reserved her answer till the next day, and came into his room with a solemn face. 'I cannot do what you wished!' she said passionately. 'It is too much to ask. My whole life has been passed in this way.' Her words and manner showed that before entering she had been struggling with herself in private, and that the contention had been strong.

Stockdale turned pale, but he spoke quietly. 'Then, Lizzy, we must part. I cannot go against my principles in this matter, and I cannot make my profession a mockery. You know how I love you, and what I would do for you; but this one thing I cannot do.'

'But why should you belong to that profession?' she burst out. 'I have got this large house; why can't you marry me, and live here with us, and not be a Methodist preacher any more? I assure you, Richard, it is no harm, and I wish you could only see it as I do! We only carry it on in winter: in summer it is never done at all. It stirs up one's dull life at this time o' the year, and gives excitement, which I have got so used to now that I should hardly know how to do 'ithout it. At nights, when the wind blows, instead of being dull and stupid, and not noticing whether it do blow or not, your mind is afield, even if you are not afield yourself; and you are wondering how the chaps are getting on; and you walk up and down the room, and look out o' window, and then you go out yourself, and know your way about as well by night as by day, and have hairbreadth escapes from old Latimer and his fellows, who are too stupid ever to really frighten us, and only make us a bit nimble.'

'He frightened you a little last night, anyhow: and I would advise you to drop it before it is worse.'

She shook her head. 'No, I must go on as I have begun. I was born to it. It is in my blood, and I can't be cured. O, Richard, you cannot think what a hard thing you have asked, and how sharp you try me when you put me between this and my love for 'ee!'

Stockdale was leaning with his elbow on the mantelpiece, his hands over his eyes. 'We ought never to have met, Lizzy,' he said. 'It was an ill day for us! I little thought there was anything so hopeless and impossible in our engagement as this.

Well, it is too late now to regret consequences in this way. I have had the happiness of seeing you and knowing you at least.'

'You dissent from Church, and I dissent from State,' she said. 'And I don't see why we are not well matched.'

He smiled sadly, while Lizzy remained looking down, her eyes beginning to overflow.

That was an unhappy evening for both of them, and the days that followed were unhappy days. Both she and he went mechanically about their employments, and his depression was marked in the village by more than one of his denomination with whom he came in contact. But Lizzy, who passed her days indoors, was unsuspected of being the cause: for it was generally understood that a quiet engagement to marry existed between her and her cousin Owlett, and had existed for some time.

Thus uncertainly the week passed on; till one morning Stockdale said to her: 'I have had a letter, Lizzy. I must call you that till I am gone.'

'Gone?' said she blankly.

'Yes,' he said. 'I am going from this place. I felt it would be better for us both that I should not stay after what has happened. In fact, I couldn't stay here, and look on you from day to day, without becoming weak and faltering in my course. I have just heard of an arrangement by which the other minister can arrive here in about a week; and let me go elsewhere.'

That he had all this time continued so firmly fixed in his resolution came upon her as a grievous surprise. 'You never loved me!' she said bitterly.

'I might say the same,' he returned; 'but I will not. Grant me one favour. Come and hear my last sermon on the day before I go.'

Lizzy, who was a church-goer on Sunday mornings, frequently attended Stockdale's chapel in the evening with the rest of the double-minded; and she promised.

It became known that Stockdale was going to leave, and a good many people outside his own sect were sorry to hear it.

The intervening days flew rapidly away, and on the evening of the Sunday which preceded the morning of his departure Lizzy sat in the chapel to hear him for the last time. The little building was full to overflowing, and he took up the subject which all had expected, that of the contraband trade so extensively practised among them. His hearers, in laying his words to their own hearts, did not perceive that they were most particularly directed against Lizzy, till the sermon waxed warm, and Stockdale nearly broke down with emotion. In truth his own earnestness, and her sad eyes looking up at him, were too much for the young man's equanimity. He hardly knew how he ended. He saw Lizzy, as through a mist, turn and go away with the rest of the congregation; and shortly afterwards followed her home.

She invited him to supper, and they sat down alone, her mother having, as was usual with her on Sunday nights, gone to bed early.

'We will part friends, won't we?' said Lizzy, with forced gaiety, and never alluding to the sermon: a reticence which rather disappointed him.

'We will,' he said, with a forced smile on his part; and they sat down.

It was the first meal that they had ever shared together in their lives, and probably the last that they would so share. When it was over, and the indifferent conversation could no longer be continued, he arose and took her hand. 'Lizzy,' he said, 'do you say we must part – do you?'

'You do,' she said solemnly. 'I can say no more.'

'Nor I,' said he. 'If that is your answer, goodbye!'

Stockdale bent over her and kissed her, and she involuntarily returned his kiss. 'I shall go early,' he said hurriedly. 'I shall not see you again.'

And he did leave early. He fancied, when stepping forth into the grey morning light, to mount the van which was to carry him away, that he saw a face between the parted curtains of Lizzy's window, but the light was faint, and the panes glistened with wet; so he could not be sure. Stockdale mounted the vehicle, and was gone; and on the following

Sunday the new minister preached in the chapel of the Moynton Wesleyans.

One day, two years after the parting, Stockdale, now settled in a midland town, came into Nether-Moynton by carrier in the original way. Jogging along in the van that afternoon he had put questions to the driver, and the answers that he received interested the minister deeply. The result of them was that he went without the least hesitation to the door of his former lodging. It was about six o'clock in the evening, and the same time of year as when he had left; now, too, the ground was damp and glistening, the west was bright, and Lizzy's snowdrops were raising their heads in the border under the wall.

Lizzy must have caught sight of him from the window, for by the time that he reached the door she was there holding it open: and then, as if she had not sufficiently considered her act of coming out, she drew herself back, saying with some constraint, 'Mr Stockdale!'

'You knew it was,' said Stockdale, taking her hand. 'I wrote to say I should call.'

'Yes, but you did not say when,' she answered.

'I did not. I was not quite sure when my business would lead me to these parts.'

'You only came because business brought you near?'

'Well, that is the fact; but I have often thought I should like to come on purpose to see you. . . . But what's all this that has happened? I told you how it would be, Lizzy, and you would not listen to me.'

'I would not,' she said sadly. 'But I had been brought up to that life; and it was second nature to me. However, it is all over now. The officers have blood-money for taking a man dead or alive, and the trade is going to nothing. We were hunted down like rats.'

'Owlett is quite gone, I hear.'

'Yes. He is in America. We had a dreadful struggle that last time, when they tried to take him. It is a perfect miracle that he lived through it; and it is a wonder that I was not killed. I was shot in the hand. It was not by aim; the shot was really meant for my cousin; but I was behind, looking on as usual, and the bullet came to me. It bled terribly, but I got home without fainting; and it healed after a time. You know how he suffered?'

'No,' said Stockdale. 'I only heard that he just escaped with his life.'

'He was shot in the back; but a rib turned the ball. He was badly hurt. We would not let him be took. The men carried him all night across the meads to Kingsbere, and hid him in a barn, dressing his wound as well as they could, till he was so far recovered as to be able to get about. Then he was caught, and tried with the others at the assizes; but they all got off. He had given up his mill for some time; and at last he went to Bristol, and took a passage to America, where he's settled.'

'What do you think of smuggling now?' said the minister gravely.

'I own that we were wrong,' said she. 'But I have suffered for it. I am very poor now, and my mother has been dead these twelve months. . . . But won't you come in, Mr Stockdale?'

Stockdale went in: and it is to be supposed that they came to an understanding, for a fortnight later there was a sale of Lizzy's furniture, and after that a wedding at a chapel in a neighbouring town.

He took her away from her old haunts to the home that he had made for himself in his native county, where she studied her duties as a minister's wife with praiseworthy assiduity. It is said that in after years she wrote an excellent tract called *Render unto Caesar; or, The Repentant Villagers*, in which her own experience was anonymously used as the introductory story. Stockdale got it printed, after making some corrections, and putting in a few powerful sentences of his own; and many hundreds of copies were distributed by the couple in the course of their married life.

NOTE: The ending of this story with the marriage of Lizzy and the minister was almost *de rigueur* in an English magazine at the time of writing. But at this late date, thirty years after, it may not be amiss to give the ending that would have been preferred by the writer to the convention used above. Moreover it corresponds more closely with the true incidents of which the tale is a vague and flickering shadow. Lizzy did not, in fact, marry the minister, but – much to her credit in the author's opinion – stuck to Jim the smuggler; and emigrated with him after their marriage, an expatrial step rather forced upon him by his adventurous antecedents. They both died in Wisconsin between 1850 and 1860. (May 1912.)

Rudyard Kipling

WILLIAM THE CONQUEROR

I

> I have done one braver thing
> Than all the Worthies did;
> And yet a braver thence doth spring,
> Which is, to keep that hid.
> *The Undertaking*

'Is it officially declared yet?'

'They've gone as far as to admit extreme local scarcity, and they've started relief-works in one or two districts, the paper says.'

'That means it will be declared as soon as they can make sure of the men and the rolling-stock. Shouldn't wonder if it were as bad as the Big Famine.'

'Can't be,' said Scott, turning a little in the long cane chair. 'We've had fifteen-anna crops in the north, and Bombay and Bengal report more than they know what to do with. They'll be able to check it before it gets out of hand. It will only be local.'

Martyn picked up the *Pioneer* from the table, read through the telegrams once more, and put up his feet on the chair-rests. It was a hot, dark, breathless evening, heavy with the smell of the newly-watered Mall. The flowers in the Club gardens were dead and black on their stalks, the little lotus-pond was a circle of caked mud, and the tamarisk-trees were white with the dust of days. Most of the men were at the band-stand in the public gardens – from the Club verandah you could hear the native Police band hammering stale waltzes – or on the polo-ground or in the high-walled fives-court, hotter than a Dutch oven. Half a dozen grooms, squatted at the heads of their ponies, waited their masters' return. From time to time a man would ride at a foot-pace into the Club compound, and list-lessly loaf over to the whitewashed barracks beside the main building. These were supposed to be chambers. Men lived in them, meeting the same faces night after night at dinner, and drawing out their office-work till the latest possible hour, that they might escape that doleful company.

'What are you going to do?' said Martyn, with a yawn. 'Let's have a swim before dinner.'

'Water's hot,' said Scott. 'I was at the bath today.'

'Play you game o' billiards – fifty up.'

'It's a hundred and five in the hall now. Sit still and don't be so abominably energetic.'

A grunting camel swung up to the porch, his badged and belted rider fumbling a leather pouch.

'*Kubber-kargaz – ki – yektraaa*,' the man whined, handing down the newspaper extra – a slip printed on one side only, and damp from the press. It was pinned on the green-baize board, between notices of ponies for sale and fox-terriers missing.

Martyn rose lazily, read it, and whistled. 'It's declared!' he cried. 'One, two, three – eight districts go under the operations of the Famine Code *ek dum*. They've put Jimmy Hawkins in charge.'

'Good business!' said Scott, with the first sign of interest he had shown. 'When in doubt hire a Punjabi. I worked under Jimmy when I first came out and he belonged to the Punjab. He has more *bundobust* than most men.'

'Jimmy's a Jubilee Knight now,' said Martyn. 'He was a good chap, even though he is a thrice-born civilian and went to the Benighted Presidency. What unholy names these Madras districts rejoice in – all *ungas* or *rungas* or *pillays* or *polliums*.'

A dog-cart drove up, and a man entered, mopping his head. He was editor of the one daily paper at the capital of a province of twenty-five million natives and a few hundred white men, and as his staff was limited to himself and one assistant, his office hours ran variously from ten to twenty a day.

'Hi, Raines; you're supposed to know everything,' said Martyn, stopping him. 'How's this Madras "scarcity" going to turn out?'

'No one knows as yet. There's a message as long as your arm coming in on the telephone. I've left my cub to fill it out. Madras has owned she can't manage it alone, and Jimmy seems to have a free hand in getting all the men he needs. Arbuthnot's warned to hold himself in readiness.'

'"Badger" Arbuthnot?'

'The Peshawur chap. Yes, and the *Pi* wires that Ellis and Clay have been moved from the North-West already, and they've taken half a dozen Bombay men, too. It's *pukka* famine, by the looks of it.'

'They're nearer the scene of action than we are; but if it comes to indenting on the Punjab this early, there's more in this than meets the eye,' said Martyn.

'Here today and gone tomorrow. Didn't come to stay for ever,' said Scott, dropping one of Marryat's novels, and rising to his feet. 'Martyn, your sister's waiting for you.'

A rough grey horse was backing and shifting at the edge of the verandah, where the light of a kerosene lamp fell on a brown calico habit and a white face under a grey felt hat.

'Right, O,' said Martyn. 'I'm ready. Better come and dine with us if you've nothing to do, Scott. William, is there any dinner in the house?'

'I'll go home first and see,' was the rider's answer. 'You can drive him over – at eight, remember.'

Scott moved leisurely to his room, and changed into the evening-dress of the season and the country: spotless white linen from head to foot, with a broad silk cummerbund. Dinner at the Martyns' was a decided improvement on the goat-mutton, twiney-tough fowl, and tinned entrées of the Club. But it was a great pity Martyn could not afford to send his sister to the Hills for the hot weather. As an Acting District Superintendent of Police, Martyn drew the magnificent pay of six hundred depreciated silver rupees a month, and his little four-roomed bungalow said just as much. There were the usual blue-and-white striped jail-made rugs on the uneven floor; the usual glass-studded Amritsar *phulkaris* draped to nails driven into the flaking whitewash of the walls; the usual half-dozen chairs that did not match, picked up at sales of dead men's effects; and the usual streaks of black grease where the leather punka-thong ran through the wall. It was as though everything had been unpacked the night before to be repacked next morning. Not a door in the house was true on its hinges. The little windows, fifteen feet up, were darkened with wasp-nests, and lizards hunted flies between the beams of the wood-ceiled roof. But all this was part of Scott's life. Thus did people live who had such an income; and in a land where each man's pay, age, and position are printed in a book, that all may read, it is hardly worth while to play at pretences in word or deed. Scott counted eight years' service in the Irrigation Department, and drew eight hundred rupees a month, on the understanding that if he served the State faithfully for another twenty-two years he could retire on a pension of some four hundred rupees a month. His working life, which had been spent chiefly under canvas or in temporary shelters where a man could sleep, eat, and write letters, was bound up with the opening and guarding of irrigation canals, the handling of two or three thousand workmen of all castes and creeds, and the payment of vast sums of coined silver. He had finished that spring, not without credit, the last section of the great Mosuhl Canal, and – much against his will, for he hated office work – had been sent in to serve during the hot weather on the accounts and supply side of the Department, with sole charge of the sweltering sub-office at the capital of the Province. Martyn knew this; William, his sister, knew it; and everybody knew it.

Scott knew, too, as well as the rest of the world, that Miss Martyn had come out to India four years before, to keep house for her brother, who, as every one, again, knew, had borrowed the money to pay for her passage, and that she ought, as all the world said, to have married long ago. Instead of this, she had refused some half a dozen subalterns, a civilian twenty years her senior, one major, and a man in the Indian Medical Department. This, too, was common property.

She had 'stayed down three hot weathers', as the saying is, because her brother was in debt and could not afford the expense of her keep at even a cheap hill-station. Therefore her face was white as bone, and in the centre of her forehead was a big silvery scar about the size of a shilling – the mark of a Delhi sore, which is the same as a 'Bagdad date'. This comes from drinking bad water, and slowly eats into the flesh till it is ripe enough to be burned out with acids.

None the less William had enjoyed herself hugely in her four years. Twice she had been nearly drowned while fording a river on horseback; once she had been run away with on a camel; had witnessed a midnight attack of thieves on her brother's camp; had seen justice administered, with long sticks, in the open under trees; could speak Urdu and even rough Punjabi with a fluency that was envied by her seniors; had altogether fallen out of the habit of writing to her aunts in England, or cutting the pages of the English magazines; had been through a very bad cholera year, seeing sights unfit to be told; and had wound up her experiences by six weeks of typhoid fever, during which her head had been shaved; and hoped to keep her twenty-third birthday that September. It is conceivable that her aunts would not have approved of a girl who never set foot on the ground if a horse were within hail; who rode to dances with a shawl thrown over her skirt; who wore her hair cropped and curling all over her head; who answered indifferently to the name of William or Bill; whose speech was heavy with the flowers of the vernacular; who could act in amateur theatricals, play on the banjo, rule eight servants and two horses, their accounts and their diseases, and look men slowly and deliberately between the eyes – yea, after they had proposed to her and been rejected.

'I like men who do things,' she had confided to a man in the Educational Department, who was teaching the sons of cloth merchants and dyers the beauty of Wordsworth's 'Excursion' in annotated cram-books; and when he grew poetical, William explained that she 'didn't understand poetry very much; it made her head ache,' and another broken heart took refuge at the Club. But it was all William's fault. She delighted

in hearing men talk of their own work, and that is the most
fatal way of bringing a man to your feet.

Scott had known her more or less for some three years,
meeting her, as a rule, under canvas when his camp and her
brother's joined for a day on the edge of the Indian Desert.
He had danced with her several times at the big Christmas
gatherings, when as many as five hundred white people came
into the station; and he had always a great respect for her
housekeeping and her dinners.

She looked more like a boy than ever when, after their meal,
she sat, one foot tucked under her, on the leather camp-sofa,
rolling cigarettes for her brother, her low forehead puckered
beneath the dark curls as she twiddled the papers. She stuck
out her rounded chin when the tobacco stayed in place, and,
with a gesture as true as a school-boy's throwing a stone,
tossed the finished article across the room to Martyn, who
caught it with one hand, and continued his talk with Scott. It
was all 'shop', – canals and the policing of canals; the sins of
villagers who stole more water than they had paid for, and the
grosser sin of native constables who connived at the thefts; of
the transplanting bodily of villages to newly-irrigated ground,
and of the coming fight with the desert in the south when the
Provincial funds should warrant the opening of the long-
surveyed Luni Protective Canal System. And Scott spoke
openly of his great desire to be put on one particular section of
the work where he knew the land and the people, and Martyn
sighed for a billet in the Himalayan foot-hills, and spoke his
mind of his superiors, and William rolled cigarettes and said
nothing, but smiled gravely on her brother because he was
happy.

At ten Scott's horse came to the door, and the evening was
ended.

The lights of the two low bungalows in which the daily
paper was printed showed bright across the road. It was too
early to try to find sleep, and Scott drifted over to the editor.
Raines, stripped to the waist like a sailor at a gun, lay in a long
chair, waiting for night telegrams. He had a theory that if a
man did not stay by his work all day and most of the night he

laid himself open to fever; so he ate and slept among his files.

'Can you do it?' he said drowsily. 'I didn't mean to bring you over.'

'About what? I've been dining at the Martyns'.'

'The famine, of course, Martyn's warned for it, too. They're taking men where they can find 'em. I sent a note to you at the Club just now, asking if you could do us a letter once a week from the south – between two and three columns, say. Nothing sensational, of course, but just plain facts about who is doing what, and so forth. Our regular rates – ten rupees a column.'

'Sorry, but it's out of my line,' Scott answered, staring absently at the map of India on the wall. 'It's rough on Martyn – very. Wonder what he'll do with his sister. Wonder what the deuce they'll do with me? I've no famine experience. This is the first I've heard of it. *Am* I ordered?'

'Oh, yes. Here's the wire. They'll put you on relief-works,' Raines went on, 'with a horde of Madrassis dying like flies; one native apothecary and half a pint of cholera-mixture among the ten thousand of you. It comes of your being idle for the moment. Every man who isn't doing two men's work seems to have been called upon. Hawkins evidently believes in Punjabis. It's going to be quite as bad as anything they have had in the last ten years.'

'It's all in the day's work, worse luck. I suppose I shall get my orders officially some time tomorrow. I'm glad I happened to drop in. Better go and pack my kit now. Who relieves me here – do you know?'

Raines turned over a sheaf of telegrams. 'McEuan,' said he, 'from Murree.'

Scott chuckled. 'He thought he was going to be cool all summer. He'll be very sick about this. Well, no good talking. 'Night.'

Two hours later, Scott, with a clear conscience, laid himself down to rest on a string cot in a bare room. Two worn bullock-trunks, a leather water-bottle, a tin ice-box, and his pet saddle sewed up in sacking were piled at the door, and the

Club secretary's receipt for last month's bill was under his pillow. His orders came next morning, and with them an unofficial telegram from Sir James Hawkins, who did not forget good men, bidding him report himself with all speed at some unpronounceable place fifteen hundred miles to the south, for the famine was sore in the land, and white men were needed.

A pink and fattish youth arrived in the red-hot noonday, whimpering a little at fate and famines, which never allowed any one three months' peace. He was Scott's successor – another cog in the machinery, moved forward behind his fellow, whose services, as the official announcement ran, 'were placed at the disposal of the Madras Government for famine duty until further orders'. Scott handed over the funds in his charge, showed him the coolest corner in the office, warned him against excess of zeal, and, as twilight fell, departed from the Club in a hired carriage with his faithful bodyservant, Faiz Ullah, and a mound of disordered baggage atop, to catch the Southern Mail at the loopholed and bastioned railway-station. The heat from the thick brick walls struck him across the face as if it had been a hot towel, and he reflected that there were at least five nights and four days of travel before him. Faiz Ullah, used to the chances of service, plunged into the crowd on the stone platform, while Scott, a black cheroot between his teeth, waited till his compartment should be set away. A dozen native policemen, with their rifles and bundles, shouldered into the press of Punjabi farmers, Sikh craftsmen, and greasy-locked Afreedee pedlars, escorting with all pomp Martyn's uniform-case, water-bottles, ice-box, and bedding-roll. They saw Faiz Ullah's lifted hand, and steered for it.

'My Sahib and your Sahib,' said Faiz Ullah to Martyn's man, 'will travel together. Thou and I, O brother, will thus secure the servants' places close by, and because of our masters' authority none will dare to disturb us.'

When Faiz Ullah reported all things ready, Scott settled down coatless and bootless on the broad leather-covered bunk. The heat under the iron-arched roof of the station might have been anything over a hundred degrees. At the last moment Martyn entered, hot and dripping.

'Don't swear,' said Scott lazily; 'it's too late to change your carriage; and we'll divide the ice.'

'What are you doing here?' said the policeman.

'Lent to the Madras Government, same as you. By Jove, it's a bender of a night! Are you taking any of your men down?'

'A dozen. Suppose I'll have to superintend relief distributions. Didn't know you were under orders too.'

'I didn't till after I left you last night. Raines had the news first. My orders came this morning. McEuan relieved me at four, and I got off at once. Shouldn't wonder if it wouldn't be a good thing – this famine – if we come through it alive.'

'Jimmy ought to put you and me to work together,' said Martyn; and then, after a pause: 'My sister's here.'

'Good business,' said Scott, heartily. 'Going to get off at Umballa, I suppose, and go up to Simla. Who'll she stay with there?'

'No-o; that's just the trouble of it. She's going down with me.'

Scott sat bolt upright under the oil lamp as the train jolted past Tarn-Taran station. 'What! You don't mean you couldn't afford –'

'Oh, I'd have scraped up the money somehow.'

'You might have come to me, to begin with,' said Scott, stiffly; 'we aren't altogether strangers.'

'Well, you needn't be stuffy about it. I might, but – you don't know my sister. I've been explaining and exhorting and entreating and commanding and all the rest of it all day – lost my temper since seven this morning, and haven't got it back yet – but she wouldn't hear of any compromise. A woman's entitled to travel with her husband if she wants to, and William says she's on the same footing. You see, we've been together all our lives, more or less, since my people died. It isn't as if she were an ordinary sister.'

'All the sisters I've heard of would have stayed where they were well off.'

'She's as clever as a man, confound her,' Martyn went on. 'She broke up the bungalow over my head while I was talking at her. 'Settled the whole *subchiz* in three hours – servants, horses, and all. I didn't get my orders till nine.'

'Jimmy Hawkins won't be pleased,' said Scott. 'A famine's no place for a woman.'

'Mrs Jim – I mean Lady Jim's in camp with him. At any rate, she says she will look after my sister. William wired down to her on her own responsibility, asking if she could come, and knocked the ground from under me by showing me her answer.'

Scott laughed aloud. 'If she can do that she can take care of herself, and Mrs Jim won't let her run into any mischief. There aren't many women, sisters or wives, who would walk into a famine with their eyes open. It isn't as if she didn't know what these things mean. She was through the Jaloo cholera last year.'

The train stopped at Amritsar, and Scott went back to the ladies' compartment, immediately behind their carriage. William, a cloth riding-cap on her curls, nodded affably.

'Come in and have some tea,' she said. 'Best thing in the world for heat-apoplexy.'

'Do I look as if I were going to have heat-apoplexy?'

'Never can tell,' said William, wisely. 'It's always best to be ready.'

She had arranged her belongings with the knowledge of an old campaigner. A felt-covered water-bottle hung in the draught of one of the shuttered windows; a tea-set of Russian china, packed in a wadded basket, stood ready on the seat; and a travelling spirit-lamp was clamped against the wood-work above it.

William served them generously, in large cups, hot tea, which saves the veins of the neck from swelling inopportunely on a hot night. It was characteristic of the girl that, her plan of action once settled, she asked for no comments on it. Life with men who had a great deal of work to do, and very little time to do it in, had taught her the wisdom of effacing as well as of fending for herself. She did not by word or deed suggest that she would be useful, comforting, or beautiful in their travels, but continued about her business serenely: put the cups back without clatter when tea was ended, and made cigarettes for her guests.

'This time last night,' said Scott, 'we didn't expect – er – this kind of thing, did we?'

'I've learned to expect anything,' said William. 'You know, in our service, we live at the end of the telegraph; but, of course, this ought to be a good thing for us all, departmentally – if we live.'

'It knocks us out of the running in our own Province,' Scott replied, with equal gravity. 'I hoped to be put on the Luni Protective Works this cold weather; but there's no saying how long the famine may keep us.'

'Hardly beyond October, I should think,' said Martyn. 'It will be ended, one way or the other, then.'

'And we've nearly a week of this,' said William. 'Shan't we be dusty when it's over?'

For a night and a day they knew their surroundings; and for a night and a day, skirting the edge of the great Indian Desert on a narrow-gauge line, they remembered how in the days of their apprenticeship they had come by that road from Bombay. Then the languages in which the names of the stations were written changed, and they launched south into a foreign land, where the very smells were new. Many long and heavily-laden grain trains were in front of them, and they could feel the hand of Jimmy Hawkins from far off. They waited in extemporized sidings blocked by processions of empty trucks returning to the north, and were coupled on to slow, crawling trains, and dropped at midnight, Heaven knew where; but it was furiously hot; and they walked to and fro among sacks, and dogs howled.

Then they came to an India more strange to them than to the untravelled Englishman – the flat, red India of palm-tree, palmyra-palm, and rice, the India of the picture-books, of *Little Henry and His Bearer* – all dead and dry in the baking heat. They had left the incessant passenger-traffic of the north and west far and far behind them. Here the people crawled to

the side of the train, holding their little ones in their arms; and
a loaded truck would be left behind, men and women cluster-
ing round and above it like ants by spilled honey. Once in the
twilight they saw on a dusty plain a regiment of little brown
men, each bearing a body over his shoulder; and when the
train stopped to leave yet another truck, they perceived that
the burdens were not corpses, but only foodless folk picked
up beside their dead oxen by a corps of Irregular troops. Now
they met more white men, here one and there two, whose
tents stood close to the line, and who came armed with written
authorities and angry words to cut off a truck. They were too
busy to do more than nod at Scott and Martyn, and stare
curiously at William, who could do nothing except make tea,
and watch how her men staved off the rush of wailing, walking
skeletons, putting them down three at a time in heaps, with
their own hands uncoupling the marked trucks, or taking
receipts from the hollow-eyed, weary white men, who spoke
another argot than theirs.

They ran out of ice, out of soda-water, and out of tea; for
they were six days and seven nights on the road, and it
seemed to them like seven times seven years.

At last, in a dry, hot dawn, in a land of death, lit by long
red fires of railway sleepers, where they were burning the dead,
they came to their destination, and were met by Jim Hawkins,
the Head of the Famine, unshaven, unwashed, but cheery, and
entirely in command of affairs.

Martyn, he decreed, then and there, was to live on trains till
further orders; was to go back with empty trucks, filling
them with starving people as he found them, and dropping
them at a famine-camp on the edge of the Eight Districts. He
would pick up supplies and return, and his constables would
guard the loaded grain-cars, also picking up people, and would
drop them at a camp a hundred miles south. Scott – Hawkins
was very glad to see Scott again – would, that same hour, take
charge of a convoy of bullock-carts, and would go south,
feeding as he went, to yet another famine-camp, far from the
rail, where he would leave his starving – there would be no
lack of starving on the route – and wait for orders by telegraph.

Generally, Scott was in all small things to do what he thought best.

William bit her underlip. There was no one in the wide world like her one brother, but Martyn's orders gave him no discretion. She came out, masked with dust from head to foot, a horseshoe wrinkle on her forehead, put there by much thinking during the past week, but as self-possessed as ever. Mrs Jim – who should have been Lady Jim, but that no one remembered to call her aright – took possession of her with a little gasp.

'Oh, I'm so glad you're here,' she almost sobbed. 'You oughtn't to, of course, but there – there isn't another woman in the place, and we must help each other, you know; and we've all the wretched people and the little babies they are selling.'

'I've seen some,' said William.

'Isn't it ghastly? I've bought twenty; they're in our camp; but won't you have something to eat first? We've more than ten people can do here; and I've got a horse for you. Oh, I'm so glad you've come! You're a Punjabi too, you know.'

'Steady, Lizzie,' said Hawkins, over his shoulder. 'We'll look after you, Miss Martyn. Sorry I can't ask you to breakfast, Martyn. You'll have to eat as you go. Leave two of your men to help Scott. These poor devils can't stand up to load carts. Saunders' (this to the engine-driver, half asleep in the cab), 'back down and get those empties away. You've "line clear" to Anundrapillay; they'll give you orders north of that. Scott, load up your carts from that B. P. P. truck, and be off as soon as you can. The Eurasian in the pink shirt is your interpreter and guide. You'll find an apothecary of sorts tied to the yoke of the second wagon. He's been trying to bolt; you'll have to look after him. Lizzie, drive Miss Martyn to camp, and tell them to send the red horse down here for me.'

Scott, with Faiz Ullah and two policemen, was already busy on the carts, backing them up to the back of the truck and unbolting the sideboards quietly, while the others pitched in the bags of millet and wheat. Hawkins watched him for as long as it took to fill one cart.

'That's a good man,' he said. 'If all goes well I shall work him – hard.' This was Jim Hawkins's notion of the highest compliment one human being could pay another.

An hour later Scott was under way; the apothecary threatening him with the penalties of the law for that he, a member of the Subordinate Medical Department, had been coerced and bound against his will and all laws governing the liberty of the subject; the pink-shirted Eurasian begging leave to see his mother, who happened to be dying three miles away: 'Only verree, verree short leave of absence, and will presently return, sar –'; the two constables, armed with staves, bringing up the rear; and Faiz Ullah, a Muhammedan's contempt for all Hindoos and foreigners in every line of his face, explaining to the drivers that though Scott Sahib was a man to be feared on all fours, he, Faiz Ullah, was Authority itself.

The procession creaked past Hawkins's camp – three stained tents under a clump of dead trees; behind them the famine-shed where a crowd of hopeless ones tossed their arms around the cooking kettles.

'Wish to Heaven William had kept out of it,' said Scott to himself, after a glance. 'We'll have cholera, sure as a gun, when the Rains come.'

But William seemed to have taken kindly to the operations of the Famine Code, which, when famine is declared, supersede the workings of the ordinary law. Scott saw her, the centre of a mob of weeping women, in a calico riding-habit and a blue-grey felt hat with a gold puggaree.

'I want fifty rupees, please. I forgot to ask Jack before he went away. Can you lend it me? It's for condensed milk for the babies,' said she.

Scott took the money from his belt, and handed it over without a word. 'For goodness sake take care of yourself,' he said.

'Oh, I shall be all right. We ought to get the milk in two days. By the way, the orders are, I was to tell you, that you're to take one of Sir Jim's horses. There's a grey Cabuli here that I thought would be just your style, so I've said you'd take him. Was that right?'

'That's awfully good of you. We can't either of us talk much about style, I'm afraid.'

Scott was in a weather-stained drill shooting-kit, very white at the seams and a little frayed at the wrists. William regarded him thoughtfully, from his pith helmet to his greased ankle-boots. 'You look very nice, I think. Are you sure you've everything you'll need – quinine, chlorodyne, and so on?'

'Think so,' said Scott, patting three or four of his shooting-pockets as the horse was led up and he mounted and rode alongside his convoy.

'Good-bye,' he cried.

'Good-bye, and good luck,' said William. 'I'm awfully obliged for the money.' She turned on a spurred heel and disappeared into the tent, while the carts pushed on past the famine-sheds, past the roaring lines of the thick, fat fires, down to the baked Gehenna of the South.

2

> So let us melt and make no noise,
>   No tear-floods nor sigh-tempests move;
> 'Twere profanation of our joys
>   To tell the laity our love.
>   *A Valediction*

It was punishing work, even though he travelled by night and camped by day; but within the limits of his vision there was no man whom Scott could call master. He was as free as Jimmy Hawkins – freer, in fact, for the Government held the Head of the Famine tied neatly to a telegraph-wire, and if Jimmy had ever regarded telegrams seriously, the death-rate of that famine would have been much higher than it was.

At the end of a few days' crawling Scott learned something of the size of the India which he served; and it astonished him. His carts, as you know, were loaded with wheat, millet, and barley, good food-grains needing only a little grinding. But the people to whom he brought the life-giving stuffs were rice-eaters. They knew how to hull rice in their mortars, but they knew nothing of the heavy stone querns of the North, and less of the material that the white man convoyed so laboriously. They clamoured for rice – unhusked paddy, such as they were accustomed to – and, when they found that there was none, broke away weeping from the sides of the cart. What was the use of these strange hard grains that choked their throats? They would die. And then and there were many of them kept their word. Others took their allowance, and bartered enough millet to feed a man through a week for a few handfuls of rotten rice saved by some less unfortunate. A few put their shares into the rice-mortars, pounded it, and made a paste with foul water; but they were very few. Scott understood, dimly that many people in the India of the South ate rice, as a rule, but he had spent his service in a grain Province, had seldom seen rice in the blade or the ear, and least of all would have believed that, in time of deadly need, men would die at arm's length of plenty, sooner than touch food they did not know. In vain the interpreters interpreted; in vain his two policemen showed by vigorous pantomime what should be done. The starving crept away to their bark and weeds, grubs, leaves, and clay, and left the open sacks untouched. But sometimes the women laid their phantoms of children at Scott's feet, looking back as they staggered away.

Faiz Ullah opined it was the will of God that these foreigners should die, and therefore it remained only to give orders to burn the dead. None the less there was no reason why the Sahib should lack his comforts, and Faiz Ullah, a campaigner of experience, had picked up a few lean goats and had added them to the procession. That they might give milk for the morning meal, he was feeding them on the good grain that these imbeciles rejected. 'Yes,' said Faiz Ullah; 'if the Sahib thought fit, a little milk might be given to some of the babies'; but, as the Sahib well knew, babies were cheap, and, for his own part, Faiz Ullah held that there was no Government order as to babies. Scott spoke forcefully to Faiz Ullah and the two policemen, and bade them capture goats where they could find them. This they most joyously did, for it was a recreation, and many ownerless goats were driven in. Once fed, the poor brutes were willing enough to follow the carts, and a few days' good food – food such as human beings died for lack of – set them in milk again.

'But I am no goatherd,' said Faiz Ullah. 'It is against my *izzat* [my honour].'

'When we cross the Bias River again we will talk of *izzat*,' Scott replied. 'Till that day thou and the policemen shall be sweepers to the camp, if I give the order.'

'Thus, then, it is done,' grunted Faiz Ullah, 'if the Sahib will have it so'; and he showed how a goat should be milked, while Scott stood over him.

'Now we will feed them,' said Scott; 'thrice a day we will feed them'; and he bowed his back to the milking, and took a horrible cramp.

When you have to keep connection unbroken between a restless mother of kids and a baby who is at the point of death, you suffer in all your system. But the babies were fed. Morning, noon and evening Scott would solemnly lift them out one by one from their nest of gunny-bags under the cart-tilts. There were always many who could do no more than breathe, and the milk was dropped into their toothless mouths drop by drop, with due pauses when they choked. Each morning, too, the goats were fed; and since they would straggle without a leader, and since the natives were hirelings, Scott was forced to give up riding, and pace slowly at the head of his flocks, accommodating his step to their weaknesses. All this was sufficiently absurd, and he felt the absurdity keenly; but at least he was saving life, and when the women saw that their children did not die, they made shift to eat a little of the strange foods, and crawled after the carts, blessing the master of the goats.

'Give the women something to live for,' said Scott to himself, as he sneezed in the dust of a hundred little feet, 'and they'll hang on somehow. But this beats William's condensed-milk trick all to pieces. I shall never live it down, though.'

He reached his destination very slowly, found that a rice-ship had come in from Burma, and that stores of paddy were available; found also an overworked Englishman in charge of the shed, and, loading the carts, set back to cover the ground he had already passed. He left some of the children and half his goats at the famine-shed. For this he was not thanked by the Englishman, who had already more stray babies than he knew what to do with. Scott's back was suppled to stooping now, and he went on with his wayside ministrations in addition to distributing the paddy. More babies and more goats were added unto him; but now some of the babies wore rags, and beads round their wrists or necks. '*That*,' said the interpreter, as though Scott did not know, 'signifies that their mothers hope in eventual contingency to resume them offeecially.'

'The sooner the better,' said Scott; but at the same time he marked, with the pride of ownership, how this or that little Ramaswamy was putting on flesh like a bantam. As the paddy-carts were emptied he headed for Hawkins's camp by the railway, timing his arrival to fit in with the dinner-hour, for it was long since he had eaten at a cloth. He had no desire to make any dramatic entry, but an accident of the sunset ordered it that, when he had taken off his helmet to get the evening breeze, the low light should fall across his forehead, and he could not see what was before him; while one waiting at the tent door beheld, with new eyes, a young man, beautiful as Paris, a god in a halo of golden dust, walking slowly at the head of his flocks, while at his knee ran small naked Cupids. But she laughed – William in a slate-coloured blouse, laughed consumedly till Scott, putting the best face he could upon the matter, halted his armies and bade her admire the kindergarten. It was an unseemly sight, but the proprieties had been left ages ago, with the tea-party at Amritsar Station, fifteen hundred miles to the northward.

'They are coming on nicely,' said William. 'We've only five-and-twenty here now. The women are beginning to take them away again.'

'Are you in charge of the babies, then?'

'Yes – Mrs Jim and I. We didn't think of goats, though. We've been trying condensed milk and water.'

'Any losses?'

'More than I care to think of,' said William, with a shudder. 'And you?'

Scott said nothing. There had been many little burials along his route – many mothers who had wept when they did not find again the children they had trusted to the care of the Government.

Then Hawkins came out carrying a razor, at which Scott looked hungrily, for he had a beard that he did not love. And when they sat down to dinner in the tent he told his tale in few words, as it might have been an official report. Mrs Jim snuffled from time to time, and Jim bowed his head judicially; but William's grey eyes were on the clean-shaven face, and it was to her that Scott seemed to speak.

'Good for the Pauper Province!' said William, her chin in her hand, as she leaned forward among the wine-glasses. Her cheeks had fallen in, and the scar on her forehead was more prominent than ever, but the well-turned neck rose roundly as a column from the ruffle of the blouse which was the accepted evening-dress in camp.

'It was awfully absurd at times,' said Scott. 'You see I didn't know much about milking or babies. They'll chaff my head off, if the tale goes north.'

'Let 'em,' said William, haughtily. 'We've all done coolie-work since we came. I know Jack has.' This was to Hawkins's address, and the big man smiled blandly.

'Your brother's a highly efficient officer, William,' said he, 'and I've done him the honour of treating him as he deserves. Remember, I write the confidential reports.'

'Then you must say that William's worth her weight in gold,' said Mrs Jim. 'I don't know what we should have done without her. She has been everything to us.' She dropped her hand upon William's, which was rough with much handling of reins, and William patted it softly. Jim beamed on the company. Things were going well with his world. Three of his more grossly incompetent men had died, and their places had been filled by their betters. Every day brought the rains nearer. They had put out the famine in five of the Eight

Districts, and, after all, the death-rate had not been too heavy – things considered. He looked Scott over carefully, as an ogre looks over a man, and rejoiced in his thews and iron-hard condition.

'He's just the least bit in the world tucked up,' said Jim to himself, 'but he can do two men's work yet.' Then he was aware that Mrs Jim was telegraphing to him, and according to the domestic code the message ran: 'A clear case. Look at them!'

He looked and listened. All that William was saying was: 'What can you expect of a country where they call a *bhistee* [a water-carrier] a *tunni-cutch*?' and all that Scott answered was: 'I shall be precious glad to get back to the Club. Save me a dance at the Christmas ball, won't you?'

'It's a far cry from here to the Lawrence Hall,' said Jim. 'Better turn in early, Scott. It's paddy-carts tomorrow; you'll begin loading at five.'

'Aren't you going to give Mr Scott one day's rest?'

'Wish I could, Lizzie. 'Fraid I can't. As long as he can stand up we must use him.'

'Well, I've had one Europe evening, at least . . . By Jove, I'd nearly forgotten! What do I do about those babies of mine?'

'Leave them here,' said William – 'we are in charge of that – and as many goats as you can spare. I must learn how to milk now.'

'If you care to get up early enough tomorrow I'll show you. I have to milk, you see; and, by the way, half of 'em have beads and things round their necks. You must be careful not to take 'em off, in case the mothers turn up.'

'You forget I've had some experience here.'

'I hope to goodness you won't overdo it.' Scott's voice was unguarded.

'I'll take care of her,' said Mrs Jim, telegraphing hundred-word messages as she carried William off, while Jim gave Scott his orders for the coming campaign. It was very late – nearly nine o'clock.

'Jim you're a brute,' said his wife, that night; and the Head of the Famine chuckled.

'Not a bit of it, dear. I remember doing the first Jandiala Settlement for the sake of a girl in a crinoline; and she was slender, Lizzie. I've never done as good a piece of work since. *He'll* work like a demon.'

'But you might have given him one day.'

'And let things come to a head now? No, dear; it's their happiest time.'

'I don't believe either of the dears know what's the matter with them. Isn't it beautiful? Isn't it lovely?'

'Getting up at three to learn to milk, bless her heart! Ye gods, why must we grow old and fat?'

'She's a darling. She has done more work under me – '

'Under *you*! The day after she came she was in charge and you were subordinate, and you've stayed there ever since. She manages you almost as well as you manage me.'

'She doesn't, and that's why I love her. She's as direct as a man – as her brother.'

'Her brother's weaker than she is. He's always coming to me for orders; but he's honest, and a glutton for work. I confess I'm rather fond of William, and if I had a daughter – '

The talk ended there. Far away in the Derajat was a child's grave more than twenty years old, and neither Jim nor his wife spoke of it any more.

'All the same, you're responsible,' Jim added, after a moment's silence.

'Bless 'em!' said Mrs Jim sleepily.

Before the stars paled, Scott, who slept in an empty cart, waked and went about his work in silence; it seemed at that hour unkind to rouse Faiz Ullah and the interpreter. His head being close to the ground, he did not hear William till she stood over him in the dingy old riding-habit, her eyes still heavy with sleep, a cup of tea and a piece of toast in her hands. There was a baby on the ground, squirming on a piece of blanket, and a six-year-old child peered over Scott's shoulder.

'Hai, you little rip,' said Scott, 'how the deuce do you expect to get your rations if you aren't quiet?'

A cool white hand steadied the brat, who forthwith choked as the milk gurgled into his mouth.

'Mornin',' said the milker. 'You've no notion how these little fellows can wriggle.'

'Oh yes, I have.' She whispered, because the world was asleep. 'Only I feed them with a spoon or a rag. Yours are fatter than mine. . . . And you've been doing this day after day, twice a day?' The voice was almost lost.

'Yes; it was absurd. Now you try,' he said, giving place to the girl. 'Look out! A goat's not a cow.'

The goat protested against the amateur, and there was a scuffle, in which Scott snatched up the baby. Then it was all to do over again, and William laughed softly and merrily. She managed, however, to feed two babies, and a third.

'Don't the little beggars take it well!' said Scott. 'I trained 'em.'

They were very busy and interested, when, lo! it was broad daylight, and before they knew, the camp was awake, and they kneeled among the goats, surprised by the day, both flushed to the temples. Yet all the round world rolling up out of the darkness might have heard and seen all that had passed between them.

'Oh,' said William, unsteadily, snatching up the tea and toast. 'I had this made for you. It's stone-cold now. I thought you mightn't have anything ready so early. Better not drink it. It's – it's stone-cold.'

'That's awfully kind of you. It's just right. It's awfully good of you, really. I'll leave my kids and goats with you and Mrs Jim; and, of course, anyone in camp can show you about the milking.'

'Of course,' said William; and she grew pinker and pinker and statelier and more stately, as she strode back to her tent, fanning herself vigorously with the saucer.

There were shrill lamentations through the camp when the elder children saw their nurse move off without them. Faiz Ullah unbent so far as to jest with the policemen, and Scott turned purple with shame because Hawkins, already in the saddle, roared.

A child escaped from the care of Mrs Jim, and, running like a rabbit, clung to Scott's boot, William pursuing with long easy strides.

'I will not go – I will not go!' shrieked the child, twining his feet round Scott's ankle. 'They will kill me here. I do not know these people.'

'I say,' said Scott, in broken Tamil, 'I say, she will do you no harm. Go with her and be well fed.'

'Come!' said William, panting, with a wrathful glance at Scott, who stood helpless and, as it were, hamstrung.

'Go back,' said Scott quickly to William. 'I'll send the little chap over in a minute.'

The tone of authority had its effect, but in a way Scott did not exactly intend. The boy loosened his grasp, and said with gravity, 'I did not know the woman was thine. I will go.' Then he cried to his companions, a mob of three-, four-, and five-year-olds waiting on the success of his venture ere they stampeded: 'Go back and eat. It is our man's woman. She will obey his orders.'

Jim collapsed where he sat; Faiz Ullah and the two policemen grinned; and Scott's orders to the cartmen flew like hail.

'That is the custom of the Sahibs when truth is told in their presence,' said Faiz Ullah. 'The time comes that I must seek new service. Young wives, especially such as speak our language and have knowledge of the ways of the Police, make great trouble for honest butlers in the matter of weekly accounts.'

What William thought of it all she did not say, but when her brother, ten days later, came to camp for orders, and heard of Scott's performances, he said, laughing: 'Well, that settles it. He'll be *Bakri* Scott to the end of his days' (*Bakri*, in the northern vernacular, means a goat). 'What a lark! I'd have given a month's pay to have seen him nursing famine babies. I fed some with *conjee* [rice-water], but that was all right.'

'It's perfectly disgusting,' said his sister, with blazing eyes. 'A man does something like – like that – and all you other men think of is to give him an absurd nickname, and then you laugh and think it's funny.'

'Ah,' said Mrs Jim, sympathetically.

'Well, *you* can't talk, William. You christened little Miss Demby the Button-quail last cold weather; you know you did. India's the land of nicknames.'

'That's different,' William replied. 'She was only a girl, and she hadn't done anything except walk like a quail, and she *does*. But it isn't fair to make fun of a man.'

'Scott won't care,' said Martyn. 'You can't get a rise out of old Scotty. I've been trying for eight years, and you've only known him for three. How does he look?'

'He looks very well,' said William, and went away with a flushed cheek. '*Bakri* Scott, indeed!' Then she laughed to herself, for she knew the country of her service. 'But it will be *Bakri* all the same'; and she repeated it under her breath several times slowly, whispering it into favour.

When he returned to his duties on the railway, Martyn spread the name far and wide among his associates, so that Scott met it as he led his paddy-carts to war. The natives believed it to be some English title of honour, and the cart-drivers used it in all simplicity till Faiz Ullah, who did not approve of foreign japes, broke their heads. There was very little time for milking now, except at the big camps, where Jim had extended Scott's idea, and was feeding large flocks on the useless northern grains. Enough paddy had come into the Eight Districts to hold the people safe, if it were only distributed quickly; and for that purpose no one was better than the big Canal officer, who never lost his temper, never gave an unnecessary order, and never questioned an order given. Scott pressed on, saving his cattle, washing their galled necks daily, so that no time should be lost on the road; reported himself with his rice at the minor famine-sheds, unloaded, and went back light by forced night-march to the next distributing centre, to find Hawkins's unvarying telegram: 'Do it again.' And he did it again and again, and yet again, while Jim Hawkins, fifty miles away, marked off on a big map the tracks of his wheels gridironing the stricken lands. Others did well – Hawkins reported at the end that they all did well – but Scott was the most excellent, for he kept good coined rupees by him, and paid for his own cart-repairs on the spot, and ran to meet all sorts of unconsidered extras, trusting to be recouped later. Theoretically, the Government should have paid for every shoe and linchpin, for every hand employed in the loading; but Government vouchers cash themselves slowly, and intelligent and efficient clerks write at great length, contesting unauthorized expenditure of eight annas. The man who wishes to make his work a success must draw on his own bank-account of money or other things as he goes.

'I told you he'd work,' said Jimmy to his wife at the end of six weeks. 'He's been in sole charge of a couple of thousand men up north on the Mosuhl Canal for a year, and he gives one less trouble than young Martyn with his ten constables; and I'm morally certain – only Government doesn't recognize moral obligations – that he's spent about half his pay to grease his wheels. Look at this, Lizzie, for one week's work! Forty miles in two days with twelve carts; two days' halt building a famine-shed for young Rogers (Rogers ought to have built it himself, the idiot!). Then forty miles back again, loading six carts on the way, and distributing all Sunday. Then in the evening he pitches in a twenty-page demi-official to me, saying that the people where he is might be "advantageously employed on relief-work", and suggesting that he put 'em to work on some broken-down old reservoir he's discovered, so as to have a good water-supply when the Rains come. He thinks he can caulk the dam in a fortnight. Look at his marginal sketches – aren't they clear and good? I knew he was *pukka*, but I didn't know he was as *pukka* as this!'

'I must show these to William,' said Mrs Jim. 'The child's wearing herself out among the babies.'

'Not more than you are, dear. Well, another two months ought to see us out of the wood. I'm sorry it's not in my power to recommend you for a V.C.'

William sat late in her tent that night, reading through page after page of the square handwriting, patting the sketches of proposed repairs to the reservoir, and wrinkling her eyebrows over the columns of figures of estimated water-supply.

'And he finds time to do all this,' she cried to herself, 'and

. . . well, I also was present. I've saved one or two babies.'

She dreamed for the twentieth time of the god in the golden dust, and woke refreshed to feed loathsome black children, scores of them, wastrels picked up by the wayside, their bones almost breaking their skin, terrible and covered with sores.

Scott was not allowed to leave his cart-work, but his letter was duly forwarded to the Government, and he had the consolation, not rare in India, of knowing that another man was reaping where he had sown. That also was discipline profitable to the soul.

'He's much too good to waste on canals,' said Jimmy. 'Any one can oversee coolies. You needn't be angry, William: he can – but I need my pearl among bullock-drivers, and I've transferred him to the Khanda district, where he'll have it all to do over again. He should be marching now.'

'He's *not* a coolie,' said William, furiously. 'He ought to be doing his regulation work.'

'He's the best man in his service, and that's saying a good deal; but if you *must* use razors to cut grindstones, why, I prefer the best cutlery.'

'Isn't it almost time we saw him again?' said Mrs Jim. 'I'm sure the poor boy hasn't had a respectable meal for a month. He probably sits on a cart and eats sardines with his fingers.'

'All in good time, dear. Duty before decency – wasn't it Mr Chucks said that?'

'No; it was Midshipman Easy,' William laughed. 'I sometimes wonder how it will feel to dance or listen to a band again, or sit under a roof. I can't believe that I ever wore a ball-frock in my life.'

'One minute,' said Mrs Jim, who was thinking. 'If he goes to Khanda, he passes within five miles of us. Of course he'll ride in.'

'Oh no, he won't,' said William.

'How do you know, dear?'

'It'll take him off his work. He won't have time.'

'He'll make it,' said Mrs Jim, with a twinkle.

'It depends on his own judgement. There's absolutely no reason why he shouldn't, if he thinks fit,' said Jim.

'He won't see fit,' William replied, without sorrow or emotion. 'It wouldn't be him if he did.'

'One certainly gets to know people rather well in times like these,' said Jim, drily; but William's face was serene as ever, and, as she prophesied, Scott did not appear.

The Rains fell at last, late, but heavily; and the dry, gashed earth was red mud, and servants killed snakes in the camp, where every one was weather-bound for a fortnight – all except Hawkins who took horse and splashed about in the wet, rejoicing. Now the Government decreed that seed-grain should be distributed to the people as well as advances of money for the purchase of new oxen; and the white men were doubly worked for this new duty, while William skipped from brick to brick laid down on the trampled mud, and dosed her charges with warming medicines that made them rub their little round stomachs; and the milch-goats throve on the rank grass. There was never a word from Scott in the Khanda district, away to the south-east, except the regular telegraphic report to Hawkins. The rude country roads had disappeared; his drivers were half mutinous; one of Martyn's loaned policemen had died of cholera; and Scott was taking thirty grains of quinine a day to fight the fever that comes if one works hard in heavy rain; but those were things he did not consider necessary to report. He was, as usual, working from a base of supplies on a railway line, to cover a circle of fifteen miles radius, and since full loads were impossible, he took quarter-loads, and toiled four times as hard by consequence; for he did not choose to risk an epidemic which might have grown uncontrollable by assembling villagers in thousands at the relief-sheds. It was cheaper to take Government bullocks, work them to death, and leave them to the crows in the way-side sloughs.

That was the time when eight years of clean living and hard condition told, though a man's head were ringing like a bell from the cinchona, and the earth swayed under his feet when he stood and under his bed when he slept. If Hawkins had seen fit to make him a bullock-driver, that, he thought, was entirely Hawkins's own affair. There were men in the North

who would know what he had done; men of thirty years'
service in his own department who would say that it was
'not half bad'; and above, immeasurably above all men of all
grades, there was William in the thick of the fight, who would
approve because she understood. He had so trained his mind
that it would hold fast to the mechanical routine of the day,
though his own voice sounded strange in his own ears, and his
hands, when he wrote, grew large as pillows or small as peas
at the end of his wrists. That steadfastness bore his body to the
telegraph-office at the railway station, and dictated a telegram
to Hawkins, saying that the Khanda district was, in his
judgement, now safe, and he 'waited further orders'.

The Madrassee telegraph-clerk did not approve of a large
gaunt man falling over him in a dead faint, not so much
because of the weight, as because of the names and blows that
Faiz Ullah dealt him when he found the body rolled under a
bench. Then Faiz Ullah took blankets and quilts and coverlets
where he found them, and lay down under them at his master's
side, and bound his arms with a tent-rope, and filled him with
a horrible stew of herbs, and set the policeman to fight him
when he wished to escape from the intolerable heat of his
coverings, and shut the door of the telegraph-office to keep
out the curious for two nights and one day; and when a light
engine came down the line, and Hawkins kicked in the door,
Scott hailed him weakly, but in a natural voice, and Faiz Ullah
stood back and took all the credit.

'For two nights, Heaven-born, he was *pagal*,' said Faiz
Ullah. 'Look at my nose, and consider the eye of the policeman. He beat us with his bound hands; but we sat upon him,
Heaven-born, and though his words were *tez*, we sweated him.
Heaven-born, never has been such a sweat! He is weaker now
than a child; but the fever has gone out of him, by the grace of
God. There remains only my nose and the eye of the constab-
eel. Sahib, shall I ask for my dismissal because my Sahib has
beaten me?' And Faiz Ullah laid his long thin hand carefully on
Scott's chest to be sure that the fever was all gone, ere he went
out to open tinned soups and discourage such as laughed at his
swelled nose.

'The district's all right,' Scott whispered. 'It doesn't make any difference. You got my wire? I shall be fit in a week. 'Can't understand how it happened. I shall be fit in a few days.'

'You're coming into camp with us,' said Hawkins.

'But look here – but – '

'It's all over except the shouting. We shan't need you Punjabis any more. On my honour, we shan't. Martyn goes back in a few weeks; Arbuthnot's returned already; Ellis and Clay are putting the last touches to a new feeder line the Government's built as relief-work. Morten's dead – he was a Bengal man, though; you wouldn't know him. 'Pon my word, you and Will – Miss Martyn – seem to have come through it as well as anybody.'

'Oh, how is she?' The voice went up and down as he spoke.

'She was in great form when I left her. The Roman Catholic Missions are adopting the 'unclaimed babies to turn them into little priests; the Basil Mission is taking some, and the mothers are taking the rest. You should hear the little beggars howl when they're sent away from William. She's pulled down a bit, but so are we all. Now, when do you suppose you'll be able to move?'

'I can't come into camp in this state. I won't,' he replied pettishly.

'Well, you *are* rather a sight, but from what I gathered there it seemed to me they'd be glad to see you under any conditions. I'll look over your work here, if you like, for a couple of days, and you can pull yourself together while Faiz Ullah feeds you up.'

Scott could walk dizzily by the time Hawkins's inspection was ended, and he flushed all over when Jim said of his work in the district that it was 'not half bad', and volunteered, further, that he had considered Scott his right-hand man through the famine, and would feel it his duty to say as much officially.

So they came back by rail to the old camp; but there were no crowds near it, the long fires in the trenches were dead and black, and the famine-sheds stood almost empty.

'You see!' said Jim. 'There isn't much more for us to do. Better ride up and see the wife. They've pitched a tent for you. Dinner's at seven. I'll see you then.'

Riding at a foot-pace, Faiz Ullah by his stirrup, Scott came to William in the brown-calico riding-habit, sitting at the dining-tent door, her hands in her lap, white as ashes, thin and worn, with no lustre in her hair. There did not seem to be any Mrs Jim on the horizon, and all that William could say was: 'My word, how pulled down you look!'

'I've had a touch of fever. You don't look very well yourself.'

'Oh, I'm fit enough. We've stamped it out. I suppose you know?'

Scott nodded. 'We shall all be returned in a few weeks. Hawkins told me.'

'Before Christmas, Mrs Jim says. Shan't you be glad to go back? I can smell the wood-smoke already'; William sniffed. 'We shall be in time for all the Christmas doings. I don't suppose even the Punjab Government would be base enough to transfer Jack till the new year?'

'It seems hundreds of years ago – the Punjab and all that – doesn't it? Are you glad you came?'

'Now it's all over, yes. It has been ghastly here. You know we had to sit still and do nothing, and Sir Jim was away so much.'

'Do nothing! How did you get on with the milking?'

'I managed it somehow – after you taught me.'

Then the talk stopped with an almost audible jar. Still no Mrs Jim.

'That reminds me I owe you fifty rupees for the condensed milk. I thought perhaps you'd be coming here when you were transferred to the Khanda district, and I could pay you then; but you didn't.'

'I passed within five miles of the camp. It was in the middle of a march, you see, and the carts were breaking down every few minutes, and I couldn't get 'em over the ground till ten o'clock that night. But I wanted to come awfully. You knew I did, didn't you?'

'I – believe – I – did,' said William, facing him with level eyes. She was no longer white.

'Did you understand?'

'Why you didn't ride in? Of course I did.'

'Why?'

'Because you couldn't, of course. I knew that.'

'Did you care?'

'If you had come in – but I knew you wouldn't – but if you *had*, I should have cared a great deal. You know I should.'

'Thank God I didn't! Oh, but I wanted to! I couldn't trust myself to ride in front of the carts, because I kept edging 'em over here, don't you know?'

'I knew you wouldn't,' said William, contentedly. 'Here's your fifty.'

Scott bent forward and kissed the hand that held the greasy notes. Its fellow patted him awkwardly but very tenderly on the head.

'And *you* knew, too, didn't you?' said William, in a new voice.

'No, on my honour, I didn't. I hadn't the – the cheek to expect anything of the kind, except ... I say, were you out riding anywhere the day I passed by to Khanda?'

William nodded, and smiled after the manner of an angel surprised in a good deed.

'Then it was just a speck I saw of your habit in the – '

'Palm-grove on the Southern cart-road. I saw your helmet when you came up from the nullah by the temple – just enough to be sure that you were all right. D'you care?'

This time Scott did not kiss her hand, for they were in the dusk of the dining-tent, and, because William's knees were trembling under her, she had to sit down in the nearest chair, where she wept long and happily, her head on her arms; and when Scott imagined that it would be well to comfort her, she needing nothing of the kind, she ran to her own tent; and Scott went out into the world, and smiled upon it largely and idiotically. But when Faiz Ullah brought him a drink, he found it necessary to support one hand with the other, or the good

whisky and soda would have been spilled abroad. There are
fevers and fevers.

But it was worse – much worse – the strained, eye-shirking
talk at dinner till the servants had withdrawn, and worst of all
when Mrs Jim, who had been on the edge of weeping from
the soup down, kissed Scott and William, and they drank one
whole bottle of champagne, hot, because there was no ice, and
Scott and William sat outside the tent in the starlight till Mrs
Jim drove them in for fear of more fever.

Apropos of these things and some others William said:
'Being engaged is abominable, because, you see, one has no
official position. We must be thankful that we've lots of
things to do.'

'Things to do!' said Jim, when that was reported to him.
'They're neither of them any good any more. I can't get five
hours' work a day out of Scott. He's in the clouds half the
time.'

'Oh, but they're so beautiful to watch, Jimmy. It will break
my heart when they go. Can't you do anything for him?'

'I've given the Government the impression – at least, I hope
I have – that he personally conducted the entire famine. But all
he wants is to get on to the Luni Canal Works, and William's
just as bad. Have you ever heard 'em talking of barrage and
aprons and wastewater? It's their style of spooning, I suppose.'

Mrs Jim smiled tenderly. 'Ah, that's in the intervals – bless
'em.'

And so Love ran about the camp unrebuked in broad
daylight, while men picked up the pieces and put them neatly
away of the Famine in the Eight Districts.

*

Morning brought the penetrating chill of the Northern
December, the layers of wood-smoke, the dusty grey blue of
the tamarisks, the domes of ruined tombs, and all the smell of
the white Northern plains, as the mail-train ran on to the mile-
long Sutlej Bridge. William, wrapped in a *poshteen* – silk
embroidered sheepskin jacket trimmed with rough astrakhan –
looked out with moist eyes and nostrils that dilated joyously.

The South of pagodas and palm-trees, the over-populated Hindu South, was done with. Here was the land she knew and loved, and before her lay the good life she understood, among folk of her own caste and mind.

They were picking them up at almost every station now – men and women coming in for the Christmas Week, with racquets, with bundles of polo-sticks, with dear and bruised cricket-bats, with fox terriers and saddles. The greater part of them wore jackets like William's, for the Northern cold is as little to be trifled with as the Northern heat. And William was among them and of them, her hands deep in her pockets, her collar turned up over her ears, stamping her feet on the platforms as she walked up and down to get warm, visiting from carriage to carriage, and everywhere being congratulated. Scott was with the bachelors at the far end of the train, where they chaffed him mercilessly about feeding babies and milking goats; but from time to time he would stroll up to William's window, and murmur: 'Good enough, isn't it?' and William would answer with sighs of pure delight: 'Good enough, indeed.' The large open names of the home towns were good to listen to. Umballa, Ludhiana, Phillour, Jullundur, they rang like the coming marriage-bells in her ears, and William felt deeply and truly sorry for all strangers and outsiders – visitors, tourists, and those fresh-caught for the service of the country.

It was a glorious return, and when the bachelors gave the Christmas ball, William was, unofficially, you might say, the chief and honoured guest among the stewards, who could make things very pleasant for their friends. She and Scott danced nearly all the dances together, and sat out the rest in the big dark gallery overlooking the superb teak floor, where the uniforms blazed, and the spurs clinked, and the new frocks and four hundred dancers went round and round till the draped flags on the pillars flapped and bellied to the whirl of it.

About midnight half a dozen men who did not care for dancing came over from the Club to play 'Waits', and – that was a surprise the stewards had arranged – before any one knew what had happened, the band stopped, and hidden voices

broke into 'Good King Wenceslaus', and William in the
gallery hummed and beat time with her foot:

> Mark my footsteps well, my page,
> Tread thou in them boldly.
> Thou shalt find the winter's rage
> Freeze thy blood less coldly!

'Oh, I hope they are going to give us another! Isn't it pretty,
coming out of the dark in that way? Look — look down.
There's Mrs Gregory wiping her eyes!'

'It's like home, rather,' said Scott. 'I remember — '

'H'sh! Listen! — dear.' And it began again:

> When shepherds watched their flocks by night —

'A-h-h!' said William, drawing closer to Scott.

> All seated on the ground,
> The Angel of the Lord came down,
> And glory shone around.
> 'Fear not,' said he (for mighty dread
> Had seized their troubled mind);
> 'Glad tidings of great joy I bring
> To you and all mankind.'

This time it was William that wiped her eyes.

THE BUCKET AND THE ROPE

A BUCKET once lay upon its side in a little shed, that was a short way down a by-lane, near to the village of Shelton.

This bucket, a large one, had been kicked over by a man who had hanged himself up by the neck, by means of an odd piece of rope that he had tied to a strong beam.

The man's name who had hanged himself was Mr Dendy, who rented a few pleasant fields that he used to plough happily, and, besides keeping a few good cows, he fattened some nice pigs.

Every servant, be he never so humble, is interested in his master, whose habits of life, goings and comings, loves and hates, are watched and commented upon. Mr Dendy's movements as well as his behaviour had always been of great interest to the bucket and to the rope; who, when together, which was often the case, for they lived in the same shed, would speak of all that Mr Dendy did, and endeavour to find out as best they might a reason for his actions.

Both were interested in any kind of life that was not like themselves, such as mankind, because both were humble and did not consider, as so many do, that they or their own kind deserved the most notice.

In order to study men, both the bucket and the rope decided to take Mr Dendy as an example of humanity, believing, as they well might, that the ways and notions of a simple countryman ought to be easier to understand than those of one more sly and cunning. They wished to study Mr Dendy in order to find out from his behaviour what other men were like; to learn from his doings how they did, to find out the causes of their sorrows and joys, so as to journey a little nearer to the Truth that is always so hard to discover.

Now and again the two friends had been a little puzzled by Mr Dendy, who did not often act as they would have expected him to, for sometimes he would seem to be troubled, when, according to the bucket's ideas of cause and effect, there was no reason for him to be so.

And now that Mr Dendy had hanged himself, pressing both of them into this last service, to forward his self-destruction, the bucket and the rope thought they would review the man's life, in the hope of finding one true reason at least for his final act.

'Is it not a little curious, if not altogether surprising,' observed the bucket, 'that we should have been put to so sad a use in helping our good master to die? Perhaps you can remember as well as I the joyful day when we were first purchased, which happened to be the very day before Mr Dendy was married.

'He married, as you know, a woman, a creature created to ease a man of the heavy burden of desire, a burden as troublesome to carry as a kicking ass.'

'And who also,' observed the rope, 'was intended to cook and prepare a man's food, to rear his children and to clean his house.'

'That should certainly be so,' said the other.

'The day we were purchased,' continued the rope, 'happened to be one of those delightful May days when all things, animate and inanimate, that exist under the sun, are entirely happy.

'I was coiled up in the shop window of Mr Johnson, the ropemaker, a man whose shirt-sleeves were always turned up, so that his hairy arms made the children stare. The sun shone upon me, and in its pleasant warmth I soon fell asleep. I dreamed of my happy childhood, when I grew up in a large field, beside a million brothers and sisters who were all beautiful flowers. But I did not sleep long, for as soon as the sun rose too high to shine into the window I awoke and looked out into the street.

'Anyone with a proper desire for knowledge, if he has eyes, can always see something of interest in what goes on in a street. He has only to look and something will be sure to come near.

'I began to watch the folk who moved along the pavement in front of the shop, and a few of them particularly attracted my notice. Two old women came by, whose feet seemed to stick to the stones at every step, while their tongues cackled and gabbled about the ill-conduct of their neighbours.

'A grand military gentleman sauntered past, who saw his own reflection in every window that he went by, and became prouder than ever. A lady who followed him at a little distance wished to see herself too, but did not dare to look, because she feared that a servant girl who walked behind might notice what she did.

'Presently there was a fine clatter of running feet; some schoolboys came by, pulling the caps from one another's heads, and then an alderman passed, who looked about him as if the town were all his own.

'After him came two young and pleasing girls, who were ready for love; they watched coyly every young man in the street, and laughed in order to show what they longed for. The clock in the church tower at the top of the town struck three, but no one seemed to give any heed to it, except a poor debtor, whose examination was to be at that very hour in the town hall, and who wished he had taken his wife's advice earlier and drowned himself.

'The clock had hardly finished striking when a young man, who had the joyful looks of a would-be bridegroom, together with a young girl entered the shop. I looked at her with admiration, and at him with pleasure. They seemed made for one another. Anyone could see that she had the sweetest of natures, that would be unlikely, for fear of being cruel, to refuse anything a man might ask of her. The man was Mr Dendy, and she was to be his wife.'

'Her arms had been opened to another before him,' murmured the bucket.

'Only a grave could have prevented that,' answered the rope; 'but allow me to continue:

'Mr Dendy came forward to the window and looked at me, together with Mr Johnson. The girl looked elsewhere. Mr Johnson's hands, that were as hairy as his arms, took me up, uncoiled me, and stretched me out. Our master examined me for a little, satisfied himself that I was what he needed, and made the purchase.'

'Mr Dendy was about twenty-nine years old then, and the young girl about eighteen,' remarked the bucket.

'So she was,' said the rope, 'but it is curious to think now what she did next. While Mr Johnson and Mr Dendy were talking, she coiled and uncoiled me, and then, in her girlish amusement, for she looked at him lovingly, she made a running noose of me, slipped it over our master's head, and pulled it tight.'

'Mr Johnson laughed, I suppose?'

'Yes, but a little uneasily. While she toyed with me,' said the rope, 'I had the chance to look at her the more narrowly. She seemed just the creature to delight any man with her sweetness and eagerness for love. She had a yielding kindness, but no wickedness in her. She showed her good nature to a young man, the son of the lawyer, who happened to pass her in a by-street when Mr Dendy slipped into a small inn. The lawyer's son looked unhappy and she allowed him to kiss her, while Mr Dendy was out of the way.'

'She had a little foot,' observed the bucket, 'and a winning gait, and had Mr Dendy peeped through the dingy bar-window, when he was having a merry jest with Farmer Pardy, he should have been glad to see that the lawyer's son thought her as nice as he did.'

'A rope would have fancied so,' said the other dryly.

'Mr Dendy had no sooner bought you,' said the bucket, 'than he went to the ironmonger's and purchased me. We were carried off together, and so we became acquainted, and that very evening I was made use of to collect the swill for the pigs; I remember even now the unpleasant smell of the rotten potatoes.'

'It was not the stink of the sour garbage that made our master hang himself,' observed the rope thoughtfully, 'for he would be often whistling when he brought you in, full of the nastiest stuff. Neither could it have been the weight of you that troubled him, for he would ever carry you jauntily, as if

the burden of a few gallons of swill was nothing to so powerful an arm as his.'

'Oh no, he never minded carrying me,' said the bucket,
'for whatever the time of year was, whether the summer sun
shone or whether a dreary autumn rain fell, Mr Dendy
would bear me along with the same sprightliness. He would
perhaps tarry at a cottage gate, and have a merry word with
the occupants, telling a droll story of country matters for the
young girls to smile at, and bidding them to ask of his kind
Betty what the fancies were that she had found the most useful in the getting of a husband.'

'We could watch nearly all that he did,' remarked the
rope, 'and he certainly appeared to be living a very happy
life: the sweet country air, the plain and wholesome food that
he ate, as well as his constant though not too tedious toil,
gave him health and joy, and he was never in want of a
shilling to spend when he needed one.'

'Only once,' observed the bucket sadly, 'did I notice Mr
Dendy act in a way that was not usual for a village man. He
was bearing me, full, along a path from a small cottage where
he bought swill. On each side of the path there were flowers,
both white and yellow. Mr Dendy set me down, a rotten
orange bobbed up on my surface. Mr Dendy rested by the
path, plucked some of the flowers, and seemed to take delight
in holding them in his hand.'

'What did he do next?' asked the rope.

'He carried the flowers home to his wife,' replied the
bucket...

'The summer pleased Mr Dendy, and so did the winter,'
said the rope.

'In the winter we saw more of him, for we were used the
more. During the winter the horses lay in, and straw had to
be carried to them, and in the winter there were more pigs to
be fattened. In the winter, too, a strong man feels his strength
and his happiness more than in the summer. He learns to
brave the keenest wind without a shudder, and cares nothing
when the rain soaks him to the skin. No weather daunted Mr
Dendy, and the more he bore with the storms outside the

pleasanter was his parlour, with its cheerful light, and the warm presence of a wife who loved him.'

'Why, then, did he hang himself?' asked the bucket.

'The winter weather was certainly not to blame,' answered the rope, 'for I cannot think of those happy days without being sure that he enjoyed them. I was stouter then, and yet I think not, for I appear to be strong enough now to hold a pretty fair burden. Mr Dendy, who is carried by me, could carry a bundle then, he thought nothing of carrying as much straw with me as was enough for three men to bear. However large the bundle was, he would somehow get it upon his back, so that the straw upon either side of him would sweep the hedges in the lane, almost as though a whole stack was out a-walking.'

'Yes, there was Mr Dendy!' exclaimed the bucket, 'a true and joyful countryman, doing his proper tasks. What could harm him? What could prevent him from living out his life contentedly and going down, as a good man should, gently into the grave? Surely never was a poor man created who meant so well.'

'Look at him now,' said the rope quietly; 'at first when he kicked you over I wondered if I should be strong enough to hold him. He struggled horribly, and I fancy that when he first felt me tighten round his throat he would have changed his mind. He tried to catch me to lessen the dreadful feeling of suffocation.'

'You must have hurt him very much,' observed the bucket, 'for his face became quite black, and his eyes bulged out of his head. I wonder you did not let him fall, for in his death agony he kicked his legs and swung round, but you held him fast. Why did he do it?'

'I believe the reason was,' replied the rope, 'that Mr Dendy did not like to see others happy.'

'That is not easy to believe,' remarked the bucket, 'when one considers how happy he was himself.'

'His wife made him so,' said the rope, 'and feeling her success with him she naturally wished to make another happy too.'

'What could be more proper?' said the bucket.

'It was this summer,' continued the rope, 'and the master, having saved a few guineas, bought for himself a new Sunday suit. "You look so well in it," his wife told him, "that you should go to church more often, for people will know how well you are getting on when they see you in your new clothes." Now, it was the time when Mr Dendy began to go to church of an evening that I noticed passing this shed the same young man who had given Betty a kiss in the by-street when Mr Dendy was drinking a glass in the little tavern. He still looked unhappy.'

'A chance for Betty to turn his sorrow into joy!' laughed the bucket.

'She wished to do so, and they met in this very shed, on a Sunday evening, when Mr Dendy was supposed to be gone to church.'

'But had he gone?' asked the bucket.

'No,' replied the rope. 'He had only put on his best clothes and walked out, as if to go. Instead of going to church, he came to this shed, took me up, and bound me round a large bundle of straw. The bundle he placed against the wall of the shed, where there was a little chink, and, creeping under the straw to hide himself, he waited.'

'For the pleasure of witnessing the kindness of his wife, I suppose,' said the bucket.

'One would have thought so,' replied the rope, 'but the look upon Mr Dendy's face when he saw what was going on did not warrant such a supposition.'

'Perhaps he thought,' reasoned the bucket, 'that Betty should have remained at home and warmed the rabbit pie for his supper; for the sermon preached by Mr Hayball always made him extremely hungry, and Betty was not to be expected to know that he was not at church. I have seen the pigs fed so often, and I know how hungry animals are, and, as food keeps a man alive and prevents him from becoming a dead carcass, it is natural that a man should wish the woman that he keeps to prepare food for him, even though she may prefer to be loving and kind to another man.'

'You should have heard Mr Dendy,' said the rope; 'he gnashed his teeth and moaned horribly, and when his wife's friend seemed to be altogether forgetting his sorrow, being come, as the lyric poet says, "Where comfort is – " Mr Dendy crept out of the bundle and hid in the lane, snarling like a bitten dog.'

'His hunger, I suppose, had gone beyond the proper bounds,' suggested the bucket.

'It is difficult,' said the rope, after a few minutes' silence, as the body swung to and fro, 'for us to decide what could have troubled this good man. No one had robbed him. No one had beaten or hurt him, and never once since they had been married had Betty refused his embraces.'

'It must have been that nosegay,' exclaimed the bucket.

E. M. Forster

THE ROAD FROM COLONUS

I

FOR NO very intelligible reason, Mr Lucas had hurried ahead of his party. He was perhaps reaching the age at which independence becomes valuable, because it is so soon to be lost. Tired of attention and consideration, he liked breaking away from the younger members, to ride by himself and to dismount unassisted. Perhaps he also relished that more subtle pleasure of being kept waiting for lunch, and of telling the others on their arrival that it was of no consequence.

So, with childish impatience, he battered the animal's sides with his heels, and made the muleteer bang it with a thick stick and prick it with a sharp one, and jolted down the hillsides through clumps of flowering shrubs and stretches of anemones and asphodel, till he heard the sound of running water, and came in sight of the group of plane trees where they were to have their meal.

Even in England those trees would have been remarkable, so huge were they, so interlaced, so magnificently clothed in quivering green. And here in Greece they were unique, the one cool spot in that hard brilliant landscape, already scorched by the heat of an April sun. In their midst was hidden a tiny Khan or country inn, a frail mud building with a broad wooden balcony in which sat an old woman spinning, while a small brown pig, eating orange peel, stood beside her. On the wet earth below squatted two children, playing some primeval game with their fingers; and their mother, none too clean either, was messing with some rice inside. As Mrs Forman would have said, it was all very Greek, and the fastidious Mr Lucas felt thankful that they were bringing their own food with them and should eat it in the open air.

Still, he was glad to be there – the muleteer had helped him off – and glad that Mrs Forman was not there to forestall his opinions – glad even that he should not see Ethel for quite half an hour. Ethel was his youngest daughter, still unmarried. She was unselfish and affectionate, and it was generally understood that she was to devote her life to her father and be the comfort of his old age. Mrs Forman always referred to her as Antigone, and Mr Lucas tried to settle down to the role of Oedipus, which seemed the only one that public opinion allowed him.

He had this in common with Oedipus, that he was growing old. Even to himself it had become obvious. He had lost interest in other people's affairs, and seldom attended when they spoke to him. He was fond of talking himself but often forgot what he was going to say, and even when he succeeded, it seldom seemed worth the effort. His phrases and gestures had become stiff and set, his anecdotes, once so successful, fell flat, his silence was as meaningless as his speech. Yet he had led a healthy, active life, had worked steadily, made money, educated his children. There was nothing and no one to blame: he was simply growing old.

At the present moment, here he was in Greece, and one of the dreams of his life was realized. Forty years ago he had caught the fever of Hellenism, and all his life he had felt that could he but visit that land, he would not have lived in vain. But Athens had been dusty, Delphi wet, Thermopylae flat, and he had listened with amazement and cynicism to the rapturous exclamations of his companions. Greece was like England: it was a man who was growing old, and it made no difference whether that man looked at the Thames or the Eurotas. It was his last hope of contradicting that logic of experience, and it was failing.

Yet Greece had done something for him, though he did not know it. It had made him discontented, and there are stirrings of life in discontent. He knew that he was not the victim of continual ill-luck. Something great was wrong, and he was pitted against no mediocre or accidental enemy. For the last month a strange desire had possessed him to die fighting.

'Greece is the land for young people,' he said to himself as he stood under the plane trees, 'but I will enter into it, I will possess it. Leaves shall be green again, water shall be sweet, the sky shall be blue. They were so forty years ago, and I will win them back. I do mind being old, and I will pretend no longer.'

He took two steps forward, and immediately cold waters were gurgling over his ankle.

'Where does the water come from?' he asked himself. 'I do not even know that.' He remembered that all the hillsides were dry; yet here the road was suddenly covered with flowing streams.

He stopped still in amazement saying: 'Water out of a tree – out of a hollow tree? I never saw nor thought of that before.'

For the enormous plane that leant towards the Khan was hollow – it had been burnt out for charcoal – and from its living trunk there gushed an impetuous spring, coating the bark with fern and moss, and flowing over the mule track to create fertile meadows beyond. The simple country folk had paid to beauty and mystery such tribute as they could, for in the rind of the tree a shrine was cut, holding a lamp and a little picture of the Virgin, inheritor of the Naiad's and Dryad's joint abode.

'I never saw anything so marvellous before,' said Mr Lucas. 'I could even step inside the trunk and see where the water comes from.'

For a moment he hesitated to violate the shrine. Then he remembered with a smile his own thought – 'the place shall be mine; I will enter it and possess it' – and leapt almost aggressively on to a stone within.

The water pressed up steadily and noiselessly from the hollow roots and hidden crevices of the plane, forming a wonderful amber pool ere it spilt over the lip of bark on to the earth outside. Mr Lucas tasted it and it was sweet, and when he looked up the black funnel of the trunk he saw sky which was blue, and some leaves which were green; and he remembered, without smiling, another of his thoughts.

Others had been before him – indeed he had a curious sense of companionship. Little votive offerings to the presiding Power were fastened on to the bark – tiny arms and legs and eyes in tin, grotesque models of the brain or the heart – all tokens of some recovery of strength or wisdom or love. There was no such thing as the solitude of nature, for the sorrows and joys of humanity had pressed even into the bosom of a tree. He spread out his arms and steadied himself against the soft charred wood, and then slowly leant back, till his body was resting on the trunk behind. His eyes closed, and he had the strange feeling of one who is moving, yet at peace – the feeling of the swimmer, who, after long struggling with chopping seas, finds that after all the tide will sweep him to his goal.

So he lay motionless, conscious only of the stream below his feet, and that all things were a stream, in which he was moving.

He was aroused at last by a shock – the shock of an arrival perhaps, for when he opened his eyes, something unimagined, indefinable, had passed over all things, and made them intelligible and good.

There was meaning in the stoop of the old woman over her work, and in the quick motions of the little pig, and in her diminishing globe of wool. A young man came singing over the streams on a mule, and there was beauty in his pose and sincerity in his greeting. The sun made no accidental patterns upon the spreading roots of the trees, and there was intention in the nodding clumps of asphodel, and in the music of the water. To Mr Lucas, who, in a brief space of time, had discovered not only Greece, but England and all the world and life, there seemed nothing ludicrous in the desire to hang within the tree another votive offering – a little model of an entire man.

'Why, here's papa, playing at being Merlin.'

All unnoticed they had arrived – Ethel, Mrs Forman, Mr Graham, and the English-speaking dragoman. Mr Lucas peered out at them suspiciously. They had suddenly become unfamiliar, and all that they did seemed strained and coarse.

'Allow me to give you a hand,' said Mr Graham, a young man who was always polite to his elders.

Mr Lucas felt annoyed. 'Thank you, I can manage perfectly well by myself,' he replied. His foot slipped as he stepped out of the tree, and went into the spring.

'Oh, papa, my papa!' said Ethel, 'what are you doing? Thank goodness I have got a change for you on the mule.'

She tended him carefully, giving him clean socks and dry boots, and then sat him down on the rug beside the lunch basket, while she went with the others to explore the grove.

They came back in ecstasies, in which Mr Lucas tried to join. But he found them intolerable. Their enthusiasm was superficial, commonplace, and spasmodic. They had no perception of the coherent beauty that was flowering around them. He tried at least to explain his feelings, and what he said was:

'I am altogether pleased with the appearance of this place. It impresses me very favourably. The trees are fine, remarkably fine for Greece, and there is something very poetic in the spring of clear running water. The people too seem kindly and civil. It is decidedly an attractive place.'

Mrs Forman upbraided him for his tepid praise.

'Oh, it is a place in a thousand!' she cried. 'I could live and die here! I really would stop if I had not to be back at Athens! It reminds me of the Colonus of Sophocles.'

'Well, *I* must stop,' said Ethel. 'I positively must.'

'Yes, do! You and your father! Antigone and Oedipus. Of course you must stop at Colonus!'

Mr Lucas was almost breathless with excitement. When he stood within the tree, he had believed that his happiness would be independent of locality. But these few minutes' conversation had undeceived him. He no longer trusted himself to journey through the world, for old thoughts, old wearinesses might be waiting to rejoin him as soon as he left the shade of the planes and the music of the virgin water. To sleep in the Khan with the gracious, kind-eyed country people, to watch the bats flit about within the globe of shade, and see the moon turn the golden patterns into silver – one such night would place him beyond relapse, and confirm him for ever in the kingdom he had regained. But all his lips could say was: 'I should be willing to put in a night here.'

'You mean a week, papa! It would be sacrilege to put in less.'

'A week then, a week,' said his lips, irritated at being corrected, while his heart was leaping with joy. All through lunch he spoke to them no more, but watched the place he should know so well, and the people who would so soon be his companions and friends. The inmates of the Khan only consisted of an old woman, a middle-aged woman, a young man and two children, and to none of them had he spoken, yet he loved them as he loved everything that moved or breathed or existed beneath the benedictory shade of the planes.

'*En route!*' said the shrill voice of Mrs Forman. 'Ethel! Mr Graham! The best of things must end.'

'Tonight,' thought Mr Lucas, 'they will light the little lamp by the shrine. And when we all sit together on the balcony, perhaps they will tell me which offerings they put up.'

'I beg your pardon, Mr Lucas,' said Graham, 'but they want to fold up the rug you are sitting on.'

Mr Lucas got up, saying to himself: 'Ethel shall go to bed first, and then I will try to tell them about my offering too – for it is a thing I must do. I think they will understand if I am left with them alone.'

Ethel touched him on the cheek. 'Papa! I've called you three times. All the mules are here.'

'Mules? What mules?'

'Our mules. We're all waiting. Oh, Mr Graham, do help my father on.'

'I don't know what you're talking about, Ethel.'

'My dearest papa, we must start. You know we have to get to Olympia tonight.'

Mr Lucas in pompous, confident tones replied: 'I always did wish, Ethel, that you had a better head for plans. You know perfectly well that we are putting in a week here. It is your own suggestion.'

Ethel was startled into impoliteness. 'What a perfectly ridiculous idea. You must have known I was joking. Of course I meant I wished we could.'

'Ah! if we could only do what we wished!' sighed Mrs Forman, already seated on her mule.

'Surely,' Ethel continued in calmer tones, 'you didn't think I meant it.'

'Most certainly I did. I have made all my plans on the supposition that we are stopping here, and it will be extremely inconvenient, indeed, impossible for me to start.'

He delivered this remark with an air of great conviction, and Mrs Forman and Mrs Graham had to turn away to hide their smiles.

'I am sorry I spoke so carelessly; it was wrong of me. But, you know, we can't break up our party, and even one night here would make us miss the boat at Patras.'

Mrs Forman, in an aside, called Mr Graham's attention to the excellent way in which Ethel managed her father.

'I don't mind about the Patras boat. You said that we should stop here, and we are stopping.'

It seemed as if the inhabitants of the Khan had divined in some mysterious way that the altercation touched them. The old woman stopped her spinning, while the young man and the two children stood behind Mr Lucas, as if supporting him.

Neither arguments nor entreaties moved him. He said little, but he was absolutely determined, because for the first time he saw his daily life aright. What need had he to return to England? Who would miss him? His friends were dead or cold. Ethel loved him in a way, but, as was right, she had other interests. His other children he seldom saw. He had only one other relative, his sister Julia, whom he both feared and hated. It was no effort to struggle. He would be a fool as well as a coward if he stirred from the place which brought him happiness and peace.

At last Ethel, to humour him, and not disinclined to air her modern Greek, went into the Khan with the astonished dragoman to look at the rooms. The woman inside received them with loud welcomes, and the young man, when no one was looking, began to lead Mr Lucas' mule to the stable.

'Drop it, you brigand!' shouted Graham, who always

declared that foreigners could understand English if they chose. He was right, for the man obeyed, and they all stood waiting for Ethel's return.

She emerged at last, with close-gathered skirts, followed by the dragoman bearing the little pig, which he had bought at a bargain.

'My dear papa, I will do all I can for you, but stop in that Khan – no.'

'Are there – fleas?' asked Mrs Forman.

Ethel intimated that 'fleas' was not the word.

'Well, I am afraid that settles it,' said Mrs Forman, 'I know how particular Mr Lucas is.'

'It does not settle it,' said Mr Lucas. 'Ethel, you go on. I do not want you. I don't know why I ever consulted you. I shall stop here alone.'

'That is absolute nonsense,' said Ethel, losing her temper. 'How can you be left alone at your age? How would you get your meals or your bath? All your letters are waiting for you at Patras. You'll miss the boat. That means missing the London operas, and upsetting all your engagements for the month. And as if you could travel by yourself!'

'They might knife you,' was Mr Graham's contribution.

The Greeks said nothing; but whenever Mr Lucas looked their way, they beckoned him towards the Khan. The children would even have drawn him by the coat, and the old woman on the balcony stopped her almost completed spinning, and fixed him with mysterious appealing eyes. As he fought, the issue assumed gigantic proportions, and he believed that he was not merely stopping because he had regained youth or seen beauty or found happiness, but because in that place and with those people a supreme event was awaiting him which would transfigure the face of the world. The moment was so tremendous that he abandoned words and arguments as useless, and rested on the strength of his mighty unrevealed allies: silent men, murmuring water, and whispering trees. For the whole place called with one voice, articulate to him, and his garrulous opponents became every minute more meaningless and absurd. Soon they would be tired and go chattering away into the sun, leaving him to the cool grove and the moonlight and the destiny he foresaw.

Mrs Forman and the dragoman had indeed already started, amid the piercing screams of the little pig, and the struggle might have gone on indefinitely if Ethel had not called in Mr Graham.

'Can you help me?' she whispered. 'He is absolutely un-manageable.'

'I'm no good at arguing – but if I could help you in any other way – ' and he looked down complacently at his well-made figure.

Ethel hesitated. Then she said: 'Help me in any way you can. After all, it is for his own good that we do it.'

'Then have his mule led up behind him.'

So when Mr Lucas thought he had gained the day, he suddenly felt himself lifted off the ground, and sat sideways on the saddle, and at the same time the mule started off at a trot. He said nothing, for he had nothing to say, and even his face showed little emotion as he felt the shade pass and heard the sound of the water cease. Mr Graham was running at his side, hat in hand, apologizing.

'I know I had no business to do it, and I do beg your pardon awfully. But I do hope that some day you too will feel that I was – damn!'

A stone had caught him in the middle of the back. It was thrown by the little boy, who was pursuing them along the mule track. He was followed by his sister, also throwing stones.

Ethel screamed to the dragoman, who was some way ahead with Mrs Forman, but before he could rejoin them, another adversary appeared. It was the young Greek, who had cut them off in front, and now dashed down at Mr Lucas' bridle. Fortunately Graham was an expert boxer, and it did not take him a moment to beat down the youth's feeble defence, and to send him sprawling with a bleeding mouth into the asphodel. By this time the dragoman had arrived, the children, alarmed at the fate of their brother, had desisted, and the rescue party, if such it is to be considered, retired in disorder to the trees.

'Little devils!' said Graham, laughing with triumph. 'That's the modern Greek all over. Your father meant money if he stopped, and they consider we were taking it out of their pocket.'

'Oh, they are terrible – simple savages! I don't know how I shall ever thank you. You've saved my father.'

'I only hope you didn't think me brutal.'

'No,' replied Ethel with a little sigh. 'I admire strength.'

Meanwhile the cavalcade reformed, and Mr Lucas, who, as Mrs Forman said, bore his disappointment wonderfully well, was put comfortably on to his mule. They hurried up the opposite hillside, fearful of another attack, and it was not until they had left the eventful place far behind that Ethel found an opportunity to speak to her father and ask his pardon for the way she had treated him.

'You seemed so different, dear father, and you quite frightened me. Now I feel that you are your old self again.'

He did not answer, and she concluded that he was not unnaturally offended at her behaviour.

By one of those curious tricks of mountain scenery, the place they had left an hour before suddenly reappeared far below them. The Khan was hidden under the green dome, but in the open there still stood three figures, and through the pure air rose up a faint cry of defiance or farewell.

Mr Lucas stopped irresolutely, and let the reins fall from his hand.

'Come, father dear,' said Ethel gently.

He obeyed, and in another moment a spur of the hill hid the dangerous scene for ever.

2

It was breakfast time, but the gas was alight, owing to the fog. Mr Lucas was in the middle of an account of a bad night he had spent. Ethel, who was to be married in a few weeks, had her arms on the table, listening.

'First the door bell rang, then you came back from the theatre. Then the dog started, and after the dog the cat. And at three in the morning a young hooligan passed by singing. Oh yes: then there was the water gurgling in the pipe above my head.'

'I think that was only the bath water running away,' said Ethel, looking rather worn.

'Well, there's nothing I dislike more than running water. It's perfectly impossible to sleep in the house. I shall give it up. I shall give notice next quarter. I shall tell the landlord plainly, "The reason I am giving up the house is this: it is perfectly impossible to sleep in it." If he says – says – well, what has he got to say?'

'Some more toast, father?'

'Thank you, my dear.' He took it, and there was an interval of peace.

But he soon recommenced. 'I'm not going to submit to the practising next door as tamely as they think. I wrote and told them so – didn't I?'

'Yes,' said Ethel, who had taken care that the letter should not reach. 'I have seen the governess, and she has promised to arrange it differently. And Aunt Julia hates noise. It will be sure to be all right.'

Her aunt, being the only unattached member of the family, was coming to keep house for her father when she left him. The reference was not a happy one, and Mr Lucas commenced a series of half articulate sighs, which was only stopped by the arrival of the post.

'Oh, what a parcel!' cried Ethel. 'For me! What can it be! Greek stamps. This is most exciting!'

It proved to be some asphodel bulbs, sent by Mrs Forman from Athens for planting in the conservatory.

'Doesn't it bring it all back! You remember the asphodels, father. And all wrapped up in Greek newspapers. I wonder if I can read them still. I used to be able to, you know.'

She rattled on, hoping to conceal the laughter of the children next door – a favourite source of querulousness at breakfast time.

'Listen to me! "A rural disaster." Oh, I've hit on something sad. But never mind. "Last Tuesday at Plataniste, in the province of Messenia, a shocking tragedy occurred. A large tree" – aren't I getting on well? – "blew down in the night and" – wait a minute – oh dear! "crushed to death the five occupants of the little Khan there, who had apparently been sitting in the balcony. The bodies of Maria Rhomaides, the aged proprietress, and of her daughter, aged forty-six, were easily recognizable, whereas that of her grandson" – oh, the rest is really too horrid; I wish I had never tried it, and what's more I feel to have heard the name Plataniste before. We didn't stop there, did we, in the spring?'

'We had lunch,' said Mr Lucas, with a faint expression of trouble on his vacant face. 'Perhaps it was where the dragoman bought the pig.'

'Of course,' said Ethel in a nervous voice. 'Where the dragoman bought the little pig. How terrible!'

'Very terrible!' said her father, whose attention was wandering to the noisy children next door. Ethel suddenly started to her feet with genuine interest.

'Good gracious!' she exclaimed. 'This is an old paper. It happened not lately but in April – the night of Tuesday the eighteenth – and we – we must have been there in the afternoon.'

'So we were,' said Mr Lucas. She put her hand to her heart, scarcely able to speak.

'Father, dear father, I must say it: you wanted to stop there. All those people, those poor half savage people, tried to keep you, and they're dead. The whole place, it says, is in ruins, and even the stream has changed its course. Father dear, if it had not been for me, and if Arthur had not helped me, you must have been killed.'

Mr Lucas waved his hand irritably. 'It is not a bit of good speaking to the governess, I shall write to the landlord and say, "The reason I am giving up the house is this: the dog barks, the children next door are intolerable, and I cannot stand the noise of running water."'

Ethel did not check his babbling. She was aghast at the

narrowness of the escape, and for a long time kept silence. At last she said: 'Such a marvellous deliverance does make one believe in Providence.'

Mr Lucas, who was still composing his letter to the landlord, did not reply.

IVY DAY IN THE COMMITTEE ROOM

OLD JACK raked the cinders together with a piece of cardboard and spread them judiciously over the whitening dome of coals. When the dome was thinly covered his face lapsed into darkness but, as he set himself to fan the fire again, his crouching shadow ascended the opposite wall and his face slowly re-emerged into light. It was an old man's face, very bony and hairy. The moist blue eyes blinked at the fire and the moist mouth fell open at times, munching once or twice mechanically when it closed. When the cinders had caught he laid the piece of cardboard against the wall, sighed and said:

'That's better now, Mr O'Connor.'

Mr O'Connor, a grey-haired young man, whose face was disfigured by many blotches and pimples, had just brought the tobacco for a cigarette into a shapely cylinder, but when spoken to he undid his handiwork again meditatively. Then he began to roll the tobacco again meditatively and after a moment's thought decided to lick the paper.

'Did Mr Tierney say when he'd be back?' he asked in a husky falsetto.

'He didn't say.'

Mr O'Connor put his cigarette into his mouth and began to search his pockets. He took out a pack of thin pasteboard cards.

'I'll get you a match,' said the old man.

'Never mind, this'll do,' said Mr O'Connor.

He selected one of the cards and read what was printed on it:

MUNICIPAL ELECTIONS

ROYAL EXCHANGE WARD

Mr Richard J. Tierney, P. L. G., respectfully solicits the favour of your vote and influence at the coming election in the Royal Exchange Ward.

Mr O'Connor had been engaged by Tierney's agent to canvass one part of the ward but, as the weather was inclement and his boots let in the wet, he spent a great part of the day sitting by the fire in the Committee Room in Wicklow Street with Jack, the old caretaker. They had been sitting thus since the short day had grown dark. It was the sixth of October, dismal and cold out of doors.

Mr O'Connor tore a strip off the card and, lighting it, lit his cigarette. As he did so the flame lit up a leaf of dark glossy ivy in the lapel of his coat. The old man watched him attentively and then, taking up the piece of cardboard again, began to fan the fire slowly while his companion smoked.

'Ah, yes,' he said, continuing, 'it's hard to know what way to bring up children. Now who'd think he'd turn out like that! I sent him to the Christian Brothers and I done what I could for him, and there he goes boozing about. I tried to make him somewhat decent.'

He replaced the cardboard wearily.

'Only I'm an old man now I'd change his tune for him. I'd take the stick to his back and beat him while I could stand over him – as I done many a time before. The mother you know, she cocks him up with this and that . . .'

'That's what ruins children,' said Mr O'Connor.

'To be sure it is,' said the old man. 'And little thanks you get for it, only impudence. He takes th'upper hand of me whenever he sees I've a sup taken. What's the world coming to when sons speaks that way to their fathers?'

'What age is he?' said Mr O'Connor.

'Nineteen,' said the old man.

'Why don't you put him to something?'

'Sure, amn't I never done at the drunken bowsy ever since he left school? "I won't keep you," I says. "You must get a job for yourself." But, sure it's worse whenever he gets a job; he drinks it all.'

Mr O'Connor shook his head in sympathy, and the old man fell silent, gazing into the fire. Someone opened the door of the room and called out:

'Hello! Is this a Freemasons' meeting?'

'Who's that?' said the old man.

'What are you doing in the dark?' asked a voice.

'Is that you, Hynes?' asked Mr O'Connor.

'Yes. What are you doing in the dark?' said Mr Hynes, advancing into the light of the fire.

He was a tall, slender young man with a light brown moustache. Imminent little drops of rain hung at the brim of his hat and the collar of his jacket-coat was turned up.

'Well, Mat,' he said to Mr O'Connor, 'how goes it?'

Mr O'Connor shook his head. The old man left the hearth, and after stumbling about the room returned with two candlesticks which he thrust one after the other into the fire and carried to the table. A denuded room came into view and the fire lost all its cheerful colour. The walls of the room were bare except for a copy of an election address. In the middle of the room was a small table on which papers were heaped.

Mr Hynes leaned against the mantelpiece and asked:

'Has he paid you yet?'

'Not yet,' said Mr O'Connor. 'I hope to God he'll not leave us in the lurch tonight.'

Mr Hynes laughed.

'O, he'll pay you. Never fear,' he said.

'I hope he'll look smart about it if he means business,' said Mr O'Connor.

'What do you think, Jack?' said Mr Hynes satirically to the old man.

The old man returned to his seat by the fire, saying:

'It isn't but he has it, anyway. Not like the other tinker.'

'What other tinker?' said Mr Hynes.

'Colgan,' said the old man scornfully.

'It is because Colgan's a working-man you say that? What's the difference between a good honest bricklayer and a publican – eh? Hasn't the working-man as good a right to be in the Corporation as anyone else – ay, and a better right than those shoneens that are always hat in hand before any fellow with a handle to his name? Isn't that so, Mat?' said Mr Hynes, addressing Mr O'Connor.

'I think you're right,' said Mr O'Connor.

'One man is a plain honest man with no hunker-sliding about him. He goes in to represent the labour classes. This fellow you're working for only wants to get some job or other.'

'Of course, the working-classes should be represented,' said the old man.

'The working-man,' said Mr Hynes, 'gets all kicks and no halfpence. But it's labour produces everything. The working-man is not looking for fat jobs for his sons and nephews and cousins. The working-man is not going to drag the honour of Dublin in the mud to please a German monarch.'

'How's that?' said the old man.

'Don't you know they want to present an address of welcome to Edward Rex if he comes here next year? What do we want kowtowing to a foreign king?'

'Our man won't vote for the address,' said Mr O'Connor. 'He goes in on the Nationalist ticket.'

'Won't he?' said Mr Hynes. 'Wait till you see whether he will or not. I know him. Is it Tricky Dicky Tierney?'

'By God! perhaps you're right, Joe,' said Mr O'Connor. 'Anyway, I wish he'd turn up with the spondulicks.'

The three men fell silent. The old man began to rake more cinders together. Mr Hynes took off his hat, shook it and then turned down the collar of his coat, displaying, as he did so, an ivy leaf in the lapel.

'If this man was alive,' he said, pointing to the leaf, 'we'd have no talk of an address of welcome.'

'That's true,' said Mr O'Connor.

'Musha, God be with them times!' said the old man. 'There was some life in it then.'

The room was silent again. Then a bustling little man with a snuffling nose and very cold ears pushed in the door. He walked over quickly to the fire, rubbing his hands as if he intended to produce a spark from them.

'No money, boys,' he said.

'Sit down here, Mr Henchy,' said the old man, offering him his chair.

'O, don't stir, Jack, don't stir,' said Mr Henchy.

He nodded curtly to Mr Hynes and sat down on the chair which the old man vacated.

'Did you serve Aungier Street?' he asked Mr O'Connor.

'Yes,' said Mr O'Connor, beginning to search his pockets for memoranda.

'Did you call on Grimes?'

'I did.'

'Well? How does he stand?'

'He wouldn't promise. He said: "I won't tell anyone what way I'm going to vote." But I think he'll be all right.'

'Why so?'

'He asked me who the nominators were; and I told him, I mentioned Father Burke's name. I think it'll be all right.'

Mr Henchy began to snuffle and to rub his hands over the fire at a terrific speed. Then he said:

'For the love of God, Jack, bring us a bit of coal. There must be some left.'

The old man went out of the room.

'It's no go,' said Mr Henchy, shaking his head. 'I asked the little shoeboy, but he said: "O, now, Mr Henchy, when I see the work going on properly I won't forget you, you may be sure.' Mean little tinker! 'Usha, how could he be anything else?'

'What did I tell you, Mat?' said Mr Hynes. 'Tricky Dicky Tierney.'

'O, he's as tricky as they make 'em,' said Mr Henchy. 'He hasn't got those little pig's eyes for nothing. Blast his soul! Couldn't he pay up like a man instead of: "O, now Mr Henchy, I must speak to Mr Fanning ... I've spent a lot of money." Mean little schoolboy of hell! I suppose he forgets the time his little old father kept the hand-me-down shop in Mary's Lane.'

'But is that a fact?' asked Mr O'Connor.

'God, yes,' said Mr Henchy. 'Did you never hear that? And the men used to go in on Sunday morning before the houses were open to buy a waistcoat or a trousers – moya! But Tricky Dicky's little old father always had a tricky little black bottle up in a corner. Do you mind now? That's that. That's where he first saw the light.'

The old man returned with a few lumps of coal which he placed here and there on the fire.

'That's a nice how-do-you-do,' said Mr O'Connor. 'How does he expect us to work for him if he won't stump up?'

'I can't help it,' said Mr Henchy. 'I expect to find the bailiffs in the hall when I go home.'

Mr Hynes laughed and, shoving himself away from the mantelpiece with the aid of his shoulders, made ready to leave.

'It'll be all right when King Eddie comes,' he said. 'Well, boys, I'm off for the present. See you later. 'Bye, 'bye.'

He went out of the room slowly. Neither Mr Henchy nor the old man said anything, but, just as the door was closing, Mr O'Connor, who had been staring moodily into the fire, called out suddenly:

''Bye, Joe.'

Mr Henchy waited a few moments and then nodded in the direction of the door.

'Tell me,' he said across the fire, 'what brings our friend in here? What does he want?'

''Usha, poor Joe!' said Mr O'Connor, throwing the end of his cigarette into the fire, 'he's hard up, like the rest of us.'

Mr Henchy snuffled vigorously and spat so copiously that he nearly put out the fire, which uttered a hissing protest.

'To tell you my private and candid opinion,' he said, 'I think he's a man from the other camp. He's a spy of Colgan's, if you ask me. Just go round and try and find out how they're getting on. They won't suspect you. Do you twig?'

'Ah, poor Joe is a decent skin,' said Mr O'Connor.

'His father was a decent, respectable man,' Mr Henchy admitted. 'Poor old Larry Hynes! Many a good turn he did in his day! But I'm greatly afraid our friend is not nineteen carat. Damn it, I can understand a fellow being hard up, but what I can't understand is a fellow sponging. Couldn't he have some spark of manhood about him?'

'He doesn't get a warm welcome from me when he comes,' said the old man. 'Let him work for his own side and not come spying around here.'

'I don't know,' said Mr O'Connor dubiously, as he took out cigarette-papers and tobacco. 'I think Joe Hynes is a straight man. He's a clever chap, too, with the pen. Do you remember that thing he wrote . . . ?'

'Some of these hillsiders and fenians are a bit too clever if you ask me,' said Mr Henchy. 'Do you know what my private and candid opinion is about some of those little jokers? I believe half of them are in the pay of the Castle.'

'There's no knowing,' said the old man.

'O, but I know it for a fact,' said Mr Henchy. 'They're Castle hacks . . . I don't say Hynes . . . No, damn it, I think he's a stroke above that . . . But there's a certain little nobleman with a cock-eye – you know the patriot I'm alluding to?'

Mr O'Connor nodded.

'There's a lineal descendant of Major Sirr for you if you like! O, the heart's blood of a patriot! That's a fellow now that'd sell his country for fourpence – ay – and go down on his bended knees and thank the Almighty Christ he had a country to sell.'

There was a knock at the door.

'Come in!' said Mr Henchy.

A person resembling a poor clergyman or a poor actor appeared in the doorway. His black clothes were tightly buttoned on his short body and it was impossible to say whether he wore a clergyman's collar or a layman's, because the collar of his shabby frock-coat, the uncovered buttons of which reflected the candle-light, was turned up about his neck. He wore a round hat of hard black felt. His face, shining with raindrops, had the appearance of damp yellow cheese save where two rosy spots indicated the cheek-bones. He opened his very long mouth suddenly to express disappointment and at the same time opened wide his very bright blue eyes to express pleasure and surprise.

'O, Father Keon!' said Mr Henchy, jumping up from his chair. 'Is that you? Come in!'

'O, no, no, no,' said Father Keon quickly, pursing his lips as if he were addressing a child.

'Won't you come in and sit down?'

'No, no, no!' said Father Keon, speaking in a discreet, indulgent, velvety voice. 'Don't let me disturb you now! I'm just looking for Mr Fanning ...'

'He's round at the *Black Eagle*,' said Mr Henchy. 'But won't you come in and sit down a minute?'

'No, no, thank you. It was just a little business matter,' said Father Keon. 'Thank you, indeed.'

He retreated from the doorway and Mr Henchy, seizing one of the candlesticks, went to the door to light him downstairs.

'O, don't trouble, I beg!'

'No, but the stairs is so dark.'

'No, no, I can see ... Thank you, indeed.'

'Are you right now?'

'All right, thanks ... Thanks.'

Mr Henchy returned with the candlestick and put it on the table. He sat down again at the fire. There was silence for a few moments.

'Tell me, John,' said Mr O'Connor, lighting his cigarette with another pasteboard card.

'Hm?'

'What is he exactly?'

'Ask me an easier one,' said Mr Henchy.

'Fanning and himself seem to me very thick. They're often in Kavanagh's together. Is he a priest at all?'

'Mmmyes, I believe so ... I think he's what you call a black sheep. We haven't many of them, thank God! but we have a few ... He's an unfortunate man of some kind ...'

'And how does he knock it out?' asked Mr O'Connor.

'That's another mystery.'

'Is he attached to any chapel or church or institution or –'

'No,' said Mr Henchy, 'I think he's travelling on his own account ... God forgive me,' he added, 'I thought he was the dozen of stout.'

'Is there any chance of a drink itself?' asked Mr O'Connor.

'I'm dry too' said the old man.

'I asked that little shoeboy three times,' said Mr Henchy, 'would he send up a dozen of stout. I asked him again now, but he was leaning on the counter in his shirt-sleeves having a deep goster with Alderman Cowley.'

'Why didn't you remind him?' said Mr O'Connor.

'Well, I wouldn't go over while he was talking to Alderman Cowley. I just waited till I caught his eye, and said: "About that little matter I was speaking to you about ..." "That'll be all right, Mr H.," he said. Yerra, sure the little hop-o'-my-thumb has forgotten about it.'

'There's some deal on in that quarter,' said Mr O'Connor thoughtfully. 'I saw the three of them hard at it yesterday at Suffolk Street corner.'

'I think I know the little game they're at,' said Mr Henchy. 'You must owe the City Fathers money nowadays if you want to be made Lord Mayor. Then they'll make you Lord Mayor. By God! I'm thinking seriously of becoming a City Father myself. What do you think? Would I do for the job?'

Mr O'Connor laughed.

'So far as owing money goes ...'

'Driving out of the Mansion House,' said Mr Henchy, 'in all my vermin, with Jack here standing up behind me in a powdered wig – eh?'

'And make me your private secretary, John.'

'Yes. And I'll make Father Keon my private chaplain. We'll have a family party.'

'Faith, Mr Henchy,' said the old man, 'you'd keep up better style than some of them. I was talking one day to old Keegan, the porter. "And how do you like your new master, Pat?" says I to him. "You haven't much entertaining now,' says I. "Entertaining!" says he. "He'd live on the smell of an oil-rag." And do you know what he told me? Now, I declare to God, I didn't believe him.'

'What?' said Mr Henchy and Mr O'Connor.

'He told me: 'What do you think of a Lord Mayor of Dublin sending out for a pound of chops for his dinner? How's that for high living?" says he. "Wisha! wisha," says I. "A pound of chops," says he, "coming into the Mansion House." "Wisha!" says I, "what kind of people is going at all now?"'

At this point there was a knock at the door, and a boy put in his head.

'What is it?' said the old man.

'From the *Black Eagle*,' said the boy, walking in sideways and depositing a basket on the floor with a noise of shaken bottles.

The old man helped the boy to transfer the bottles from the basket to the table and counted the full tally. After the transfer the boy put his basket on his arm and asked:

'Any bottles?'

'What bottles?' said the old man.

'Won't you let us drink them first?' said Mr Henchy.

'I was told to ask for the bottles.'

'Come back tomorrow,' said the old man.

'Here, boy!' said Mr Henchy, 'will you run over to O'Farrell's and ask him to lend us a corkscrew – for Mr Henchy, say. Tell him we won't keep it a minute. Leave the basket there.'

The boy went out and Mr Henchy began to rub his hands cheerfully, saying:

'Ah, well, he's not so bad after all. He's as good as his word, anyhow.'

'There's no tumblers,' said the old man.

'O, don't let that trouble you, Jack,' said Mr Henchy. 'Many's the good man before now drank out of the bottle.'

'Anyway, it's better than nothing,' said Mr O'Connor.

'He's not a bad sort,' said Mr Henchy, 'only Fanning has such a loan of him. He means well, you know, in his own tinpot way.'

The boy came back with the corkscrew. The old man opened three bottles and was handing back the corkscrew when Mr Henchy said to the boy:

'Would you like a drink, boy?'

'If you please, sir,' said the boy.

The old man opened another bottle grudgingly, and handed it to the boy.

'What age are you?' he asked.

'Seventeen,' said the boy.

As the old man said nothing further, the boy took the bottle, said: 'Here's my best respects, sir, to Mr Henchy,' drank the contents, put the bottle back on the table and wiped his mouth with his sleeve. Then he took up the corkscrew and went out of the door sideways, muttering some form of salutation.

'That's the way it begins,' said the old man.

'The thin edge of the wedge,' said Mr Henchy.

The old man distributed the three bottles which he had opened and the men drank from them simultaneously. After having drunk each placed his bottle on the mantelpiece within hand's reach and drew in a long breath of satisfaction.

'Well, I did a good day's work today,' said Mr Henchy, after a pause.

'That so, John?'

'Yes. I got one or two sure things in Dawson Street, Crofton and myself. Between ourselves, you know, Crofton (he's a decent chap, of course), but he's not worth a damn as a canvasser. He hasn't a word to throw to a dog. He stands and looks at the people while I do the talking.'

Here two men entered the room. One of them was a very fat man, whose blue serge clothes seemed to be in danger of falling from his sloping figure. He had a big face which resembled a young ox's face in expression, staring blue eyes and a grizzled moustache. The other man, who was much younger and frailer, had a thin, clean-shaven face. He wore a very high double collar and a wide-brimmed bowler hat.

'Hello, Crofton!' said Mr Henchy to the fat man. 'Talk of the devil . . .'

'Where did the booze come from?' asked the young man. 'Did the cow calve?'

'O, of course, Lyons spots the drink first thing!' said Mr O'Connor, laughing.

'Is that the way you chaps canvass,' said Mr Lyons, 'and Crofton and I out in the cold and rain looking for votes?'

'Why, blast your soul,' said Mr Henchy, 'I'd get more votes in five minutes than you two'd get in a week.'

'Open two bottles of stout, Jack,' said Mr O'Connor.

'How can I?' said the old man, 'when there's no cork-screw?'

'Wait now, wait now!' said Mr Henchy, getting up quickly. 'Did you ever see this little trick?'

He took two bottles from the table and, carrying them to the fire, put them on the hob. Then he sat down again by the fire and took another drink from his bottle. Mr Lyons sat on the edge of the table, pushed his hat towards the nape of his neck and began to swing his legs.

'Which is my bottle?' he asked.

'This, lad,' said Mr Henchy.

Mr Crofton sat down on a box and looked fixedly at the other bottle on the hob. He was silent for two reasons. The first reason, sufficient in itself, was that he had nothing to say; the second reason was that he considered his companions beneath him. He had been a canvasser for Wilkins, the Conservative, but when the Conservatives had withdrawn their man and, choosing the lesser of two evils, given their support to the Nationalist candidate, he had been engaged to work for Mr Tierney.

In a few minutes an apologetic 'Pok!' was heard as the cork flew out of Mr Lyons' bottle. Mr Lyons jumped off the table, went to the fire, took his bottle and carried it back to the table.

'I was just telling them, Crofton,' said Mr Henchy, 'that we got a good few votes today.'

'Who did you get?' asked Mr Lyons.

'Well, I got Parkes for one, and I got Atkinson for two, and I got Ward of Dawson Street. Fine old chap he is, too — regular old toff, old Conservative! "But isn't your candidate a Nationalist?" said he. "He's a respectable man," said I. "He's in favour of whatever will benefit this country. He's a big ratepayer," I said. "He has extensive house property in the city and three places of business, and isn't it to his own advantage to keep down the rates? He's a prominent and respected citizen," said I, "and a Poor Law Guardian, and he doesn't belong to any party, good, bad, or indifferent." That's the way to talk to 'em.'

'And what about the address to the King?' said Mr Lyons, after drinking and smacking his lips.

'Listen to me,' said Mr Henchy. 'What we want in this country, as I said to old Ward, is capital. The King's coming here will mean an influx of money into this country. The citizens of Dublin will benefit by it. Look at all the factories down by the quays there, idle! Look at all the money there is in the country if we only worked the old industries, the mills, the ship-building yards and factories. It's capital we want.'

'But look here, John,' said Mr O'Connor. 'Why should we welcome the King of England? Didn't Parnell himself . . .'

'Parnell,' said Mr Henchy, 'is dead. Now, here's the way I look at it. Here's this chap come to the throne after his old mother keeping him out of it till the man was grey. He's a man of the world, and he means well by us. He's a jolly fine, decent fellow, if you ask me, and no damn nonsense about him. He just says to himself: "The old one never went to see these wild Irish. By Christ, I'll go myself and see what they're like." And are we going to insult the man when he comes over here on a friendly visit? Eh? Isn't that right, Crofton?'

Mr Crofton nodded his head.

'But after all now,' said Mr Lyons argumentatively, 'King Edward's life, you know, is not the very . . .'

'Let bygones be bygones,' said Mr Henchy. 'I admire the man personally. He's just an ordinary knockabout like you and me. He's fond of his glass of grog and he's a bit of a rake, perhaps, and he's a good sportsman. Damn it, can't we Irish play fair?'

'That's all very fine,' said Mr Lyons. 'But look at the case of Parnell now.'

'In the name of God,' said Mr Henchy, 'where's the analogy between the two cases?'

'What I mean,' said Mr Lyons, 'is we have our ideals. Why, now, would we welcome a man like that? Do you think now after what he did Parnell was a fit man to lead us? And why, then, would we do it for Edward the Seventh?'

'This is Parnell's anniversary,' said Mr O'Connor, 'and don't let us stir up any bad blood. We all respect him now that he's dead and gone – even the Conservatives,' he added, turning to Mr Crofton.

Pok! The tardy cork flew out of Mr Crofton's bottle. Mr Crofton got up from his box and went to the fire. As he returned with his capture he said in a deep voice:

'Our side of the house respects him, because he was a gentleman.'

'Right you are, Crofton!' said Mr Henchy fiercely. 'He was the only man that could keep that bag of cats in order. "Down, ye dogs! Lie down, ye curs!" That's the way he treated them. Come in, Joe! Come in!' he called out, catching sight of Mr Hynes in the doorway.

Mr Hynes came in slowly.

'Open another bottle of stout, Jack,' said Mr Henchy. 'O, I forgot there's no corkscrew! Here, show me one here and I'll put it at the fire.'

The old man handed him another bottle and he placed it on the hob.

'Sit down, Joe,' said Mr O'Connor, 'we're just talking about the Chief.'

'Ay, ay!' said Mr Henchy.

Mr Hynes sat on the side of the table near Mr Lyons but said nothing.

'There's one of them, anyhow,' said Mr Henchy, 'that didn't renege him. By God, I'll say for you, Joe! No, by God, you stuck to him like a man!'

'O, Joe,' said Mr O'Connor suddenly. 'Give us that thing you wrote – do you remember? Have you got it on you?'

'O, ay!' said Mr Henchy. 'Give us that. Did you ever hear that, Crofton? Listen to this now: splendid thing.'

'Go on,' said Mr O'Connor. 'Fire away, Joe.'

Mr Hynes did not seem to remember at once the piece to which they were alluding, but, after reflecting a while, he said:

'O, that thing is it . . . Sure, that's old now.'

'Out with it, man!' said Mr O'Connor.

''Sh, 'sh,' said Mr Henchy. 'Now Joe!'

Mr Hynes hesitated a little longer. Then amid the silence he took off his hat, laid it on the table and stood up. He seemed to be rehearsing the piece in his mind. After a rather long pause he announced:

THE DEATH OF PARNELL.
6th October, 1891

He cleared his throat once or twice and then began to recite:

> He is dead. Our Uncrowned King is dead.
>   O, Erin, mourn with grief and woe
> For he lies dead whom the fell gang
>   Of modern hypocrites laid low.
>
> He lies slain by the coward hounds
>   He raised to glory from the mire;
> And Erin's hopes and Erin's dreams
>   Perish upon her monarch's pyre.
>
> In palace, cabin or in cot
>   The Irish heart where'er it be
> Is bowed with woe – for he is gone
>   Who would have wrought her destiny.
>
> He would have had his Erin famed,
>   The green flag gloriously unfurled,
> Her statesman, bards, and warriors raised
>   Before the nations of the World.
>
> He dreamed (alas, 'twas but a dream!)
>   Of Liberty: but as he strove
> To clutch that idol, treachery
>   Sundered him from the thing he loved.
>
> Shame on the coward, caitiff hands
>   That smote their Lord or with a kiss
> Betrayed him to the rabble-rout
>   Of fawning priests – no friends of his.
>
> May everlasting shame consume
>   The memory of those who tried
> To befoul and smear the exalted name
>   Of one who spurned them in his pride.

He fell as fall the mighty ones,
  Nobly undaunted to the last,
And death has now united him
  With Erin's heroes of the past.

No sound of strife disturbs his sleep!
  Calmly he rests: no human pain
Or high ambition spurs him now
  The peaks of glory to attain.

They had their way: they laid him low.
  But Erin, list, his spirit may
Rise, like the Phoenix from the flames,
  When breaks the dawning of the day,

The day that brings us Freedom's reign.
  And on that day may Erin well
Pledge in the cup she lifts to Joy
  One grief — the memory of Parnell.

Mr Hynes sat down again on the table. When he had finished his recitation there was a silence and then a burst of clapping: even Mr Lyons clapped. The applause continued for a little time. When it had ceased all the auditors drank from their bottles in silence.

Pok! The cork flew out of Mr Hynes' bottle, but Mr Hynes remained sitting flushed and bareheaded on the table. He did not seem to have heard the invitation.

'Good man, Joe!' said Mr O'Connor, taking out his cigarette papers and pouch the better to hide his emotion.

'What do you think of that, Crofton?' cried Mr Henchy. 'Isn't that fine? What?'

Mr Crofton said that it was a very fine piece of writing.

Virginia Woolf

THE MARK ON THE WALL

PERHAPS it was the middle of January in the present year that I looked up and saw the mark on the wall. In order to fix a date it is necessary to remember what one saw. So now I think of the fire; the steady film of yellow light upon the page of my book; the three chrysanthemums in the round glass bowl on the mantelpiece. Yes, it must have been the winter time, and we had just finished our tea, for I remember that I was smoking a cigarette when I looked up and saw the mark on the wall for the first time. I looked up through the smoke of my cigarette and my eye lodged for a moment upon the burning coals, and that old fancy of the crimson flag flapping from the castle tower came into my mind, and I thought of the cavalcade of red knights riding up the side of the black rock. Rather to my relief the sight of the mark interrupted the fancy, for it is an old fancy, an automatic fancy, made as a child perhaps. The mark was a small round mark, black upon the white wall, about six or seven inches above the mantelpiece.

How readily our thoughts swarm upon a new object, lifting it a little way, as ants carry a blade of straw so feverishly, and then leave it ... If that mark was made by a nail, it can't have been for a picture, it must have been for a miniature – the miniature of a lady with white powdered curls, powder-dusted cheeks, and lips like red carnations. A fraud of course, for the people who had this house before us would have chosen pictures in that way – an old picture for an old room. That is the sort of people they were – very interesting people, and I think of them so often, in such queer places, because one will never see them again, never know what happened next. They wanted to leave this house because they wanted to change their style of furniture, so he said, and he was in process of saying that in his opinion art should have ideas behind it when we were torn asunder, as one is torn from the old lady about to pour out tea and the young man about to hit the tennis ball in the back garden of the suburban villa as one rushes past in the train.

But for that mark, I'm not sure about it; I don't believe it was made by a nail after all; it's too big, too round, for that. I might get up, but if I got up and looked at it, ten to one I shouldn't be able to say for certain; because once a thing's done, no one ever knows how it happened. Oh! dear me, the mystery of life; the inaccuracy of thought! The ignorance of humanity! To show how very little control of our possessions we have — what an accidental affair this living is after all our civilization — let me just count over a few things lost in one lifetime, beginning, for that seems always the most mysterious of losses — what cat would gnaw, what rat would nibble — three pale blue canisters of book-binding tools? Then there were the bird cages, the iron hoops, the steel skates, the Queen Anne coal-scuttle, the bagatelle board, the hand organ — all gone, and jewels, too. Opals and emeralds, they lie about the roots of turnips. What a scraping paring affair it is to be sure! The wonder is that I've any clothes on my back, that I sit surrounded by solid furniture at this moment. Why, if one wants to compare life to anything, one must liken it to being blown through the Tube at fifty miles an hour — landing at the other end without a single hairpin in one's hair! Shot out at the feet of God entirely naked! Tumbling head over heels in the asphodel meadows like brown paper parcels pitched down a shoot in the post-office! With one's hair flying back like the tail of a race-horse. Yes, that seems to express the rapidity of life, the perpetual waste and repair; all so casual, all so haphazard. . .

But after life. The slow pulling down of thick green stalks so that the cup of the flower, as it turns over, deluges one with purple and red light. Why, after all, should one not be born there as one is born here, helpless, speechless, unable to focus one's eyesight, groping at the roots of the grass, at the toes of the Giants? As for saying which are trees, and which are men and women, or whether there are such things, that one won't be in a condition to do for fifty years or so. There will be nothing but spaces of light and dark, intersected by thick stalks, and rather higher up perhaps, rose-shaped blots of an indistinct colour – dim pinks and blues – which will, as time goes on, become more definite, become – I don't know what. . .

And yet that mark on the wall is not a hole at all. It may even be caused by some round black substance, such as a small rose leaf, left over from the summer, and I, not being a very vigilant housekeeper – look at the dust on the mantelpiece, for example, the dust which, so they say, buried Troy three times over, only fragments of pots utterly refusing annihilation, as one can believe.

The tree outside the window taps very gently on the pane . . . I want to think quietly, calmly, spaciously, never to be interrupted, never to have to rise from my chair, to slip easily from one thing to another, without any sense of hostility, or obstacle. I want to sink deeper and deeper, away from the surface, with its hard separate facts. To steady myself, let me catch hold of the first idea that passes . . . Shakespeare . . . Well, he will do as well as another. A man who sat himself solidly in an arm-chair, and looked into the fire, so – A shower of ideas fell perpetually from some very high Heaven down through his mind. He leant his forehead on his hand, and people, looking in through the open door – for this scene is supposed to take place on a summer's evening – But how dull this is, this historical fiction! It doesn't interest me at all. I wish I could hit upon a pleasant track of thought, a track indirectly reflecting credit upon myself, for those are the pleasantest thoughts, and very frequent even in the minds of modest mouse-coloured people, who believe genuinely that they dislike to hear their own praises. They are not thoughts directly praising oneself; that is the beauty of them; they are thoughts like this:

'And then I came into the room. They were discussing botany. I said how I'd seen a flower growing on a dust heap on the site of an old house in Kingsway. The seed, I said, must have been sown in the reign of Charles the First. What flowers grew in the reign of Charles the First?' I asked – (but I don't remember the answer). Tall flowers with purple tassels to them perhaps. And so it goes on. All the time I'm dressing up the figure of myself in my own mind, lovingly, stealthily, not openly adoring it, for if I did that, I should catch myself out, and stretch my hand at once for a book in self-protection. Indeed, it is curious how instinctively one protects the image of oneself from idolatry or any other handling that could make it ridiculous, or too unlike the original to be believed in any longer. Or is it not so very curious after all? It is a matter of great importance. Supposing the looking-glass smashes, the image disappears, and the romantic figure with the green of forest depths all about it is there no longer, but only that shell of a person which is seen by other people – what an airless, shallow, bald, prominent world it becomes! A world not to be lived in. As we face each other in omnibuses and underground railways we are looking into the mirror; that accounts for the vagueness, the gleam of glassiness, in our eyes. And the novelists in future will realize more and more the importance of these reflections, for of course there is not one reflection but an almost infinite number; those are the depths they will explore, those the phantoms they will pursue, leaving the description of reality more and more out of their stories, taking a knowledge of it for granted, as the Greeks did and Shakespeare perhaps – but these generalizations are very worthless. The military sound of the word is enough. It recalls leading articles, cabinet ministers – a whole class of things indeed which, as a child, one thought the thing itself, the standard thing, the real thing, from which one could not depart save at the risk of nameless damnation. Generalizations bring back somehow Sunday in London, Sunday afternoon walks, Sunday luncheons, and also ways of speaking of the dead, clothes, and habits – like the habit of sitting all together in one room until a certain hour, although nobody liked it. There was a rule for everything. The rule for tablecloths at that particular period was that they should be made of tapestry with little yellow compartments marked upon them, such as you may see in photographs of the carpets in the corridors of the royal palaces. Tablecloths of a different kind were not real tablecloths. How shocking, and yet how wonderful it was to discover that these real things, Sunday luncheons, Sunday walks, country houses, and tablecloths were not entirely real, were indeed half phantoms, and the damnation which visited the disbeliever in them was only a sense of illegitimate freedom. What now takes the place of those things I wonder, those real standard things? Men perhaps, should you be a woman; the masculine point of view which governs our lives, which sets the standard, which established Whitaker's Table of Precedency, which has become, I suppose, since the war, half a phantom to many men and women, which soon, one may hope, will be laughed into the dustbin where the phantoms go, the mahogany sideboards and the Landseer prints, Gods and Devils, Hell and so forth, leaving us all with an intoxicating sense of illegitimate freedom – if freedom exists. . .

In certain lights that mark on the wall seems actually to project from the wall. Nor is it entirely circular. I cannot be sure, but it seems to cast a perceptible shadow, suggesting that if I ran my finger down that strip of the wall it would, at a certain point, mount and descend a small tumulus, a smooth tumulus like those barrows on the South Downs which are, they say, either tombs or camps. Of the two I should prefer them to be tombs, desiring melancholy like most English people, and finding it natural at the end of a walk to think of the bones stretched beneath the turf. . . There must be some book about it. Some antiquary must have dug up those bones and given them a name. . . What sort of a man is an antiquary, I wonder? Retired Colonels for the most part, I daresay, leading parties of aged labourers to the top here, examining clods of earth and stone, and getting into correspondence with the neighbouring clergy, which, being opened at breakfast time, gives them a feeling of importance, and the comparison of arrow-heads necessitates cross-country journeys to the county towns, an agreeable necessity both to them and to their elderly wives, who wish to make plum jam or to clean out the study, and have every good reason for keeping that great question of the camp or the tomb in perpetual suspension, while the Colonel himself feels agreeably philosophic in accumulating evidence on both sides of the question. It is true that he does finally incline to believe in the camp; and, being opposed, indites a pamphlet which he is about to read at the quarterly meeting of the local society when a stroke lays him low, and his last conscious thoughts are not of wife or child, but of the camp and that arrow-head there, which is now in the case at the local museum, together with the foot of a Chinese murderess, a handful of Elizabethan nails, a great many Tudor clay pipes, a piece of Roman pottery, and the wineglass that Nelson drank out of – proving I really don't know what.

No, no, nothing is proved, nothing is known. And if I were to get up at this very moment and ascertain that the mark on the wall is really – what shall we say? – the head of a gigantic old nail, driven in two hundred years ago, which has now, owing to the patient attrition of many generations of house-maids, revealed its head above the coat of paint, and is taking its first view of modern life in the sight of a white-walled fire-lit room, what should I gain? – Knowledge? Matter for further speculation? I can think sitting still as well as standing up. And what is knowledge? What are our learned men save the descendants of witches and hermits who crouched in caves and in woods brewing herbs, interrogating shrew-mice and writing down the language of the stars? And the less we honour them as our superstitions dwindle and our respect for beauty and health of mind increases.... Yes, one could imagine a very pleasant world. A quiet, spacious world, with the flowers so red and blue in the open fields. A world without professors or specialists or house-keepers with the profiles of policemen, a world which one could slice with one's thought as a fish slices the water with his fin, grazing the stems of the water-lilies, hanging suspended over nests of white sea eggs. ... How peaceful it is down here, rooted in the centre of the world and gazing up through the grey waters, with their sudden gleams of light, and their reflections – if it were not for Whitaker's Almanack – if it were not for the Table of Precedency!

I must jump up and see for myself what that mark on the wall really is – a nail, a rose-leaf, a crack in the wood?

Here is nature once more at her old game of self-preservation. This train of thought, she perceives, is threatening mere waste of energy, even some collision with reality, for who will ever be able to lift a finger against Whitaker's Table of Precedency? The Archbishop of Canterbury is followed by the Lord High Chancellor; the Lord High Chancellor is followed by the Archbishop of York. Everybody follows somebody, such is the philosophy of Whitaker; and the great thing is to know who follows whom. Whitaker knows, and let that, so Nature counsels, comfort you, instead of enraging you; and if you can't be comforted, if you must shatter this hour of peace, think of the mark on the wall.

I understand Nature's game – her prompting to take action as a way of ending any thought that threatens to excite or to pain. Hence, I suppose, comes our slight contempt for men of action – men, we assume, who don't think. Still, there's no harm in putting a full stop to one's disagreeable thoughts by looking at a mark on the wall.

Indeed, now that I have fixed my eyes upon it, I feel that I have grasped a plank in the sea; I feel a satisfying sense of reality which at once turns the two Archbishops and the Lord High Chancellor to the shadows of shades. Here is something definite, something real. Thus, waking from a midnight dream of horror, one hastily turns on the light and lies quiescent, worshipping the chest of drawers, worshipping solidity, worshipping reality, worshipping the impersonal world which is a proof of some existence other than ours. That is what one wants to be sure of. . . . Wood is a pleasant thing to think about. It comes from a tree; and trees grow, and we don't know how they grow. For years and years they grow, without paying any attention to us, in meadows, in forests, and by the side of rivers – all things one likes to think about. The cows swish their tails beneath them on hot afternoons; they paint rivers so green that when a moorhen dives one expects to see its feathers all green when it comes up again. I like to think of the fish balanced against the stream like flags blown out; and of water-beetles slowly raising domes of mud upon the bed of the river. I like to think of the tree itself: first the close dry sensation of being wood; then the grinding of the storm; then the slow, delicious ooze of sap. I like to think of it, too, on winter's nights standing in the empty field with all leaves close-furled, nothing tender exposed to the iron bullets of the moon, a naked mast upon an earth that goes tumbling, tumbling, all night long. The song of birds must sound very loud and strange in June; and how cold the feet of insects must feel upon it, as they make laborious progresses up the creases of the bark, or sun themselves upon the thin green awning of the leaves, and look straight in front of them with diamond-cut red eyes. . . . One by one the fibres snap beneath the im-mense cold pressure of the earth, then the last storm comes and, falling, the highest branches drive deep into the ground again. Even so, life isn't done with; there are a million patient, watchful lives still for a tree, all over the world, in bedrooms, in ships, on the pavement, lining rooms, where men and women sit after tea, smoking cigarettes. It is full of peaceful thoughts, happy thoughts, this tree. I should like to take each one separately – but something is getting in the way. . . . Where was I? What has it all been about? A tree? A river? The Downs? Whitaker's Almanack? The fields of asphodel? I can't remember a thing. Everything's moving, falling, slipping, vanishing. . . . There is a vast upheaval of matter. Someone is standing over me and saying:

'I'm going out to buy a newspaper.'

'Yes?'

'Though it's no good buying newspapers. . . . Nothing ever happens. Curse this war; God damn this war! . . . All the same, I don't see why we should have a snail on our wall.'

Ah, the mark on the wall! It was a snail.

D. H. Lawrence

THE HORSE DEALER'S DAUGHTER

'WELL, Mabel, and what are you going to do with yourself?'
asked Joe, with foolish flippancy. He felt quite safe himself.
Without listening for an answer, he turned aside, worked a
grain of tobacco to the tip of his tongue, and spat it out. He
did not care about anything, since he felt safe himself.

The three brothers and the sister sat round the desolate
breakfast table, attempting some sort of desultory consultation. The morning's post had given the final tap to the family
fortunes, and all was over. The dreary dining-room itself, with
its heavy mahogany furniture, looked as if it were waiting to
be done away with.

But the consultation amounted to nothing. There was a
strange air of ineffectuality about the three men, as they
sprawled at table, smoking and reflecting vaguely on their own
condition. The girl was alone, a rather short, sullen-looking
young woman of twenty-seven. She did not share the same life
as her brothers. She would have been good-looking, save for
the impassive fixity of her face, 'bull-dog', as her brothers
called it.

There was a confused tramping of horses' feet outside. The
three men all sprawled round in their chairs to watch. Beyond
the dark holly-bushes that separated the strip of lawn from the
highroad, they could see a cavalcade of shire horses swinging
out of their own yard, being taken for exercise. This was the
last time. These were the last horses that would go through
their hands. The young men watched with critical, callous
look. They were all frightened at the collapse of their lives, and
the sense of disaster in which they were involved left them no
inner freedom.

Yet they were three fine, well-set fellows enough. Joe, the

eldest, was a man of thirty-three, broad and handsome in a hot, flushed way. His face was red, he twisted his black moustache over a thick finger, his eyes were shallow and restless. He had a sensual way of uncovering his teeth when he laughed, and his bearing was stupid. Now he watched the horses with a glazed look of helplessness in his eyes, a certain stupor of downfall.

The great draught-horses swung past. They were tied head to tail, four of them, and they heaved along to where a lane branched off from the highroad, planting their great hoofs floutingly in the fine black mud, swinging their great rounded haunches sumptuously, and trotting a few sudden steps as they were led into the lane, round the corner. Every movement showed a massive, slumbrous strength, and a stupidity which held them in subjection. The groom at the head looked back, jerking the leading rope. And the cavalcade moved out of sight up the lane, the tail of the last horse, bobbed up tight and stiff, held out taut from the swinging great haunches as they rocked behind the hedges in a motion like sleep.

Joe watched with glazed hopeless eyes. The horses were almost like his own body to him. He felt he was done for now. Luckily he was engaged to a woman as old as himself, and therefore her father, who was steward of a neighbouring estate, would provide him with a job. He would marry and go into harness. His life was over, he would be a subject animal now.

He turned uneasily aside, the retreating steps of the horses echoing in his ears. Then, with foolish restlessness, he reached for the scraps of bacon-rind from the plates, and making a faint whistling sound, flung them to the terrier that lay against the fender. He watched the dog swallow them, and waited till the creature looked into his eyes. Then a faint grin came on his face, and in a high, foolish voice he said:

'You won't get much more bacon, shall you, you little b——?'

The dog faintly and dismally wagged its tail, then lowered its haunches, circled round, and lay down again.

There was another helpless silence at the table. Joe sprawled uneasily in his seat, not willing to go till the family conclave was dissolved. Fred Henry, the second brother, was erect, clean-limbed, alert. He had watched the passing of the horses with more *sang-froid*. If he was an animal, like Joe, he was an animal which controls, not one which is controlled. He was master of any horse, and he carried himself with a well-tempered air of mastery. But he was not master of the situations of life. He pushed his coarse brown moustache upwards, off his lip, and glanced irritably at his sister, who sat impassive and inscrutable.

'You'll go and stop with Lucy for a bit, shan't you?' he asked. The girl did not answer.

'I don't see what else you can do,' persisted Fred Henry.

'Go as a skivvy,' Joe interpolated laconically.

The girl did not move a muscle.

'If I was her, I should go in for training for a nurse,' said Malcolm, the youngest of them all. He was the baby of the family, a young man of twenty-two, with a fresh, jaunty *museau*.

But Mabel did not take any notice of him. They had talked at her and round her for so many years, that she hardly heard them at all.

The marble clock on the mantel-piece softly chimed the half-hour, the dog rose uneasily from the hearthrug and looked at the party at the breakfast table. But still they sat on in ineffectual conclave.

'Oh, all right,' said Joe suddenly, *à propos* of nothing. 'I'll get a move on.'

He pushed back his chair, straddled his knees with a downward jerk, to get them free, in horsy fashion, and went to the fire. Still he did not go out of the room; he was curious to know what the others would do or say. He began to charge his pipe, looking down at the dog and saying, in a high, affected voice:

'Going wi' me? Going wi' me are ter? Tha'rt goin' further than tha counts on just now, dost hear?'

The dog faintly wagged its tail, the man stuck out his jaw and covered his pipe with his hands, and puffed intently, losing himself in the tobacco, looking down all the while at the dog with an absent brown eye. The dog looked up at him in mournful distrust. Joe stood with his knees stuck out, in real horsy fashion.

'Have you had a letter from Lucy?' Fred Henry asked of his sister.

'Last week,' came the neutral reply.

'And what does she say?'

There was no answer.

'Does she *ask* you to go and stop there?' persisted Fred Henry.

'She says I can if I like.'

'Well, then, you'd better. Tell her you'll come on Monday.'

This was received in silence.

'That's what you'll do then, is it?' said Fred Henry, in some exasperation.

But she made no answer. There was a silence of futility and irritation in the room. Malcolm grinned fatuously.

'You'll have to make up your mind between now and next Wednesday,' said Joe loudly, 'or else find yourself lodgings on the kerbstone.'

The face of the young woman darkened, but she sat on immutable.

'Here's Jack Fergusson!' exclaimed Malcolm, who was looking aimlessly out of the window.

'Where?' exclaimed Joe, loudly.

'Just gone past.'

'Coming in?'

Malcolm craned his neck to see the gate.

'Yes,' he said.

There was a silence. Mabel sat on like one condemned, at the head of the table. Then a whistle was heard from the kitchen. The dog got up and barked sharply. Joe opened the door and shouted:

'Come on.'

After a moment a young man entered. He was muffled up in overcoat and a purple woollen scarf, and his tweed cap, which he did not remove, was pulled down on his head. He was of medium height, his face was rather long and pale, his eyes looked tired.

'Hello, Jack! Well, Jack!' exclaimed Malcolm and Joe. Fred Henry merely said, 'Jack.'

'What's doing?' asked the newcomer, evidently addressing Fred Henry.

'Same. We've got to be out by Wednesday. – Got a cold?'

'I have – got it bad, too.'

'Why don't you stop in?'

'*Me* stop in? When I can't stand on my legs, perhaps I shall have a chance.' The young man spoke huskily. He had a slight Scotch accent.

'It's a knock-out, isn't it,' said Joe boisterously, 'if a doctor goes round croaking with a cold. Looks bad for the patients, doesn't it?'

The young doctor looked at him slowly.

'Anything the matter with *you*, then?' he asked sarcastically.

'Not as I know of. Damn your eyes, I hope not. Why?'

'I thought you were very concerned about the patients, wondered if you might be one yourself.'

'Damn it, no, I've never been patient to no flaming doctor, and hope I never shall be,' returned Joe.

At this point Mabel rose from the table, and they all seemed to become aware of her existence. She began putting the dishes together. The young doctor looked at her, but did not address her. He had not greeted her. She went out of the room with the tray, her face impassive and unchanged.

'When are you off then, all of you?' asked the doctor.

'I'm catching the eleven-forty,' replied Malcolm. 'Are you goin' down wi' th' trap, Joe?'

'Yes, I've told you I'm going down wi' th' trap, haven't I?'

'We'd better be getting her in then. – So long, Jack, if I don't see you before I go,' said Malcolm, shaking hands.

He went out, followed by Joe, who seemed to have his tail between his legs.

'Well, this is the devil's own,' exclaimed the doctor, when he was left alone with Fred Henry. 'Going before Wednesday, are you?'

'That's the orders,' replied the other.

'Where, to Northampton?'

'That's it.'

'The devil!' exclaimed Fergusson, with quiet chagrin.

And there was silence between the two.

'All settled up, are you?' asked Fergusson.

'About.'

There was another pause.

'Well, I shall miss yer, Freddy, boy,' said the young doctor.

'And I shall miss thee, Jack,' returned the other.

'Miss you like hell,' mused the doctor.

Fred Henry turned aside. There was nothing to say. Mabel came in again, to finish clearing the table.

'What are *you* going to do, then, Miss Pervin?' asked Fergusson. 'Going to your sister's, are you?'

Mabel looked at him with her steady, dangerous eyes, that always made him uncomfortable, unsettling his superficial ease.

'No,' she said.

'Well, what in the name of fortune *are* you going to do? Say what you mean to do,' cried Fred Henry, with futile intensity.

But she only averted her head, and continued her work. She folded the white table-cloth, and put on the chenille cloth.

'The sulkiest bitch that ever trod!' muttered her brother.

But she finished her task with perfectly impassive face, the young doctor watching her interestedly all the while. Then she went out.

Fred Henry stared after her, clenching his lips, his blue eyes fixing in sharp antagonism, as he made a grimace of sour exasperation.

'You could bray her into bits, and that's all you'd get out of her,' he said, in a small, narrowed tone.

The doctor smiled faintly.

'What's she *going* to do, then?' he asked.

'Strike me if *I* know!' returned the other.

There was a pause. Then the doctor stirred.

'I'll be seeing you tonight, shall I?' he said to his friend.

'Ay – where's it to be? Are we going over to Jessdale?'

'I don't know. I've got such a cold on me. I'll come round to the Moon and Stars, anyway.'

'Let Lizzie and May miss their night for once, eh?'

'That's it – if I feel as I do now.'

'All's one –'

The two young men went through the passage and down to the back door together. The house was large, but it was servantless now, and desolate. At the back was a small bricked house-yard, and beyond that a big square, gravelled fine and red, and having stables on two sides. Sloping, dank, winter-dark fields stretched away on the open sides.

But the stables were empty. Joseph Pervin, the father of the family, had been a man of no education, who had become a fairly large horse dealer. The stables had been full of horses, there was a great turmoil and come-and-go of horses and of dealers and grooms. Then the kitchen was full of servants. But of late things had declined. The old man had married a second time, to retrieve his fortunes. Now he was dead and everything was gone to the dogs, there was nothing but debt and threatening.

For months, Mabel had been servantless in the big house, keeping the home together in penury for her ineffectual brothers. She had kept house for ten years. But previously, it was with unstinted means. Then, however brutal and coarse everything was, the sense of money had kept her proud, confident. The men might be foul-mouthed, the women in the kitchen might have bad reputations, her brothers might have illegitimate children. But so long as there was money, the girl felt herself established, and brutally proud, reserved.

No company came to the house, save dealers and coarse men. Mabel had no associates of her own sex, after her sister went away. But she did not mind. She went regularly to church, she attended to her father. And she lived in the memory of her mother, who had died when she was fourteen, and whom she had loved. She had loved her father, too, in a different way, depending upon him, and feeling secure in him, until at the age of fifty-four he married again. And then she had set hard against him. Now he had died and left them all hopelessly in debt.

She had suffered badly during the period of poverty. Nothing, however, could shake the curious sullen, animal pride that dominated each member of the family. Now, for Mabel, the end had come. Still she would not cast about her. She would follow her own way just the same. She would always hold the keys of her own situation. Mindless and persistent, she endured from day to day. Why should she think? Why should she answer anybody? It was enough that this was the end, and there was no way out. She need not pass any more darkly along the main street of the small town, avoiding every eye. She need not demean herself any more, going into the shops and buying the cheapest food. This was at an end. She thought of nobody, not even of herself. Mindless and persistent, she seemed in a sort of ecstasy to be coming nearer to her fulfilment, her own glorification, approaching her dead mother, who was glorified.

In the afternoon she took a little bag, with shears and sponge and a small scrubbing brush, and went out. It was a grey, wintry day, with saddened, dark-green fields and an atmosphere blackened by the smoke of foundries not far off. She went quickly, darkly along the causeway, heeding nobody, through the town to the churchyard.

There she always felt secure, as if no one could see her, although as a matter of fact she was exposed to the stare of everyone who passed along under the churchyard wall. Nevertheless, once under the shadow of the great looming church, among the graves, she felt immune from the world, reserved within the thick churchyard wall as in another country.

Carefully she clipped the grass from the grave, and arranged the pinky-white, small chrysanthemums in the tin cross. When this was done, she took an empty jar from a neighbouring grave, brought water, and carefully, most scrupulously sponged the marble headstone and the coping-stone.

It gave her sincere satisfaction to do this. She felt in immediate contact with the world of her mother. She took minute pains, went through the park in a state bordering on pure happiness, as if in performing this task she came into a subtle, intimate connection with her mother. For the life she followed here in the world was far less real than the world of death she inherited from her mother.

The doctor's house was just by the church. Fergusson, being a mere hired assistant, was slave to the countryside. As he hurried now to attend to the outpatients in the surgery, glancing across the graveyard with his quick eye, he saw the girl at her task at the grave. She seemed so intent and remote, it was like looking into another world. Some mystical element was touched in him. He slowed down as he walked, watching her as if spell-bound.

She lifted her eyes, feeling him looking. Their eyes met. And each looked again at once, each feeling, in some way, found out by the other. He lifted his cap and passed on down the road. There remained distinct in his consciousness, like a vision, the memory of her face, lifted from the tombstone in the churchyard, and looking at him with slow, large, portentous eyes. It *was* portentous, her face. It seemed to mesmerize him. There was a heavy power in her eyes which laid hold of his whole being, as if he had drunk some powerful drug. He had been feeling weak and done before. Now the life came back to him, he felt delivered from his own fretted, daily self.

He finished his duties at the surgery as quickly as might be, hastily filling up the bottles of the waiting people with cheap drugs. Then, in perpetual haste, he set off again to visit several cases in another part of his round, before teatime. At all times he preferred to walk, if he could, but particularly when he was not well. He fancied the motion restored him.

The afternoon was falling. It was grey, deadened, and wintry, with a slow, moist, heavy coldness sinking in and deadening all the faculties. But why should he think or notice? He hastily climbed the hill and turned across the dark-green fields, following the black cinder-track. In the distance, across a shallow dip in the country, the small town was clustered like smouldering ash, a tower, a spire, a heap of low, raw, extinct houses. And on the nearest fringe of the town, sloping into the dip, was Oldmeadow, the Pervins' house. He could see the stables and the outbuildings distinctly, as they lay towards him on the slope. Well, he would not go there many more times! Another resource would be lost to him, another place gone: the only company he cared for in the alien, ugly little town he was losing. Nothing but work, drudgery, constant hastening from dwelling to dwelling among the colliers and the iron-workers. It wore him out, but at the same time he had a craving for it. It was a stimulant to him to be in the homes of the working people, moving as it were through the innermost body of their life. His nerves were excited and gratified. He could come so near, into the very lives of the rough, inarticulate, powerfully emotional men and women. He grumbled, he said he hated the hellish hole. But as a matter of fact it excited him, the contact with the rough, strongly-feeling people was a stimulant applied direct to his nerves.

Below Oldmeadow, in the green, shallow, soddened hollow of fields, lay a square, deep pond. Roving across the landscape, the doctor's quick eye detected a figure in black passing through the gate of the field, down towards the pond. He looked again. It would be Mabel Pervin. His mind suddenly became alive and attentive.

Why was she going down there? He pulled up on the path on the slope above, and stood staring. He could just make sure of the small black figure moving in the hollow of the failing day. He seemed to see her in the midst of such obscurity, that he was like a clairvoyant, seeing rather with the mind's eye than with ordinary sight. Yet he could see her positively enough, whilst he kept his eye attentive. He felt, if he looked away from her, in the thick, ugly falling dusk, he would lose her altogether.

He followed her minutely as she moved, direct and intent, like something transmitted rather than stirring in voluntary activity, straight down the field towards the pond. There she stood on the bank for a moment. She never raised her head. Then she waded slowly into the water.

He stood motionless as the small black figure walked slowly

and deliberately towards the centre of the pond, very slowly, gradually moving deeper into the motionless water, and still moving forward as the water got up to her breast. Then he could see her no more in the dusk of the dead afternoon.

'There!' he exclaimed. 'Would you believe it?'

And he hastened straight down, running over the wet, soddened fields, pushing through the hedges, down into the depression of callous wintry obscurity. It took him several minutes to come to the pond. He stood on the bank, breathing heavily. He could see nothing. His eyes seemed to penetrate the dead water. Yes, perhaps that was the dark shadow of her black clothing beneath the surface of the water.

He slowly ventured into the pond. The bottom was deep, soft clay, he sank in, and the water clasped dead cold round his legs. As he stirred he could smell the cold, rotten clay that fouled up into the water. It was objectionable in his lungs. Still, repelled and yet not heeding, he moved deeper into the pond. The cold water rose over his thighs, over his loins, upon his abdomen. The lower part of his body was all sunk in the hideous cold element. And the bottom was so deeply soft and uncertain, he was afraid of pitching with his mouth underneath. He could not swim, and was afraid.

He crouched a little, spreading his hands under the water and moving them round, trying to feel for her. The dead cold pond swayed upon his chest. He moved again, a little deeper, and again, with his hands underneath, he felt all around under the water. And he touched her clothing. But it evaded his fingers. He made a desperate effort to grasp it.

And so doing he lost his balance and went under, horribly, suffocating in the foul earthy water, struggling madly for a few moments. At last, after what seemed an eternity, he got his footing, rose again into the air and looked around. He gasped, and knew he was in the world. Then he looked at the water. She had risen near him. He grasped her clothing, and drawing her nearer, turned to take his way to land again.

He went very slowly, carefully, absorbed in the slow progress. He rose higher, climbing out of the pond. The water was now only about his legs; he was thankful, full of relief to be out of the clutches of the pond. He lifted her and staggered on to the bank, out of the horror of wet, grey clay.

He laid her down on the bank. She was quite unconscious and running with water. He made the water come from her mouth, he worked to restore her. He did not have to work very long before he could feel the breathing begin again in her; she was breathing naturally. He worked a little longer. He could feel her live beneath his hands; she was coming back. He wiped her face, wrapped her in his overcoat, looked round into the dim, dark-grey world, then lifted her and staggered down the bank and across the fields.

It seemed an unthinkably long way, and his burden so heavy he felt he would never get to the house. But at last he was in the stable-yard, and then in the house-yard. He opened the door and went into the house. In the kitchen he laid her down on the hearthrug, and called. The house was empty. But the fire was burning in the grate.

Then again he kneeled to attend to her. She was breathing regularly, her eyes were wide open and as if conscious, but there seemed something missing in her look. She was conscious in herself, but unconscious of her surroundings.

He ran upstairs, took blankets from a bed, and put them before the fire to warm. Then he removed her saturated, earthy-smelling clothing, rubbed her dry with a towel, and wrapped her naked in the blankets. Then he went into the dining-room, to look for spirits. There was a little whisky. He drank a gulp himself, and put some into her mouth.

The effect was instantaneous. She looked full into his face, as if she had been seeing him for some time, and yet had only just become conscious of him.

'Dr Fergusson?' she said.

'What?' he answered.

He was divesting himself of his coat, intending to find some dry clothing upstairs. He could not bear the smell of the dead, clayey water, and he was mortally afraid for his own health.

'What did I do?' she asked.

'Walked into the pond,' he replied. He had begun to shudder like one sick, and could hardly attend to her. Her eyes remained full on him, he seemed to be going dark in his mind, looking back at her helplessly. The shuddering became quieter in him, his life came back in him, dark and unknowing, but strong again.

'Was I out of my mind?' she asked, while her eyes were fixed on him all the time.

'Maybe, for the moment,' he replied. He felt quiet, because his strength had come back. The strange fretful strain had left him.

'Am I out of my mind now?' she asked.

'Are you?' he reflected a moment. 'No,' he answered truthfully, 'I don't see that you are.' He turned his face aside. He was afraid now, because he felt dazed, and felt dimly that her power was stronger than his, in this issue. And she continued to look at him fixedly all the time. 'Can you tell me where I shall find some dry things to put on?' he asked.

'Did you dive into the pond for me?' she asked.

'No,' he answered. 'I walked in. But I went in overhead as well.'

There was silence for a moment. He hesitated. He very much wanted to go upstairs to get into dry clothing. But there was another desire in him. And she seemed to hold him. His will seemed to have gone to sleep, and left him, standing there slack before her. But he felt warm inside himself. He did not shudder at all, though his clothes were sodden on him.

'Why did you?' she asked.

'Because I didn't want you to do such a foolish thing,' he said.

'It wasn't foolish,' she said, still gazing at him as she lay on the floor, with a sofa cushion under her head. 'It was the right thing to do. I knew best, then.'

'I'll go and shift these wet things,' he said. But still he had not the power to move out of her presence, until she sent him. It was as if she had the life of his body in her hands, and he could not extricate himself. Or perhaps he did not want to.

Suddenly she sat up. Then she became aware of her own immediate condition. She felt the blankets about her, she knew her own limbs. For a moment it seemed as if her reason were going. She looked round, with wild eye, as if seeking something. He stood still with fear. She saw her clothing lying scattered.

'Who undressed me?' she asked, her eyes resting full and inevitable on his face.

'I did,' he replied, 'to bring you round.'

For some moments she sat and gazed at him awfully, her lips parted.

'Do you love me then?' she asked.

He only stood and stared at her, fascinated. His soul seemed to melt.

She shuffled forward on her knees, and put her arms round him, round his legs, as he stood there, pressing her breasts against his knees and thighs, clutching him with strange, convulsive certainty, pressing his thighs against her, drawing him to her face, her throat, as she looked up at him with flaring, humble eyes, of transfiguration, triumphant in first possession.

'You love me,' she murmured, in strange transport, yearning and triumphant and confident. 'You love me. I know you love me, I know.'

And she was passionately kissing his knees, through the wet clothing, passionately and indiscriminately kissing his knees, his legs, as if unaware of everything.

He looked down at the tangled wet hair, the wild, bare, animal shoulders. He was amazed, bewildered, and afraid. He had never thought of loving her. He had never wanted to love her. When he rescued her and restored her, he was a doctor, and she was a patient. He had had no single personal thought of her. Nay, this introduction of the personal element was very distasteful to him, a violation of his professional honour. It was horrible to have her there embracing his knees. It was horrible. He revolted from it, violently. And yet – and yet – he had not the power to break away.

She looked at him again, with the same supplication of powerful love, and that same transcendent, frightening light of triumph. In view of the delicate flame which seemed to come from her face like a light, he was powerless. And yet he had never intended to love her. He had never intended. And something stubborn in him could not give way.

'You love me,' she repeated, in a murmur of deep, rhapsodic assurance. 'You love me.'

Her hands were drawing him, drawing him down to her. He was afraid, even a little horrified. For he had, really, no intention of loving her. Yet her hands were drawing him towards her. He put out his hand quickly to steady himself, and grasped her bare shoulder. A flame seemed to burn the hand that grasped her soft shoulder. He had no intention of loving her: his whole will was against his yielding. It was horrible. And yet wonderful was the touch of her shoulders, beautiful the shining of her face. Was she perhaps mad? He had a horror of yielding to her. Yet something in him ached also.

He had been staring away at the door, away from her. But his hand remained on her shoulder. She had gone suddenly very still. He looked down at her. Her eyes were now wide with fear, with doubt, the light was dying from her face, a shadow of terrible greyness was returning. He could not bear the touch of her eyes' question upon him, and the look of death behind the question.

With an inward groan he gave way, and let his heart yield towards her. A sudden gentle smile came on his face. And her eyes, which never left his face, slowly, slowly filled with tears. He watched the strange water rise in her eyes, like some slow fountain coming up. And his heart seemed to burn and melt away in his breast.

He could not bear to look at her any more. He dropped on his knees and caught her head with his arms and pressed her face against his throat. She was very still. His heart, which seemed to have broken, was burning with a kind of agony in his breast. And he felt her slow, hot tears wetting his throat. But he could not move.

He felt the hot tears wet his neck and the hollows of his neck, and he remained motionless, suspended through one of man's eternities. Only now it had become indispensable to him to have her face pressed close to him; he could never let her go again. He could never let her head go away from the close clutch of his arm. He wanted to remain like that for ever, with his heart hurting him in a pain that was also life to him. Without knowing, he was looking down on her damp, soft brown hair.

Then, as it were suddenly, he smelt the horrid stagnant smell of that water. And at the same moment she drew away from him and looked at him. Her eyes were wistful and unfathomable. He was afraid of them, and he fell to kissing her, not knowing what he was doing. He wanted her eyes not to have that terrible, wistful, unfathomable look.

When she turned her face to him again, a faint delicate flush was glowing, and there was again dawning that terrible shining of joy in her eyes, which really terrified him, and yet which he now wanted to see, because he feared the look of doubt still more.

'You love me?' she said, rather faltering.

'Yes.' The word cost him a painful effort. Not because it wasn't true. But because it was too newly true, the *saying* seemed to tear open again his newly-torn heart. And he hardly wanted it to be true, even now.

She lifted her face to him, and he bent forward and kissed her on the mouth, gently, with the one kiss that is an eternal pledge. And as he kissed her his heart strained again in his breast. He never intended to love her. But now it was over. He had crossed over the gulf to her, and all that he had left behind had shrivelled and become void.

After the kiss, her eyes again slowly filled with tears. She sat still, away from him, with her face drooped aside, and her hands folded in her lap. The tears fell very slowly. There was complete silence. He too sat there motionless and silent on the hearthrug. The strange pain of his heart that was broken seemed to consume him. That he should love her? That this was love! That he should be ripped open in this way! — Him, a doctor! — How they would all jeer if they knew! — It was agony to him to think they might know.

In the curious naked pain of the thought he looked again to her. She was sitting there drooped into a muse. He saw a tear fall, and his heart flared hot. He saw for the first time that one of her shoulders was quite uncovered, one arm bare, he could see one of her small breasts; dimly, because it had become almost dark in the room.

'Why are you crying?' he asked, in an altered voice.

She looked up at him, and behind her tears the consciousness of her situation for the first time brought a dark look of shame to her eyes.

'I'm not crying, really,' she said, watching him half frightened.

He reached his hand, and softly closed it on her bare arm.

'I love you! I love you!' he said in a soft, low vibrating voice, unlike himself.

She shrank, and dropped her head. The soft, penetrating grip of his hand on her arm distressed her. She looked up at him.

'I want to go,' she said. 'I want to go and get you some dry things.'

'Why?' he said. 'I'm all right.'

'But I want to go,' she said. 'And I want you to change your things.'

He released her arm, and she wrapped herself in the blanket, looking at him rather frightened. And still she did not rise.

'Kiss me,' she said wistfully.

He kissed her, but briefly, half in anger.

Then, after a second, she rose nervously, all mixed up in the blanket. He watched her in confusion, as she tried to extricate herself and wrap herself up so that she could walk. He watched her relentlessly, as she knew. And as she went, the blanket trailing, and as he saw a glimpse of her feet and her white leg, he tried to remember her as she was when he had wrapped her in the blanket. But then he didn't want to remember, because she had been nothing to him then, and his nature revolted from remembering her as she was when she was nothing to him.

A tumbling, muffled noise from within the dark house startled him. Then he heard her voice:– 'There are clothes.' He rose and went to the foot of the stairs, and gathered up the garments she had thrown down. Then he came back to the fire, to rub himself down and dress. He grimaced at his own appearance when he had finished.

The fire was sinking, so he put on coal. The house was now quite dark, save for the light of a street-lamp that shone in faintly from beyond the holly trees. He lit the gas with matches he found on the mantel-piece. Then he emptied the pockets of his own clothes, and threw all his wet things in a heap into the scullery. After which he gathered up her sodden clothes, gently, and put them in a separate heap on the copper-top in the scullery.

It was six o'clock on the clock. His own watch had stopped. He ought to go back to the surgery. He waited, and still she did not come down. So he went to the foot of the stairs and called:

'I shall have to go.'

Almost immediately he heard her coming down. She had on her best dress of black voile, and her hair was tidy, but still damp. She looked at him – and in spite of herself, smiled.

'I don't like you in those clothes,' she said.

'Do I look a sight?' he answered.

They were shy of one another.

'I'll make you some tea,' she said.

'No, I must go.'

'Must you?' And she looked at him again with the wide, strained, doubtful eyes. And again, from the pain of his breast, he knew how he loved her. He went and bent to kiss her, gently, passionately, with his heart's painful kiss.

'And my hair smells so horrible,' she murmured in distraction. 'And I'm so awful, I'm so awful! Oh no, I'm too awful.' And she broke into a bitter, heart-broken sobbing. 'You can't want to love me, I'm horrible.'

'Don't be silly, don't be silly,' he said, trying to comfort her, kissing her, holding her in his arms. 'I want you, I want to marry you, we're going to be married, quickly, quickly – to-morrow if I can.'

But she only sobbed terribly, and cried:

'I feel awful. I feel awful. I feel I'm horrible to you.'

'No, I want you, I want you,' was all he answered, blindly, with that terrible intonation which frightened her almost more than her horror lest he should *not* want her.

Katherine Mansfield

FEUILLE D'ALBUM

HE really was an impossible person. Too shy altogether. With absolutely nothing to say for himself. And such a weight. Once he was in your studio he never knew when to go, but would sit on and on until you nearly screamed, and burned to throw something enormous after him when he did finally blush his way out – something like the tortoise stove. The strange thing was that at first sight he looked most interesting. Everybody agreed about that. You would drift into the café one evening and there you would see, sitting in a corner, with a glass of coffee in front of him, a thin dark boy, wearing a blue jersey with a little grey flannel jacket buttoned over it. And somehow that blue jersey and the grey jacket with the sleeves that were too short gave him the air of a boy that has made up his mind to run away to sea. Who has run away, in fact, and will get up in a moment and sling a knotted handkerchief containing his nightshirt and his mother's picture on the end of a stick, and walk out into the night and be drowned. . . Stumble over the wharf edge on his way to the ship, even. . . He had black close-cropped hair, grey eyes with long lashes, white cheeks and a mouth pouting as though he were determined not to cry. . . . How could one resist him? Oh, one's heart was wrung at sight. And, as if that were not enough, there was his trick of blushing. . . Whenever the waiter came near him he turned crimson – he might have been just out of prison and the waiter in the know. . .

'Who is he, my dear? Do you know?'

'Yes. His name is Ian French. Painter. Awfully clever, they say. Someone started by giving him a mother's tender care. She asked him how often he heard from home, whether he had enough blankets on his bed, how much milk he drank a day. But when she went round to his studio to give an eye to his socks, she rang and rang, and though she could have sworn she heard someone breathing inside, the door was not answered. . . . Hopeless!'

Someone else decided that he ought to fall in love. She summoned him to her side, called him 'boy', leaned over him so that he might smell the enchanting perfume of her hair, took his arm, told him how marvellous life could be if one only had the courage, and went round to his studio one evening and rang and rang. . . . Hopeless.

'What the poor boy really wants is thoroughly rousing,' said a third. So off they went to cafés and cabarets, little dances, places where you drank something that tasted like tinned apricot juice, but cost twenty-seven shillings a bottle and was called champagne, other places, too thrilling for words, where you sat in the most awful gloom, and where someone had always been shot the night before. But he did not turn a hair. Only once he got very drunk, but instead of blossoming forth, there he sat, stony, with two spots of red on his cheeks, like, my dear, yes, the dead image of that rag-time thing they were playing, like a 'Broken Doll'. But when she took him back to his studio he had quite recovered, and said 'good night' to her in the street below, as though they had walked home from church together. . . . Hopeless.

After heaven knows how many more attempts – for the spirit of kindness dies very hard in women – they gave him up. Of course, they were still perfectly charming, and asked him to their shows, and spoke to him in the café but that was all. When one is an artist one has no time simply for people who won't respond. Has one?

'And besides I really think there must be something rather fishy somewhere . . . don't you? It can't all be as innocent as it looks! Why come to Paris if you want to be a daisy in the field? No, I'm not suspicious. But –'

He lived at the top of a tall mournful building overlooking the river. One of those buildings that look so romantic on rainy nights and moonlight nights, when the shutters are shut, and the heavy door, and the sign advertising 'a little apartment to let immediately' gleams forlorn beyond words. One of those buildings that smell so unromantic all the year round, and where the concierge lives in a glass cage on the ground floor, wrapped up in a filthy shawl, stirring something in a saucepan and ladling out tit-bits to the swollen old dog lolling on a bead cushion. . . . Perched up in the air the studio had a wonderful view. The two big windows faced the water; he could see the boats and the barges swinging up and down, and the fringe of an island planted with trees, like a round bouquet. The side window looked across to another house, shabbier still and smaller, and down below there was a flower market. You could see the tops of huge umbrellas, with frills of bright flowers escaping from them, booths covered with striped awning where they sold plants in boxes and clumps of wet gleaming palms in terracotta jars. Among the flowers the old women scuttled from side to side, like crabs. Really there was no need for him to go out. If he sat at the window until his white beard fell over the sill he still would have found something to draw. . .

How surprised those tender women would have been if they had managed to force the door. For he kept his studio as neat as a pin. Everything was arranged to form a pattern, a little 'still life' as it were – the saucepans with their lids on the wall behind the gas stove, the bowl of eggs, milk jug and teapot on the shelf, the books and the lamp with the crinkly paper shade on the table. An Indian curtain that had a fringe of red leopards marching round it covered his bed by day, and on the wall beside the bed on a level with your eyes when you were lying down there was a small neatly printed notice: GET UP AT ONCE.

Every day was much the same. While the light was good he slaved at his paintings, then cooked his meals and tidied up the place. And in the evenings he went off to the café, or sat at home reading or making out the most complicated list of expenses headed: 'What I ought to be able to do it on,' and ending with a sworn statement . . . 'I swear not to exceed this amount for next month. Signed, Ian French.'

Nothing very fishy about this; but those far-seeing women were quite right. It wasn't all.

One evening he was sitting at the side window eating some prunes and throwing the stones on to the tops of the huge umbrellas in the deserted flower market. It had been raining – the first real spring rain of the year had fallen – a bright spangle hung on everything, and the air smelled of buds and moist earth. Many voices sounding languid and content rang out in the dusky air, and the people who had come to close their windows and fasten the shutters leaned out instead. Down below in the market the trees were peppered with new green. What kind of trees were they? he wondered. And now came the lamplighter. He stared at the house across the way, the small shabby house, and suddenly, as if in answer to his gaze, two wings of windows opened and a girl came out on to the tiny balcony carrying a pot of daffodils. She was a strangely thin girl in a dark pinafore, with a pink handkerchief tied over her hair. Her sleeves were rolled up almost to her shoulders and her slender arms shone against the dark stuff.

'Yes, it is quite warm enough. It will do them good,' she said, putting down the pot and turning to someone in the room inside. As she turned she put her hands up to the hand-kerchief and tucked away some wisps of hair. She looked down at the deserted market and up at the sky, but where he sat there might have been a hollow in the air. She simply did not see the house opposite. And then she disappeared.

His heart fell out of the side window of his studio, and down to the balcony of the house opposite – buried itself in the pot of daffodils under the half-opened buds and spears of green. . . . That room with the balcony was the sitting room, and the one next door to it was the kitchen. He heard the clatter of the dishes as she washed up after supper, and then she came to the window, knocked a little mop against the ledge, and hung it on a nail to dry. She never sang or unbraided her hair, or held out her arms to the moon as young girls are supposed to do. And she always wore the same dark pina-fore and the pink handkerchief over her hair. . . . Whom did she live with? Nobody else came to those two windows, and yet she was always talking to someone in the room. Her mother, he decided, was an invalid. They took in sewing. The father was dead. . . . He had been a journalist – very pale, with long moustaches, and a piece of black hair falling over his forehead.

By working all day they just made enough money to live on, but they never went out and they had no friends. Now when he sat down at his table he had to make an entirely new set of sworn statements. . . . Not to go to the side window before a certain hour: signed Ian French. Not to think about her until he had put away his painting things for the day: signed, Ian French.

It was quite simple. She was the only person he really wanted to know, because she was, he decided, the only other person alive who was just his age. He couldn't stand giggling girls, and he had no use for grown-up women. . . . She was his age, she was – well, just like him. He sat in his dusky studio, tired, with one arm hanging over the back of his chair, staring in at her window and seeing himself in there with her. She had a violent temper; they quarrelled terribly at times, he and she. She had a way of stamping her foot and twisting her hands in her pinafore . . . furious. And she very rarely laughed. Only when she told him about an absurd little kitten she once had who used to roar and pretend to be a lion when it was given meat to eat. Things like that made her laugh. . . . But as a rule they sat together very quietly; he, just as he was sitting now, and she with her hands folded in her lap and her feet tucked under, talking in low tones, or silent and tired after the day's work. Of course, she never asked him about his pictures, and of course he made the most wonderful drawings of her which she hated, because he made her so thin and so dark. . . . But how could he get to know her? This might go on for years. . .

Then he discovered that once a week, in the evenings, she went out shopping. On two successive Thursdays she came to the window wearing an old-fashioned cape over the pinafore, and carrying a basket. From where he sat he could not see the the door of her house, but on the next Thursday evening at the same time he snatched up his cap and ran down the stairs. There was a lovely pink light over everything. He saw it glowing in the river, and the people walking towards him had pink faces and pink hands.

He leaned against the side of his house waiting for her and he had no idea of what he was going to do or say. 'Here she comes,' said a voice in his head. She walked very quickly, with small, light steps; with one hand she carried the basket, with the other she kept the cape together. . . . What could he do? He could only follow. . . . First she went into the grocer's and spent a long time in there, and then she went into the butcher's where she had to wait her turn. Then she was an age at the draper's matching something, and then she went to the fruit shop and bought a lemon. As he watched her he knew more surely than ever he must get to know her, now. Her composure, her seriousness and her loneliness, the very way she walked as though she was eager to be done with this world of grown-ups all was so natural to him and so inevitable.

'Yes, she is always like that,' he thought proudly. 'We have nothing to do with these people.'

But now she was on her way home and he was as far off as ever. . . . She suddenly turned into the dairy and he saw her through the window buying an egg. She picked it out of the basket with such care – a brown one, a beautifully shaped one, the one he would have chosen. And when she came out of the dairy he went in after her. In a moment he was out again, and following her past his house across the flower market, dodging among the huge umbrellas and treading on the fallen flowers and the round marks where the pots had stood. . . . Through her door he crept and up the stairs after, taking care to tread in time with her so that she should not notice. Finally, she stopped on the landing, and took the key out of her purse. As she put it into the door he ran up and faced her.

Blushing more crimson than ever, but looking at her severely he said, almost angrily: 'Excuse me, Mademoiselle, you dropped this.'

And he handed her an egg.

Joyce Cary

GOVERNMENT BABY

'SHE's coming, Caffin.' Two grinning faces appeared outside the mosquito house. The wire mesh gave them the look of early press photographs, grey and blurred.

Caffin, a pale, fat young man, lying on the bed in a singlet, glared savagely at them.

'Can't you let me sleep?' he growled. 'I got a head like a sore tooth.'

'But you told us to tell you – it's that mish girl that brought the tracts yesterday.'

'Damn it all, why does she come now?'

'Oh well, it's all right, it's only because you said to tell you.'

They smiled at Caffin and Caffin glared at them. The smiles were now a little doubtful and Caffin felt the doubt. He got up slowly, swearing to himself, dressed even to a necktie, drank a hasty gin to steady his legs, and stepped out into the afternoon sun.

His two hosts peering out of the top windows of the store bungalow across the glaring earth of the station, watched him intercept the girl at the opening of the mission road.

He took off his hat, she jumped off her bicycle with a quick eager gesture. Caffin stooped forward, hollowing his back and wriggling his behind in a Chaplin pose. The two men in the store laughed, and Billson, who was the agent in charge, a man of fifty who did not laugh easily, said in a tone of surprised pleasure: 'That chap – he really is –'

Caffin accosted the girl. He gave another wriggle and raised his hat high into the air. The two watchers suddenly exploded with laughter. They could not contain themselves. Billson did not seem the same man. The tall dignified agent, with his thick grey hair and reserved critical expression, fell back into a chair, kicked up his legs and crowed. He clasped himself. He could not bear it. With a violent effort he controlled himself, sat up and wiped his eyes.

'You couldn't believe it unless you saw it – what a nerve –'

Meanwhile Caffin, his head swimming, played his part.

'I read the tract you left at the store, Miss, and I was wondering if you had any more of the same kind.'

'Oh, I'm so glad you liked it.' She was a short, thick-set girl with a snub nose and round chin. She was neither plain nor pretty; an ordinary girl, but Caffin liked her skin and her expression. The first told him that she was young and new to Africa, the second that she was full of life and enthusiasm. He leant towards her giving his bottom another wriggle for the pleasure of his admirers, and said earnestly, 'You don't mind me speaking to you like this, Miss.'

'Of course not –'

'Well, Miss, I only thought you might have heard something –'

The delighted watchers, now including every white man in the station, saw Caffin's modest air of repentant sinner, the girl's eager and encouraging glances and gestures while he led her slowly towards the deeper shade of the bush road down which they disappeared. The bicycle left leaning against a tree was the only relic of the episode. Billson stared at it as if at something solid left over from a dream. 'You couldn't believe it,' he murmured. 'What a nerve.'

This was Caffin's first visit to Dabbi. He had been sacked from some temporary job further down the river and had invited himself to stay with Billson who had once met him on a boat. Caffin was a well-known character. There were many stories about him and all of them created the idea of a complete liar, soaker, coward, and thief. But Dabbi thought them a little too good.

Saxby, the district officer, had used these very words at the club, 'Perhaps a little too good, Billson.'

'Oh, of course, the chaps pile it on,' Billson agreed.

All the same, Caffin had a gratifying reception at the club that night. At least he had shown unusual gifts.

'And where's the lady friend?' Saxby asked him.

'She had to go back to her Bible class. She asked me to go along, but I said I was shy.'

The club which was held that night in the store compound down by the river, laughed heartily. Caffin didn't laugh. He was a post-war hero and his pose was the hard-boiled, the bored, the victim of fate.

'She'll change you yet, Caffy.'

'You bet,' he said. 'Back to the fold.'

There was another laugh, but Caffin said gloomily, 'I can't keep off 'em.'

Saxby, who had been as generous as anyone in his appreciation of the artist, said, 'You're a wonderful chap, Caffin – how do you do it?'

'There's only one thing to tell a girl – that you're bad – rotten bad.'

'You tell 'em the truth, Caffy,' said a young soldier.

'Yes, they won't believe it – not a really nice girl.'

Again the club laughed; Saxby, good husband, good father, laughed more than anyone. 'I see – that's the idea.'

After this Caffin met the girl every day, although, of course, he complained bitterly of the necessity, saying in a disgusted voice. 'Why do I do it – it's just silly – and me feeling rotten too.'

In the evening he reported to the club, imitating the girl's voice, 'Oh, Mr Caffin, you mustn't think so badly of yourself.' Then in his own voice, 'Miss Smith – Martha – I may call you Martha, mayn't I – you're so kind, too trustful.'

The club roared with laughter. Caffin said in a mournful voice, 'It makes you tired.'

Another night he described his first attempt at a kiss. The lady, it appeared, had been greatly shocked.

'What did she do, Caffy?'

'All the usual things.' Caffin sighed. 'She said I was a disgusting beast.'

'She believes in the truth, too.'

'And she said she didn't see any need for that sort of thing.'

'Do they all say that?'

'All of 'em. I don't know why I go on.'

'And what did you do then?'

'Oh, the usual. I told her I couldn't help my feelings and that she was a crool, hard-hearted girl.'

'And then?'

'Well, then, of course, I did it again.'

'What, kissed her?'

'Yes, God knows why. There's no kick for me in green apples. But it was the next move.'

'Did you though?' Saxby strove to call up the idea of this unconventional act. 'And what did she say to that?'

'Oh, the usual thing – she asked me to forgive her.'

'To forgive *you*?'

'For being so crool and hard-hearted. And, of course, she wanted some more, a lot more.'

'A lot more what?'

'Why, kisses.' Caffin said this word with such concentrated misery and disgust that the club burst into a shout of joy. 'It makes you sick,' he said, 'but I suppose it's my own fault – why do I do it, why?'

The next night he arrived in such extreme depression that the club actually cheered him. The whole circle broke into laughter and cries of encouragement as soon as he came into the firelight. He accepted his triumph with a gesture of despair, fell into his seat and sat bent forward for about five minutes gazing at the ground with his head between his hands.

'Come on, Caffy, what's the latest? Did she propose?'

He shook his head slightly but he did not groan. He never over-acted a part; it is quite probable that he did not act at all. He played the part, modelled no doubt on some hero of the post-war magazine, some Huxley neurote or coffee-stall philosopher, so often, that it was himself.

'Spit it out, Caffy – we'll hold your hand.'

Caffin took a drink. 'It's only something she said tonight – but you wouldn't believe it.'

'Now then, Caffy.'

'Well, you know what sort she is – she gets her feelings in a

big way,' and he sighed. 'She wouldn't be a mish if she didn't
– I can't blame her – I just asked for it.'

'Go on, Caffy, what did she say?'

The club implored. Even Saxby gave his official encouragement. 'Now then, Caffin, you mustn't disappoint us.'

'She said, "God sent you to me".'

'No, no, Caffy.'

'Try another, Caffy.'

'No, Caffy, a thin tale.'

Caffin sat up. 'Damn it all, don't you understand anything –
why, a girl like that – it's the shock of their lives – they don't
know anything – I bet you that one never had a doll, not a real
baby doll – teddy bear's the style, don't raise any awkward
ideas or nasty feeling – they're brought up in a bag and when a
chap tickles 'em a bit through a moth 'ole, it's like a revelation
from 'eaven – if they 'aven't been smothered already –' in his
excitement Caffin began to drop aitches. But the club repeated
from all sides, 'No, no, Caffy.'

The joke was that Caffin took the thing seriously, it
appeared that he valued himself as an expert on seduction
and female psychology. He had a weak side; a faith, almost a
religion. 'No, no, Caffy,' everyone cried, and he shouted,
'Damn it all, I tell you – that's nothing – lots of girls – it's just
the natural thing – give 'em a chance, that's all.'

'No, no, Caffy, that's a bit too good.'

At last Caffin got up and went away. He was huffed.

The club was surprised and a little conscience-smitten. The
Dabbi staff at that time were thoroughly good fellows, all of
them, sociable and good-natured. Saxby had the name for
making happy stations, and he deserved it. He was an excellent
district officer, hard-working, conscientious with a strong,
natural sympathy for the natives, and he had never stood on
his official dignity.

He took his pipe from his mouth, looked after Caffin with a
startled air and said, 'He isn't wounded in his feelings, I
hope.'

They reassured him. 'It's all right, sir, he had to go.'

'I'm afraid he was hurt. I must drop in tomorrow and say

something.' He put back his pipe and reflected. Gradually a chuckle rose through his huge form. 'Funny sort of chap.'

'Shouldn't believe everything he tells you,' Billson said.

'Well, I don't know.' Saxby puffed and reflected. A serious expression appeared on several faces. The Dabbi club was accustomed after sunset now and then to hear some thoughtful remark from Saxby, on politics or religion, and it received these always with respect and appreciation.

There was a slight pause. A boy pushed inwards the faggots burning beside the circle of chairs and blew on their red points. They burst at once into a bright, high flame in which the features of Saxby, Billson, and even the young soldier suddenly acquired striking light and shade. They seemed like a circle of deep-eyed philosophers, pondering the nature of things.

'Well, I don't know,' Saxby said again, 'about that girl, for instance.'

There was a respectful pause.

'Some people do have extraordinary ideas,' Saxby said, puffing. He looked round with impressive gravity. 'Extraordinary.'

'It's the religion,' Billson suggested. 'I been to chapel myself and you wouldn't believe how some of them talk.'

'H'm yes, but it's not only the talk – it's – well – it's a different kind of – well – almost outlook.'

There was another long pause while everyone contemplated the bottles glistening in the firelight.

'And then, of course, they really do believe in God,' Billson said.

'Why not?' the young soldier asked in a surprised voice.

This startled everyone. Saxby cautiously turned his big face towards the young man, Billson opened his mouth to speak and then thought better of it.

The subaltern was a perfectly ordinary young man from an excellent school, neither tall nor short, dark nor fair, with brown eyes and a neat little brown moustache. He had never done anything to make anyone even suspect that he had any ideas about anything except drill, polo, and beer.

There was a pause. Billson's mouth remained open. Saxby was pondering. He knew by experience that you had to be careful with soldiers. They not only picked up the most extraordinary stuff but sometimes they believed it, really believed it. It could be most embarrassing, especially in a mixed company. He glanced at Billson and slightly moved an eyebrow. Billson shut his mouth. Saxby said in a thoughtful voice, 'I see that Robert Lynd wants to change the law about maidens.'

At once everyone began to discuss the future of cricket. This was a favourite subject with Saxby, who took a sensible and serious view of the state of the game. He was never content to say, 'Let it alone.' No better subject could have been suggested to take discussion away from a dangerous subject. Saxby had that excellent tact which does not appear like tact. The young soldier and Billson both had strong views on cricket, and when the philosopher's circle broke up for dinner an hour later, everyone felt that kind of gratification which follows upon an expansion of feeling and imagination.

Saxby called at the store next afternoon to ask Caffin to tennis, but the young man was out. For a while he was not seen even at the club. Billson said that he was spending all his time at the mission. There was even a rumour that he had attended the mission chapel.

All the same, the announcement of his engagement to Miss Martha Smith caused surprise in the station and a kind of confusion. It was discussed in Caffin's absence, during the whole of one evening, and no one could fail to notice the flat and disappointed tone of the speakers. Even Saxby was a little put out.

'I'm afraid friend Caffin has lost his character,' he said. 'He can't be such a blackguard as they say.'

'Nature's been too much for him.'

'Or the climate.'

'Perhaps he was tight,' the young soldier suggested.

But no one would accept this whitewashing. 'Caffy's always more or less tight – but it never affects his form. No, she's caught him – another good man gone.'

Caffin himself was not seen at all until one evening Saxby met him on the town road going towards the mission. He was whistling in a particularly lively manner.

But as soon as he caught sight of the district officer, his shoulders drooped, his forehead wrinkled. He lived up to his ideal. Saxby congratulated him and he answered in a tone of gloomy despair, 'Just when I got nicely settled in with old Billson – but what can a chap do?'

Saxby told the story at the club which agreed that Caffin was a bit of a fraud, that he had always been a poser. The next day Caffin took a lift in the company car to railhead. Miss Smith saw him off at the store. She was obviously in bridal spirits; everyone who saw her described her as quite pretty in her excitement. Billson, who had lent Caffin ten pounds for his trip and necessary expenses, said that after all Caffy had done pretty well for himself.

There was no more news of Caffin for two months. He was then said to be in Spanish Muni with a high yellow señorita. Billson was furious. 'The dirty little swine,' he shouted. 'He's bilked me.'

The others were sympathetic but much amused. They were also, of course, sympathetic with the poor girl at the mission who was said to be suffering a good deal, but there was a ring of pleasure even in Saxby's tone when he said at the club, 'So after all there was something in those stories about Caffin.'

'I wonder what he got out of it.'

'Probably everything she had.'

'Did you ever hear how he bought an ejaw girl for fifteen shillings and hired her out?'

'No, but I can well believe it.'

Everyone began to tell stories about Caffin's mean tricks and the meanest gave the most pleasure.

The station had been a little surprised at Caffin's disappearance, but everyone was astonished when the rumour went round that the girl Smith, though ill with unhappiness, was growing plumper every day.

Saxby spoke of it to the missionaries, a couple called Beatty, who said there was nothing in it. The Beattys in fact could not believe their own eyes. It was the nursing sister who had to make them understand that the symptoms had exactly the same meaning in Martha Smith, though she was white, as in any of the pagan girls who disturbed the mission every year with unexpected babies.

'It's incredible,' Beatty said to Saxby, 'quite incredible – a most respected family in the West Country.'

Beatty was a small, fair man with very blue eyes. He had a habit of bending towards you while he talked, as if asking for your sympathy and understanding. Probably he knew by experience that missionaries could not expect fair judgement. He was plainly in distress about Martha Smith.

'And do you know her explanation – the only explanation she vouchsafed to give us?'

'No.'

'That he thought she couldn't really love him.'

'My God, what a blackguard Caffin is,' Saxby pondered. 'Seemed quite an ordinary sort of lad – it's really astonishing –' Suddenly he caught Beatty's eye, whose pained expression warned him that he was smiling. He became at once grave. 'Poor girl, I suppose you'll send her home?'

'She won't go home.'

'Oh, I see – yes – naturally – in that state.'

'But I can't turn her out, can I?'

'No, I suppose not – certainly not.'

Beatty went away quite stooped with anxiety and perplexity. However, a few days later, Miss Martha Smith suddenly turned up at the station rest-house. It seemed that Beatty had solved his problem after all. Little Mrs Beatty explained that matter to Billson who, although he no longer went to chapel, had once belonged to a congregation. 'Poor, poor girl,' she cried. 'We didn't know what to do – my piccaninnies are so sharp and quick, even the quite, quite little ones, poor neglected darlings. But we brought it all to prayer and really, we were wonderfully answered – the poor girl softened at once. She saw what harm she was doing us.'

'I suppose she hasn't got a ring or anything?'

'I don't think so, Mr Billson, why?'

'Well, Mrs Beatty, that chap Caffin took ten pounds off me to buy things for the wedding – and so, of course, if he did send her a ring, it's really out of my property.'

'Oh, I'm sure she'll give anything back – she's really a very nice girl. She's been accusing herself of selfishness towards us and really, it was a little selfish of her not to think of the mission sooner.'

'Well, if you would just mention about the ring. I wouldn't like to intrude myself.'

'Of course, Mr Billson – that's six tins of tomato soup, isn't it, and you've made an allowance for the flour with the weevils. Of course, I was sure you had.'

Miss Smith was very retiring. None saw her at all except in the late evening, when a short figure, in a cloak which gave it almost a conical shape, was sometimes seen moving quickly towards the garden by the bush road.

No one troubled her. It was supposed that she was waiting for her steamer ticket. Saxby took care that regular supplies of wood, water, chickens, and yam were delivered at the rest-house, and gave his cook-general orders to keep an eye on her commissariat.

After a month, however, even Saxby began to wonder how long the girl would stay. He sent a discreet note asking when she would need transport. When did her boat sail? She wrote back to say that she had no boat and she did not mean to sail.

Saxby was uneasy. He felt that the girl was suffering and that she needed help of some kind. He appealed to the Beattys who came at once to the office.

'But what can I do, Mr Saxby? She ought to go home, of course. But I can't turn her out into the bush, can I?'

'No, but couldn't you persuade her?'

'Terribly, terribly obstinate,' Mrs Beatty said. 'I always said she was the difficult type – poor thing. I noticed it at once – especially her neck.'

'Her neck?'

'Terribly, terribly short. Poor girl, nothing could ever teach her. What are we to do, Mr Saxby – it's such a dreadful anxiety for us at the mission – and the poor girl must be suffering so terribly too. Even though it is her own selfishness.'

'I was told you had a little meeting with her,' Saxby said.

They gazed at him. Suddenly Mrs Beatty understood and with a little smile for the layman's ignorance of terms, she murmured, 'He means when we brought it to prayer, dear.'

'Oh yes, but it's no good. We tried – we've tried everything, Mr Saxby.' His blue eyes implored Saxby to believe him, to understand his difficulties.

'Poor, poor, girl,' Mrs Beatty murmured. 'I feel so terribly sorry for her. I wonder, Mr Saxby, is this a good sixpence?' Mrs Beatty had taken advantage of the visit to cash a cheque. 'Yes, I was sure it was – some of the new ones are so yellow, aren't they?'

Beatty said in a tone unexpectedly decisive, as if, having given up hope of sympathy, he fell back on his rights. 'Besides, we have no jurisdiction – since she left the mission.'

Saxby understood this very well. The Beattys did not intend to do anything further. Having been successful by the aid of prayer in removing Miss Smith from the mission, they were leaving her to providence. Saxby was indignant and alarmed.

But he was a conscientious man. He put on a tie, took an early whisky, and went to the rest-house and knocked on the side of the doorway with his stick. 'Excuse me, it's Saxby.'

'Come in.'

The hut was in twilight, and at first he could see only a dark bundle of shawls or cloaks in the middle of the bed, under the looped-up net. Then he perceived a white face, thin and small, projecting from the top of this bundle. He could not recognize this face, thin and hollow-cheeked, and for some reason this increased his confusion: as if he found himself confronted by something altogether beyond his expectation.

Perspiring, he murmured another apology and began to make his little prepared speech of sympathy and encouragement. He meant to explain to the girl that she must not feel ashamed or shy, that everybody knew how badly she had been treated. But he had barely uttered three words before it struck him that the girl resented his interference. There was an awkward silence. Then with an inspiration, he said, 'I just called to know about the chickens.'

The girl said nothing.

'You're getting them all right? You're all right for supplies? Because if there's any difficulty – the least difficulty, I hope you'll let me know at once,' Saxby said firmly. He then wished her good night, stepped quickly out into the compound and made his way home at speed. He was distressed, but on the whole pleased with himself. He had got out, he thought, with the least damage to anybody's feelings.

But he was still anxious about Miss Smith and, as her case was not official, he put it to the club that evening. He wanted popular support, so to speak.

'The best thing you could have done, sir.'

'Well, I thought, as she obviously wanted to be left alone –'

'Of course she does.'

'Better not seem to notice her at all – that's the kindest thing,' Billson said.

Saxby was reassured, and had just put up his feet on the foot-rest when the young soldier arrived from the polo pit, sweating and crying out for a drink. He said at once, 'Has anyone seen that girl lately? Why doesn't the parson come to see her?'

'She won't have him,' Billson said. 'She's got some funny notion, you know, that she disgraced the mission and that there oughtn't to be any connection. Besides, they say she ought to go home and she won't.'

'I don't care, he ought to come and pray with her at the least. Hi, boy, where's that cold drink?'

Everyone looked with new interest and curiosity at the young soldier. Billson opened his mouth, hesitated a moment and then asked boldly, 'You think it would do her good?'

'Oh, I don't know about that, but it's his job I should think. Cheeroh, sir.' He raised his glass to Saxby.

Saxby was pondering. Everyone was pondering. Now and then someone looked doubtfully at the young man. At last Saxby said in his most thoughtful voice, 'Prayer, that's an interesting question.'

The club continued to ponder, but with rather a blank expression of eye as if faced by a huge bare wall. Saxby and Billson finally looked at the subaltern. Saxby's expression was at once inquiring and a little apprehensive. He was both curious and alarmed. Probably he regretted already his impulsive plunge into a subject so tricky.

The young man with a most cheerful and knowing air was holding up his glass to the firelight. He closed one eye and said, 'It's not too bad, this beer of yours, Billson – to look at.'

Every expression at once showed relief, and Saxby said, 'If you can call lager, beer. Now, real beer –'

Meanwhile one would suppose that there was a tremendous scandal. The Beattys expected it. So did the station.

But there was no scandal at Dabbi. For some reason no one was particularly shocked about this case, and nobody talked about it very much. It did not strike the imagination. Visitors to Dabbi might be there for half an hour before they heard of it and even then they seemed unable to get any definite flavour out of it.

' At the rest-house, you say – seven months gone –'

The rest-house at Dabbi was a round hut with a broken thatch set a little crooked on the walls. It looked as if, slightly fuddled, it had dozed off in the sun a year or two before, with its hat on one ear. The visitors might gaze at it with hopeful interest but this interest faded quickly; they found it like any other rest-house in any of a hundred rather dull little bush stations where there was no butter, no potatoes, no ice; where newspapers were a fortnight old, the library consisted of two Edgar Wallaces and somebody's *Auction Bridge* with all the middle pages torn out, and nothing ever happened except in the native town which was a perfect nuisance in any case.

' Seven months gone – and Caffin's in Patagonia.'

' A bit tough on the girl – how's she taken it?'

'Well, of course, we don't see much of her.'

'Keeps herself to herself?'

'That's it – in fact she don't show up at all.'

By this time interest had entirely disappeared.

'But he's in Patagonia, is he? What do they do there?' and they talked sheep or currency or revolutions.

It was tax time and Saxby was extremely busy. He liked, however, to be busy, and he always made time to see that the rest-house was looked after. He would inspect it twice a day to make sure that the prison gang had swept the compound and brought the water. He built a neat private way to the latrine, of straw mats, from the back door. Saxby was not called 'dear old Saxby' for nothing. He was a most good-natured man. Also he felt a real admiration for Miss Smith. He would say, 'She might have made it damned awkward for everybody, but she's been no trouble at all. That girl has real guts.'

Some time before, he had written complaining that the station doctor had not yet returned from leave, and pointing out that a station with half a company of troops was entitled to a doctor.

For six weeks this had no effect. The wires were not even acknowledged. Then in May, when Saxby had given up all hope of a doctor, just before six o'clock in the evening of the fourth, a telegram came from headquarters: 'Clear the line M.O. Bing due Dabbi fourth. Stop. Resdt.'

'Good God,' Saxby said, and then he began to laugh. He went down to the club with the wire in his hand. 'Do you know who they're sending us for M.O.? – Bing.'

'No, sir.'

'Not really.'

'Not old Bing. Good Lord, what a joke.' The young soldier gave a shout of laughter, and two people began simultaneously to tell a story about Bing. The rest were smiling even before they heard it. The very idea of Bing made them smile. Bing, or Major Bing, as he preferred to be called, was then one of the biggest jokes in the service.

'A perfect terror,' Saxby said smiling. 'He tried to diet me once. In fact, he did put me off my palm oil chop.'

'Did you ever hear how he wanted to cut my liver out – well, part of it –' Billson laughed heartily at the recollection and having told the story, said, 'My God, Major Bing is really –'

'And due today,' Saxby said.

'Today. By Jove.'

There was a thoughtful pause. Then the young soldier got up. 'I think I'll just have a look round the barracks,' and ten minutes later Billson refused a third gin.

'It's not because of old Bing,' he said, but the club laughed.

Yet next morning, when the lorry arrived at last with Bing's loads, there were groans from all sides. Bing was a joke to the imagination, but in fact he meant trouble for everyone, insults, contempt, and hard work.

Bing's car was close behind the lorry. He was a short plump man with a purple face and a curled up moustache, like two little rolls of barbed wire; who leant so far backwards as he walked, or rather strutted, that he seemed likely every moment to fall on his own spurs. He always wore uniform, with his war ribbons; sometimes major's uniform, but usually a khaki coat with shoulder straps which looked like army uniform from a little distance. No one more military than Bing could be imagined. He ought, of course, to have been in the Ram corps, and, like many Ram corps men, he was a student of tactics. He used to cross-examine company commanders about Napoleon's battles, and prove to the whole station that they knew nothing about war and oughtn't to be soldiers at all.

Bing's first visit was expected by the soldiers, and two fatigues had been cleaning up barracks from dawn. Saxby, too, having sent him an invitation for breakfast, ordered an unusually light meal. But Bing did not begin on Saxby's diet, or Billson's liver, or the company latrines. He was one of those men who had an infallible nose for the place where the most trouble was to be found, the biggest stink, and, of course, it was usually a place quite unnoticed or long overlooked by the inhabitants. Bing always took his victims unawares, on their exposed side, in flank or rear, and having engaged battle, he massed his artillery and blew a hole in their line before they knew what was happening.

He stopped his car at the rest-house and charged through the doorway. For twenty minutes his loud voice volleyed from within. While Saxby, in great surprise, was still wondering what the noise was about, he came marching across the station, already hot as a griddle, to the divisional office.

'Look here, Saxby,' he bawled, without greeting, 'what the devil do you think you're playing at with this woman Smith?'

Saxby nearly fell out of his chair. 'Playing –' he said.

'Playing – playing – damn it, I said playing – by God,' he stared at Saxby with amazement, 'I don't believe he realizes it now –'

'Realizes what?'

'The situation, man, the very urgent and critical situation – dammit, right under your nose for about six months – but I suppose you've been absorbed in chasing an odd sixpence through the cash book –'

'My dear Bing, I know that Miss Smith was – ah –'

'And do you know the regulations of your own silly department? No, dammit, he don't! Talk about the efficiency of our civil services. Do – you – realize – that it's absolutely impossible for that woman to have her baby here – that she ought to have gone home two months ago, as I damn well told her.'

Saxby was now perturbed as well as astonished.

'But, Bing, I don't think she wants to go home. Naturally, she rather shrinks from it.'

'What's that got to do with it? When it's laid down in black and white that no white woman is allowed to have babies except in a station on the schedule. Perhaps you can show me Dabbi on the schedule, or perhaps not.' Bing spoke this with an ironical inflexion which had, during the war, thrown regimental sergeant-majors into confusion.

'But white babies have been born in Dabbi. Mrs Beatty had one last year.'

'What? Where? Oh, in the damn mission.' Bing hated all missions, which he considered to be a military necessity, like rum and No. 3 pills. 'I'm talking about civilian babies,' he said with hearty contempt.

'But this is a civilian baby. Miss Smith was a missionary.'

'Not at all. They drummed her out of the mission. She's in a Government rest-house, in a Government station, and she's in my charge. She's in exactly the same position as an official wife, and her baby is a Government baby.'

'But Bing, think of her feelings, going home in that state!'

'Feelings be damned.' Bing has no more sympathetic imagination than a mule, and much less than a horse. 'Do you understand the nature of an order?' he snapped.

'Really, Bing.' Saxby was growing slightly annoyed. He thought that Bing was making unnecessary trouble. Bing grew redder. He could not bear the least opposition. 'I know my duty,' he said; and no one but Bing could have said such a thing with the same dramatic air. He swelled up his chest, bringing the medal ribbons into great prominence. The ribbons no doubt meant something to Bing, his religion, his idea of things, including himself and his duty, and he entered into that idea with great enthusiasm and energy – an energy overwhelming to Saxby. Saxby, a most dutiful man, was embarrassed by the very word duty. He said mildly, 'All the same, we have to be careful.'

'Careful be damned. There's the regulations. The woman's in my charge, and I'll thank you to arrange for deporting her by the next boat. That means leaving here this afternoon. I've told her to be ready for an examination at nine, so you'd better go now. And I'm reporting to the P.M.O. by the next mail.' He made for the door.

Saxby, heavy and slow-moving as he was, rushed after him. 'But, my dear Bing, I can't absolutely order the poor girl to –'

'You'll have to. She told me she'd rather shoot herself than go.'

'What!' Saxby, with a look of horror, rushed for his hat.

'You needn't be alarmed.' Bing looked his military contempt of a civilian panic. 'She hasn't got a gun. I asked her.' He marched off.

Saxby fell back in his chair and cursed Bing. Then he laughed, and mopped his forehead. 'My God, what a – really – Bing is –'

But he knew he would have to act. Bing was an autocrat by nature and education. All doctors tend to autocracy, and Government doctors are tyrants. Ram corps doctors are also tyrants. But Major Bing was worse than any Ram corps doctor, because he was not a real major; he was the dictator who must always act the tyrant because otherwise people will remember his lowly origin.

Saxby sighed and pondered. What was he to do? What could he say to that unlucky girl? Really, it was a terrible position for anybody. He reflected deeply for some time. A bugle sounded from the barracks for the guard-changing; five minutes to nine.

Saxby remembered that at nine Bing was going back to the rest-house. He suddenly felt a deep sense of alarm, so urgent that he was half-way to the rest-house before he had decided what to say.

As he knocked at the door, he was startled to see the girl move quickly across it, as if in flight. He went in at once, but she was already seated on the bed. She glared at him, panting.

'What do you want?' she asked furiously.

'I'm awfully sorry if I seem to intrude, but Doctor Bing came to see me just now.'

'I'm not going home.'

'But Bing tells me –'

'I'm not going home like this–' She made a gesture full of rage, throwing out her hands, like a leper who says, 'See my horrible body.' 'Why should I? You can't make me –'

Saxby was startled by this passionate violence. What had happened to that nice little mission girl? It was incredible that she should have changed into this excitable woman with huge, furious eyes. He stood astonished while she declared in the same dramatic manner that she would do what she liked with herself, that she didn't belong to anybody now.

'Of course not,' Saxby murmured. 'I don't want to interfere at all – but Doctor Bing –'

She made as if to spring up from the bed, and Saxby hastily stepped back. His bald head knocked upon something dangling. He looked up and saw a rope hanging from a rafter. It was thrown loosely over the palm rib, and it had a running noose at the lower end. A box stood below, slightly to one side.

Saxby stared at the rope, and then at the girl. His mouth opened. He was shocked out of his discretion.

'But you didn't mean –' Saxby said. 'It's too –'

The girl sat motionless, staring at him. She did not blink an eye, and Saxby faltered into silence. They gazed at each other, shocked. It was as though a mutual discovery, flashing through the air, had turned it into a heavy medium in which neither could move.

Suddenly the girl's face twisted, her eyes turned aside, and she said in a faint voice, 'I was just putting up –' She looked round, as if for inspiration. Saxby found one before he realized it. 'Oh, yes, very convenient – hang things up.'

'The lamp,' she said.

'Yes, of course – the lamp,' and his face relaxed. He put a hand to his forehead.

'Hullo,' said a voice outside. 'It's Bing.'

The girl sprang up. She and Saxby together grabbed at the rope. Saxby's long arm reached it, tore it down and jerked it behind his back. He heard the girl's voice in his ear, full of contemptuous rage: 'No one can stop me. I'll do what I like.'

Bing was already in the doorway. The girl sank back suddenly on the box.

'Hullo.' Bing stared at her suspiciously. 'Got your orders?'

'Not from me,' Saxby exclaimed hastily. 'I'm not taking the responsibility.'

'I'm not going,' the girl said.

'What do you mean, responsibility?' Bing glared at Saxby.

'The patient must be consulted.'

'The patient,' Bing snapped. 'But all that is decided. What do you think service regulations are for?' His tone might have referred to Holy Writ. 'I suppose it means nothing to you, miss, where your baby is born, but it's my duty to see that you don't have it in a place already scheduled as unfit for babies.'

'Nothing to me?' she looked at him in amazement and rage. Then suddenly her expression changed in a manner very surprising to both the men. It was as though something had escaped from behind the girl's hard, furious mask, by eyes and lips and even cheeks, so that the eyes looked beyond Bing and the rest-house wall, the compressed lips softened and stood open, the cheeks were coloured with life. 'Mine,' she said.

Saxby, as well as Bing, stared uncomprehendingly while the girl's colour deepened, her lips trembled, and her eyes, a moment before as hard as agate, sparkled with tears. Suddenly she made that gesture, common in the pregnant woman, as if to clasp her womb between her hands. 'Oh, how wicked I have been – how ungrateful.'

'Now, now,' Bing said sharply. 'No hysterics. Please control yourself, and answer my question. Do you understand that you must go home? Do you understand the nature of an order, a Government order?'

Saxby, still perspiring, terrified of Bing's roughness, said hastily in a cajoling voice, 'You see, Miss – ah – in Major Bing's view, you are to a certain extent, in Government charge.'

The girl gazed at him as if through a window at a new discovered sky. 'Yes, yes, in Government charge – of course I'll do anything.'

Suddenly she caught Bing's hand and kissed it. 'God sent you to me.'

Robert Graves

THE LOST CHINESE

JAUME GELABERT was a heavily-built, ill-kempt, morose Majorcan lad of seventeen. His father had died in 1936 at the siege of Madrid, but on the losing side, and therefore without glory or a dependant's pension; his mother a few years later. He lived by himself in a dilapidated cottage near our village of Muleta, where he cultivated a few olive terraces and a lemon grove. On my way down for a swim from the rocks, three hundred feet below, I would cut through Jaume's land and, if we happened to meet, always offered him an American cigarette. He would then ask if I were taking a bathe, to which I answered either: 'You have divined my motive correctly,' or: 'Yes, doctors say it benefits the health.' Once I casually remarked that my blue jeans had grown too tight and, rather than throw them away, I wondered if they might come in handy for rough work. 'I could perhaps use them,' he answered, fingering the solid denim. To say 'thank you' would have been to accept charity and endanger our relationship; but next day he gave me a basket of cherries, with the excuse that his tree was loaded and that June cherries were not worth marketing. So we became good neighbours.

This was June 1952 – just before Willie Fedora appeared in Muleta and rented a cottage. The United States Government was paying Willie a modest disability grant, in recognition of 'an anxiety neurosis aggravated by war service in Korea', which supported him nicely until the tide of tourism sent prices rocketing. Brandy then cost a mere twelve pesetas a litre, not thirty-six as now; and brandy was his main expense.

Our small foreign colony, mostly painters, at first accepted Willie. But the tradition here is that instead of drinking, playing bridge, sun-bathing, and discussing one another's marital hazards, as at expensive resorts with more easily accessible beaches, foreigners *work*. We meet only in the evening around a café table, when our mail has arrived. Occasional parties are thrown, and sometimes we hire the village bus for a Sunday bullfight; otherwise we keep ourselves to ourselves. Willie disliked this unsociable way of life. He would come calling on trivial pretexts, after breakfast, just when we were about to start work, and always showed his independence by bringing along a four-litre straw-covered flask of cheap brandy – which he called 'my samovar' – slung from his shoulder. To shut the door in Willie's face would have been churlish; to encourage him, self-destructive. Usually, we slipped out by the back door and waited until he had gone off again.

Willie wrote plays; or, rather, he laboured at the same verse play for months and months, talking about it endlessly but making no progress. The hero of *Vercingetorix* (Willie himself disguised in a toga) was one of Julius Caesar's staff-captains in the Gallic War. Whenever Willie began his day's work on *Vercingetorix* he needed to down half a pint of brandy, because of the fearful load of guilt which he carried with him and which formed the theme of his Roman drama. Apparently towards the end of the Korean War, a senior officer had put Willie in charge of five hundred captured Chinese Communists but, when he later marched them to the pen, a bare three hundred were left. The remainder could neither have been murdered, nor committed suicide, nor escaped; yet they had disappeared. 'Disappeared into thin air!' he would repeat tragically, tilting the samovar. Any suggestion that these Chinamen had existed only on paper – a 3 scrawled in the heat of battle, we pointed out, might easily be read as a 5 – enraged Willie. 'Goddam it!' he would shout, pounding the table. 'I drew rations and blankets for five hundred. Laugh *that* off!'

Before long, we shut our doors against Willie. Let him finish his play, we said, rather than talk about it; and none of us felt responsible for his lost Chinese. Yet every night they haunted his dreams, and often he would catch glimpses of them skulking behind trees or barns even by day.

Now, it is an old custom at Muleta to support the Catholic China Missions, and on 'China Day' the school children paint their faces yellow, slant their eyebrows and dress themselves up in the Oriental clothes, of uncertain origin, which the Mother Superior of our Franciscan convent distributes from a long, deep, camphor-scented chest. They drive around in a tilt-cart and collect quite a lot of money; though who ultimately benefits from it remains a mystery, because (as I told the incredulous Mother Superior) no foreign missions have been tolerated in China for some years. Unfortunately, the young Chinese came tapping at Willie's cottage window one afternoon and scared him out of his wits. Accidently smashing his samovar against a wine barrel as he stumbled into the café, Willie collapsed on the terrace. When he felt better, we recommended a Palma doctor. He groaned at us: 'You jump off a cliff! I'm through with you all. I'm going native.'

Willie did go native. To the surprise of Muleta, he and Jaume Gelabert struck up a friendship. Jaume, already branded as the son of a Red, had earned a reputation for violence at that year's *fiesta* of San Pedro, Muleta's patron saint. The Mayor's sharp-tongued son, who owned a motorcycle and led the *atlotes*, or village bucks, made Jaume his victim. 'Behold the Lord of La Coma!' Paco sneered. Jaume went pale. '"Lord of La Coma" comes badly from you, Paco, you loud-mouthed wencher! Your own uncle robbed my widowed mother of her share in the estate, and the whole village knew it, though they were too cowardly to protest.' Paco then extemporized a *copeo*, a satiric verse of the sort current on San Pedro's Day:

> The Lord of La Coma he lives in disgrace:
> He never eats crayfish nor washes his face!

A group of *atlotes* took up the chorus, dancing in a ring around Jaume:

> Ho, ho, that's how we go —
> He never eats crayfish nor washes his face!

Jaume pulled a stake from the baker's fence and ran amok, felling Paco and a couple of other *atlotes* before he was disarmed by Civil Guards and shoved without ceremony into the village lock-up. The Justice of the Peace, Paco's father, bound Jaume over after a stern caution. At Muleta, no decent man ever uses force: all fighting is done either with the tongue or with money.

The two social outcasts became such close friends that it spared us further responsibility for Willie's health. He had de- -cided to learn Majorcan from Jaume. This old language, not unlike Provençal, is in domestic use throughout the island, though discountenanced by the Government. Willie had a natural linguistic gift, and within three months could chatter fluent Majorcan – the sole foreigner in Muleta (except my children, who went to school there) who ever achieved the feat. Willie gratefully insisted on teaching Jaume how to write plays, having once majored in dramatic composition at a Midwestern university, and meanwhile laid *Vercingetorix* aside. By the spring, Jaume had finished *The Indulgent Mother*, a Majorcan comedy based on the life of his great-aunt Catalina. In return he had made Willie eat solid food, such as bean porridge and *pa'mb'oli*, and drink more red wine than brandy. Jaume did not question Willie's account of those lost Chinese, but argued that the command of five hundred prisoners must have been too great a burden for so young a soldier as Willie; and that omniscient God had doubtless performed a miracle and cut down their numbers. 'Suppose someone were to give me five hundred sheep!' he said. 'How would I manage them all single-handed? One hundred, yes; two hundred, yes; three hundred, perhaps; five hundred would be excessive.'

'But, if so, why do these yellow devils continue to haunt me?'

'Because they are heathen and blaspheme God! Pay no attention! And if they ever plague you, eat rather than drink!'

In 1953, Muleta suffered a financial crisis. Foul weather ruined the olive prospects, blighted the fruit blossom, and sent numerous terraces rumbling down. Moreover, Dom Enrique, our parish priest, had ordered a new altar and rebuilt the chancel at extravagant cost; while neglecting the church roof, part of which fell in after a stormy night. One consequence was that the village could not afford to hire the Palma Repertory Troupe for their usual San Pedro's Day performance. But Dom Enrique heard about Jaume's play, read it, and promised to raise a cast from the *Acción Católica* girls and their *novios*: if Willie would stage-manage the show, and Jaume devote its takings to the Roof Fund.

This plan naturally met with a good deal of opposition among the village elders: Willie, now nicknamed 'Don Coñac', and Jaume the violent Red, seemed most unsuitable playwrights. Dom Enrique, however, had felt a certain sympathy for Jaume's use of the stake, and also noted the happy improvement in Willie's health under Jaume's care. He preached a strong sermon against the self-righteous and the uncharitable and, having got his way, cleverly cast Paco as the juvenile lead. Nevertheless, to avoid any possible scandal, he laid it down that rehearsals must follow strict rules of propriety: the girls' mothers should either attend or send proxies. He himself would always be present.

The Indulgent Mother, which combined the ridiculous with the pathetic, in a style exploited by Menander, Terence, Plautus and other ancient masters, was an unqualified success. Although no effort of Willie's or Dom Enrique's, as joint stage-managers, could keep the cast from turning their backs on the audience, gagging, mumbling, hamming, missing their cues, and giggling helplessly at dramatic moments, the Roof Fund benefited by fifteen hundred pesetas; and a raffle for a German wrist-watch (left on the beach two years previously) brought in another eight hundred. The *Baleares* printed a paragraph on the remarkable young playwright, Don Jaime Gelabert, below the heading: 'Solemn Parochial Mass at Muleta; Grandiose Popular Events.' Paco and his *novia*, the heroine, also secured a niche in the news.

Meanwhile Willie, whom the *Baleares* unfortunately named 'Don Guillermo Coñac, the transatlantic theatrician', had celebrated Jaume's debut a little too well, singing Negro spirituals in the village streets until long after midnight. When at last he fell insensible, Paco and the other *atlotes* pulled off his clothes and laid him naked on a vault in the churchyard, with the samovar under his head. He was there discovered by a troop of black-veiled old *beatas*, or religious women, on the way to early Mass – an appalling scandal! Jaume had gone straight home, after the final curtain, to escape congratulations. In the morning, however, he pieced the story together from village gossip, caught Paco outside the café and threw him into the Torrent, where he broke an ankle. This time, Jaume would have been tried in the capital for attempted homicide, had Willie not intervened. 'Punish Jaume,' he warned the Mayor, 'and you will force me to sue your son. I have witnesses who can testify to his shameless behaviour, and the United States Government is behind me.'

Jaume and I remained on good terms. I told him: 'Jaume, in my view you acted correctly. No true friend could have done less under such provocation.'

Winter and spring went swiftly by, and another San Pedro's Day was on us. Willie visited Dom Enrique at the Rectory and offered to stage-manage a new play of Jaume's: *The Difficult Husband.* He did not arrive drunk but (as they say in Ireland) 'having drink taken', and when he announced that this comedy had merits which would one day make it world famous, Dom Enrique could hardly be blamed for excusing himself. A deceased widow, the Lady of La Coma, had just left the Church a small fortune, on the strength of which his parishioners trusted him to re-engage the Palma Repertory Troupe as in previous years.

Bad news further aggravated this setback. Jaume, due for the draft, had counted on being sent to an anti-aircraft battery, three miles away, from where he could get frequent leave; in fact, the Battery commander had promised to arrange the matter. But something went wrong – Paco's father may have spoken a word in the Captain's ear – and Jaume was ordered to Spanish Morocco.

Willie, with streaming eyes, promised to irrigate the lemon grove, plough around the olive trees, plant the beans when the weather broke, and wait patiently for Jaume's return. But two hundred phantom Chinese took advantage of his loneliness to prowl among the trees and tap at the kitchen window. Willie's samovar filled and emptied, filled and emptied four or five times a week; he neglected the lemon grove, seldom bothered with meals, and locked the cottage door against all callers: at all costs he must finish an English translation of *The Difficult Husband*. I met him one morning in the postman's house, where he was mailing a package to the States. He looked so thin and lost that, on meeting the Mayor, I suggested he should take some action. 'But what would you have me do?' cried the Mayor. 'He is committing no crime. If he is ill, let him consult the Doctor!' That afternoon, Willie saw Toni Coll digging a refuse pit below the cottage: convinced that this was to be his own grave, he sought sanctuary in the church organ-loft, drank himself silly, and was not discovered for twenty-four hours. Dom Enrique and his mother carried him to the Rectory, where they nursed him until the American Embassy could arrange his transfer to the States. At New York, a veterans' reception committee met Willie, and he was sent to a Pittsburgh army hospital. On New Year's Day, 1955, he broke his neck falling out of a window, apparently pursued by Chinese oppressors. I felt bad about him.

If Muleta expected to hear no more about Jaume's comedy, Muleta erred. Just before the rockets soared up in honour of San Pedro two years later, Mercurio the postman (who also acts as our telegraphist) tugged at my sleeve. 'Don Roberto,' he said, 'I have a telegram here from New York for a certain William Schenectady. Do you know the individual? It came here three days ago, and none of your friends recognize the name. Could he be some transitory tourist?'

'No: this is for our unfortunate Don Coñac,' I told him. In Spain only the middle name counts, being the patronymic, and Willie's passport had read 'William Schenectady Fedora'.

'A sad story,' sighed Mercurio. 'How can telegrams benefit the dead, who are unable even to sign a receipt? And there is no means of forwarding the message . . .'

'I'll sign, since that's what worries you,' I said. 'Probably it contains birthday greetings from some old aunt, who has remained ignorant of his fate. If so, I'll tear it up.'

After the fun was over, I remembered the cable. It ran:

WILLIAM SCHENECTADY FEDORA : MULETA : MAJORCA :
SPAIN : MAGNIFICENT BRAVO BRAVO BRAVO STOP
DIFICTUL HUSBAN SENSACIONAL FUST THE PLOY
NEEDED ON BIRDWAY WIT NEUMANN DIRECION HARP-
VICKE IN THE LED STOP AIRMALLING CONTRACT
STOP PROPOSE FOLOV UP WIT PRESONAL VISIT SO
ONEST KINDLY REPLAY STOP REGARDS
EVERETT SAMSTAG EMPIRE STAT ENTERPRIXES
NEW YORK

I frowned. My neighbour Len Simkin was always talking about
Sammy Samstag, the Broadway impresario, and had even
promised Willie to interest him in *Vercingetorix*; but somehow
this cable did not seem like a joke. Who would waste ten
dollars on kidding a dead man? Yet, if it wasn't a joke, why
did Samstag send no prepaid reply coupon?

I tackled Mercurio, who admitted that such a form had, as it
happened, come with the cable for Don Coñac; adding: 'But
since Don Coñac is no more, perhaps some other foreigner
may care to dispatch a telegram with its help.'

So I cabled Samstag:

INTERESTED IN YOUR INTEREST STOP WILL ADVISE
AUTHOR OF DIFFICULT HUSBAND CURRENTLY ON
SAFARI TO GRANT OPTION IF FINANCIALLY COMMEN-
SURATE WITH YOUR TRIPLE BRAVO STOP REGARDS

To explain that Willie was no longer available, and that the
job of protecting Jaume fell to me, would have exceeded the
prepaid allowance, so I signed 'Fedora'. 'Currently on safari'
was cablese for 'at present trailing his rifle through North
Africa, but will be back next week', and sounded far more
opulent.

At the café, I met Len, a young-old fabricator of abstract
mobiles. He had once briefly taken a very small part in an off-
Broadway play, but was Muleta's sole contact with the Great

White Way. 'A pity poor Willie's dead,' I said, when Len had finished his scathing comments on last night's performance by the Palma Repertory Troupe. 'He might have got you a speaking part in this new Broadway play. Willie always admired your delivery.'

'I don't get the joke,' Len grumbled. 'That wack gave me the creeps! One of those "creative artists" who create chaos. A few drinks from the old samovar, and I could *see* those goddamned Chinese! I bet they infiltrated into his coffin, and pulled the lid down after them.'

'If you take my front-page news like that, Len,' I told him, 'you'll not be offered even a walk-on!'

'Still, I don't get it . . .'

'Well, you will – as soon as Sammy Samstag turns up here toting an enormous box of Havanas, and you're left in a corner smoking your foul *Peninsulares*.'

'Neumann directing? Harwicke in the lead as Vercingetorix?'

'No, the title isn't *Vercingetorix*. It's *The Difficult Husband*. Otherwise you've guessed right.'

'You're very fonny, don't you, Mister?' Len stalked away, then wheeled angrily, and came out with a splendid curtain line: 'In my opinion, jokes about dead Americans stink!'

When Jaume stepped from the Palma-Muleta bus, looking bigger and more morose than ever, no one rolled out the red carpet. That evening I found him alone in his cottage, cooking a bean and blood-pudding stew over the wood fire; and accepted an invitation to share it. Jaume asked for details on Willie's death, and wept to hear about the open window.

'He was a brother to me,' he choked. 'So magnanimous, so thoughtful! And since he could not manage this little property by himself, I had asked Toni Coll to tend the trees, and go half-shares in the lemons and oil. Toni has just paid me two thousand pesetas. We are not friends, but he would have lost face with the village by neglecting my land while I was doing my service. He even repaired the terrace that fell before my departure.'

I had brought along a bottle of red Binisalem wine, to celebrate Samstag's cable.

'Poor Willie, how wildly enthusiastic he would have been,' Jaume sighed, when I read it to him. 'And how he would have drunk and sung! This comes too late. Willie always wanted me to enjoy the success that his frailties prevented him from attaining.'

'May he rest in peace!'

'I had no great theatrical ambition,' Jaume continued, after a pause. 'Willie forced me to write first *The Indulgent Mother*, and then *The Difficult Husband*.'

'Did they take you long?'

'*The Indulgent Mother*, yes. Over the second I did not need to rack my brains. It was a gift.'

'Yet Señor Samstag, a most important person, finds the result magnificent. That is certainly a triumph. You have a copy of the play?'

'Only in Majorcan.'

'Do you realize, Jaume, what will happen if *The Difficult Husband* pleases Broadway?'

'Might they pay me?'

'Pay you, man? Of course! With perhaps five per cent of the gross takings, which might mean fifty thousand dollars a week. Say it ran for a couple of years, you'd amass ... let me work it out – well, some two hundred and fifty thousand dollars.'

'That means nothing to me. What part of a peseta is a dollar?'

'Listen: if things go well, you may earn *twelve million pesetas* ... And even if the play proved a dead failure, you'd get two hundred thousand, merely by selling Señor Samstag the right to stage it!'

'Your talk of millions confuses me. I would have accepted five hundred pesetas for the job.'

'But you would equally accept twelve million?'

'Are these people mad?'

'No, they are clever businessmen.'

'You make fun of me, Don Roberto!'

'I do not.'

'Then, at least, you exaggerate? What I want to know is whether this telegram will help me to buy a donkey and re-tile my roof.'

'I can promise you an avalanche of donkeys!'

Two days later the contract came, addressed to Willie. Its thirty pages covered all possible contingencies of mutual and reciprocal fraud on the part of author and producer, as foreseen by the vigilant Dramatists Guild of the Authors League of America; and dealt with such rich minor topics as Second Class Touring Rights, Tabloid Versions, Concert Tour Versions, Foreign Language Performances, and the sale of dolls or other toys based on characters in the play . . .

I was leafing through the document on the café terrace that afternoon, when Len entered. 'There's a man at my place,' he gasped excitedly, 'name of Bill Truscott, who says he's Willie's agent! Bill and I were at Columbia together. Nice guy. He seems sort of puzzled to find no Willie . . . See here: could it be that you weren't kidding me about his Broadway show the other day?'

'I never kid. Got no sense of humour.'

'Is that so? Well, anyhow, I told Bill you might be able to help him. Come along!'

Bill Truscott, a gaunt Bostonian, welcomed us effusively. 'I sent *The Difficult Husband* to Samstag's office ten days ago,' he said, 'and a spy I keep there sent word that the old s.o.b. was jumping my claim. Doesn't like agents, favours the direct approach. But let's get this straight: is Fedora really dead? My spy swears that he cabled Samstag from this place.'

'Correct. He's dead. Yet he promised to meet Samstag and discuss this document' – I tapped the contract – 'which maybe you'd better have a look at. Tell me, do you speak Spanish? Jaume Gelabert has no English or French.'

'Gelabert? Who's Gelabert? Never heard of him.'

'Author of *The Difficult Husband*. Fedora's only the translator.'

'Only the translator – are you sure? How extremely tense! That changes everything. I took it for Fedora's own work . . .

What sort of a guy is this Gelabert? Any previous stage successes?'

'He made a hit with *The Indulgent Mother*,' I said, kicking Len under the table. 'He's a simple soul – you might call him a recluse.'

'Know of any arrangement between Fedora and Gelabert as to the translator's fee?'

'I can't think that they made one. Fedora drank, and did the job by way of a favour to Gelabert, who had been caring for him. . . . Are you worried about your commission?'

'*Am* I worried? However, Gelabert will need an agent, and, after all, Fedora sent the play to my office. Len will vouch for me, won't you, Len?'

'I'm sure he will, Mr Truscott,' I said, 'and you'll vouch for him. Len needs some vouching for.'

'I'm on my knees, Don Roberto,' Len whined, grovelling gracefully.

I let him grovel awhile, and asked Truscott: 'But didn't Fedora acknowledge Gelabert's authorship in a covering letter?'

'He did, I remember, mention a local genius who had defended him against some Chinese and was now setting off to fight the Moors, while he himself guarded the lemon grove – and would I please try enclosed play on Samstag; but that's as far as it went, except for some passages in a crazy foreign language, full of x's and y's.'

'I gather the letter has disappeared?'

Truscott nodded gloomily.

'In fact, you can't prove yourself to be Fedora's agent, let alone Gelabert's?'

No reply. I pocketed the contract and rolled myself a cigarette, taking an unnecessarily long time about it. At last I said: 'Maybe Gelabert would appoint you his agent; but he's a difficult man to handle. Better leave all the talking to me.'

'That's very nice of you . . . I surely appreciate it. I suppose you've seen a copy of *The Difficult Husband*?'

'Not yet.'

'Which makes two of us! You see: after reading Fedora's

crazy letter, I tossed the typescript, unexamined, to my secretary Ethel May, who, for all that she was the dumbest operator on Thirty-eighth Street, had beautiful legs and neat habits. Hated to throw away anything, though – even gift appeals. She filed it under "Try Mr Samstag". Ethel May got married and quit. Then, one day, I came down with the grippe, and that same evening Sam wanted a script in a hurry – some piece by a well-known author of mine. I called Ethel May's replacement from my sickbed and croaked: "Send off the Samstag script at once! Special messenger." The poor scared chick didn't want to confess that she'd no notion what the hell I was talking about. She chirped: "Certainly, Chief!" and went away to search the files. As a matter of fact, said script was still in my brief case – grippe plays hell with a guy's memory. Scratching around, the chick comes across *The Difficult Husband*, and sends Sam that. A stroke of genius! – I must give her a raise. But Sam is short on ethics. He bypassed my office and cabled Fedora, hoping he'd sign along the dotted line, and remember too late that he should have got my expert advice on what's bound to be the trickiest of contracts. If ever there was a thieving dog!'

'Yes,' I said, '*if* Fedora had been the author, and *if* you'd been his agent, you'd have a right to complain. But, let's face it, you've no standing at all. So calm down! I suggest we call on Gelabert. He can probably supply supper.'

Night had fallen windily, after a day of unseasonable showers; and the path to Jaume's cottage is no easy one at the best of times. The ground was clayey and full of puddles; water cascaded from the trees. I lent Truscott a flashlight; but twice he tripped over an olive root and fell. He reached the cottage (kitchen, stable, well, single bedroom) in poor shape. I gave Jaume a brief outline of the situation, and we were soon sharing his *pa'mb'oli*: which means slices of bread dunked in unrefined olive oil, rubbed with a half tomato and sprinkled with salt. Raw onion, bitter olives, and a glass of red wine greatly improved the dish. *Pa'mb'oli* was something of a test for Truscott, but he passed it all right, apart from letting oil drip on his muddied trousers.

He asked me to compliment Jaume on 'this snug little shack. Say that I envy him. Say that we city folk often forget what real dyed-in-the-wool *natural* life can be!' Then he talked business. 'Please tell our host that he's been sent no more than a basic contract. I'm surprised at the size of the advance, though: three thousand on signature, and two thousand more on the first night! Sam must think he's on to a good thing. Nevertheless, my long experience as a dramatic agent tells me that we can easily improve these terms, besides demanding a number of special arrangements. Fedora is dead; or we could fiction him into the contract as the author. Unlike Gelabert, he was a non-resident American citizen, and therefore non-liable to any tax at all on the property. Maybe we can still fiction it that way ....'

'What is he saying?' asked Jaume.

'He wants to act as your agent in dealing with Señor Samstag, whom he doesn't trust. The rest of his speech is of no interest.'

'Why should I trust this gentleman more than he trusts the other?'

'Because Willie chose Señor Truscott as his agent, and Samstag got the play from him.'

Jaume solemnly held out his hand to Truscott.

'You were Willie's friend?' he asked. I translated.

'He was a very valued client of mine.' But when Truscott produced an agency agreement from his brief case, I gave Jaume a warning glance.

Jaume nodded. 'I sign only what I can read and understand,' he said. 'My poor mother lost her share of the La Coma inheritance by trusting a lawyer who threw long words at her. Let us find a reliable notary public in the capital.'

Truscott protested: 'I'm not representing Gelabert until I'm sure of my commission.'

'Quit that!' I said sharply. 'You're dealing with a peasant who can't be either bullied or coaxed.'

A cable came from Samstag: he was arriving by Swissair next day. Mercurio asked Len, who happened to be in the postman's house, why so many prodigal telegrams were flying to and fro. Len answered: 'They mean immense wealth for young Gelabert. His comedy, though rejected by Dom Enrique two years ago, is to be staged in New York.'

'That moral standards are higher here than in New York does not surprise me,' Mercurio observed. 'Yet dollars are dollars, and Jaume can now laugh at us all, whatever the demerits of his play.'

Len brought the cable to my house, where he embarrassed me by paying an old debt of two hundred pesetas (which I had forgotten), in the hope that I might deal him into the Broadway game. 'I don't need much . . . just an itty-bitty part,' he pleaded.

Why dash his hopes? Pocketing the two hundred pesetas, I said that his friend Bill would surely recommend him to Samstag.

News of Jaume's good fortune ran through the village two or three times, each time gaining in extravagance. The final version made Samstag a millionaire second cousin from Venezuela who, reading the *Baleares* account of *The Indulgent Mother*, had appointed him his heir. I asked Jaume to say no more than that he was considering the American offer: it might yet prove unacceptable.

Truscott and I met Samstag's plane at Palma airport. Spying Truscott among the crowd, he darted forward with scant respect for the Civil Guard who was shepherding the new arrivals through Customs, and grabbed his hand. 'By all that's holy, Bill,' he cried, 'I'm glad to see you. This solves our great mystery! So that anonymous package emanated from you, did it?'

'Yes, it did, Sammy,' said Truscott, 'and, like all packages I've ever sent you, it was marked all over with my office stamp.'

'Why, yes, my secretary did guess it might be yours, and called you at once – but you were sick, and I couldn't get confirm –'

The Civil Guard then unslung his rifle and used the barrel-end to prod Samstag, a small dark roly-poly of a man, back into line. Finally he emerged with his baggage and guessed that

I was Mr William Fedora. When Truscott undeceived him, he grew noticeably colder towards me; but the two were soon as thick as thieves, and no less suspicious of each other. Climbing into our taxi, Samstag lighted a large cigar, and turned away from me; so I asserted myself as a principal in the business. 'I can use one of those,' I said, stretching out a finger and thumb.

Startled, Samstag offered me his case. 'Take a couple,' he begged.

I took five, smelt and pinched them all, rejected three. 'Don't mind me, boys!' I said through a fragrant cloud of smoke. 'You haggle about the special arrangements. I'll manage the rest.'

At this reminder of our compact, Truscott hastily enlarged on the strong hold I had on Señor Gelabert, assuring Samstag that without me he would get nowhere. Samstag gave him a noncommittal 'Oh yes?' and then back to his discussion of out-of-town performances prior to a possible London *premiere*. Just before we sighted the village round the bend of our road, I tapped Samstag on the arm: 'Look here, Sam, what told you that *The Difficult Husband* was God's gift to Broadway?'

'Not *what* but *who*?' he answered cheerfully. 'It was Sharon, of course! Sharon always knows. She said: "Pappy, believe me, this is going to be the hottest ticket in town." So I cabled Fedora, and flew. She's only fourteen, my Sharon, and still studying at Saint Teresa's. You should see her grades: lousy isn't the word! And yet she always *knows*. ... Takes a script, sniffs it, reads three lines here, four there; spends a couple of minutes on Act Two; skips to the final curtain. ... Then' – Samstag lowered his voice and ended in a grave whisper – 'then she goddamwell *pronounces*!'

'So you haven't read the script either? That makes three of us. What about having a look at it after supper? Or, to save time and eyesight, we might have Len Simkin – another Thespian chum of yours, Sam – read it aloud to us?'

'If you insist. Perhaps Señor Gelabert has a copy. I haven't brought one myself – came here for business, not to hear a dramatic reading.'

In fact, nobody had a script. But that did not prevent Sam-

stag and Truscott from arguing Special Arrangements together at the village inn all the rest of the day, until everything
seemed sewed up. The meeting with Señor Gelabert, they
congratulated themselves, would be a mere formality.

Hair slicked, shoes well brushed, Jaume arrived at our ren-
dezvous in his Sunday best, and showed impressive *sang-froid*.
Early cares, ill luck, and the tough barrack life at Melilla had
made a man of him. After profuse congratulations, which
Jaume shrugged off, Samstag sent for the village taxi and
invited us both to dinner in Palma. Len, to his disappointment,
was left behind. We chose *Aqui Estamos*, Majorca's most
select restaurant, where Samstag kept slapping Jaume's
shoulders and crying '¡Amigo!', varied with '¡Magnifico!', and
asking me to translate Sharon's appreciative comments on the
play, one of which was: 'The name part couldn't be more like
you, Pappy!' ('¡El papel titular corresponde precisamente contigo,
Papaito!') At this Jaume, now full of crayfish, asparagus, roast
turkey, wild strawberries and champagne, smiled for the first
time that evening. We wound up around 3 a.m. drinking
more and worse champagne to the sound of *flamenco* in a gipsy
night club. Truscott and Samstag, who were flying back together at 8 a.m., had let themselves go properly; their good-
byes could not have been warmer.

However, Jaume had stood by his guns: declining to commit
himself until he could read the amended contract and get it
approved by a reliable notary. Nor would he anticipate his
good fortune by the purchase of so much as a pig, let alone an
ass.

When Truscott finally sent me the document, Len offered his
expert advice gratis – he knew all about Broadway contracts,
and could tell at a glance whether anything were wrong.
'Maybe Bill and Sammy did a crooked deal together,' he
suggested. 'Of course, he's an old friend of mine, but in show
business . . .'

Shaking Len off, I took the contract to Jaume's cottage. 'A
letter from Señor Samstag is attached,' I told him. 'Shall I
read it first, or shall I first translate this document?'

'The document first, if you please.'

I read: 'Whereas the Author, a member of the Dramatists Guild of the Authors League of America Inc. (hereinafter called the "Guild") has been preparing the book of a certain play or other literary property now entitled *The Difficult Husband*. And whereas the Producer etc., etc., desires to produce the said play in the United States and Canada, etc., etc. . . . Now therefore, in consideration of the premises and the mutual promises and covenants herein contained and other good and valuable considerations, it is agreed:

'FIRST: The Author hereby (a) warrants that he is the author of the said play and has a right to enter into this agreement –'

Jaume interrupted: 'But I am not a member of this Guild!'

'Never mind you can apply for membership.'

'And if they won't accept a foreigner?'

'Don't worry! Señor Truscott will fix you up. Let's get on: "The Author (b) agrees that on compliance with this contract –"'

'Maybe, Don Roberto, you should translate the letter first.'

'Very well, then. . . . It says here that Señor Samstag greatly enjoyed his visit to Majorca, and is delighted that we all see eye to eye, and that it only remains for you to sign the attached instrument, your agent, Señor Truscott, having agreed with him on the terms.

'Then, wait a bit . . . then the tone of the letter changes. While still considering the play to be superb, Señor Samstag suggests certain radical changes in the treatment. It is by no means good theatre yet, he writes. The Difficult Husband, for instance, remains too static a character; his actions are predictable, and so is the eventual victory of his wife. In a sophisticated play, the leading man's character must develop; and this development must be substantiated by brisk dialogue. Here, the Husband should grow gradually less difficult, more *human*, as the action advances. Also, he should be granted an occasional small victory over his wife . . .'

Jaume's eyes were smouldering. 'He says that, does he, the imbecile?'

I tried to smooth him down. 'After all, show-business people are apt to understand the market. They study it year in, year out.'

'Read on!'

'He insists that the scene where the couple quarrel about household accounts must be changed. Let the husband, instead, teach his wife how to manage something else, something *visible* – say, a television set or a garbage disposer. "In the theatre we want to *see* things," he writes. "Then, when the wife wins his permission to take a long cruise and pretends that she has gone, but stays ashore to save household money – this is most unconvincing! Let her go for her health, really go, and fall in love with a handsome adventurer on the ship! Her husband can get comically jealous at the beginning of the Third Act –"'

'Stop!' Jaume roared. 'Why does this fellow first telegraph that my play is magnificent, and now want to change it altogether, though offering me the same immense sum of money?'

'Patience, Jaume! He cabled "Bravo!" because he hadn't read your play. Now he writes the reverse because he still hasn't read it. Knowing you to be inexperienced, he naturally entrusts *The Difficult Husband* to his assistants, who are expert play-doctors. The suggestions you so dislike emanate from these play-doctors. If you will not rewrite the play, that task necessarily falls to them, or to someone working under their direction.'

'Then it will no longer be mine?'

'Oh yes, it will be! You're protected by the contract. Your name will flash out in red, green, and yellow neon lights from the front of the theatre, and you will get the big money. Play-doctors get no more than their salaries. They can't *write* plays; they can only rewrite them.'

'Willie would never have agreed!'

'Are you sure?'

'Willie would not have changed a single word! He had a stubborn nature.'

'Well, I admit that this letter sounds nonsense – not that I've read *The Difficult Husband* . . . But you are faced by a clear choice. Either fight for every word of your play, and be lucky if you keep one in ten; or else refuse to sign the contract.'

'Enough, enough, Don Roberto! My mind is made up. The devil take this contract! If Señor Samstag's assistants care to rewrite my play, very good! Let them spin a coin to decide who shall be the author. I will sell *The Difficult Husband* outright, making no conditions whatsoever, except that Señor Samstag must pay me a sum down, in pesetas, and – *pff!* – that's it! . . . What might he pay?'

I told him: 'Fortunately it's not a case of buying your *name*: he's only buying your story. Since the Señorita Samstag believes in it so strongly, he might be good for ten thousand dollars – around half a million pesetas. That's nothing for a producer like Samstag.'

Jaume said slowly: 'Not having yet signed my agreement with Señor Truscott, I am still my own master. Let us telegraph Señor Samstag that, if he flies here again, a new one page contract will be awaiting him at the notary's.'

'And Señor Truscott?'

'For three hundred thousand I can become the Lord of La Coma, which is in the market now; so, since Señor Truscott envies me this cottage, he may have it and welcome. I will add a terrace or two, to round off the property. As for the lemon grove and olives, which are worth far more, they are yours, Don Roberto.'

'Many thanks, Jaume; but I want nothing but your friendship. We should dispatch your message at once.'

Three days later Samstag flew in, delighted not to find Bill Truscott about. 'Agents create unnecessary complications between friends, don't you think?' he asked us. A one-page contract in legal Spanish was easily agreed upon, and Samstag had arranged for the necessary pesetas. They went straight into an account which Jaume opened at the Bank of Spain.

As we drove home from Palma, Jaume said the last word on the subject: 'What can be done with a man who complains that a play is dramatically bad before he even reads it? *The Difficult Husband*, as many Majorcans know, though perhaps few Americans, enjoyed a remarkable success at the *Cine Moderno* some years ago. My poor mother took me there. The film ran for three whole weeks. Only an imbecile would wish to change its plot. It was called – what was it called? – ah, now I remember: "*La Vida con Papa*". How does one say that in English, Don Roberto?'

V. S. Pritchett

HANDSOME IS AS HANDSOME DOES

In the morning the Corams used to leave the Pension, which was like a white box with a terra-cotta lid among its vines on the hill above the town, and walk through the dust and lavish shade to the beach. They were a couple in their forties.

He had never been out of England before, but she had spent half her youth in foreign countries. She used to wear shabby saffron beach-pyjamas with a navy-blue top which the sun had faded. She was a short, thin woman, ugly yet attractive. Her hair was going grey, her face was clay-coloured, her nose was big and long and she had long yellowish eyes. In this beach-suit she looked rat-like, with that peculiar busyness, inquisitiveness, intelligence and even charm of rats. People always came and spoke to her and were amused by her conversation. They were startled by her ugly face and her shabbiness, but they liked her lazy voice, her quick mind, her graceful good manners, the look of experience and good sense in her eyes.

He was a year older. On the hottest days, when she lay bare-backed and drunk with sunlight, dozing or reading a book, he sat awkwardly beside her in a thick tweed jacket and a white hat pulled down over his eyes. He was a thickset, ugly man; they were an ugly pair. Surly, blunt-speaking, big-boned, with stiff short fair hair that seemed to be struggling and alight in the sun, he sat frowning and glaring almost wistfully and tediously from his round blue eyes. He had big hands like a labourer's. When people came to speak to her, he first of all edged away. His instinct was to avoid all people. He wanted to sit there silently with her, alone. But if the people persisted, then he was rude to them, rude, uncouth and quarrelsome. Then she had to smooth away his rudeness and distract attention from it. But he would ignore the person to whom she was talking and looking down at her would say, 'What are you getting at me for, Julia?' There was a note of angry self-pity in his voice. She liked a man of spirit.

This started quarrels. They were always quarrelling. They quarrelled about their car, their food, where they would sit, whether on the beach or at cafés, whether they would read upstairs or downstairs. He did not really know he was quarrelling. The trouble was that everything seemed difficult to him. He had thoughts, but he could not get them out. They were tied up in knots like snakes, squeezing and suffocating him. Whenever he made a suggestion or offered an opinion, his short brow became contorted with thick frowns, like a bull's forehead, and he coloured. He lowered his forehead, not as if he were going to charge with fury, but as if he were faced with the job of pushing some impossible rock uphill. He was helpless.

She would see this and, cunningly, tactfully, she would make things easy for him. They had no children and, because of the guilt she felt about this and because of the difficulties he saw everywhere, they had become completely dependent on each other.

First of all they were alone at the Pension. There were themselves and Monsieur Pierre. He was the proprietor. At meal-times they all sat together. Monsieur Pierre was a plump grey man of sixty, with a pathetic, mean little mouth, a monocle in his eye. He was a short and vain little dandy and was given to boastfulness. The town was a gay place in the summer, like a pink flower opening by the peacock sea, and Monsieur Pierre was the butterfly that flutters about it. He had the hips of a woman. He was full of learned little proverbs, and precise little habits. Certain hours he would devote to lying on a couch and reading detective stories in a darkened room. At another time he would sit in his dining-room with a patent cigarette-making machine, winding the handle, meddling with the mechanism, turning out the cigarettes. He gave a lick to each one as it came out. 'So he won't have to offer you one,' Coram said.

In the afternoon Monsieur Pierre made a great fuss. Appearing in yellow vest and red trousers, he took out a new bicycle done in grey enamel and glittering with plated bars, gears, brakes, acetylene lamps and elaborate looped wires. He mounted by a tree and, talking excitedly as if he were about to depart on some dangerous journey to the Alps or the Himalayas, he would whizz giddily down to the beach with his towel and striped gown on the carrier.

'You are going to bathe this afternoon?' Monsieur Pierre asked. 'I am going.' It was a question he put to the Englishman regularly at lunch-time. Monsieur Pierre would boast of his love of the sea.

Coram frowned and coloured, and a veil of wetness, as if tears were being generated by the struggle within, came to his eyes.

'What's he say?' he asked his wife at last, for he understood French poorly.

'He wants to know whether we are going to bathe with him.'

'Him!' said Coram in a surly voice. 'Him bathe! He can't swim. He can't swim a yard. He just goes down to look at the women.'

'Please, Tom!' she said in a sharp lowered voice. 'You mustn't say that in front of him. He understands more than you think.'

Monsieur Pierre sat at the head of the table, grey hair parted in the middle, monocle on expressionless face.

'He's a fraud,' Coram said in his blunt grumbling voice. 'If he understands English, why does he pretend he don't?'

'Parlez français, Monsieur Coram,' came the neat, spinsterly correcting voice of the Frenchman.

'Oui,' said the wife very quickly, smiling the long enchanting smile which transformed her ugly face. 'Il *faut*.'

Monsieur Pierre smiled at her and she smiled at him. He liked her bad accent. And she liked him very much, but for her husband's sake she had to pretend to dislike him. Her life was full of pretences, small lies and exaggerations which she contrived for her husband's sake.

But Coram disliked the Frenchman from the beginning. When Monsieur Pierre saw the Corams had a car, he per-

suaded them to take him about the country; he would show
them its beauties. Sitting like a little duke in the car, he pointed
out the torrid towns raked together like heaps of earthenware
in the mountain valleys, the pale stairways of olives going up
hills where no grass grew and the valleys filled with vines.
Driving in the fixed, unchanging sunlight, Monsieur Pierre
directed them to sudden sights of the sea in new bays more
extravagant in colour. Coram frowned. It was all right for
his wife. She had been to such places before. Her family had
always been to such places. This was the thing which always
awed him when he thought about her; pleasure had been
natural to her family for generations. But for him it was un-
natural. All this was too beautiful. He had never seen anything
like it. He could not speak. At noon when the mountains of the
coast seemed to lie head down to the sea like savage, panting
and silver animals, or in the evening when the flanks and
summits were cut by sharp purple shadows and the sea
became like some murmuring lake of milky opal, he felt the
place had made a wound in him. He felt in his heart the suspended anger of a man torn between happiness and pain. After
his life in the villas and chemical factories of the Midlands, where
the air was like an escape of gas and the country brick-bruised
and infected, he could not believe in this beautiful country.
Incredulous, he mistrusted.

'Garsong!' (There was a café near the harbour where the
Corams used to sit for an hour before dinner.) 'Garsong –
Encore – drinks!' That was the only way he could melt his
mistrust.

Coram could not explain why. He was thwarted like his
country. All he could do was frown and take it out of Monsieur Pierre.

'He's a mean squirt,' Coram said.

'He's a liar,' he said.

'Look at him making those cigarettes.'

'We've known him a week, and what's he do but cadge
drinks and rides in the car. He's a fraud.'

His wife listened. Her husband was a man without subtlety
or wit, quite defenceless before unusual experience. He was a

child. Every day she was soothing this smouldering aching struggle that was going on inside him.

After they had been there a week a newcomer arrived at the Pension. He arrived one morning by the early train, walking down from the station with his new light suitcase. He was a young man in his twenties, tall, dark, aquiline, a Jew.

'We will call you Monsieur Alex,' said Monsieur Pierre with his French love of arranging things.

'That is charming,' said the Jew.

He spoke excellent English, a little too perfect, a little too round in the vowels, and excellent French, almost too pure. He talked easily. He had heard, he said, that there were some excellent pictures in the churches of the mountain towns.

'Rather sweet isn't he?' said Mrs Coram. The Jew was grave and handsome. Coram was admiring too, but he was more cautious.

'Yeah. He looks all right,' he said.

His mother was French, the young Jew told them on the first evening, his father German. But they had both come from Austria originally. He had cousins in every country in Europe. He had been educated in England. Slender, with long hands, a little coarse in complexion in the Jewish way, he had grey and acute sepia eyes. He was so boyish, so free in his talk about himself, so shy and eager in his laugh – and yet – how could Mrs Coram describe it? – he seemed ancient, like some fine statue centuries old that has worn and ripened in the sun. He was thick-lipped and had a slight lisping hesitance of speech, and this sense of the ancient and profound came perhaps from his habit of pausing before he spoke as if judiciously cogitating. Mrs Coram would sit there expectant and curious. She was used to the hesitations, the struggles with thought of her husband; but there was this difference: when the Jew spoke at last, what he said was serious, considered, a charming decoration of commentary upon their discussions.

Monsieur Pierre always longed for fresh worlds to patronize; he was delighted with Alex. Too delighted for Coram and even for his wife. She could not help being on the point of jealousy when Alex sat and talked to the Frenchman. Coram bluntly wanted to rescue the young man from 'the fraud'.

'You know what's wrong . . . with this place,' Coram said to Alex. 'There's no industry.'

'Oh, but surely agriculture, the wine,' said Alex.

'Yeah, I know,' said Coram. 'I mean real industry . . .'

'My husband's a chemist, industrial chemist,' she explained.

'I mean,' said Coram, grinding on and frowning quizzically, 'they just sit around and grow wine and batten on the visitors, like this feller. What a town like this wants is a couple of good whore-shops and a factory . . .'

'Tom!' said Mrs Coram. 'How exotic you've become.'

'I expect ample provision has been made,' said the Jew.

'No,' said Coram, in his halting, muddling, bullying tone, 'but you see what I mean.'

He screwed up his eyes. He wished to convey that he had not quite found the words for what he had meant really to say.

The odd thing about the young Jew was that although he seemed to be rich and was cultivated, he had no friends in the town. The young always arrived in troops and car-loads at this place. The elderly were often in ones and twos, but the young – never. Mrs Coram detected a curious loneliness in him. Polite and formal, he sometimes seemed not to be there. Why had he come? Why to this Pension? It was a cheap place, and obviously he had money. Why alone? There were no relations, no women. When he went out he saw no one, spoke to no one. Why not? Alone he visited the mountain churches. He was equable, smiling, interested, happy – yet alone. He liked to be alone, it seemed, and yet when they spoke to him, when Coram – urged by her – asked him to come down to the beach or drive in the car, he came without hesitation, with the continuous effortless good manners and curious lack of intimacy that he always had. It baffled her. She wanted to protect and mother him.

'The Jewboy,' Coram called him. His wife hated this. They quarrelled.

'Stop using that stupid expression,' she said.

'He is,' said her husband. 'I've nothing against him. He's clever. But he's a Jewboy. That's all.' He was not against the Jewboy. He even liked him. They talked together. Coram almost felt protective to him too.

'Aren't you being rather vulgar?' she said to her husband.

One effect the Jew had on them was to make them stop having this kind of quarrel in public. Coram did not change. He was as uncouth as ever. But his wife restrained herself. In mortification she heard his crude stumbling words and quickly interrupted them, smoothed them away hastily so that Alex should not notice them. Either she was brushing her husband away out of hearing, first of all, or she was working with every nerve to transform her husband in the young man's eyes. At the end of the day she was exhausted.

One evening when they went up to bed in the hot room at the top of the house, she said to her husband:

'How old is he, Tom? Twenty-two?'

Coram stared at her. He did not know.

'Do you realize,' she said, 'we're nearly old enough to be his parents?' She had no children. She thought about him as her son.

She took off her clothes. The room was hot. She lay on the bed. Coram, slow and methodical, was taking off his shoes. He went to the window and emptied out the sand. He did not answer. He was working out how old he would have been if the young man had been his son. Before he found an answer, she spoke again.

'One forgets he must think we're old,' she said. 'Do you think he does? Do you think he realizes how much older we are? When I look at him it seems a century and then other times we might all be the same age . . .'

'Jews look older than they are,' said Coram.

Her questioning voice stopped. Tom was hanging up his jacket. Every time he took off a garment he walked heavily across the room. Her questions went on silently in her mind. Twenty-two? And she was forty. What did he think of her? What did he think of her husband? Did her husband seem crude and vulgar? Did he seem slow-minded? What did the

young man think of both of them? Did he notice things? Did
he notice their quarrels? And why did he like to spend time
with them, talk to them, go about with them? What was he
thinking, what was he feeling? Why was he so friendly and yet
ultimately so unapproachable?

She lay on her side with her slight knees bent. Out of her
shabby clothes her body was thin but graceful. Her shoulders
were slender, but there were lines on her neck, a reddish stain
spreading over her breast bone, a stain hard with exposure to
years. Her small breasts were loose and slack over the ribs.
The skin creasing under them was sallow. She ran her hands
over her hips. She moved her hands round and round on her
small flat belly, caressing herself where she knew her body was
beautiful. It seemed only a few days ago that this had been the
body of a young girl. She was filled with sadness for her
husband and herself. She could hear the beating of her heart.
She found herself listening for the steps of the young man on
the stairs. Her heart beat louder and louder. To silence it she
said in an anxious voice to her husband, lowering her knees:

'Tom – you haven't stopped wanting me.' She knew her
voice was false.

He was taking off his shirt.

'What do you want?' he said.

His face looked grotesque as it looked out of the shirt top.
'Nothing,' she said.

Tom took off his shirt and looked out of the window. You
could see the white farms of the valley with their heavy walls
from the window. The peasants kept their dogs chained, and
when there was a moon they barked, a dozen or more of them,
one after the other, all down the valley.

'If those dogs – start tonight – we won't sleep,' he said. He
came to the bed and waited for her to get under the sheet. She
felt his big-boned body beside her and smelled his sharp,
curious smell.

'God,' he said. He felt stupefied in this place. In five
minutes he was asleep. But she lay awake. Forty, she was
thinking. A woman of forty with a son. No son. She heard, as
she lay awake, the deep breathing of her husband, the curious

whistlings of his breath. She lay thinking about her life, puzzling, wondering. Why had she no son? She dozed. She awakened. She threw back the sheet and sleeplessly sighed. If she slept it was only in snatches, and she woke up with her heart beating violently and to find herself listening for the sound of a step on the stairs. There was a sensation of inordinate hunger and breathlessness in her body.

Sometimes the young Jew waited for them in the morning and went down with them to the beach. He carried her basket for her or her book. He went back for things.

'Tom,' she said in front of her husband, 'has no manners.'

She walked between them and talked excitedly to the young man about characters in books, or foreign towns, or pictures. She laughed and Coram smiled. He listened with wonder to them.

They sat on the beach. Under his clothes the Jew wore a black bathing-suit. He undressed at once and went into the water. His body was alien and slender, the skin burned to the colour of dark corn. He dived in and swam far out into the blue water, beyond the other bathers. He did not laugh or wave or call back, but in his distant, impersonal way he swam far out with long easy strokes. After a mile he lay floating in the sun. He seemed to pass the whole morning out there. She could see his black head. To be young like that and lie in the sea in the sun! And yet how boring to lie there for so long. She would have sudden pangs of anxiety. She would talk of the cold current that came out in the deeper water, from the harbour. She was always glad and relieved when she saw his head moving towards the shore. When he came out of the water he seemed to be dry at once, as if some oil were in his skin. She would see only beads of water at the back of his neck on the short black hair.

'You can swim!' she said.

He smiled.

'Not much,' he said. 'Why don't you?'

The question pleased her. She was astonished by the pleasure it gave her.

'I'm not allowed,' she said with animation. 'Tell me, what were you doing out there? You were such a long time.'

His dark eyes were large and candid as he turned to her and she caught her breath. There were three or four black freckles on his skin. Her older yellow eyes returned his innocent gaze. Good heavens, she thought. With eyes like that he ought to be a girl. But she did not know and did not feel that her eyes were older than his.

'I was nearly asleep,' he said. 'The sea is like a mattress.'

He and Coram had a scientific discussion about the possibility of sleeping on the sea.

It was absurd of her, she knew, but she was disappointed. Had he not thought of them, of her? She had been thinking of him all the time.

Coram sat beside them. He talked about the business scandals and frauds in the chemical trade. The quick-minded Jew understood all these stories long before Coram got to their elaborate end. Coram had an obsession with fraud. His slow mind was angry about that kind of quickness of mind which made fraud possible. Coram sat inert, uncomprehending, quite outside the gaiety on the beach. He was not gloomy or morose. He was not sulking. His blue eyes glistened and he had the wistful face of a dog trying to understand. He sat struggling to find words which would convey all that he had felt in this fortnight. He considered the sea and the young man for a long time. Then he undressed. Out of his dark red bathing-dress his legs were white and were covered with thick golden hairs. His neck was pink where the sun had caught it. He walked down awkwardly over the pebbles, scowling because of the force of the sun, and straddled knee-deep into the water. Then he flung himself on it helplessly, almost angrily, and began clawing at it. He seemed to swim with clenched fists. They could see him clawing and crawling as the slow swell lifted him up. For a hundred yards he would swim not in a straight line but making a half circle from the beach, as if he were incapable of swimming straight or of knowing where he was going. When he waded out with the water drenching from him there was a look of grievance on his face.

'That water's dirty,' he said when he got back. The Mediterranean was a fraud: it was too warm, thick as syrup. He sat dripping on his wife's books.

One morning when he came back and was drying himself, rubbing his head with the towel, he caught sight of Monsieur Pierre. The Frenchman was sitting not many yards away. Short-sighted, no doubt Monsieur Pierre had not seen them. Beside him were his towels, his red slippers, his red swimming-helmet, his cigarette case, his striped bathing-gown and his jar of coconut oil. He was in his bathing-dress. More than ever, but for his short grey hair, he looked like a pot-bellied middle-aged woman as he rubbed coconut oil on his short brown arms. His monocle was in his eye. He looked like a Lesbian in his monocle.

Coram scowled.

'You see,' he blurted in a loud voice. 'He hasn't been in. He won't go in either. He just comes – down here – all dolled up – to look at the women.'

'Not so loud,' his wife said. 'Please.' She looked with anxiety at the Jew. 'Poor Monsieur Pierre,' said Mrs Coram. 'Remember his age. He's sixty. Perhaps he doesn't want to go in. I bet you won't be swimming when you're sixty.'

'He can swim very well,' said the young Jew politely. 'I went out with him a couple of days ago from the other beach.' He pointed over the small headland. 'He swam out to the ship in the bay. That is three miles.'

'There, Tom!' cried his wife.

She was getting bored with these attacks on Monsieur Pierre.

'He's a fraud, a rotten fraud,' said Tom in his smouldering, struggling voice.

'But Alex was with him!' she said.

'I don't care who was with him,' said Tom. 'He's a fraud. You wait till you know him better,' said Tom bluntly to the Jew. 'Believe me, he's a rotten little blackmailer.'

'Ssh. You don't know that. You mustn't repeat things,' she said.

'Well, you know it as well as I do,' Tom said.

'Quiet, Tom, please,' his wife said. 'He's sitting there.'

'He blackmails his brother-in-law,' Tom persisted. He was addressing himself to the Jew.

'Well, what of it?'

She was angry. Monsieur Pierre could easily hear. And she was angry, trembling with anger, because she did not want the young man to see the uncouthness of her husband and her mortification at it.

'Pierre's sister married a motor millionaire. That's where Pierre gets his money. He waits till his brother-in-law has a new woman and then goes to his sister and pitches the tale to her. She goes to her husband, makes a jealous scene and, to keep her quiet, he gives her what she wants for Pierre.'

'You don't know that,' she said.

'I know it as well as you do,' he said. 'Everyone in the town knows it. He's a fraud.'

'Well, don't *shout*. And use some other word. It's a bore,' she said.

'I've no respect for a man who doesn't earn his living,' Coram said. Oh, God, she thought, now he's going to quarrel with this boy.

The Jew raised an eyebrow.

'Doesn't he keep the Pension?' the Jew inquired calmly.

'You mean his servants keep it,' blustered Coram. 'Have you ever seen him do a stroke?'

'Well,' his wife said, 'we can't all be like you, Tom. My family never earned a penny in their lives. They would have been horrified at the idea.'

She was speaking not with irony but with indignation. At once she knew she had gone too far. She had failed for once to soothe, to smooth away.

'Ay! Didn't want the dirty work,' Coram said, dropping into his Midland accent. He was not angry. He was, from his own stolid point of view, reasonable and even genial. He wondered why she was 'getting at' him.

'Why, dearest,' she said, knowing how irony hurt his vanity. 'You've hit it. You've hit it in one. Bravo. They had no illusions about the nobility of work.' She was ridiculing him.

'You don't believe in the nobility of work, do you?' she said to the Jew. 'My husband's got a slave's mind,' she said.

'Working is a habit, like sleeping and eating,' said the Jew seriously in his lazy and too perfect enunciation. It had the well-oiled precision of a complexity of small pistons in an impersonal machine. She had heard him speak French and German with an equal excellence. It was predestined.

Living with her husband, always dealing with the inarticulate, she had injured her own full capacity to speak. The Jew stirred her tongue and her lips. She felt an impulse to put her lips to his, not in love, but to draw some of the magic of exposition from him. She wanted her head to be joined to his head in a kiss, her brow to be against his. And then his young face and his dark hair would take the lines from her face and would darken her greyness with the dark, fresh, gleaming stain of youth. She could never really believe that her hair was grey. Her lips were tingling and parted as, lost in this imagination, she gazed at him; innocent and cool-eyed, he returned her look. She did not lower her eyes. How young she had been! A shudder of weakness took her shoulders and pain spread like a burn from her throat and over her breasts into the pit of her stomach. She moistened her lips. She saw herself driving in the August sun on an English road twenty years ago, a blue tarred road that ran dazzling like steel into dense trees and then turned and vanished. That day with its climate and the resinous smells of the country always came back when she thought of being young. She was overwhelmed.

The sun had gone in and the sea was grey and sultry and, in this light, the water looked heavier and momentous, higher and deeper at the shore, like a swollen wall. The sight of the small lips of foam was like the sight of thirst, like the sudden inexplicable thirst she had for his lips.

Then she heard Tom's voice. It was explanatory. Sitting with people who were talking, he would sometimes slowly come to conclusions about a remark which had struck him earlier in the conversation. He would cling to this, work upon it, struggle with it. She often laughed affectionately at this lagging of his tortoise mind.

The frowns were deep in the thick pink skin of his forehead, the almost tearful glare was in his eyes:

'They didn't want the dirty work,' he said. He was addressing the young man. 'They have butlers. They have a grown man to answer door-bells and bring letters. Her family had. They corrupt people by making them slaves . . .'

The Jew listened politely. Coram felt he hadn't said what he meant. The frown deepened as the clear eyes of the Jew looked at his troubled face.

'I was on a jury,' Coram said. 'We had to try a man . . .'

'Oh, Tom, not that story about the butler who stole elevenpence. Yes, Tom was on a jury and a man got six months for obtaining a meal value elevenpence from an A.B.C. or a Lyons or some place . . .'

'Yes,' said Coram eagerly, his glaring eyes begging the Jew to see his point.

He wanted to explain that a man corrupts by employing servants. No, not that. What Coram really meant in his heart was that he would not forgive his wife for coming from a rich family. And yet something more than that, too, something not so ridiculous but more painful. He was thinking of some fatal difference between his wife and himself and their fatal difference from society. He was thinking of the wound which this place by the beautiful sea had made in him. He struggled, gave it up.

But she looked scornfully at him. She wiped him out of her sight. She was angry with him for exposing his stupidity before the young Jew. She had fought against it in the last few days; she had been most clever in concealing it. But now she had failed. The thing was public.

She got up angrily from the beach.

'Pick up my book,' she said to her husband. The Jew did not quite hide his astonishment. She saw him gaze, and was angrier still with herself. Tactfully he let her husband pick up the book.

They walked back to the Pension. All the way along the road she scarcely spoke to her husband. Once in their room, she pulled off her hat and went to the mirror. She saw him reflected in the glass, standing with a look of heavy resentment on his face, bewildered by her.

She saw her own face. The skin was swollen with anger and lined too. Her grey hair was untidy. She was shocked by her physical deterioration. She was ugly. When she heard the young man's step on the stairs she could have wept. She waited: he did not close his door. This was more than she could bear. She turned upon her husband. She raised her voice. She wanted the young man to hear her rage.

Why had she married such an oaf, such a boor? Her family had begged her not to marry him. She mocked him. He failed at everything. There he was, stuck at forty, stuck in his career, stuck for life.

Sometimes he blurted out things in the quarrel, but most of the time he was speechless. He stood at the foot of the bed with his tweed coat in his hand, looking at her with heavy blue eyes, his face reddening under the insults, his tongue struggling to answer, his throat moving. He was not cold, but hot with goading. Yet he did nothing. The forces inside him were locked like wrestlers at each other's throats, muddled, powerless. As the quarrel exhausted itself, she sank on to the bed. She was fascinated by his hulking incapacity. She had always been fascinated. From the very beginning.

He had not moved during all this, but when she lay down on the bed with her head in the pillow he went quietly to the clothes peg and hung up his coat. He stood there rolling up his sleeves. He was going to wash. But she heard him move. She suddenly could not bear that he moved away, even those two steps, from her. She could not bear that he should say to himself, 'One of Julia's scenes. Leave her alone. She'll get over it,' and, taking his opportunity, slip away and go on as if nothing had happened.

She sat up on the edge of the bed. Tears were stinging her cheeks.

'Tom!' she called out. 'What are we going to do? What are we going to do?'

He turned guiltily. She had made him turn.

'I want a child, Tom. What are we going to do? I must have a child.'

Her tone made his blood run cold. There was something wild and horror-struck in her voice. It sounded like a piercing voice crying out in a cavern far away from any other living creature, outraged, animal and incomprehensible.

God, he thought. Are we going over all that again? I thought we'd resigned ourselves to that.

He wanted to say, 'You're forty. You can't have a child.' But he could not say that to her. He suspected that she was acting. He said instead what she so often said to him; it seemed to be the burden of their isolated lives.

'Quiet,' he said. 'People will hear.'

'All you ever think of!' she cried out. 'People. Drift. Do nothing.'

They went down the tiled stairs to the dining-room. The sun had come out again, but it was weak. A thin film of cloud was rising in the east. The shutters of the dining-room were always closed early in the morning, and by noon the house was cool and dark. Before his guests came down, Monsieur Pierre used to go round the room with a fly-swatter. Then the wine was brought in a bucket of water and he put it down beside his chair and waited. A clock clucked like some drowsy hen on the wall, and the coloured plates, like crude carnival wheels, glowed in the darkened room on the black carved shelves of the cupboard. Mrs Coram came into the room and she heard the dust blowing outside in the breeze and the leaves moving in the vines. A bolt tapped on the shutters.

Their faces were dark in the room, all the faces except Mrs Coram's. Her face was white and heavily powdered. She had been afraid that when she saw Alex she would be unable to speak, but would choke and have to run from the table. To her surprise, when she saw him standing by his chair in the room, with his brown bare arm on the chair top, she was able to speak. So easily that she talked a great deal.

'Red wine or white? The wishes of women are the wishes of

God,' said Monsieur Pierre to her, paying himself a compliment at the same time.

She began to mock the young man. He laughed. He enjoyed the mockery. 'The wishes of women are the sorrows of Satan,' he said satanically. She went on to mockery of Monsieur Pierre. He was delighted. She repeated in her own way the things which her husband said about him.

'Monsieur Pierre is a fraud,' she said. 'He goes to the beach. He pretends he goes there to swim. Don't you believe it! He goes there to look at the girls. And Alex – he has got a motor inside him. He goes straight out and anchors. You think he's swimming. But he's only floating.'

'I can swim ten miles,' said Monsieur Pierre. He took a small mouthful of wine and boasted in a neat, deprecating way. 'I once swam half across the Channel.'

'Did you?' said the young man with genuine interest.

And once Monsieur Pierre had started to boast, he could not be stopped. She egged him on.

'Challenge him,' said Coram morosely to the young man, chewing a piece of meat.

'I challenge him,' said Monsieur Pierre.

But not at the town beach, he said, at the one beyond. It was true he rarely swam at the town beach. He liked to be alone when he swam . . . solitude . . . freedom . . .

'You bet he does,' grunted Coram.

'And Monsieur Coram too,' said Monsieur Pierre.

'I have been in once,' Coram said.

'So have they!' she exclaimed.

When they got up from the table, Coram took his wife aside. He saw through it all, he said to her; it was a device of Monsieur Pierre's to get a drive in his car. She was astonished at this remark. Before today she would not have been astonished, she would have tried to smooth away the difficulties he saw and the suspicions. But now everything was changed. He was like a stranger to her. She saw it clearly; he was mean. Men of his class who had worked their way up from nothing were often mean. Such a rise in the world was admired. She had once often admired it. Now it amused her and made her contemptuous. Mean! Why had she never thought of that before? She had been blind.

When lunch was over, it was their habit in the house to go to their rooms and sleep. She waited. First Monsieur Pierre went into his room, with his yellow novel. The Jew and her husband lingered. 'The best thing about this place is the drinks,' he was saying. 'They're cheap. You can have as much as you like. Down at those hotels in the town they don't leave the bottle on the table.' He was flushed and torpid. After a while he said:

'I'm going up.'

'I'm staying here. I shall take a deck-chair outside. That room's too hot,' she said.

He hesitated. 'Go, go,' she almost cried. She looked at the black shining hair of the young man, his full lips, the brown bare arms that came out of the blue vest, the large dark hands, redder with the flush of blood. They were spread on the table, stroking the cloth. She could feel, in imagination, those palms on her body. Her heart raced and shook her. She and he would be alone. She would talk to him, she would not listen to him, he should not have his own words, perfect, predestined and impersonal. It was she who would talk. She would make him halt and stammer. She would break through this perfection of impersonal speech. She would talk and make him know her. She would bring herself close to him with words, and then with touch. She would touch him. He was young, he was without will: he would touch her. She saw in her mind the open door of his room. She thought all this as her husband hesitated, stupefied, by the table.

But when he went and she was alone with Alex her heart stopped and there were no words in her throat. Her whole body was trembling, the bones of her knees were hard to her hands.

'I think,' Alex suddenly said as he had often said before, 'I think I shall go for a walk. I'll be back for the swim,' he said.

She gasped. She looked with intent irony at him. She saw him get up from the table and, in his oddly studied way, as if there were meat in his solitude no one else could know, he went.

'You fool,' she said to herself. But as she stared out of the open door and heard his cool footsteps on the gravel outside until the sound of the breeze in the vines licked them away, she felt lost with relief.

In a deck-chair under the mulberry tree she thought about herself and her husband. It was the time of year when the fruit of the mulberry falls. The berries dropped on to the gravel, into the tank where the frogs croaked at night and on to the table. They broke there. Sometimes they dropped like small hard hearts into her lap and when she picked them off they crushed in her fingers and the red juice ran out. She breathed deeply, almost panting in her chair.

She had married an outcast. Her relations had said that and they had been right. Some of those who had been right – her mother and father, for example – were dead. Tom's father had had a small boot-repairing business in Leicester. He worked in the front room of their house, with its bay window. Coram. Repairs While You Wait. That man and his wife had had seven children. Imagine such a life! Tom had studied, won scholarships, passed examinations. All his life he had been different from his brothers and sisters. Now his job was chemistry. Once he was going to be a famous chemist. Instead he got commercial jobs in the laboratories of big firms. He did not belong to the working class any more. He did not belong to her class. He did not belong to the class of the comfortable professional people he now met. He did not belong anywhere. He was lost, rough, unfinished, ugly, unshaped by the wise and harmonious hand of a good environment.

And she had really been the same. That was what had brought them together. He was ugly in life, she was ugly in body; two ugly people cut off from all others, living in their desert island.

Her family were country gentry, not very rich, with small private incomes and testy, tiresome genteel habits. The males went into the army. The females married into the army. You saw one and you had seen them all. She had always been small and thin; her long nose, her long mouth, her almost yellowish eyes and dead clay skin made her ugly. She had to be clever and lively, had to have a will or no one would have noticed her. At one time she supposed she would marry one of those tedious young men with dead eyes and little fair moustaches who were 'keen' on gunnery and motor cars. She had thrown herself at them – thrown herself at them, indeed, like a bomb. That didn't suit the modern militarists. They had the tastes of clerks. They fingered their moustaches, looked dead and embarrassed at her, said they couldn't bear 'highbrow' girls, and got away as quickly as they could. They were shocked because she didn't wear gloves. The naked finger seemed an indecency to them. 'I could be a General's wife by now if I'd worn gloves,' she used to say. Before they could throw her out and treat her as the bright, noisy, impossible woman who appears in every family, she threw them out.

So she married Tom. She got away from her home, went to live with a friend, met Tom and married him. There was a row. 'The toothpaste man,' her relations called him. Thought she was going to live in a chemist's shop. He became a stick to beat her family with; he was going to be a great man, a great scientist – she flogged them. He was going to be a much greater man than those 'keen' subalterns with their flannel bags, dance records and little moustaches, or those furtive majors, guilty with self-love.

She looked back on these days. She had always expected something dramatic and sudden to happen. But – what was it? – Tom had not become a great man. The emergence from his class had become really an obsession, and a habit. He was struggling to emerge long after he had emerged. He was always spending his energy on reacting from something which no longer existed. He lived – she could never quite understand it – in the grip of some thwarting inward conflict, his energy went into this invisible struggle. The veins and the muscles swelled as if they would burst. Torn between dealing with her, that is with the simple business of giving her simple natural happiness, and himself, he was paralysed. And they had had no children. Whose fault was that? At first it was a mercy because they were poor, but later? She slept with him. Her body had grown old trying to tear a child from him. Afterwards she attacked him. He listened, stupefied.

Why had this happened to her? And why had she this guilt towards him so that now she pitied him and spent all her day coming between him and difficulty? She had sown her disappointment in him, he had sown his frustration in her. Why? And why did they live in a circle they could not break? Why did they live so long in it until suddenly she was forty, a greyhaired woman?

She went over these things, but she was not thinking and feeling them only. There was the soft stroke of a pulse between her breasts, making her breathless with every throb. Movement came to her blood from the sight of the blowing vines and the red soil of the olive fields and out of the windwhitened sky. Her lips parted in thirst for the articulate lips of the young Jew. She could not sleep or read.

At last she went into the cool house. The flies, driven indoors by the wind, were swimming in the darkness. She went up the stairs to her room.

'Get up,' she said to her husband. 'We must go.'

He couldn't go in these clothes, she said. He must get the car. She bullied him. She changed into a green dress. Grumbling, he changed.

She looked out of the window. Alex was not coming. She could see the valley and the trees flowing and silvered by the wind. Dust was blowing along the roads between the earth and sun giving it a weird and brilliant light like the glitter of silica in granite.

Tom went downstairs. His clothes were thrown all over the room.

'We're waiting,' he said when she came down. The black car was there and Monsieur Pierre. He stood by it as if he owned it.

'Women,' said Monsieur Pierre, 'are like the bon Dieu. They live not in time but in eternity.'

Coram glared at him. Alex was there, tall and impersonal. He had come back, he said, some other way. He gravely considered Monsieur Pierre's remark. He made a quotation from a poet. This was obscure to her and everyone.

'Where the hell's this picnic going to be?' said Coram.

They disputed about where they should sit. That is, she said one thing and her husband another. At last Monsieur Pierre was in front and she and the young man were at the back. Coram got in and sulked. No one had answered his question. 'If anyone knows where they're going they'd better drive,' he said. 'The far beach,' she called out. 'Well, in God's name!' he muttered. Still he drove off.

'Are you crowded at the back?' he said later in a worried voice. A sudden schoolgirl hilarity took her.

'We like it,' she cried loudly, giggling. And pressed her legs against Alex.

She was immediately ashamed of her voice. Before she could stop herself, she cried out:

'I've got my young man.'

She swaggered her arm through his and laughed loudly close to his face. She was horrified at herself. He laughed discreetly, in a tolerant elderly way at her. So they bumped and brushed over the bad roads to the beach. Coram swore it would break the springs of his car, this damfool idea. She could see the sweat on her husband's thick pink neck. She goaded him. She called to him not to crawl, not to bump them about, not to take the town road but the other. Coram turned angrily to her.

She wanted to show the young man: You see, I don't care. I don't care how revolting I am. I don't care for anything. I hate everything except a desire that is in me. There is nothing but that.

The car topped the hill and she turned her head to look back upon the town. She was surprised. Two belfries stood above the roofs. She had never seen them before. The clay-coloured houses were closely packed together by the hills, and those that were in the sun stood out white and tall. The roofs went up in tiers and over each roof a pair of windows stared like foreign eyes. The houses were a phalanx of white and alien witnesses. She was startled to think that she had brought her life to a place so strange to her. She and her husband had lived in the deeply worn groove of their lives even on this holiday, and had not noticed the place. Her mood quietened.

The outlying villas of this side of the town were newer and the air burned with the new resinous odour of the pines and the two flames of the sea and sky.

'I often come this way,' said the Jew, 'because there is more air. Do you know the waiter in the café by the harbour? On one hot day last year he chased his wife's lover down the street, loosing off a revolver. He breaks out once a year. The rest of the time he is the perfectly contented complaisant husband. If the café were up here, it would not happen. Or perhaps he might only be complaisant once a year. Probably our whole emotional life is ruled by temperature and air currents.'

She looked at him. 'You have read your Huxley,' she said dryly, 'haven't you?' But afterwards she felt repentant because she thought if he was showing off, it was because he was young. '*I* could cure him of that.'

Presently the car stopped. They had got to the beach. They sat for a minute in the car studying it. It was a long beach of clean sand, looped between two promontories of rock, a wilder beach than the one by the town where people came to picnic. Now there was no one on it. And here the sea was not the pan of enamelled water they had known but was open and stood up high from the beach like a loose tottering wall, green, wind-torn, sun-shot and riotous. The sky was whitened on the horizon. The lighthouse on the red spit eight miles across the bay seemed to be racing through the water like a periscope. The whole coast was like groups of reddened riders driving the waves into a corral.

'The east wind,' said Monsieur Pierre, from his window, considering it.

They got out of the car. They walked on the sand and the waves unrolled in timed relay along the shore. The three men and Mrs Coram stood singly, separated by the wind, gazing at the tumult. They spoke and then turned to see where their words had gone. The wind had swept them from their lips and no one could hear.

Alex stayed behind, but soon he ran forward in his bathing-dress.

'You're not going!' Tom said. The sea was too wild. The Jew did not hear him and ran down to the shore.

'Oh!' Mrs Coram said anxiously and moved to Pierre.

Without a word the Jew had dived in. Now he was swimming out. She held Pierre's arm tightly and then slowly the grip of her fingers relaxed. She smiled and then she laughed. It was like watching a miracle to see Alex rise and sink with those tall waves, strike farther out and play like some remote god with their dazzling falls. Sometimes he seemed to drop like a stone to the sea's floor and then up he shot again as if he had danced to the surface. She watched him, entranced.

'He's fine,' she called. She looked for Tom. He was standing back from them, looking resentfully, confusedly, at the sea. Suddenly all her heart was with the swimmer and her mind felt clean by the cleansing sea. Her fear for him went. She adored his danger in the water and the way he sought it, the way he paused and went for the greatest waves and sailed through.

'Tom!' she called.

Before he knew what she wanted, Coram said:

'I'm not going out in that.'

'Pierre is,' she called. 'Aren't you?'

The old man sat down on the shingle. Yes, he was going in, he said.

Alex came back. He came out and stood by the water, unable to leave it. He was fifty yards from them. Suddenly he had dived in again. Then he came out once more and stood throwing stones into the sea. She saw him crouch and his long arm fling out as he threw the stone. He was smiling when he came back to them.

They sat down and talked about the rough water. They were waiting for Pierre to go in. He did nothing. He sat down there and talked. The Jew eyed him. Eagerly he wanted Pierre to come. The time passed, and Pierre said this sea was nothing. He began to boast of a time when he had been in a yacht which had been dismasted in a gale. 'I looked death in the face,' he said. Coram glowered, and winked at the Jew.

The Jew grew tired of waiting and said he was going to try the other end of the beach. She watched him walk away over the sand. Like a boy he picked up stones to throw as he went. She was hurt that he went away from her and yet she admired him more for this. She leaned back on her elbow; the soft stroke of pleasure and pain was beating between her breasts, a stroke for every step of his brown legs across the sand, a stroke for every fall of the sea on the shore. She saw him at last run down to the water and go in. He went far out of sight until there was a crest of fear to every breath of longing in her. He has gone far enough, she thought, far enough away from me.

She stood up. If she could fly in this wind over the sea and, like a gull, call to him from overhead and, pretending to be pursued, make him follow her to the shore! Then, to her surprise, he was suddenly on the shore again, standing as he had done before, studying the waves he had just been through. He stood there a long time and afterwards sat down and watched them. She called to him. It was too far. Timelessly he lived in his far-away youth. What was he doing, what was he thinking as he sat there remote in the other world of his youth?

Now Pierre had the beach to himself and there were no near competitors, he walked away and undressed. Presently he came back, short and corpulent in his bathing-dress and his red slippers. He asked particularly that Mrs Coram should be careful with his eyeglass. He fastened his helmet. Dandified, deprecating, like the leading dancer in a beauty chorus, he stood before them.

'I float naturally in the sea,' he observed, as if he were a scientific exhibit, 'because the balance of displacement in my case is exact.'

He went to the sea's edge like royalty, pausing every few yards to nod.

'Look,' she said.

It was odd, for the moment, to be alone with her husband,

to feel that just he and she saw this as they alone had seen
many other things in the world.

'He won't go in,' said Coram.

Pierre had reached the sea's edge. Impertinently a large wave
broke and he stood, surprised, like an ornament in a spread
lace doiley of surf. It swilled his ankles. He waited for it to
seethe back a little and then he bent and wetted his forehead.
He paused again. A green wave stood up on end, eight feet
high, arched and luminous like a carved window in a cathedral.
It hung waiting to crash. But before it crashed an astonishing
thing happened. The fat little man had kicked up his heels and
dived clean through it. They saw the soles of his red rubber
shoes as he went through and disappeared. There he was on
the other side of the wave in the trough and then, once again,
he dived through the next wave and the next, clambering over
the surf-torn ridges like a little beetle. The foam spat round
him, suds of it dabbed his face. Now his head in its red bathing-
helmet bobbed up in dignified surprise at the top of a wave,
now he was trudging out farther and farther into the riotous
water.

'He's floating,' said Tom.

'He's swimming,' she said.

They talked and watched. She looked down the beach for
Alex. He was lying full length in the sun.

Pierre was far out. How far they could not tell. Sometimes
they saw the head bobbing in the water, sometimes they could
not see him. They lost him. It was difficult to see against the
flash of the sun. Nearer to them the emerald water fell in its
many concussions on the shore and the shingle sang as the
undertow drew back. She saw with surprise the lighthouse still
racing, periscope-like, through the waves, dashing through the
water and yet going nowhere. Why does he stay there, why
doesn't he come back? She looked avidly to the young man
stretched on the shore.

'Let's go up to the car and have a drink,' said Tom.

'No,' she said. 'Wait.'

She looked up for Pierre. He was not straight ahead of them.

'Where is Pierre?'

Ah, there he was; he was far out, swimming as far as they could see parallel to the beach.

She got up and walked along the beach. The mounting chaos of the sea was like the confusion of her heart. The sea had broken loose from the still sky and the stable earth; her life was breaking loose too from everything she had known. Her life was becoming free and alarmed. The prostration of each wave upon the sand mocked her with the imagination of desire for ever fulfilling and satiate; satiate and fulfilling. She walked dazed and giddily towards Alex as if she were being blown towards him. Her dress blew and the wind wetted her eyes. She lifted her arms above her head and the wind blew into her legs, drove back her skirts. She paused. Did he see her? Did he see her miming her passion with the wind?

She marched back to her husband. The wind caught and blew her almost unwillingly fast towards him.

'Tom!' she said. 'I shall have a child by someone else.'

He looked at her, in his habitual startled stupor. He hated this sea, this beach, this extraordinary country. He simply did not believe in it. Those words seemed like the country, wild and incredible. He just did not believe them, any more than he believed that the wind could speak. God, he thought she'd had her scene for the day and had got over it.

He was struggling.

'I have decided,' she said. It was an ultimatum.

He smiled because he could not speak.

'You don't believe me.'

'If you say so, I believe you.'

She had terrified him. He was like a man blundering about a darkened room. Say? What could he say? She'd be crying before the night was out that she could never leave him. Or would she? He was relieved to see her walk away and to sink back into his habitual stupor. When she had gone he wanted to seize her and shake her. He saw another man lying naked on her; the picture enraged him and yet it gave him the happiness of an inexpressible jealousy. Then tears came to his eyes and he felt like a child.

She was walking away looking for Pierre and thinking, 'He doesn't believe me. He's a lout.'

She watched Pierre as she walked. An old man, a nice old man, a funny old man. And very brave. Two unconcerned men, making no fuss, one old and one young: Pierre and the Jew.

The grace of the Jew, the comic strength of Pierre – they belonged to a free, articulate world. She was opposite to Pierre now. The sea was heavy in his course, the waves weightier there, and once or twice a roller cracked at the crest as he was swimming up it. But he was coming in, she saw, very slowly coming in. He was coming in much farther down. She came back to Tom.

'Look,' she jeered. She seemed to have forgotten her earlier words. 'You said he couldn't swim!' Coram screwed up his eyes. She walked down once more to the place where Pierre would land. The roar of the waves was denser and more chaotic. Tom followed her down. Pierre hardly seemed nearer. It was long waiting for him to come in.

At this end of the beach there was rock. It ran out from the promontory into the water. She climbed up to get a better view. Suddenly she called out in a controlled voice:

'Tom. Come here. Look '

He climbed up and followed her. She was looking down. When he got there he looked down too. 'Hell!' he said.

Below them was a wide cavern worn by the sea with two spurs of rock running out into the water from either side of it. The enormous waves broke on the outer spurs and then came colliding with each other and breaking against the tables of rock submerged in the water, jostled, punched and scattered in green lumps into the cave. With a hollow boom they struck and then swept back on the green tongue of the undertow. The place was like a wide gulping mouth with jagged teeth. Mr and Mrs Coram could not hear themselves speak, though they stood near together looking down at the hole with wonder and fear.

'Tom,' she said, clutching his arm. He pulled his arm away. He was frightened too.

'Tom!' she said. 'Is he all right?'

'What?'

'Pierre – he's not coming in here?' she said.

He looked at the hole and drew back.

'Tom, he is. He is!' she cried out suddenly in a voice that stopped his heart. 'He's drifting. He's drifting in here. These rocks will kill him.'

Tom glared at the sea. He could see it as plainly as she. He backed away.

'The damn fool,' Tom said. 'He's all right.'

'He's not. Look.'

He was drifting. He had been drifting all the time they had talked. They had thought he was swimming parallel to the beach, but all the time he had been drifting.

They could see Pierre plainly. In five minutes he would be borne beyond the first spur and would be carried into the hole.

As he came nearer they saw him at battle. They saw him fighting and striking out with his arms and legs. His cap had come loose and his grey hair was plastered over his head. His face had its little air of deprecation, but he was gasping and spitting water, his eyes were stern and bewildered as if he had not time to decide which of the waves that slapped him on the face was his opponent. He was like a man with dogs jumping up at his waving arms. The Corams were above him on the rock and she called out and signalled to him but he did not look up.

'Are you all right?' she called.

'Course he's all right,' said Coram.

It seemed to her that Pierre refused to look up, but kept his eyes lowered. Increasingly as he got into the outer breakers he had the careless, dead look of a body that cannot struggle any more and helplessly allows itself to be thrown to its pursuers. The two watchers stood hypnotized on the rock. Then Mrs Coram screamed. A wave, larger than the rest, seemed to dive under Pierre and throw him half out of the water. His arms absurdly declaimed in space and a look of dazed consternation was on his face as he dropped into the trough. The sun in the sky flashed like his own monocle upon him and the rich foam.

'Quick. He is going,' she cried to her husband, clambering down the rock to the beach.

'Come on,' she said. He followed her down. She ran towards the surf. 'We'll make a chain. Quick. Take my hand. He's finished. We'll get him before he goes.'

She stretched out her hand.

'Get Alex,' she said. 'Run and get him. We'll make a chain. Quickly run and get him.'

But Tom drew back. He drew back a yard, two yards, he retreated up the beach, backing away.

'No,' he said angrily, waving his arm as though thrusting her away. Yet she was not near him or touching him.

'Tom!' she called. 'Quick. You can swim. I'll come.'

'No,' he said.

She did not see for a moment that the look of angry stupor on his face was fear, that he was prepared to let Pierre drown; and then, as he half ran up the beach, she saw it. He would not go in himself. He would not fetch Alex. He was going to stand there and let Pierre drown. 'Tom,' she called. She saw his thick red glistening face, his immovable glowering struggling stare. He stood like a chained man. He would stand there like that doing nothing and let Pierre drown. She was appalled.

So she ran. She ran down the beach, calling, waving to the Jew.

It happened that he had got up and was wandering idly along the surf towards them. He heard her cry and thought she was calling out with the excitement of the wind. Then he saw.

'Quick,' she called. 'Pierre is drowning.'

She clutched his arm as the Jew came up to her. He gave a glance, jerked away her arm, and ran swiftly along the beach. She followed him. She saw him smile as he ran, the slight gleam of his teeth. When he got near the rock he broke into a short laugh of joy and rushed into the water. In two strokes he was there.

She feared for both of them. She saw a wave rise slowly like an animal just behind Pierre and a second greater one, green as ice and snowy with fluttering spume, following it closely. The two swimmers stared with brief, almost polite surprise at each other. Then the Jew flung himself bodily upon Pierre. An arm shot up. Their legs were in the air. They were thrown like two wrestlers in the water. There was a shout. The Jew came up, his arm went out and his hand – the big hand she had seen upon the table that morning in the Pension – caught the old man under the armpit. They were clear of the rock. They swayed like waltzing partners and then the enormous wave picked them both up, tossed them to its crest and threw them headlong over and over on the shore. The falling wave soaked Mrs Coram as they fell.

Monsieur Pierre crawled dripping up the shingle and sank down panting. His face was greenish in colour, his skin purple with cold. He looked astonished to be out of the sea. The Jew had a lump the size of an egg on his shin.

'I thought I was finished,' Pierre said.

'I'll get some brandy,' Mrs Coram said.

'No,' he said. 'It is not necessary.'

'You saved his life,' she said excitedly to the Jew.

'It was nothing,' he said. 'I found myself the current out there is strong.'

'I could do nothing against the current,' Pierre said. 'I was finished. That,' he said in his absurd negligent way, 'is the second time I have looked death in the face.'

'Rub yourself with the towel,' she said.

He did not like being treated as an old man.

'I'm all right,' he said. After all, once he had attempted to swim the Channel. Perhaps they would believe now he was a swimmer.

'It is always you good swimmers who nearly drown,' she said tactfully.

'Yes,' Pierre boasted, becoming proud as he warmed up. 'I nearly drowned! I nearly drowned! Ah yes, I nearly drowned.'

The emotion of the rescue had driven everything else from her mind. The scene was still in front of her. She looked with fear still at the careless water by the rock where only a few minutes ago she had seen him nearly go. Never would she forget his expressionless head in the water. With the eyelids lowered it had looked grave, detached, like a guillotined head. She was shivering: her fingers were still tightly clenched. Supposing now they had Monsieur Pierre dead beside them. How near they had been to death! She shuddered. The sea, green and dark as a blown shrub, with its slop of foam, sickened her.

He is not very grateful, she thought. And she said aloud:

'Monsieur Pierre, but for Alex you would be dead.'

'Ah yes,' said Pierre, turning to the Jew not very warmly. 'I must express my warmest thanks to you. That is the second time I have looked . . .'

'You get no credit,' she said to Alex in English just in her husband's way. It was odd how she had his habit in a time of stress. 'He thinks he's immortal.'

'Parlez français,' said Pierre.

'She says,' said Alex quickly, 'that you are immortal.'

All this time she was standing up. One side of her dress had been soaked by the wave which had borne them in. As she talked she could see Tom standing forty yards off. He was standing by the car as if for protection and half turned from the sight of the sea. She was still too much in the excitement of the rescue, going over it again and again, to realize that she was looking at him or to know what she thought of him.

'We must get you home,' she said to Pierre, 'quickly.'

'There is no hurry,' he said with dignity. 'Sit down, Madame. Calm yourself. When one has looked death in the face . . .'

She obeyed. She was surprised they thought her not calm. She sat next to Alex as all the afternoon, when he had gone off, she had wished to do. She looked at his arms, his chest and his legs as if to find the courage shining off his body.

'It was nothing.' She could see that this was true. It had been nothing to him. One must not exaggerate. He was young. His black hair was thick and shining and young. His eyes were young too. He had, as she had always thought, that peculiarly ancient and everlasting youth of the Greek statues that are sometimes unearthed in this Mediterranean soil. He was equable and in command of himself, he was at the beginning

of everything, at the beginning of the mind and the body.
There was no difficulty anywhere, it was all as easy as that
smile of his when he ran into the water. Had she been like that
when she was young? How had she been? Had everything
been easy? No, it had been difficult. She could not remember
truly, but she could not believe she had ever been as young as
he was young. Without knowing it, she touched his bare leg
with two of her fingers and ran them down to his knee. The
skin was firm.

'You're cold,' she said. The coldness startled her. He had
probably never slept with a woman. She found herself, as she
touched that hard body which did not move under her touch,
pitying the woman who might have slept with this perfect,
impersonal, impenetrable man.

There was resentment against his perfection, his laugh in
the water, his effortless achievement. He showed no weakness.
There was no confusion in him. There was no discernible vice.
She could not speak.

And now, as she calmed down and saw Tom, her heart
started. She saw, really saw him for the first time since the
rescue and went up the tiring shingle to him. He was still
standing against the car.

'The damn fool,' Coram said before his wife could speak.
'Trying to drown others besides himself. They're all alike.'

'It is no thanks to you that we saved him,' she said. 'Leave
it to me! You ran away!' she said angrily.

'I didn't,' he said. 'Drown myself for a fool like that? What
do you take me for? He wasn't drowning anyway.'

'He was,' she said. 'And you ran away. You wouldn't even
go for Alex. I had to go.'

'No need to shout,' he said. She stood below him on the
shingle and he winced as if she were throwing stones at him.
'These people get me down in this place,' he said, 'going into
a sea like that.'

'You ran away when I called,' she insisted.

'Are you saying I'm a coward?' he said.

He looked at her small, shrilling figure. She was ugly when
she was in a temper, like a youth, gawky, bony, unsensual.

Now she had joined all the things that were against him. The beauty of this country was a fraud, a treachery against the things he had known. He saw the red street of his childhood, heard the tap of his father's hammer, the workers getting off the trams with their packages and little bags in their hands, the oil on their dungarees. He heard the swing door of his laboratory, the drum of machines and smoke drooping like wool through the Midland rain, saw the cold morning placards. That was his life. The emeralds and ultramarine of this sea and the reddened, pine-plumed coast made him think of those gaudy *cocottes* he had seen in Paris. The beauty was corruption and betrayal.

He did not know how to say this. It was confused in his mind. He blustered. He glared. She saw through the glowering eyes the piteous struggle, the helpless fear. He was ugly. He stood there blustering and alone with his dust-covered car, an outcast.

'I'm saying you could have helped,' she said.

She looked in anger at him. Her heart was beating loudly, her blood was up. It was not the rescue – she half realized now – which had stirred her – but the failure to rescue. From the very moment when he had run away, something in her had run after him, clamouring for him, trying to drag him back. Now, his muddle seemed to drag her in too.

'Help that swine!' he said.

Pierre and Alex came to the car carrying their towels.

'You think of no one but yourself,' she said to her husband in front of them. 'For God's sake let's get home.'

Everyone looked at her apprehensively. Coram got into the car and she, determined not to let him escape one moment of her contempt, sat beside him. Pierre and Alex were at the back. In silence they drove from the beach and over the hill from which the white town could be seen stacked closely in the sun, like a pack of tall cards. As the car crawled through the narrow streets which were crowded in the evenings with holiday-makers and workers who came up from the harbour or down from the fields, Pierre put his head out of the window He waved to friends sitting in cafés.

'I nearly drowned!' he called out. 'I nearly drowned.'

'Drowned?' people laughed, getting up from their tables.

'For the second time in my life,' he called, 'I have looked death in the face.'

'Tiens!'

'Yes, I nearly . . .'

Coram trod on the accelerator. Pierre fell back into his seat, his little scene cut short, as they swerved up the dusty road to the Pension.

Coram was silent. They got out and he went to put the car away. Pierre went to his room and she and Alex went up the stairs of the shuttered house to their rooms. She was ahead of him. When she got to his landing she saw his door was open. She turned and said:

'May I see what you are like?'

'Of course,' he said.

She went into his room and he followed her. The shutters were closed and the room was dark and cool. There was the white shape of the bed, the pile of books by its side, the white enamel basin on its iron stand and his suitcase on a chair. He went to push open the shutters.

'Oh, don't do that,' she said. But one shutter slipped open. Her face was white and hard, tragically emptied of all expression as she looked at his polite face.

There was nothing.

She went over and lay on his bed. He raised his eyebrows slightly. She saw him raise them.

'They are hard in this house,' she said. 'The beds.'

'A bit,' he said.

She leant up on one elbow.

'You were plucky,' she said, 'this afternoon. But my husband ran away.'

'Oh, no,' he said. 'He had not changed. He had not been in.'

'He ran away,' she said. 'He wouldn't even go and fetch you.'

'One could not expect . . .' Alex began.

'You mean you are young?' she said.

'Yes,' said Alex.

'My husband is my age,' she said in a hard voice. 'Turned forty.'

'I admired what you did,' she said.

He murmured something politely. She got up and sat on the edge of the bed.

'My skirt,' she said, 'was soaked. Look.'

She pulled it above her knees. 'Feel it,' she said.

He came close to her and felt the frock. She stared into his eyes as he touched the cloth. She was shivering.

'Close the door,' she said suddenly. 'I must take it off. I don't want Monsieur Pierre to see me.' He closed the door. While his back was turned she picked up the hem of her frock and pulled it over her head. She stood bare-legged in her white underclothes. The shoulder strap slipped over her arm. She knew that he saw her white breast.

'In England this might be misunderstood,' she said with a loud nervous laugh. 'But not in France.' She laughed and stared, frightened at him.

'I'm old enough to be your mother, aren't I?'

'Well, not quite,' he said.

She was nearly choking. She could nearly scream. She was ugly and hideous. She had wanted to show him what she was. 'Feel how cold I am,' she said, putting out her leg. He put his hand on her white thigh. It was soft and warm. He was puzzled.

'Do you mind?' she said. She lay back on the bed. Tears came into her eyes when she spoke.

'You are young,' she said. 'Come and sit here.'

He came and sat on the edge of the bed beside her. He was very puzzled. She took his hand. But there was no desire in her. It had gone. Where had it gone? She dropped his hand and stared helplessly at him. She saw that he did not want her and that it had not occurred to him to want her. If she had drawn his head down to her breast she would have been cold to his touch. There was no desire, but only shame and anger in her heart.

'I suppose,' she said suddenly, with a false yawn, 'that this is a little unconventional.'

To her astonishment he got up.

'Have you ever been in love?' she asked in a mocking voice to call him back. 'Hardly, I expect, not yet. You are only a child.'

Before he could answer she said:

'Too young to sleep with a woman.'

Now he looked embarrassed and angry. She laughed. She got up. She was delighted she had made him angry.

She took her frock and waited. Perhaps he would attempt to kiss her. She stood waiting for him. But he did not move. Slowly a horror of what she was doing came over her. There was no desire. She saw, too, a remote fear of her in his brown eyes.

'Thank you,' she said. She put the frock against her breast and went to the door. She hoped for one more humiliation when she opened it: that she should be seen, half naked, leaving his room. But there was no one on the stairs.

From the landing window as she went up she saw the familiar picture. The military rows of the vines in the red soil. The shadow-pocked mountains, the pines. It was like a post-card view taken in the sun, the sun not of today but of other days, a sun which was not warm but the indifferent, hard, dead brilliance of the past itself, surrounding her life.

She lay down on the bed and sobbed with misery and shame as a broken creature will abase itself before a bloodless, un-approachable idol. She sobbed because of her ugliness and of the ugliness of having no desire. She had abased and humili-ated herself. When had the desire gone? Before Alex had rushed to the rescue into the sea it had been there. When?

It had gone when she had heard her husband's refusal and had seen the fear and helplessness in his eyes, the muddle in his heart. Her desire had not gone winged after the rescuer, but angry, hurt, astounded and shocked towards her husband. She knew this.

She stopped weeping and listened for him. And in this clarity of the listening mind she knew she had not gone to Alex's room to will her desire to life or even to will it out of him, but to abase herself to the depths of her husband's abasement. He dominated her entirely, all her life; she wished to be no better than he. They were both of them like that; helpless, halted, tangled people, outcasts in everything they did.

She heard him coming up the stairs.

'Tom,' she called. 'Tom.'

She went avidly to the door.

That evening in the quietness after dinner some friends of Pierre's came in to hear about his escape. He wore his yachting cap that night. Death, he said, had no terrors for him, nor had the sea. In his case the balance of displacement was exact; once already he had looked death in the face. . . . He was the hero. He did not once refer to his rescuer. Two of the guests were English, a Colonel and his wife, and to them Coram, also, told the story. He stumbled over his words. He lumbered on. They sat under the massed black leaves of the mulberry tree.

Mrs Coram sat there calm, clever and experienced, as she always was. Here and there, as she always did, she helped her husband over the story. 'Let me tell you what happened,' she said, smiling. They turned to her with relief, and Coram himself was grateful.

Wonderful story she always tells, they said. Ought to write. Why didn't she take it up? 'Go on, Mrs Coram, give us the lowdown.'

They all laughed, except Pierre, under the trees. He was out of his depth in so much quick English.

It was ridiculous, she said, in her quickest voice, glancing at Alex, to go out in a sea like that. She described the scene.

'Tom tried to persuade him not to go, but he would. You know how vain they are,' she said. 'And then,' she said as they laughed with approval and caught the excitement of her story. 'Poor Tom had to go in to rescue him.'

She looked at them. Her eyes were brilliant, her whole body alive with challenge as she glanced from her visitors to Alex and Tom.

'B . . .' Tom began.

'Alex was at the other end of the beach and Tom had to go in and rescue him,' she repeated.

She looked at all of them with defiance and a pause of pity for Alex; at Tom, like a cracking whip before a too docile lion. The Corams against the world.

Graham Greene

THE DESTRUCTORS

I

IT was on the eve of August Bank Holiday that the latest recruit became the leader of the Wormsley Common Gang. No one was surprised except Mike, but Mike at the age of nine was surprised by everything. 'If you don't shut your mouth,' somebody once said to him, 'you'll get a frog down it.' After that Mike had kept his teeth tightly clamped except when the surprise was too great.

The new recruit had been with the gang since the beginning of the summer holidays, and there were possibilities about his brooding silence that all recognized. He never wasted a word even to tell his name until that was required of him by the rules. When he said 'Trevor' it was a statement of fact, not as it would have been with the others a statement of shame or defiance. Nor did anyone laugh except Mike, who finding himself without support and meeting the dark gaze of the new-comer opened his mouth and was quiet again. There was every reason why T., as he was afterwards referred to, should have been an object of mockery – there was his name (and they substituted the initial because otherwise they had no excuse not to laugh at it), the fact that his father, a former architect and present clerk, had 'come down in the world' and that his mother considered herself better than the neighbours. What but an odd quality of danger, of the unpredictable, established him in the gang without any ignoble ceremony of initiation?

The gang met every morning in an impromptu car-park, the site of the last bomb of the first blitz. The leader, who was known as Blackie, claimed to have heard it fall, and no one was precise enough in his dates to point out that he would have been one year old and fast asleep on the down platform of

Wormsley Common Underground Station. On one side of the car-park leant the first occupied house, No. 3, of the shattered Northwood Terrace – literally leant, for it had suffered from the blast of the bomb and the side walls were supported on wooden struts. A smaller bomb and some incendiaries had fallen beyond, so that the house stuck up like a jagged tooth and carried on the further wall relics of its neighbour, a dado, the remains of a fireplace. T., whose words were almost confined to voting 'Yes' or 'No' to the plan of operations proposed each day by Blackie, once startled the whole gang by saying broodingly, 'Wren built that house, father says.'

'Who's Wren?'

'The man who built St Paul's.'

'Who cares?' Blackie said. 'It's only Old Misery's.'

Old Misery – whose real name was Thomas – had once been a builder and decorator. He lived alone in the crippled house, doing for himself: once a week you could see him coming back across the common with bread and vegetables, and once as the boys played in the car-park he put his head over the smashed wall of his garden and looked at them.

'Been to the loo,' one of the boys said, for it was common knowledge that since the bombs fell something had gone wrong with the pipes of the house and Old Misery was too mean to spend money on the property. He could do the redecorating himself at cost price, but he had never learnt plumbing. The loo was a wooden shed at the bottom of the narrow garden with a star-shaped hole in the door: it had escaped the blast which had smashed the house next door and sucked out the window-frames of No. 3.

The next time the gang became aware of Mr Thomas was more surprising. Blackie, Mike and a thin yellow boy, who for some reason was called by his surname Summers, met him on the common coming back from the market. Mr Thomas stopped them. He said glumly, 'You belong to the lot that play in the car-park?'

Mike was about to answer when Blackie stopped him. As the leader he had responsibilities. 'Suppose we are?' he said ambiguously.

'I got some chocolates,' Mr Thomas said. 'Don't like 'em myself. Here you are. Not enough to go round, I don't suppose. There never is,' he added with sombre conviction. He handed over three packets of Smarties.

The gang were puzzled and perturbed by this action and tried to explain it away. 'Bet someone dropped them and he picked 'em up,' somebody suggested.

'Pinched 'em and then got in a bleeding funk,' another thought aloud.

'It's a bribe,' Summers said. 'He wants us to stop bouncing balls on his wall.'

'We'll show him we don't take bribes,' Blackie said, and they sacrificed the whole morning to the game of bouncing that only Mike was young enough to enjoy. There was no sign from Mr Thomas.

Next day T. astonished them all. He was late at the rendez-vous, and the voting for that day's exploit took place without him. At Blackie's suggestion the gang was to disperse in pairs, take buses at random and see how many free rides could be snatched from unwary conductors (the operation was to be carried out in pairs to avoid cheating). They were drawing lots for their companions when T. arrived.

'Where you been, T.?' Blackie asked. 'You can't vote now. You know the rules.'

'I've been *there*,' T. said. He looked at the ground, as though he had thoughts to hide.

'Where?'

'At Old Misery's.' Mike's mouth opened and then hurriedly closed again with a click. He had remembered the frog.

'At Old Misery's?' Blackie said. There was nothing in the rules against it, but he had a sensation that T. was treading on dangerous ground. He asked hopefully, 'Did you break in?'

'No. I rang the bell.'

'And what did you say?'

'I said I wanted to see his house.'

'What did he do?'

'He showed it to me.'

'Pinch anything?'

'No.'

'What did you do it for then?'

The gang had gathered round: it was as though an impromptu court were about to form and to try some case of deviation. T. said, 'It's a beautiful house,' and still watching the ground, meeting no one's eyes, he licked his lips first one way, then the other.

'What do you mean, a beautiful house?' Blackie asked with scorn.

'It's got a staircase two hundred years old like a corkscrew. Nothing holds it up.

'What do you mean, nothing holds it up. Does it float?'

'It's to do with opposite forces, Old Misery said.'

'What else?'

'There's panelling.'

'Like in the Blue Boar?'

'Two hundred years old.'

'Is Old Misery two hundred years old?'

Mike laughed suddenly and then was quiet again. The meeting was in a serious mood. For the first time since T. had strolled into the car-park on the first day of the holidays his position was in danger. It only needed a single use of his real name and the gang would be at his heels.

'What did you do it for?' Blackie asked. He was just, he had no jealousy, he was anxious to retain T. in the gang if he could. It was the word 'beautiful' that worried him – that belonged to a class world that you could still see parodied at the Wormsley Common Empire by a man wearing a top hat and a monocle, with a haw-haw accent. He was tempted to say, 'My dear Trevor, old chap,' and unleash his hell hounds. 'If you'd broken in,' he said sadly – that indeed would have been an exploit worthy of the gang.

'This was better,' T. said. 'I found out things.' He continued to stare at his feet, not meeting anybody's eye, as though he were absorbed in some dream he was unwilling – or ashamed – to share.

'What things?'

'Old Misery's going to be away all tomorrow and Bank Holiday.'

Blackie said with relief, 'You mean we could break in?'

'And pinch things?' somebody asked.

Blackie said, 'Nobody's going to pinch things. Breaking in – that's good enough, isn't it? We don't want any court stuff.'

'I don't want to pinch anything,' T. said. 'I've got a better idea.'

'What is it?'

T. raised eyes, as grey and disturbed as the drab August day. 'We'll pull it down,' he said. 'We'll destroy it.'

Blackie gave a single hoot of laughter and then, like Mike, fell quiet, daunted by the serious implacable gaze. 'What'd the police be doing all the time?' he said.

'They'd never know. We'd do it from inside. I've found a way in.' He said with a sort of intensity, 'We'd be like worms, don't you see, in an apple. When we came out again there'd be nothing there, no staircase, no panels, nothing but just walls, and then we'd make the walls fall down – somehow.'

'We'd go to jug,' Blackie said.

'Who's to prove? and anyway we wouldn't have pinched anything.' He added without the smallest flicker of glee, 'There wouldn't be anything to pinch after we'd finished.'

'I've never heard of going to prison for breaking things,' Summers said.

'There wouldn't be time,' Blackie said. 'I've seen house-breakers at work.'

'There are twelve of us,' T. said. 'We'd organize.'

'None of us know how . . .'

'I know,' T. said. He looked across at Blackie. 'Have you got a better plan?'

'Today,' Mike said tactlessly, 'we're pinching free rides . . .'

'Free rides,' T. said. 'You can stand down, Blackie, if you'd rather . . .'

'The gang's got to vote.'

'Put it up then.'

Blackie said uneasily, 'It's proposed that tomorrow and Monday we destroy Old Misery's house.'

'Here, here,' said a fat boy called Joe.

'Who's in favour?'

T. said, 'It's carried.'

'How do we start?' Summers asked.

'He'll tell you,' Blackie said. It was the end of his leadership. He went away to the back of the car park and began to kick a stone, dribbling it this way and that. There was only one old Morris in the park, for few cars were left there except lorries: without an attendant there was no safety. He took a flying kick at the car and scraped a little paint off the rear mudguard. Beyond, paying no more attention to him than to a stranger, the gang had gathered round T.; Blackie was dimly aware of the fickleness of favour. He thought of going home, of never returning, of letting them all discover the hollowness of T.'s leadership, but suppose after all what T. proposed was possible – nothing like it had ever been done before. The fame of the Wormsley Common car-park gang would surely reach around London. There would be headlines in the papers. Even the grown-up gangs who ran the betting at the all-in wrestling and the barrow-boys would hear with respect of how Old Misery's house had been destroyed. Driven by the pure, simple and altruistic ambition of fame for the gang, Blackie came back to where T. stood in the shadow of Misery's wall.

T. was giving his orders with decision: it was as though this plan had been with him all his life, pondered through the seasons, now in his fifteenth year crystallized with the pain of puberty. 'You,' he said to Mike, 'bring some big nails, the biggest you can find, and a hammer. Anyone else who can better bring a hammer and a screwdriver. We'll need plenty of them. Chisels too. We can't have too many chisels. Can anybody bring a saw?'

'I can,' Mike said.

'Not a child's saw,' T. said. 'A real saw.'

Blackie realized he had raised his hand like any ordinary member of the gang.

'Right, you bring one, Blackie. But now there's a difficulty. We want a hacksaw.'

'What's a hacksaw?' someone asked.

'You can get 'em at Woolworth's,' Summers said.

The fat boy called Joe said gloomily, 'I knew it would end in a collection.'

'I'll get one myself,' T. said. 'I don't want your money. But I can't buy a sledge-hammer.'

Blackie said, 'They are working on No. 15. I know where they'll leave their stuff for Bank Holiday.'

'Then that's all,' T. said. 'We meet here at nine sharp.'

'I've got to go to church,' Mike said.

'Come over the wall and whistle. We'll let you in.'

2

On Sunday morning all were punctual except Blackie, even Mike. Mike had had a stroke of luck. His mother felt ill, his father was tired after Saturday night, and he was told to go to church alone with many warnings of what would happen if he strayed. Blackie had had difficulty in smuggling out the saw, and then in finding the sledge-hammer at the back of No. 15. He approached the house from a lane at the rear of the garden, for fear of the policeman's beat along the main road. The tired evergreens kept off a stormy sun: another wet Bank Holiday was being prepared over the Atlantic, beginning in swirls of dust under the trees. Blackie climbed the wall into Misery's garden.

There was no sign of anybody anywhere. The loo stood like a tomb in a neglected graveyard. The curtains were drawn. The house slept. Blackie lumbered nearer with the saw and the sledge-hammer. Perhaps after all nobody had turned up: the plan had been a wild invention: they had woken wiser. But when he came closer to the back door he could hear a confusion of sound hardly louder than a hive in swarm: a clickety-clack, a bang bang bang, a scraping, a creaking, a sudden painful crack. He thought: it's true, and whistled.

They opened the back door to him and he came in. He had at once the impression of organization, very different from the old happy-go-lucky ways under his leadership. For a while he wandered up and down stairs looking for T. Nobody addressed him: he had a sense of great urgency, and already he could begin to see the plan. The interior of the house was being carefully demolished without touching the outer walls. Summers with hammer and chisel was ripping out the skirting-boards in the ground floor dining-room: he had already smashed the panels of the door. In the same room Joe was heaving up the parquet blocks exposing the soft wood floor-boards over the cellar. Coils of wire came out of the damaged skirting and Mike sat happily on the floor clipping the wires.

On the curved stairs two of the gang were working hard with an inadequate child's saw on the banisters – when they saw Blackie's big saw they signalled for it wordlessly. When he next saw them a quarter of the banisters had been dropped into the hall. He found T. at last in the bathroom – he sat moodily in the least cared-for room in the house, listening to the sounds coming up from below.

'You've really done it,' Blackie said with awe. 'What's going to happen?'

'We've only just begun,' T. said. He looked at the sledge-hammer and gave his instructions. 'You stay here and break the bath and the wash-basin. Don't bother about the pipes. They come later.'

Mike appeared at the door. 'I've finished the wire, T.,' he said.

'Good. You've just got to go wandering round now. The kitchen's in the basement. Smash all the china and glass and bottles you can lay hold of. Don't turn on the taps – we don't want a flood – yet. Then go into all the rooms and turn out drawers. If they are locked get one of the others to break them open. Tear up any papers you find and smash all the ornaments. Better take a carving-knife with you from the kitchen. The bedroom's opposite here. Open the pillows and tear up the sheets. That's enough for the moment. And you, Blackie, when you've finished in here crack the plaster in the passage up with your sledge-hammer.'

'What are you going to do?' Blackie asked.

'I'm looking for something special,' T. said.

It was nearly lunch-time before Blackie had finished and went in search of T. Chaos had advanced. The kitchen was a shambles of broken glass and china. The dining-room was stripped of parquet, the skirting was up, the door had been taken off its hinges, and the destroyers had moved up a floor. Streaks of light came in through the closed shutters where they worked with the seriousness of creators – and destruction after all is a form of creation. A kind of imagination had seen this house as it had now become.

Mike said, 'I've got to go home for dinner.'

'Who else?' T. asked, but all the others on one excuse or another had brought provisions with them.

They squatted in the ruins of the room and swapped unwanted sandwiches. Half an hour for lunch and they were at work again. By the time Mike returned, they were on the top floor, and by six the superficial damage was completed. The doors were all off, all the skirtings raised, the furniture pillaged and ripped and smashed – no one could have slept in the house except on a bed of broken plaster. T. gave his orders – eight o'clock next morning, and to escape notice they climbed singly over the garden wall, into the car-park. Only Blackie and T. were left: the light had nearly gone, and when they touched a switch, nothing worked – Mike had done his job thoroughly.

'Did you find anything special?' Blackie asked.

T. nodded. 'Come over here,' he said, 'and look.' Out of both pockets he drew bundles of pound notes. 'Old Misery's savings,' he said. 'Mike ripped out the mattress, but he missed them.'

'What are you going to do? Share them?'

'We aren't thieves,' T. said. 'Nobody's going to steal anything from this house. I kept these for you and me – a celebration.' He knelt down on the floor and counted them out – there were seventy in all. 'We'll burn them,' he said, 'one by one,' and taking it in turns they held a note upwards and lit the top corner, so that the flame burnt slowly towards their fingers. The grey ash floated above them and fell on their heads like

age. 'I'd like to see Old·Misery's face when we are through,'
T. said.

'You hate him a lot?' Blackie asked.

'Of course I don't hate him,' T. said. 'There'd be no fun
if I hated him.' The last burning note illuminated his brooding
face. 'All this hate and love,' he said, 'it's soft, it's hooey.
There's only things, Blackie,' and he looked round the room
crowded with the unfamiliar shadows of half things, broken
things, former things. 'I'll race you home, Blackie,' he said.

3

Next morning the serious destruction started. Two were missing – Mike and another boy whose parents were off to Southend and Brighton in spite of the slow warm drops that had
begun to fall and the rumble of thunder in the estuary like
the first guns of the old blitz. 'We've got to hurry,' T. said.

Summers was restive. 'Haven't we done enough?' he said.
'I've been given a bob for slot machines. This is like work.'

'We've hardly started,' T. said. 'Why, there's all the floors
left and the stairs. We haven't taken out a single window.
You voted like the others. We are going to *destroy* this house.
There won't be anything left when we've finished.'

They began again on the first floor picking up the top floor-
boards next to the outer wall, leaving the joists exposed. Then
they sawed through the joists and retreated into the hall, as
what was left of the floor heeled and sank. They had learnt
with practice, and the second floor collapsed more easily. By
the evening an odd exhilaration seized them as they looked
down the great hollow of the house. They ran risks and made
mistakes: when they thought of the windows it was too late to
reach them. 'Cor,' Joe said, and dropped a penny down into the
dry rubble-filled well. It cracked and span amongst the broken
glass.

'Why did we start this?' Summers asked with astonishment;
T. was already on the ground, digging at the rubble, clearing a

space along the outer wall. 'Turn on the taps,' he said. 'It's too dark for anyone to see now, and in the morning it won't matter.' The water overtook them on the stairs and fell through the floorless rooms.

It was then they heard Mike's whistle at the back. 'Something's wrong,' Blackie said. They could hear his urgent breathing as they unlocked the door.

'The bogies?' Summers asked.

'Old Misery,' Mike said. 'He's on his way.' He put his head between his knees and retched. 'Ran all the way,' he said with pride.

'But why?' T. said. 'He told me . . .' He protested with the fury of the child he had never been, 'It isn't fair.'

'He was down at Southend,' Mike said, 'and he was on the train coming back. Said it was too cold and wet.' He paused and gazed at the water. 'My, you've had a storm here. Is the roof leaking?'

'How long will he be?'

'Five minutes. I gave Ma the slip and ran.'

'We better clear,' Summers said. 'We've done enough, anyway.'

'Oh no, we haven't. Anybody could do this –' 'this' was the shattered hollowed house with nothing left but the walls. Yet walls could be preserved. Façades were valuable. They could build inside again more beautifully than before. This could again be a home. He said angrily, 'We've got to finish. Don't move. Let me think.'

'There's no time,' a boy said.

'There's got to be a way,' T. said. 'We couldn't have got thus far . . .'

'We've done a lot,' Blackie said.

'No. No, we haven't. Somebody watch the front.'

'We can't do any more.'

'He may come in at the back.'

'Watch the back too.' T. began to plead. 'Just give me a minute and I'll fix it. I swear I'll fix it.' But his authority had gone with his ambiguity. He was only one of the gang. 'Please,' he said.

'Please,' Summers mimicked him, and then suddenly struck home with the fatal name. 'Run along home, Trevor.'

T. stood with his back to the rubble like a boxer knocked groggy against the ropes. He had no words as his dreams shook and slid. Then Blackie acted before the gang had time to laugh, pushing Summers backward. 'I'll watch the front, T.,' he said, and cautiously he opened the shutters of the hall. The grey wet common stretched ahead, and the lamps gleamed in the puddles. 'Someone's coming, T. No, it's not him. What's your plan, T.?'

'Tell Mike to go out to the loo and hide close beside it. When he hears me whistle he's got to count ten and start to shout.'

'Shout what?'

'Oh, "Help", anything.'

'You hear, Mike,' Blackie said. He was the leader again. He took a quick look between the shutters. 'He's coming, T.'

'Quick, Mike. The loo. Stay here, Blackie, all of you till I yell.'

'Where are you going, T.?'

'Don't worry. I'll see to this. I said I would, didn't I?'

Old Misery came limping off the common. He had mud on his shoes and he stopped to scrape them on the pavement's edge. He didn't want to soil his house, which stood jagged and dark between the bomb-sites, saved so narrowly, as he believed, from destruction. Even the fan-light had been left unbroken by the bomb's blast. Somewhere somebody whistled. Old Misery looked sharply round. He didn't trust whistles. A child was shouting: it seemed to come from his own garden. Then a boy ran into the road from the car-park. 'Mr Thomas,' he called, 'Mr Thomas.'

'What is it?'

'I'm terribly sorry, Mr Thomas. One of us got taken short, and we thought you wouldn't mind, and now he can't get out.'

'What do you mean, boy?'

'He's got stuck in your loo.'

'He'd no business. . . . Haven't I seen you before?'

'You showed me your house.'

'So I did. So I did. That doesn't give you the right to . . .'

'Do hurry, Mr Thomas. He'll suffocate.'

'Nonsense. He can't suffocate. Wait till I put my bag in.'

'I'll carry your bag.'

'Oh no, you don't. I carry my own.'

'This way, Mr Thomas.'

'I can't get in the garden that way. I've got to go through the house.'

'But you *can* get in the garden this way, Mr Thomas. We often do.'

'You often do?' He followed the boy with a scandalized fascination. 'When? What right? . . .'

'Do you see . . . ? the wall's low.'

'I'm not going to climb walls into my own garden. It's absurd.'

'This is how we do it. One foot here, one foot there, and over.' The boy's face peered down, an arm shot out, and Mr Thomas found his bag taken and deposited on the other side of the wall.

'Give me back my bag,' Mr Thomas said. From the loo a boy yelled and yelled. 'I'll call the police.'

'Your bag's all right, Mr Thomas. Look. One foot there. On your right. Now just above. To your left.' Mr Thomas climbed over his own garden wall. 'Here's your bag, Mr Thomas.'

'I'll have the wall built up,' Mr Thomas said, 'I'll not have you boys coming over here, using my loo.' He stumbled on the path, but the boy caught his elbow and supported him. 'Thank you, thank you, my boy,' he murmured automatically. Somebody shouted again through the dark. 'I'm coming, I'm coming,' Mr Thomas called. He said to the boy beside him, 'I'm not unreasonable. Been a boy myself. As long as things are done regular. I don't mind you playing round the place Saturday mornings. Sometimes I like company. Only it's got to be regular. One of you asks leave and I say Yes. Sometimes I'll say No. Won't feel like it. And you come in at the front door and out at the back. No garden walls.'

'Do get him out, Mr Thomas.'

'He won't come to any harm in my loo,' Mr Thomas said,

stumbling slowly down the garden. 'Oh, my rheumatics,' he said. 'Always get 'em on Bank Holiday. I've got to go careful. There's loose stones here. Give me your hand. Do you know what my horoscope said yesterday? "Abstain from any dealings in first half of week. Danger of serious crash." That might be on this path,' Mr Thomas said. 'They speak in parables and double meanings.' He paused at the door of the loo. 'What's the matter in there?' he called. There was no reply.

'Perhaps he's fainted,' the boy said.

'Not in my loo. Here, you, come out,' Mr Thomas said, and giving a great jerk at the door he nearly fell on his back when it swung easily open. A hand first supported him and then pushed him hard. His head hit the opposite wall and he sat heavily down. His bag hit his feet. A hand whipped the key out of the lock and the door slammed. 'Let me out,' he called, and heard the key turn in the lock. 'A serious crash,' he thought, and felt dithery and confused and old.

A voice spoke to him softly through the star-shaped hole in the door. 'Don't worry, Mr Thomas,' it said, 'we won't hurt you, not if you stay quiet.'

Mr Thomas put his head between his hands and pondered. He had noticed that there was only one lorry in the car-park, and he felt certain that the driver would not come for it before the morning. Nobody could hear him from the road in front, and the lane at the back was seldom used. Anyone who passed there would be hurrying home and would not pause for what they would certainly take to be drunken cries. And if he did call 'Help', who, on a lonely Bank Holiday evening, would have the courage to investigate? Mr Thomas sat on the loo and pondered with the wisdom of age.

After a while it seemed to him that there were sounds in the silence – they were faint and came from the direction of his house. He stood up and peered through the ventilation-hole – between the cracks in one of the shutters he saw a light, not the light of a lamp, but the wavering light that a candle might give. Then he thought he heard the sound of hammering and scraping and chipping. He thought of burglars – perhaps they had employed the boy as a scout, but why should burglars

engage in what sounded more and more like a stealthy form of
carpentry? Mr Thomas let out an experimental yell, but nobody answered. The noise could not even have reached his
enemies.

4

Mike had gone home to bed, but the rest stayed. The question
of leadership no longer concerned the gang. With nails, chisels,
screwdrivers, anything that was sharp and penetrating they
moved around the inner walls worrying at the mortar between
the bricks. They started too high, and it was Blackie who hit
on the damp course and realized the work could be halved if
they weakened the joints immediately above. It was a long,
tiring, unamusing job, but at last it was finished. The gutted
house stood there balanced on a few inches of mortar between
the damp course and the bricks.

There remained the most dangerous task of all, out in the
open at the edge of the bomb-site. Summers was sent to watch
the road for passers-by, and Mr Thomas sitting on the loo,
heard clearly now the sound of sawing. It no longer came
from his house, and that a little reassured him. He felt less
concerned. Perhaps the other noises too had no significance.

A voice spoke to him through the hole. 'Mr Thomas.'

'Let me out,' Mr Thomas said sternly.

'Here's a blanket,' the voice said, and a long grey sausage
was worked through the hole and fell in swathes over Mr
Thomas's head.

'There's nothing personal,' the voice said. 'We want you to
be comfortable tonight.'

'Tonight,' Mr Thomas repeated incredulously.

'Catch,' the voice said. 'Penny buns – we've buttered
them, and sausage-rolls. We don't want you to starve, Mr
Thomas.'

Mr Thomas pleaded desperately. 'A joke's a joke, boy. Let
me out and I won't say a thing. I've got rheumatics. I got to
sleep comfortable.'

'You wouldn't be comfortable, not in your house, you wouldn't. Not now.'

'What do you mean, boy?' But the footsteps receded. There was only the silence of night: no sound of sawing. Mr Thomas tried one more yell, but he was daunted and rebuked by the silence – a long way off an owl hooted and made away again on its muffled flight through the soundless world.

At seven next morning the driver came to fetch his lorry. He climbed into the seat and tried to start the engine. He was vaguely aware of a voice shouting, but it didn't concern him. At last the engine responded and he backed the lorry until it touched the great wooden shore that supported Mr Thomas's house. That way he could drive right out and down the street without reversing. The lorry moved forward, was momentarily checked as though something were pulling it from behind, and then went on to the sound of a long rumbling crash. The driver was astonished to see bricks bouncing ahead of him, while stones hit the roof of his cab. He put on his brakes. When he climbed out the whole landscape had suddenly altered. There was no house beside the car-park, only a hill of rubble. He went round and examined the back of his car for damage, and found a rope tied there that was still twisted at the other end round part of a wooden strut.

The driver again became aware of somebody shouting. It came from the wooden erection which was the nearest thing to a house in that desolation of broken brick. The driver climbed the smashed wall and unlocked the door. Mr Thomas came out of the loo. He was wearing a grey blanket to which flakes of pastry adhered. He gave a sobbing cry. 'My house,' he said. 'Where's my house?'

'Search me,' the driver said. His eye lit on the remains of a bath and what had once been a dresser and he began to laugh. There wasn't anything left anywhere.

'How dare you laugh,' Mr Thomas said. 'It was my house. My house.'

'I'm sorry,' the driver said, making heroic efforts, but when he remembered the sudden check to his lorry, the crash of bricks falling, he became convulsed again. One moment the house had stood there with such dignity between the bomb-sites like a man in a top hat, and then, bang, crash, there wasn't anything left – not anything. He said, 'I'm sorry. I can't help it, Mr Thomas. There's nothing personal, but you got to admit it's funny.'

Angus Wilson

AFTER THE SHOW

ALL the way home in the taxi and in the lift up to her flat on the seventh floor Mrs Liebig kept on talking. Sometimes she spoke of the play, making comments to Maurice in the form of questions to which she did not await the answer. The lights of Regent Street and Oxford Street flashed momentarily through the taxi window, caught in the saxe-blue spangles of the ornament that crowned her almost saxe-blue neatly waved hair, reflected in the mirror of her powder compact which seemed always to occupy her attention in taxis. 'Was the father of the girl a fraud then?' she asked, and, 'Why didn't the mother make him work?' 'I suppose,' she said, 'that the old man had used him to get rid of his mistress.' Then, 'What a play,' she exclaimed, 'for a boy of your age to take his grandmother to! But it's clever, of course, too clever, I think. There weren't any real animals you know, in the cage. That was clever.'

More often she commented on family affairs. 'Your father needs a real rest,' she said, 'let's hope your mother sees that he gets it. It's not the way to take holidays – mixing business up with pleasure. Of course your mother will want to spend a lot of time with her own people, that's only natural. They have a very nice house, you know, the Engelmanns in Cologne. Or they used to have. Anything might have happened to it now. But she *must* think of your father all the same. That won't be much of a holiday for Norman, talking German all the time. Though he's a wonderful linguist, your father, you know.'

Once she said, 'Well we must try to imagine what they are doing now,' but the effort was apparently too great for her, because she went straight on, 'Lending her house to those Parkinsons. What a thing for your mother to do! But then they don't have to think about money, so there'd be no sense in all the trouble of letting.' Her tone was at once reverent and sarcastic.

Maurice said nothing, indeed he hardly stirred, except once or twice to light Mrs Liebig's cigarette with the lighter she handed him from her bag. She shared his parents' constant concern that he should have perfect manners with women. After the theatre, his slim body, usually so loosely and naturally elegant, remained tense – a tailor's-dummy woodenness perhaps more in keeping with the slightly over-careful elegance of his clothes than his usual poise. A tension too came into the expression of his large dark eyes, ordinarily a trifle cow-like in their placid, liquid sensuality. It was not so much that he remained hypnotically bewitched by the play's deception, but rather that he dreaded returning from its dramatic reality to the fraudulent flatness of his own life. He seemed to strain every nerve to keep the play in action, to spin out at least its mood from the theatre into the commonplace texture of his own life. His apprehension announced his experience that the task was vain, his nervous elation a certain fear that he might on this occasion succeed. It was the same, too, with every theatrical performance from Shakespeare to musical comedy. In addition to this adolescent histrionic restlessness, however, there was a somewhat plodding seriousness which demanded a peculiarly strong response to 'good' plays.

Tonight, after *The Wild Duck*, then, his earnest good taste reinforced his emotions in their struggle against the invasion of his grandmother's voice. The underlying Jewish cockney note of her cracked contralto jarred more than usual and he could not condemn his unfeeling snobbery without also condemning his mother, for Mrs Norman Liebig was forever saying that 'Grandmother's voice was such a pity'.

As they entered the hall of the flat, old Mrs Liebig's well-corseted plump body collided as usual against one of the giant-size Japanese pots as she searched for the light switch, but she still continued to talk. 'Well, there it is,' she said, 'so the poor little girl committed suicide. No wonder with a father who was a liar and did nothing all day. All the same,'

she said, and the electric light shone brightly upon heavily
rouged high cheek-bones, 'I don't think a little girl like that
would shoot herself. More likely the mother – tied to such a
man.'

Maurice took her black moiré silk evening coat off her
shoulders, and folded it carefully, smoothing the squirrel-skin
collar; then he said, 'Gregers Werle was a fanatic. In his false
determination to expose the truth, he destroyed the poetry in
Hedwig's life and drove her to her death.' His voice was a
shade higher than usual and its normal slight sibilance had a
hissing edge. Even Mrs Liebig was struck by the fierceness of
his tone, she looked up for a moment from the telephone pad
on which the maid had noted a message. 'Oh, it's a dreadful
thing all right,' she said, 'to destroy young people's dreams.'
But there was a limit to her sentiment, or perhaps she remembered her own comfortable, prosaic childhood, for she added,
'What a way to bring a child up! With all those fancies. No,'
she said emphatically, 'it's not the sort of thing I'd have gone
to if you hadn't taken me. But I'm glad I've seen it. The acting
was fine.'

In the sitting-room the brown velvet sofa and easy chairs
looked hot and uninviting on this warm spring evening.
Mrs Liebig automatically moved one or two of the daffodils in
the thick shell-shaped white earthenware vase. She crossed the
room and drew the long heavy velvet curtains, shutting out
the night breeze. 'Go on, Maurice,' she said, 'help yourself,
tuck in.' And she slapped the handle of the silver-shaded green
metal cocktail wagon. 'Your father said you could have two
beers or one whisky.'

Maurice gave himself a lager and turned to his grandmother, but she answered his gesture before he spoke, 'No,
I'll have my nightcap after my bath,' she said, but she helped
herself to a large canapé of prawns in aspic from a white-and-
gold-painted metal table. 'Go on,' she said again, 'tuck in.'

Maurice surveyed the array of gelatinous hors d'oeuvres.
The Norman Liebigs also always had a mass of foodstuff
awaiting their return from the theatre, but true to her German
origin, Mrs Norman saw that everything was cooked at home.

Maurice could hear his mother's disapproving tones – 'Poor Grandmother lives from Selfridge's cooked provision counter' – so he contented himself with a cheese straw.

Mrs Liebig trotted out of the room and came back with the rubber ice container from the refrigerator. She dropped a square of ice with the tongs into Maurice's beer and kissed his forehead. She was happy to have for a while a man to wait on. 'So there you are, my dear,' she said. 'That was your Uncle Victor phoned while we were out. Ah, well, some trouble again. Money for the dogs or for that Sylvia. It comes to the same thing, my dear. In any case it can wait for tomorrow.'

At the mention of his Uncle Victor's name, Maurice's curved nostril dilated for a moment, adding to the camel-like arrogance of his thin, sensitive face. Mrs Liebig flushed above her rouged cheek-bones to her temples.

'Oh, there's no good putting your head in the air at your Uncle's name, my dear. He hasn't had your father's luck nor his brain. But business brains aren't everything. I know. I've got them. I've made money, but that's not all in life.' Her grandson's complete stillness seemed to anger her, for she added loudly, 'Who built your father's business up, eh? And they can't do anything now, you know, my dear, unless *I* agree. I'm still a director. What does your mother say to that?'

To this attack on his mother, Maurice answered quietly, 'We see Aunt Paula regularly.'

It had all the effect he desired. Mrs Liebig's large dark eyes narrowed with fury. 'All right, you see your Aunt Paula. So do I. And she's a clever buyer and she knows it. But that's not flesh and blood. What if your Uncle Victor did leave her? How did she treat him? I can't understand your father. He knows the world. He knows well enough that Paula only married Victor because she thought he would be a success. And when he wasn't, she turned to and made success for herself. All right, she's a clever girl. But all the time she let him know it. That's not love.'

'Father helped Uncle Victor for years,' Maurice said coldly. He took out an orange-wood stick and began to clean his nails.

'And you've got clean nails and he hasn't,' Mrs Liebig cried. 'Very good. Yes, your father helped Victor. So did I. So should we all, his family. Rose sends him money from New York. It's flesh and blood, my dear. I could hardly *tell* Rose that your father doesn't see Victor any more. She asked me how the hell can they be like that when they're brothers. And now *you're* not to see Victor. Your mother told me, "We don't wish Maurice to meet Victor." She wants to have it every way. The Liebigs are no good because they have no culture. "Norman doesn't care for music. I want Maurice to care for things besides money." Very well. Your Uncle Victor cares for things besides money and he's a Liebig. He's a good artist. His cartoons made money and then those film people changed their minds and so he didn't make any more money. Oh, yes, your mother likes artists, but she doesn't like them to be out of work. I know.'

Maurice rose and picked up a book from the table. 'I can't listen to you if you talk about Mother like this,' he said.

'What do you mean you can't listen? A boy of your age,' Mrs Liebig cried. 'You'll listen to what I choose to tell you, my dear. You're going to Cambridge and you're going to be a lawyer. Nothing to do with the rag business for Gertrude Liebig's son. Well, designing dresses and selling them has more art in it than arguing in law courts. You listen to sense for once instead of to your "Wild Ducks". Mustn't meet your own uncle. You're old enough to decide for yourself.'

She was breathless by now with anger and sweating through through her heavy make-up. She put her hand to her breast.

'That's the sort of fool I am, upsetting myself for a foolish boy. All this has nothing to do with you,' she shouted, 'discussing your uncle at your age. Why, you're only just seventeen.' She drew her compact, plump little body to its full five feet four. 'I'm going to have my bath,' she said and walked trimly out of the room, teetering a little as always in her very high heels.

Maurice arranged himself negligently on the striped period Regency couch in order to control his rising hysteria. Because these people, his father, his mother, his grandmother had conditioned him to love them, they had no scruple in tearing him apart. 'Very well,' as his grandmother said, they had him emotionally, but his mind remained entirely indifferent, even contemptuous – no, not contemptuous, for that involved some engagement – to them. He chose carefully the words in which he set his thoughts – 'emotionally', 'involved', 'engagement' – for words shaped one's thinking. He could forgive them working off their loneliness, their ambitions, their nervous exhaustion on him; what he could not forgive – or rather accept, for forgiveness suggested some demand on his part and he asked nothing of them – what he could not *accept* was this inclusion in their empty, flat lives. Yes, even his mother, with her cultural aspirations; it was almost easier for someone with ideas to accept a woman like his grandmother with her tough, vulgar pushing ways.

Carefully adjusting the sharp creases of his chocolate-brown trousers as he crossed his legs, he applied himself to Burke's speeches. Through the clever passion and the stirring elegance of the oratory he tried to control his impatience, his furious wish to have the years pass more quickly so that he could live a proper life of high responsibility, of tempered adult courage. For this age of mediocrity, of grubbing merchants and sordid artisans – this age of Liebigs would pass; he and his generation would see to that. But meanwhile, if only something would happen – something real and not just on the stage.

When Mrs Liebig emerged from the bath-room, she poked her head round the sitting-room door. Between the folds of her gold thread dressing-gown, her breasts showed sagging; her face was flat, dead with vanishing cream; her blued hair frizzed out from a silver hair-net. 'How's your book, Maurice?' she asked with a smile. Anger was soon gone with her. 'We must get the man to the T.V., my dear. It's not right for it to go wrong like this. I paid a lot of money for that machine. Get me my night-cap,' she said, 'I'll be back in a minute. On the rocks,' she added. She had brought the phrase back from her visit to her daughter Rose in New York and she loved to use it.

When she returned to her strong whisky, she settled down

to her favourite half an hour's chat before bed. She had the impression that the daily routine of her life left no time for real conversation, although she had never been silent even at the height of her active career as Madame Clara, modiste.

She tried this evening to keep her talk off family matters. 'I don't know what I shall do next winter,' she said. 'The Palace is closing down. There's not another hotel like it in Madeira. They've known me since before your grandfather died. The head porter always asks after you – the young gentleman with the books.'

As Maurice made no answer, she tried hard to connect with him. 'The boys still dive, you know,' she said. 'Crabs and sponges.' The words in her mouth brought Maurice no evocation of sub-tropical romance. 'I wonder if Senhora Paloes will be at Biarritz this year. She plays very high stakes. These Brazilians are so rich, you know, my dear.' But her annual holidays – Madeira in February, Biarritz in June – were so much a routine even to her, that she could find little to say of them.

'Well,' she asked, 'who are you meeting tomorrow? The Clarkson girl or Betty Lewis?'

'I'm going out with some friends from school,' Maurice said firmly to avoid his grandmother's roguish innuendo, but to no avail.

'You prefer the little blondes, don't you, Maurice? She was very pretty, that girl in the stalls.'

Despite his annoyance at her noticing his glances in the theatre, he did not wish to appear priggish, so he said, 'Yes, wasn't she?'

'That's what I tell your mother,' Mrs Liebig said. 'Let Maurice find his girls for himself. Always arranging theatre parties for the Clarksons or dinner dances with Adela Siegl's girl. He'll go out with his old grandmother when he's with *me*, I said. Let him find his girls for himself.'

Maurice did not wish to side too openly with her against his mother, so he merely smiled.

'And tomorrow evening a nice show for *me*,' Mrs Liebig continued, 'a nice musical show – *The Pajama Game*. Rose saw it in New York. She said it was tops. Not a show for *you* this time. A show for the children. For the old girl.' She laughed in delight at her little joke – a harsh braying jay sound that seemed almost to call forth an answering note from the telephone.

'Oh, my dear, so late,' Mrs Liebig exclaimed. 'You answer, Maurice. Is it Victor? What does he want? I can't speak now. It's too late.' She chattered on, so that Maurice had to stop one ear with a finger to hear his correspondent.

'You're wanted at once,' he said. 'Sylvia is very ill. Uncle Victor's not there. They can't find him.'

'Well, I can't go like this,' Mrs Liebig was indignant. 'What's she got? A pain or something?'

'It's very urgent,' Maurice said, speaking gravely as though the person at the other side might hear Mrs Liebig's levity. 'She's had an accident.'

'Oh, my God!' Mrs Liebig cried. 'The damned fool girl. Poor Victor! Well, what can I do?'

'Mrs Liebig will come as soon as possible. I shall come immediately,' Maurice said into the telephone. 'I'm Mrs Victor Liebig's nephew.'

Mrs Liebig got up from her chair, drawing the gold and green dressing-gown round her, slopping a little in her mules. 'You can't go *there*,' she said. 'What do you mean "Mrs Victor Liebig's nephew"? You've never seen the girl?'

Maurice said, 'Someone must go. The woman on the phone wouldn't say exactly, but she implied that it wasn't an accident. I think she wanted to say that Sylvia had tried to kill herself.' His eyes were no longer flat and dead. 'She couldn't find anyone else,' he said, as though that clinched the matter.

But for his grandmother it did not. 'Oh, my God!' she cried. 'What does Victor want to mix up with such little fools for? I should never have agreed to meet the girl,' she added, as though her recognition of her son's mistress had given the girl aspirations above her station, encouraged her to ideas of suicide.

Maurice seemed not to hear her. 'You'd better get dressed as soon as you can and follow me over there,' he said and

moved to the door. Mrs Liebig ran after him, holding her
dressing-gown round her with one hand, she put the other on
his arm. 'I don't know what . . .' she said. 'Norman will never
forgive me. You'll have to answer to your mother, you know.
You're not to meet Victor and now you rush off to see his girl.
I don't know . . .' Maurice went out of the room. She followed
him, shouting into the darkness of the hall. 'They're not
married, you know.' She knew perfectly well that he knew, she
shouted it as though it were a threat. Only the click of the
front door latch answered her.

At first, in the taxi, sailing down an empty Baker Street,
Maurice was only aware that monotony had been broken;
held up by lights at the Edgware Road junction, however,
he became nervous of what he would find at the end of his
journey. The urgent and mysterious voice on the telephone
had enveloped him at once in drama; he couldn't at that moment have handed over his part to his grandmother, however
little he knew his lines. Now, however, apprehension made
him search for evasions: if the Liebigs were in the caste, he
thought, even courtesy Liebigs like Sylvia, it was bound to
turn out to be some sordid melodrama. With the taxi in progress again, he felt the elation of duty; if the cause he was
serving had neither quite the glory nor the high intent that he
would have liked, at least there was a cause to serve – and this,
as all his little group knew well, was what their generation had
been cheated of. Besides how few of his friends were likely to
be involved with mistresses who tried to commit suicide, he
reflected with a glow of pride.

Pride, however, has its fall, and as the taxi-driver braked
sharply to avoid a drunk at Westbourne Grove, Maurice was
jolted into disgust at his childishness. He blushed with shame
as though one of his friends – Gervase or Selwyn Adcock –
had heard his thoughts. They were all agreed, of course, the
whole group, that sin today was as drab and inglorious as
virtue. 'Simply the blowsy Britannia on the reverse of the fake
coin,' Gervase had said last term. By the time the taxi drew up
at 42, Branksome Terrace, Maurice had found many reasons to
support his anxious dislike of his self-imposed chivalry.

As he looked out at the dirty mid-Victorian house with its peeling stucco and straggles of grimy Virginia creeper, he saw a world whose unfamiliarity daunted him. He longed for the central heating, the books, the modern reading lamp, the iced drink, of his bedroom in his grandmother's flat. There were theatres too cheap and squalid to play in. Maurice was about to tear up his contract and tell the taxi-driver to take him home, when the front door opened and a thin, dark-haired young woman in blue jeans came out on to the steps. 'Mr Liebig,' she called, in an over-refined, slightly petulant voice. 'Mr Liebig? This is the house.' Maurice got out and paid the fare.

'I'm Freda Cherrill,' the young woman said. 'The person who phoned to you.' Her thin, yellowish face looked so drawn and tired, and her voice was so languid that Maurice felt that he dared not question her. She drew him into a little ill-lit hall and bent her long neck – yellow and grubby above her blue and white striped shirt – down towards him. Her large dark eyes were vacant rather than sad. Her breath came scented but a little sour as she whispered into his face. 'I'd better give you all the gen before you go in,' she said, and pointing towards the door at their side. 'She's in there.'

Maurice felt able to assert himself. 'Is the doctor with her?' he asked.

'I'm afraid not,' Miss Cherrill replied a little petulantly. 'He was dining in Putney, but he's on his way.'

'But surely,' Maurice cried, 'there was some doctor nearer.'

'I only know Dr Waters,' Miss Cherrill replied. 'She doesn't seem to have a doctor of her own.' Her languid voice became quite sharp with disapproval. 'So naturally I had to send for mine. He's always been very good with my anaemia and he's a very understanding man.'

'I don't know what has happened,' Maurice said, cutting through her petulance with a certain hauteur.

'Well, I couldn't very well say everything on the phone, could I?' Miss Cherrill was quite annoyed. 'She doesn't want Mr Morello and everybody else involved.'

'Where is my uncle?' Maurice asked.

'Oh!' Miss Cherrill said scornfully, 'if we knew that. ...
She's comfortable enough now. I kept walking her up and
down the room at first, I thought I had to keep her awake, she
was so dozey, but Dr Waters said she hadn't taken enough to
make it serious and in any case with aspirins ...'

'So she *has* tried to commit suicide.'

'I told you so,' Miss Cherrill said angrily.

'I didn't quite understand.'

'Well, you can see the telephone's in the hall. She asked
me not to bring everybody into it. Morello's room's only
down there.' She pointed along the hall. 'I don't know them,'
she spoke quite loudly in her annoyance. 'I heard her crying.
My room's next door. It went on for ages so I went in.'

'You've been very good,' Maurice said. 'Thank you.'

'It was lucky I was washing my hair,' Miss Cherrill replied
– 'I nearly always go out of a Wednesday. Besides, it's not
often anything happens in life, is it?'

Maurice felt disgusted by his own emotions expressed from
another mouth, so he said, 'I think I'd better go in and see her.'

'Of course,' Miss Cherrill said, 'someone ought to be very
stern with her. I told her myself that it could have meant a
police case, and would do now if I hadn't had a word with
Dr Waters. Not that he probably won't be pretty sharp with
her himself, I expect. She's *got* to be frightened.' All Miss
Cherrill's sympathy, even her pleasure at events out of the
ordinary were dissipating now that someone else was taking
over: she was very tired, she was going out the next evening
and her hair was still filthy. 'Well,' she said in final tones, 'I'm
glad there's somebody else here she knows at last. She's still
very weepy and a bit dazed. She's been awfully sick, you know.'

'I'm afraid,' said Maurice, 'that she doesn't know me at all.
We've never met.' Miss Cherrill stared at him in disgust.

'Well,' she said, 'I suppose it's all right. You're very young,
aren't you? But it's only someone to sit with her. And, anyway, she doesn't seem to have any real people.' She opened
Sylvia's door and peered in. 'She's all right for you to come in,'
she said, and then her refined petulance leaving her for a moment, 'The smell of sick isn't too bad, is it? I've drenched the

room in eau-de-Cologne.' She whispered loudly and with relish. Maurice said nothing; even the faintest smell of vomit made his stomach heave in protest.

Apart from the double bed in the corner and one broken-down, hair-oil-stained armchair, the room seemed as bare as it was large. The only dressing-table was made from something that looked like an inverted packing-case. On it were crowded lotions, creams and powders; above it hung some home-made contraption that had brought the electricity by means of a profusion of wires from its lonely eminence in the centre of the high ceiling. The walls were cream-distempered and dirty; someone had started to cover one of them with a cheap 'modernistic' wallpaper. Over an old towel-horse hung a black skirt, a white muslin blouse, stockings and underwear. There were books and magazines in scattered heaps on the matting-covered floor; an uncovered typewriter crowded, with a portable gramophone and records, the small top of a rickety varnished bedside table. On the walls were pinned, in profuse disorder, Victor's drawings, giving the room the appearance of a school art exhibition. In the bed Sylvia lay. Against the blue whiteness of her face the bed linen showed grey, and the pillow-case shone greasy under her thick but dirty fair hair.

Despite all the pallor and the grubbiness, however, she looked so young and delicious to Maurice – especially so much younger than he had expected, no older perhaps than he was – that he was unable to speak and he felt the giddiness and trembling of the legs which lust always brought to his repressed body. Her eyes seemed to him extraordinarily sensual under their drowsing, half closed, red lids; her white cheeks were nevertheless plump about their high pommets and her heavy lips were half opened in a Greuze-like pout. She looked altogether like some eighteenth-century print of a young dying harlot – ostensibly a morality, in fact a bait for prurient eyes.

Maurice felt embarrassedly that Miss Cherrill's eyes were upon him, putting his manhood to the test. He summoned all his wits to find something to say – something that would mark his authority. Before he could find words, however, Sylvia's sobbing swelled to convulsive breathing and then burst into a loud, hysterical weeping – the hideous, uncontrolled crying of a frightened, spoilt child. With children Maurice knew himself to be powerless.

Miss Cherrill looked at him for a moment, then she walked over and shook Sylvia roughly. 'Stop that noise at once,' she said. 'You'll look a fool if the doctor finds you like this.' Her action had no effect except that Sylvia hit out at her flat bosom.

'Go away,' she cried. 'Go away all of you. I won't see you or your bloody doctor.'

It seemed to Maurice that if he could do nothing with Sylvia, he could at least order Miss Cherrill about. 'I think you'd better leave us,' he said.

'I'm sure I've no wish to stay,' Miss Cherrill replied. 'This has been a lesson to me, I can tell you.'

Maurice opened the door for her. 'Thank you very much for all you have done,' he said, but she went without looking at him.

He stood for a moment staring at Sylvia. He was embarrassed at the pleasure her crying brought to him. It was not, however, his first intimation of the quirks of sexual desire. He hastened to efface the disturbing emotion with redoubled kindness. 'I should like very much to help you if I can.' The words when they came seemed very inadequate and stiffly formal; their effect on Sylvia however, was immediate.

'Get out of here, get out of here,' she screamed. 'I want to be left alone.'

The request seemed to Maurice so reasonable that he was about to walk out, when Sylvia leaned over the side of the bed and, picking up a slipper from the floor, she threw it at his head. Her half-doped aim was feebly wide of the mark. Nevertheless, it produced a strange effect on Maurice; he walked very deliberately over to the bed and smacked Sylvia's face. Then he kissed her clumsily and excitedly on the mouth. Her breath, sour through the eau-de-Cologne fumes, checked his excitement. The whole chain of his behaviour was so surprising to him that he just sat on the bed and stared not at Sylvia but slightly over her head.

'You look like a fish,' she said. She was not crying now, but he realized that her ordinary speaking voice was strangely husky.

'I'm sorry,' he said, 'I came here to help you.'

'You do,' she said.

To Maurice her strangely direct but slightly goofy manner recalled so much that he had heard in the theatre. If he had met neither the tragedy nor even the melodrama for which he had been prepared, here surely at least was English comedy at its best. He tried to forget the appearance of the room. Decor was after all an overrated aspect of the stage. He, too, must be laconic, off hand, bohemian, modern.

'Why did you do it?' he asked.

The question, alas, only brought on crying so violent that he could hardly hear himself speak. 'You'll only bring Miss Cherrill back,' he shouted.

'She's an interfering cow,' Sylvia sobbed. 'I hate her.'

'She's been very kind, I should have thought.'

'She wasn't, she just wanted to gloat.'

'Oh! please,' Maurice cried, 'don't let's discuss that. Can't you tell me what's wrong?'

'Why should I?' Sylvia asked, 'I don't know you.'

This, however, seemed unreasonable, so Maurice said, 'Why did you get Miss Cherrill to ring up my grandmother if you didn't want our help?'

This again set Sylvia crying. 'You think I didn't mean to do it. You think I got frightened. That's what you'll tell Victor, isn't it? It's easy to say someone is just a hysteric.' And when he made no answer, 'Go on, that's what you think, isn't it?' she cried.

It was, in fact, what Maurice was thinking, as far as he could in her presence; but as he had had no experience of hysterics, he did not feel fully justified in making the judgement; and, in any case, if she was, it was surely most important to calm her, since both shaking and slapping which he had always supposed to be the sovereign remedies had failed. 'I think you must be very unhappy,' he said, 'and if I can help you I should like to do so.' It was not perhaps the high purpose in life which his generation was seeking, but it was a sincere wish.

It did, indeed, also succeed in calming Sylvia a little. 'I'm in such a mess,' she said, 'such a terrible mess. I've let myself love a man who's a liar, a real hopeless liar. And that's a terrible thing to do!' She announced this gravely as one of the profound, the ultimate truths of life. 'He says there isn't someone else,' she said, 'but I know better. I know her name. It's Hilda. Isn't it awful?' She began once more to sob.

Maurice could not feel this so deeply, but he said, 'It's not a very nice name certainly.'

Sylvia immediately began to pound on his leg with her small clenched fists. 'Oh, you silly little fool,' she shouted, 'Victor's left me. Can't you understand? He's left me. All Thursday I guessed he was going and I said to him, "Victor, if you don't love me any more, well then tell me. I can take it," I said. But he just smiled, smiled to madden me. "You want me to get mad at you," I said, "so that you can have your excuse. Well, I'm not going to do it. I can take the truth," I told him. Well,' she cried, turning suddenly on Maurice, 'if I am hard and tough before I should be, what made me that way? What's life done for little Sylvia Wright?'

If she had intended an answer to this vital question, Maurice was not to hear it, for at that moment there was a noise of braking outside the house, of voices raised, of bells rung. Among the voices Maurice could hear his grandmother's. He moved to the door, wishing that he could kiss Sylvia again before Mrs Liebig came on the scene.

'You can't even bother to listen to me and yet you ask me how it happened. I think you are despicable,' Sylvia said.

It was true that he had ceased listening to her as soon as a rival noise came to attract his attention, but then her torrent of words had been so sudden and so uncontrolled.

'You think because I've been in prison . . .'

'I knew nothing about that,' Maurice interrupted. 'But in any case I can't let my grandmother stand out there for ever.'

When he came into the hall, a little old woman in a dressing-gown was making her way crabwise and very slowly down the stairs. 'Everyone's in such a hurry nowadays,' she said, 'I'm coming as quickly as I can.'

'I think they're ringing for me,' Maurice said.

'Well, I didn't suppose they were ringing for *me*,' the old woman replied, but she began slowly and with heavy dragging of her feet to go back up the stairs.

Before Maurice could get to the front door, however, another door at the end of the passage opened and a plump, dark young man, also in a dressing-gown, stuck his head out. 'If that ringing's for you,' he said, 'I should be obliged if you'd answer it quickly.' Before Maurice could answer, he added, 'If you're connected with Mrs Liebig I may as well tell you now that I have the whole matter under review.' The door closed again and he was gone.

When Maurice opened the front door he found a clean-shaven, middle-aged man in evening dress standing on the step. He was smoking a pipe and looked, Maurice thought, like a naval officer. There was no sign of Mrs Liebig.

'Liebig?' asked the man shortly. It was clear that he found the name unpleasant to pronounce.

'Are you Dr Waters?' Maurice asked; he had already resented the delay in the doctor's arrival sufficiently to pronounce his name with equal distaste.

'Yes, yes,' said Dr Waters impatiently. 'I'd better see this young woman as soon as possible.'

'I'm her nephew,' Maurice announced himself. 'I think she's all right now.'

'That's really for me to decide, old chap. It's far from what Miss Cherrill said. I suppose she's with the girl.'

'No,' Maurice said, 'she's gone up to her room.'

Dr Waters turned and grinned boyishly, 'Well, I dare say we can get over that little loss,' he said. 'Lead the way, old chap, will you?'

Maurice indicated Sylvia's door. 'If you don't mind I think I ought to look for my grandmother. I heard her voice out-side.'

'There's an old girl knocking daylight out of a taxi-driver,' Dr Waters said, and he knocked on Sylvia's door. Maurice, wondering if the doctor were drunk, went out into the darkness.

There indeed was Mrs Liebig arguing with a taxi-driver. She had reacted to the emergency by putting on a pair of royal blue slacks, a short fur coat and a cyclamen silk scarf wound turbanwise around her head. It was the costume in which she had braved the air raids, but as Maurice's memory did not go back to this time, he felt only acute embarrassment at her appearance.

When she saw her grandson, she called raucously, 'Well, it's all right, my dear, he's going to wait.' She came up the steps puffing and grumbling. 'What do they think we are?' she asked. 'Paupers? "You'll get good money," I told him. Ring for another taxi? What does he mean? I'll pay him to wait. I've got the money. "Ring up and perhaps there aren't any more taxis," I told him. "I'm an old woman!" I told him. "Do you think I want to wait about all night in a place like this?" '

Maurice said sharply, 'Sylvia's been very ill. The doctor's with her now. She tried to kill herself but she only made herself sick.'

'Well, there you are,' Mrs Liebig said, 'Victor should never have picked up with her.'

'You've no need to worry about *him*,' Maurice said bitterly. 'He's left her for some other woman.' And when he saw that his grandmother was about to defend her son, he interrupted violently, 'He's lucky not to have a murder on his hands.'

'Murder?' Mrs Liebig said. 'Don't talk nonsense. You don't know what you are talking about. A boy of your age mixed up in all this. Where's her own people, anyway? What's her mother doing? My God, what a rotten world we live in.'

At his grandmother's words, all Maurice's heroic mood shrivelled inside of him. He felt that he had simply muddled the whole affair; he had never inquired about Sylvia's parents. 'She's very young,' he said hesitatingly; he could think of nothing else to express what he felt for Sylvia.

'Young,' Mrs Liebig echoed scornfully. 'That's the trouble.

A lot of children's nonsense, the lot of you. Well, where is the girl?' And when Maurice moved towards Sylvia's door, she pushed past him and brusquely forced her way in.

Sylvia was lying back on the pillows – a ghostlike little waif. To Maurice's eyes she seemed to have faded surprisingly far out of life in the short while he had been gone.

'Well,' said Dr Waters, 'she's going to be all right. Aren't you, young woman? If she'd taken anything but aspirins she'd be dead. As it is I've given her an injection just to help nature along.'

Maurice who was sceptical of the knowledge of general practitioners assumed the air of an educated mission school-boy before the tribal witch doctor; but Mrs Liebig exclaimed knowingly, 'Ah, there you are.'

Dr Waters now assumed a stern look. 'I need to know a bit more about all this, though. I'll have to examine the patient a bit further. I must ask you to wait outside,' he announced.

'Yes, yes,' Mrs Liebig cried, 'you can't be here when doctor's examining her, Maurice. That wouldn't do at all.' Maurice moved towards the door. 'I'll call you when doctor's done,' Mrs Liebig said.

Dr Waters swung on her angrily. 'Will you kindly follow him. I want to talk to the young woman alone.'

Mrs Liebig's face was crimson, 'Don't you order me about,' she cried, 'I've no intention of leaving this girl in here with you.'

It was Dr Waters's turn to approach apoplexy. 'I would remind you, Madam,' he said, 'that it may well be my duty to turn this matter over to the police with unpleasant consequences for those responsible for this girl's welfare.'

Mrs Liebig was too astonished to reply. Maurice looked for some contradiction of the doctor's innuendo from Sylvia, but she had only faded further away into the ghost world. 'Now then,' Dr Waters cried sharply. 'Out with the lot of you.'

In the passage Mrs Liebig gave it to Maurice good and proper. 'Can't you behave like a gentleman?' she asked. 'Good God! What would your father say? So I've had to wait for my old age to watch my grandson stand by and see me insulted. How do you know he's a doctor?' she asked. 'What's he doing in there with that girl? They're pretty filthy, some of these doctors; I could tell you stories. What does Victor think I am? To be at the beck and call of every little tart he picks up off the street – his own mother!' And so on.

Maurice said nothing; indeed he heard very little – his thoughts were entirely upon Sylvia, a little puzzling at her sudden languishing, but in the main just dwelling on her.

It was over ten minutes before Dr Waters emerged from the room. Mrs Liebig was already urging that they should leave. 'Let her stew in her own dirty juice,' she said. 'She got what she was after with her tricks. Good God! I should think Victor *has* left her, and if he never takes up with her again, good riddance to bad rubbish.'

Dr Waters cut into all this abruptly. 'I think she'll be all right now,' he said. 'I apologize if I seemed rude but one must have a free hand in these affairs. I should like,' he added, 'someone to stay with her. She's still a little hysterical, and I can't say that I'm surprised. Besides, when that husband of hers comes back, heaven knows what may happen. Can I rely on one of you to stop with her?'

Mrs Liebig's expression was so unpromising that Dr Waters seemed finally to decide on Maurice as his assistant, despite his youth. He took him by the arm and drew him aside, 'If that brute comes back and pesters her,' he said, 'you may tell him that I shall be over in the morning and that I shall have one or two very unpleasant words to say to him. You can say,' he chuckled sardonically, 'that if he's so anxious for a thrashing he may well get it from an unexpected quarter. Filthy brute! Keep her quiet,' he added. 'Poor little creature!'

Before he left the house, he bowed to Mrs Liebig. 'Good-night to you, Madam,' he said. But she did not acknowledge his salute.

Back in the bedroom, Maurice had scarcely time to register the charm of Sylvia's wan smile, before the old crab-sidling woman came hobbling in. Like Dr Waters, she disregarded Mrs Liebig, so that Maurice began to wonder whether his grandmother's trousers, so unsuitable to her age, had robbed her of all claim on public respect.

'Mr Morello wants to see you right away,' the old woman mumbled to him.

'I shan't be a few minutes,' he said to Mrs Liebig and, determined on his new authority, he was gone from the room before she could protest.

Mr Morello seemed also to accept Maurice's authority; indeed he appeared anxious to counter with a demonstration of his own powers of command. He had changed his dressing-gown for a dark, rather too carefully 'city' suit and had seated himself at a large roll-topped desk which loomed incongruously in the obvious bed-sitting-room. His stature as landlord was asserted only in the neat divan bed and the unvarnished 'modernistic' wardrobe and chest-of-drawers – a setting two whole 'bed-sitter' social grades above the furnishings he provided for his tenants. Even to Maurice's eye Mr Morello seemed ill at ease in his authority. His plump young face was smooth with massage, the bluish stubble of his heavy jowl was carefully powdered; but on his neck was an angry boil and his fingers seemed unable to leave it alone.

'I'm afraid this can't go on, you know,' he said. His voice was surprisingly light for so heavy a man; his accent was Birmingham.

Maurice looked round the room and sat down on the divan. 'Of course, of course,' Mr Morello said. He was clearly embarrassed at his failure as host. 'You'll excuse this spot,' he said, and when Maurice did not answer, he added in extenuation, 'It's a boil, you know. There's nothing to do but wait for them to come to a head.' Feeling that he had gone too far perhaps in excuses, he sat back in his swivel chair and folded his hands over his stomach. 'I know things are difficult,' he said with paternal pomposity. 'It's a very bad time indeed for artists.' He spoke with the authority of a gamekeeper pronouncing on the part-ridge season. 'We all get to the end of our tether at times. Some quite small trouble or other comes along and we break. I've felt like that with this boil.' He laughed deprecatingly but it was clear that he did not feel the irritation to be a small one. To

Maurice he seemed so like a vulgar parody of his form master that he expected him to add, 'But do *I* break down and try to commit suicide?'

Instead Mr Morello pushed out his thick underlip, looking like a sea elephant. 'This house is a good part of my living,' he announced, 'and I can't have it getting a bad name. This sort of thing might easily lose me tenants. Good tenants. Paying tenants,' he added ominously. 'With all due allowance and having every sympathy I hope, if it happens again they'll have to go. Will you please tell Mrs Liebig that, when she's recovered enough to face the facts of the situation.' He paused and then as though resolving the situation from superior wisdom, he said, 'It may well be a good thing to frighten her a bit.'

Maurice was annoyed at the man's patronizing tone; he felt dissatisfied too with his own lack of command over the situation. He searched for some means of asserting himself; then, 'I think it was quite unnecessary of Miss Cherrill to have shouted my aunt's private affairs about the house.'

Only his dislike of Mr Morello had made him speak and he immediately expected a sharp rebuff, but the landlord only pouted like a fat, cross baby. 'I don't want any trouble with Miss Cherrill, please,' he said pleadingly. 'She's a good, paying tenant. I'm sure I'm glad to have made contact with one of Mrs Liebig's family,' he smiled. 'It's a thousand pities she's had such bad luck. There's money to be made in dancing today. Really good dancing.' He was clearly a man who prided himself on knowing how things stood in the world of today. 'But there you are, accidents may happen to anyone.'

Maurice could make nothing of this so he did not reply.

'Well,' Mr Morello cried cheerily, 'she'll be all right with you there, I can see.' He got up and opened the door for Maurice; he was clearly anxious to efface his previous insufficient manners. 'I feel a lot happier for our little chat,' he said. 'You really must excuse me receiving you in this state.' Once more his fingers went up to the boil on his neck. 'If there's hot water or anything needed I'm sure Martha will be glad to oblige.'

Mrs Liebig was standing in the hall when Maurice came out.

'Ah, good God, there you are,' she cried, 'do you think I'm made of money? Keeping that taxi there all night.'

As though to underline her anxiety, the door-bell buzzed loudly; and when Maurice opened it, there was indeed the taxi-driver.

'All right, all right,' Mrs Liebig cried, 'I'm coming. Do you think you're going to lose your money?'

The little, greyfaced old taxi-driver seemed so cowed by her that he only said, 'Well, it's a long time, lady.'

'A long time?' Mrs Liebig cried, 'there's illness here; of course it's a long time. Well, Maurice are you ready?'

'I must stay here. The doctor asked me to.' Maurice tried to sound as casual as he could manage, but he felt, though he could not explain why, that his whole future happiness depended upon his getting his way about this.

'Stay here? Good God! The girl's all right now. Stay here? Of course you can't stay here with that girl alone in her bedroom, a young man of your age. What good would you be anyway, a boy like you?'

'The doctor . . .' Maurice began, but she broke in furiously.

'What do we know about the doctor, anyway? You and your doctors – you wait until you know a bit more about life,' she added darkly.

Maurice's thin face was tensed. 'Either you or I must stay,' he said, 'unless we're to risk a death on our hands.' Perhaps it was the sibilance of his voice betraying to her his emotional state, or perhaps it was the fear that she might indeed have to stay; whatever the cause Mrs Liebig gave a hard little laugh. 'All right,' she cried, 'I wash my hands. You and your morbid ideas. But *you* must explain to your mother. I hope you enjoy upsetting everybody like this, for that's what you're doing.'

To Maurice's surprise she then went into Sylvia's room and, crossing to the bed, kissed the girl warmly on both cheeks. 'Maurice is staying to see you're a good girl,' she said. 'Now, don't you worry. You're a good girl, even if you are a little fool. Victor'll find his luck again. You don't have to blame yourself. That Paula must give him a divorce. You'll see, it'll turn out all right. Oh, yes,' she cried, turning to Maurice, 'I know. Happy endings aren't good enough for your clever ways. It's all got to be deaths and suicides and wild ducks. But Sylvia isn't such a little fool as that. She'll be all right.' She kissed the girl again.

Once more Maurice felt surprise, for Sylvia looked at Mrs Liebig with little girl's rounded eyes. 'Thank you,' she whispered gently, 'you've been so very kind. You've helped me to believe again a little.'

Mrs Liebig only said, 'Now you sleep, my dear, and you let her sleep, Maurice.'

Now that he was alone with Sylvia, Maurice was completely bewildered. He had asserted his right to remain on the stage, but of what the play was about he was entirely ignorant. For two years now, since his sixteenth birthday, he had been schooling himself to the sense of authority, the power of command, the heroic role which he and his friends in the Upper Sixth were determined to assume. They had discussed it so often, schooled themselves for the task of leadership which would fall to their generation – leadership out of the desert of the television world, out of the even more degrading swamps of espresso bar rebellion. They had fed themselves on high purposes and self discipline, on gallantry and panache, on Carlyle and Burke. Now for the first time he was called upon to control a situation, however paltry the occasion, and yet the situation seemed to drift by while he stood, like a night stroller on the towing-path scarcely able to distinguish water from land. He was emerging not as the hero leader but as that feeble figure, the homme moyen sensuel – the 'hero' type of all the literature that he and his friends most despised. And he saw no way out of it.

Sylvia accepted his silence at first, lying back on her pillows. With the eyes closed, her face seemed strangely smooth and empty of life; she looked both older and lost. Gradually her underlip protruded in a silky pout and her forehead wrinkled in a frown. To Maurice she now appeared like a sullen, bored child; but as he could make no sense of all that he had seen and heard of her, he tried to ignore this new ugly impression that she made on him. Suddenly the frown and the pout disappeared; opening her eyes, she looked at him tragically. 'Why do you think God hates me so?' she asked.

A question based on so many doubtful premises shocked Maurice deeply; such melodramatic speech from such attractive lips disturbed him even more.

Sylvia sensed his disquiet, she let her hand fall on the eiderdown in front of her in a gesture of hopelessness. 'Oh God! always trying to find a way out, always trying to find someone else to put the blame on, even poor old God. Do you ever hate yourself like hell?' she asked.

This question was somewhat easier for Maurice to answer, although he found its formulation hardly more to his taste. 'Quite often,' he said. 'I should think most people of any intelligence or feeling do at some time or other.'

Sylvia seemed to ponder for a moment. 'You understand things so well and yet you're so young,' she said simply.

It was so exactly what Maurice had hoped to think of himself, and yet so exactly what he now doubted, that he looked at her covertly to see if she was speaking sarcastically; but her expression was one of childlike wonderment.

'How old are you?' she asked.

'Almost eighteen.'

'Almost,' she said, and she smiled. 'That makes me terribly old. I'm twenty-three,' she said.

'That's not old, really,' Maurice tried not to sound a little disappointed.

'Almost eighteen and you know so much. I wish you could teach me some of it.' Sylvia's wondering far-away voice would not have disgraced a performance of Marie Rose.

His age was not exactly what Maurice wished to harp upon, and her praise, though pleasing, was an indulgence high purpose did not allow him. 'I'm afraid there isn't much point in our discussing these things unless you tell me why you wanted,' he paused a moment and then, determinedly realistic, ended, 'to kill yourself. Something Miss Cherrill said made me think . . .' he went on and then stopped again – to speak about pregnancy was embarrassing, but then Dr Waters's suggestion about Uncle Victor's depraved sexual tastes was an even less possible topic of conversation.

Sylvia's pupils contracted to two minute forget-me-nots. 'What did Miss Cherrill say?' she asked, her husky voice now edgy.

'That you were going to have a baby . . .'

Maurice wished now that he had set about assuming control in a different way, but he was left little time to regret, for Sylvia burst out in fury, 'That lying cow,' she said. 'Anyway, I've got a bloody sight better chance than her. No man would give her one. How dare she open her filthy mouth about my affairs? I'll have it out with her now.' She began to lift herself with difficulty from the bed.

Maurice put his hand on to her arm. 'No,' he said, 'you must stay where you are. Perhaps I misunderstood her.'

For whatever reason, Sylvia seemed willing to accept his restraint. 'And if I *were* going to, as if I shouldn't know where to go to get rid of it. Better than that silly bitch would,' she said and lay back on the pillows once more, smiling to herself.

Maurice's silence weighed down upon her satisfaction, however, and broke it. She turned to him angrily again, 'You think I'm pretty sordid, don't you?' she asked.

'I wasn't making any judgement. I was just trying to understand, that's all,' he replied. The words came out automatically and he blushed not only for their priggishness but for their untruth – he *had* been thinking the whole episode sordid.

'Well, you *should* think it sordid – sordid and disgusting. For that's what it is. You've no idea of the foul things . . .'

'I think I have,' Maurice said. 'Dr Waters told me something.'

Sylvia began to giggle. 'What did *he* say?'

Maurice found this quite difficult; to begin with he wasn't quite sure if he had interpreted Dr Waters aright, and then he was also very uncertain if his interpretation might not be nonsense. He knew there were such sexual deviations, but applied to Sylvia and Victor it seemed absurd. He did not want to make a fool of himself.

'Come on,' said Sylvia sharply. 'What did he say?'

So urged, Maurice blurted it out crudely, 'He said Victor made you beat him and that was why you'd . . .'

Sylvia, to his consternation, roared with laughter. 'Dr Waters is a fool,' she said. 'Dr Waters made a pass, and that was naughty of Dr Waters, so Sylvia told him where he could put his pass.'

It was, perhaps, the theatricality of her manner that suddenly decided Maurice. All his bewilderment suddenly vanished as a pattern formed before him. 'That's not true. None of what you've been saying is true – to Dr Waters or to Morello or to Grandmother or to me. You just make up stories about yourself.'

Sylvia leaned quickly out of the bed and smacked his face. 'You get out of here,' she said, 'go on, get out.'

Maurice rose, there seemed nothing else to do but go. He had not moved, however, before she burst into tears.

'It's true,' she cried. 'Oh God! it's true. But what else is there to do when I'm so unhappy. That or get out of it, out of all this useless meaningless squalor. I'm so unhappy,' she said again, 'and so bored. What's the point of life? Oh, it's different for you . . .'

'No,' said Maurice, 'it isn't.' And he told her of his own despair and boredom. She listened for a while like an attentive child, then she seemed to grow restless with her own silence. Once or twice she tried to break in but Maurice was intent on confiding his troubles. At last she cried, 'Well then, if you feel like that, what's the hope for someone like me? You don't know what real dull respectability is like, or worse still this sort of sordid disreputable life.'

Then in her turn she told her story – a more vivid recitation than Maurice's. The large family, the dead drudgery of the Luton newspaper shop her parents owned, running away to London, film extra work, Woolworth's soap counter, hostess at a little club, Victor.

It was at once a story so familiar to Maurice from what he had read in the newspapers and so personal from her vivid narration, that he was spellbound. He only interrupted her once, 'And prison?' he asked.

'Oh, the whole thing's a prison,' she cried.

'Is all this true that you're telling me?' he demanded. 'No, I shouldn't have said that. Only it's all so difficult.'

'Oh, yes, you should,' she replied. 'How can you believe me when I've told you so many lies. But it *is* true. Not what I've said before. That about prison was just to make myself interesting. It wasn't even true about Victor. He hasn't been unfaithful. He just didn't come back tonight because it's all so hopeless. He feels he can't help me and he's right, nobody can. I'm no use.'

It was now Maurice knew that he ought to convince her of what life could be, *was* going to be when his generation got their chance, but he found himself taking advantage of a quite different chance. He got up and kissed her. When he found that she lay so passive in his embrace, his shyness left him and he kissed her excitedly if a little clumsily on mouth and cheeks, ears and neck. She lay purring like a white cat that has found warmth.

'It's nice,' she said in her husky voice, 'we're both young and that's right, isn't it?'

He had hardly started to stroke her arms again a little clumsily before she seemed to become drowsy. Then she pushed him away – but gently.

'No,' she said, 'it's no good. Victor and I belong to each other. It may be hell but that's the way it is.' Maurice noticed for the first time that her voice had assumed a faint American note. 'Victor and I are downhillers,' she said. 'You're not. Look,' she went on, 'I like you. You understand so much and you've helped. I need a friend who I can talk to. Will you be my friend?'

Maurice could not remember feeling so depressed, but he summoned all his courage to assent.

'I want to sleep now,' she said. 'And you must go, because if Victor comes back he'll be worried if you're here and I'm too tired to face any more trouble.'

'The doctor said . . .' Maurice began.

'Please, don't make it worse.'

'All right,' Maurice said, 'but you won't be silly again.'

'Cross my heart,' she said. 'Come and see me again. I like to hear you talk.'

Maurice moved to the door. 'Of course, I shall come tomorrow to see how you are.'

Sylvia seemed to hesitate, then she smiled lazily, 'Okay,' she said, 'but don't come before five. I'm going to have a lovely long sleep,' and she curled down among the grubby sheets and blankets.

Maurice could find no taxi until he reached Marble Arch and by that time he was so absorbed in trying to sort out his emotions that he preferred to walk home.

He too slept long and heavily. Mrs Liebig was already lunching when he woke. She seemed anxious at first that he should have been involved in last night's trouble. 'I don't know what to say to Norman,' she said. 'He ought to be pleased that you did so much for his brother's girl. But heaven knows what your mother may say. I can't tell their ideas. Better say nothing. Yes, that's it,' she cried, 'tell them nothing. Do you hear, you're to tell them nothing. 'All the same you behaved well, Maurice.'

When she found that he ate a good lunch, she seemed less worried. 'Victor's got in a fine mess,' she said. 'All the same it's his life. That Paula must give him a divorce. I shall tell her. She's got a good job; what's she want to hang on to him for?' But when Maurice asked her if she had arranged to see Aunt Paula, she answered vaguely. 'Time enough,' she said. 'Besides it's all nonsense. You're not to think any more of it, do you hear? At your age. There's quite enough with your wild ducks. All that Sylvia and Victor. It's a lot of nonsense. It's just the way they live.' And with that she dismissed the subject. She was more intent that he should meet her on time for *The Pajama Game*.

Maurice found himself near Westbourne Grove long before five o'clock, but he passed the time impatiently in a tearoom. When at last five o'clock sounded from a nearby church, he ran all the way to Sylvia's house for fear that she might be annoyed at his lack of punctuality. When Sylvia opened the door, his fears seemed to be realized, for she scowled at him.

Her appearance in daylight surprised him; she was shorter than he had expected, and as a result her plumpness seemed a little gross. Her breasts reared at him aggressively through her tight white sweater and her hips seemed almost tyre-like beneath her tighter black skirt. Heavy, bright lipstick made her cheeks seem waxen. Her fair hair fell loosely across her forehead. All in all, however, she sharpened his desire.

'Oh! hullo,' she said a little crossly. 'I'm nearly ready. You'd better come in while I finish my face. Victor's expecting us at the club.'

In the bedroom she put on an Elvis Presley record on the gramophone and sat before the mirror doing her eyebrows. Maurice tried to make conversation but her inattention and the deafening volume of 'Blue Suede Shoes' made it impossible. He sat on the bed and stared disconsolately into the distance. When at last she had finished, he met her turning glance with a smile. She smiled in return and stopped the record, 'Elvis the pelvis,' she said, but there seemed to be no possible reply.

'It's only a little drinking club,' she announced, 'but we always go there.' Before they left the house, she added, 'It was sweet of you to come round.'

The club was up three flights of bare wooden stairs and very dark when you entered. The radiogram here was playing Dickie Valentine. There were only three people sitting at the bar and none of them was Victor.

'Hullo, Sylvia,' the barman said, and a thin dark girl cried, 'Sylvia, darling!'

'Hullo,' said Sylvia, 'I expected Victor.'

'He's gone to the little boys' room,' said the girl. 'He'll be back in a jiffy.'

'This is Maurice,' Sylvia said. 'Maurice, meet Joy and Davy. King of his own frontier,' she added and laughed depressedly.

'What's it to be?' Davy asked.

'Gin,' said Sylvia. 'Gin and what, Maurice?'

But Maurice was seized with panic. He must be gone before

Victor returned. 'I really think I'll have to go,' he said, 'I've got to be at the theatre.'

'Oh God!' cried Sylvia, 'do you really go to the theatre? It's ghastly.'

'I haven't been to the theatre for years,' Joy announced. 'We always go to the pictures.'

'I'm afraid I must go, though,' Maurice said.

'Well, yours was a quick one all right,' Davy said.

Just as Maurice was stumbling out on to the top step in the darkness, he found Sylvia beside him. 'I'm being bloody, I know,' she said, 'but that's how it has to be.' Once more her accent was American. 'I do need your friendship though. More than you know. I can't go on with it all much longer, even for Vic's sake. Can I call on you to help if things get too bad?'

Maurice was afraid of falling down the stairs so it was with difficulty that he said, 'Yes, of course.'

'It may be sooner than you think. It may be tonight,' Sylvia answered and kissed him on the mouth. Then she went back into the club room. Maurice stumbled down the stairs.

All the way back in the taxi from *The Pajama Game* Mrs Liebig hummed 'Fernando's Hideaway'. 'That was a good show,' she said. 'Something to take away with you.' She was tired, however, and had her nightcap in bed. Maurice sat up and read Burke's chivalrous challenge to arms in defence of the fair, unhappy Queen of France. He found it difficult, however, to feel sufficiently for Marie Antoinette's wrongs and once or twice he half rose from his chair, thinking that he had heard the ring of the telephone.

Muriel Spark

YOU SHOULD HAVE SEEN THE MESS

I AM now more than glad that I did not pass into the grammar school five years ago, although it was a disappointment at the time. I was always good at English, but not so good at the other subjects!!

I am glad that I went to the secondary modern school, because it was only constructed the year before. Therefore, it was much more hygienic than the grammar school. The secondary modern was light and airy, and the walls were painted with a bright, washable gloss. One day, I was sent over to the grammar school, with a note for one of the teachers, and you should have seen the mess! The corridors were dusty, and I saw dust on the window ledges, which were chipped. I saw into one of the classrooms. It was very untidy in there.

I am also glad that I did not go to the grammar school, because of what it does to one's habits. This may appear to be a strange remark, at first sight. It is a good thing to have an education behind you, and I do not believe in ignorance, but I have had certain experiences, with educated people, since going out into the world.

I am seventeen years of age, and left school two years ago last month. I had my A certificate for typing, so got my first job, as a junior, in a solicitor's office. Mum was pleased at this, and Dad said it was a first-class start, as it was an old-established firm. I must say that when I went for the interview, I was surprised at the windows, and the stairs up to the offices were also far from clean. There was a little waiting-room, where some of the elements were missing from the gas fire, and the carpet on the floor was worn. However, Mr Heygate's office, into which I was shown for the interview, was better. The furniture was old, but it was polished, and there was a good carpet, I will say that. The glass of the bookcase was very clean.

I was to start on the Monday, so along I went. They took me to the general office, where there were two senior short-hand-typists, and a clerk, Mr Gresham, who was far from smart in appearance. You should have seen the mess!! There was no floor covering whatsoever, and so dusty everywhere. There were shelves all round the room, with old box files on them. The box files were falling to pieces, and all the old papers inside them were crumpled. The worst shock of all was the tea-cups. It was my duty to make tea, mornings and after-noons. Miss Bewlay showed me where everything was kept. It was kept in an old orange box, and the cups were all cracked. There were not enough saucers to go round, etc. I will not go into the facilities, but they were also far from hygienic. After three days, I told Mum, and she was upset, most of all about the cracked cups. We never keep a cracked cup, but throw it out, because those cracks can harbour germs. So Mum gave me my own cup to take to the office.

Then at the end of the week, when I got my salary, Mr Heygate said, 'Well, Lorna, what are you going to do with your first pay?' I did not like him saying this, and I nearly passed a comment, but I said, 'I don't know.' He said, 'What do you do in the evenings, Lorna? Do you watch Telly?' I did take this as an insult, because we call it T.V. and his remark made me out to be uneducated. I just stood, and did not answer, and he looked surprised. Next day, Saturday, I told Mum and Dad about the facilities, and we decided I should not go back to that job. Also, the desks in the general office were rickety. Dad was indignant, because Mr Heygate's concern was flourishing, and he had letters after his name.

Everyone admires our flat, because Mum keeps it spotless, and Dad keeps doing things to it. He has done it up all over, and got permission from the Council to remodernize the kitchen. I well recall the Health Visitor, remarking to Mum, 'You could eat off your floor, Mrs Merrifield.' It is true that you could eat your lunch off Mum's floors, and any hour of the day or night you will find every corner spick and span.

Next, I was sent by the agency to a publisher's for an interview, because of being good at English. One look was enough!! My next interview was a success, and I am still at Low's Chemical Co. It is a modern block, with a quarter of an hour rest period, morning and afternoon. Mr Marwood is very smart in appearance. He is well spoken, although he has not got a university education behind him. There is special lighting over the desks, and the typewriters are the latest models.

So I am happy at Low's. But I have met other people, of an educated type, in the past year, and it has opened my eyes. It so happened that I had to go to the doctor's house, to fetch a prescription for my young brother, Trevor, when the epidemic was on. I rang the bell, and Mrs Darby came to the door. She was small, with fair hair, but too long, and a green maternity dress. But she was very nice to me. I had to wait in their living-room, and you should have seen the state it was in! There were broken toys on the carpet, and the ash trays were full up. There were contemporary pictures on the walls, but the furniture was not contemporary, but old-fashioned, with covers which were past standing up to another wash, I should say. To cut a long story short, Dr Darby and Mrs Darby have always been very kind to me, and they meant everything for the best. Dr Darby is also short and fair, and they have three children, a girl and a boy, and now a baby boy.

When I went that day for the prescription, Dr Darby said to me, 'You look pale, Lorna. It's the London atmosphere. Come on a picnic with us, in the car, on Saturday.' After that I went with the Darbys more and more. I liked them, but I did not like the mess, and it was a surprise. But I also kept in with them for the opportunity of meeting people, and Mum and Dad were pleased that I had made nice friends. So I did not say anything about the cracked lino, and the paintwork all chipped. The children's clothes were very shabby for a doctor, and she changed them out of their school clothes when they came home from school, into those worn-out garments. Mum always kept us spotless to go out to play, and I do not like to say it, but those Darby children frequently looked like the Leary family, which the Council evicted from our block, as they were far from houseproud.

One day, when I was there, Mavis (as I called Mrs Darby by then) put her head out of the window, and shouted to the boy, 'John, stop peeing over the cabbages at once. Pee on the lawn.' I did not know which way to look. Mum would never say a word like that from the window, and I know for a fact that Trevor would never pass water outside, not even bathing in the sea.

I went there usually at the week-ends, but sometimes on week-days, after supper. They had an idea to make a match for me with a chemist's assistant, whom they had taken up too. He was an orphan, and I do not say there was anything wrong with that. But he was not accustomed to those little extras that I was. He was a good-looking boy, I will say that. So I went once to a dance, and twice to films with him. To look at, he was quite clean in appearance. But there was only hot water at the week-end at his place, and he said that a bath once a week was sufficient. Jim (as I called Dr Darby by then) said it was sufficient also, and surprised me. He did not have much money, and I do not hold that against him. But there was no hurry for me, and I could wait for a man in a better position, so that I would not miss those little extras. So he started going out with a girl from the coffee bar, and did not come to the Darbys very much then.

There were plenty of boys at the office, but I will say this for the Darbys, they had lots of friends coming and going, and they had interesting conversation, although sometimes it gave me a surprise, and I did not know where to look. And sometimes they had people who were very down and out, although there is no need to be. But most of the guests were different, so it made a comparison with the boys at the office, who were not so educated in their conversation.

Now it was near the time for Mavis to have her baby, and I was to come in at the week-end, to keep an eye on the children, while the help had her day off. Mavis did not go away to have her baby, but would have it at home, in their double bed, as they did not have twin beds, although he was a doctor. A girl I knew, in our block, was engaged, but was let down, and even

she had her baby in the labour ward. I was sure the bedroom
was not hygienic for having a baby, but I did not mention it.

One day, after the baby boy came along, they took me in the
car to the country, to see Jim's mother. The baby was put in a
carry-cot at the back of the car. He began to cry, and without a
word of a lie, Jim said to him over his shoulder, 'Oh shut
your gob, you little bastard.' I did not know what to do, and
Mavis was smoking a cigarette. Dad would not dream of
saying such a thing to Trevor or I. When we arrived at Jim's
mother's place, Jim said, 'It's a fourteenth-century cottage,
Lorna.' I could well believe it. It was very cracked and old, and
it made one wonder how Jim could let his old mother live in
this tumble-down cottage, as he was so good to everyone else.
So Mavis knocked at the door, and the old lady came. There
was not much anyone could do to the inside. Mavis said, 'Isn't
it charming, Lorna?' If that was a joke, it was going too far.
I said to the old Mrs Darby, 'Are you going to be re-housed?'
but she did not understand this, and I explained how you
have to apply to the Council, and keep at them. But it was
funny that the Council had not done something already, when
they go round condemning. Then old Mrs Darby said, 'My
dear, I shall be re-housed in the Grave.' I did not know where
to look.

There was a carpet hanging on the wall, which I think was
there to hide a damp spot. She had a good TV set, I will say
that. But some of the walls were bare brick, and the facilities
were outside, through the garden. The furniture was far from
new.

One Saturday afternoon, as I happened to go to the Darbys,
they were just going off to a film and they took me too. It was
the Curzon, and afterwards we went to a flat in Curzon Street.
It was a very clean block, I will say that, and there were good
carpets at the entrance. The couple there had contemporary
furniture, and they also spoke about music. It was a nice place,
but there was no Welfare Centre to the flats, where people
could go for social intercourse, advice, and guidance. But they
were well-spoken, and I met Willy Morley, who was an artist.
Willy sat beside me, and we had a drink. He was young, dark,

with a dark shirt, so one could not see right away if he was clean. Soon after this, Jim said to me, 'Willy wants to paint you, Lorna. But you'd better ask your Mum.' Mum said it was all right if he was a friend of the Darbys.

I can honestly say that Willy's place was the most unhygienic place I have seen in my life. He said I had an unusual type of beauty, which he must capture. This was when we came back to his place from the restaurant. The light was very dim, but I could see the bed had not been made, and the sheets were far from clean. He said he must paint me, but I told Mavis I did not like to go back there. 'Don't you like Willy?' she asked. I could not deny that I liked Willy, in a way. There was something about him, I will say that. Mavis said, 'I hope he hasn't been making a pass at you, Lorna.' I said he had not done so, which was almost true, because he did not attempt to go to the full extent. It was always unhygienic when I went to Willy's place, and I told him so once, but he said, 'Lorna, you are a joy.' He had a nice way, and he took me out in his car, which was a good one, but dirty inside, like his place. Jim said one day, 'He has pots of money, Lorna,' and Mavis said, 'You might make a man of him, as he is keen on you.' They always said Willy came from a good family.

But I saw that one could not do anything with him. He would not change his shirt very often, or get clothes, but he went round like a tramp, lending people money, as I have seen with my own eyes. His place was in a terrible mess, with the empty-bottles, and laundry in the corner. He gave me several gifts over the period, which I took as he would have only given them away, but he never tried to go to the full extent. He never painted my portrait, as he was painting fruit on a table all that time, and they said his pictures were marvellous, and thought Willy and I were getting married.

One night, when I went home, I was upset as usual, after Willy's place. Mum and Dad had gone to bed, and I looked round our kitchen which is done in primrose and white. Then I went into the living room, where Dad has done one wall in a patterned paper, deep rose and white, and the other walls pale rose, with white woodwork. The suite is new, and Mum keeps everything beautiful. So it came to me, all of a sudden, what a fool I was, going with Willy. I agree to equality, but as to me marrying Willy, as I said to Mavis, when I recall his place, and the good carpet gone greasy, not to mention the paint oozing out of the tubes, I think it would break my heart to sink so low.

Kingsley Amis

INTERESTING THINGS

GLORIA DAVIES crossed the road towards the Odeon on legs that weaved a little, as if she was tipsy or rickety. She wasn't either really; it was just the high-heeled shoes, worn for the first time specially for today. The new hoop ear-rings swayed from her lobes, hitting her rhythmically on the jaws as she walked. No. They were wrong. They had looked fine in her bedroom mirror, but they were wrong, somehow. She whipped them off and stuffed them into her handbag. Perhaps there'd be a chance to try them again later, when it was the evening. They might easily make all the difference then.

She stopped thinking about the ear-rings when she found she couldn't see Mr Huws-Evans anywhere in the crowd of people waiting for their friends on the steps of the Odeon. She knew at once then that he hadn't really meant it. After all, what could an Inspector of Taxes (Assessment Section) see in an eighteen-year-old comptometer operator? How stuck-up she'd been, congratulating herself on being the first girl in the office Mr Huws-Evans had ever asked out. Just then a tall man who'd been standing close by took off his beige mackintosh hat with a drill-like movement, keeping his elbow close to his chest. It was Mr Huws-Evans.

'Hallo, Gloria,' he said. He watched her for a bit, a smile showing round the curly stem of the pipe he was biting. Then he added: 'Didn't you recognize me, Gloria?'

'Sorry, Mr Huws-Evans, I sort of just didn't see you.' The hat and the pipe had put her off completely, and she was further confused by being called Gloria twice already.

He nodded, accepting her apology and explanation. He put his hat on again with a ducking gesture, then removed his pipe. 'Shall we go in? Don't want to miss the News.'

While Mr Huws-Evans bought two two-and-fourpennies

Gloria noticed he was carrying a string bag full of packets of
potato crisps. She wondered why he was doing that.

It was very dark inside the cinema itself, and Mr Huws-
Evans had to click his fingers for a long time, and tremendously
loudly, before an usherette came. The Odeon was often full
on a Saturday when the football team was playing away, and
Gloria and Mr Huws-Evans couldn't help pushing past a lot
of people to get to their seats. A good deal of loud sighing,
crackling of sweet-packets and uncoiling of embraces marked
their progress. At last they were settled in full view of the
screen, on which the Duke of Edinburgh was playing polo.
Mr Huws-Evans asked Gloria loudly whether she could see all
right, and when she whispered that she could he offered her a
chocolate. 'They're rather good,' he said.

Almost nothing happened while the films were shown. The
main feature was on first. As soon as Gloria could tell that it
was old-fashioned she was afraid she wouldn't enjoy it. Nobody did anything in it, they just talked. Some of the talking
made Mr Huws-Evans laugh for a long time at a time, and once
or twice he nudged Gloria. When he did this she laughed too,
because it was up to her to be polite and not spoil his pleasure.
The film ended with a lot of fuss about a Gladstone bag
and people falling into each other's arms in a daft, put-on
way.

Gloria kept wondering if Mr Huws-Evans was going to put
his arm round her. She'd never yet gone to the pictures in
male company without at least this happening, and usually
quite a lot more being tried on, but somehow Mr Huws-Evans
didn't seem the man for any of that. He was older than her
usual escorts, to start with, and to go on with there was something about that mackintosh hat and that string bag which
made it hard to think of him putting his arm round anyone,
except perhaps his mother. Once she caught sight of his hand
dangling over the arm of the seat towards her, and she moved
her own hand carefully so that he could take hold of it easily if
he wanted to, but he didn't. He leaned rather closer to her to
light her cigarettes than he strictly needed to, and that was all.

After a pair of tin gates had been shown opening in a slow

and dignified way, there was about half an hour of advertisements while everybody whistled the tunes that were playing. The cereals and the detergents came up, then a fairly long and thorough episode about razor-blades. During it Mr Huws-Evans suddenly said: 'It's a damned scandal, that business.'

'What's that, then?'

'Well, all this business about the modern shave. All these damned gadgets and things. It's just a way of trying to get you to use a new blade every day, that's all.'

'Oh, I get you. You mean because the –'

'Mind you, with the kind of blade some of these firms turn out you've got to use a new blade. I grant them that.' He laughed briefly. 'If you don't want to skin yourself getting the beard off, that is. And of course they don't give a damn how much they spend on publicity. It's all off tax. Doesn't really cost them a bean.'

Gloria was going to say 'How's that, then?' but Mr Huws-Evans's manner, that of one with a comprehensive explanation on instant call, warned her not to. She said instead: 'No, of course it doesn't.'

He looked at her with mingled scepticism and wistfulness, and ended the conversation by saying violently: 'Some of these firms.'

While the lights went down again, Gloria thought about this brief exchange. It was just the kind of talk older men went in for, the sort of thing her father discussed with his buddies when they called to take him down to the pub, things to do with the Government and pensions and jobs and the Russians, things that fellows who went dancing never mentioned. She saw, on the other hand, that that kind of talk wasn't only tied up in some way with getting old, it also had to do with money and a car, with speaking properly and with being important. So a girl would show herself up for a lump with no conversation and bad manners if she gave away to an older man the fact that uninteresting things didn't interest her. Next time Mr Huws-Evans got on to them she must do better.

The second film promised to be full of interesting things. There were some lovely dresses, the star looked just like another star Gloria had often wished she looked like, and there was a scene in a kind of flash night-club with dim lights, men in tail coats and a modern band. The star was wearing a terrific evening dress with sequins and had a white fur round her shoulders. A man with a smashing profile sitting at the bar turned and saw her. Her eyes met his for a long moment. Gloria swallowed and leant forward in her seat.

Mr Huws-Evans nudged Gloria and said: 'Don't think much of this, do you? What about some tea?'

'Oh, we haven't got to go yet, have we?'

'Well, we don't want to sit through this, do we?'

Gloria recollected herself. 'No, right you are, then.'

They moved effortfully back along the row, taking longer this time because some of the embraces were slower in un-coiling. In the foyer, Gloria said: 'Well, thank you very much, Mr Huws-Evans, I enjoyed the film ever so much,' but he wasn't listening; he was looking wildly about as if he'd just found himself in a ladies' cloakroom, and beginning to say: 'The crisps. I've left them inside.'

'Never mind, don't you worry, it won't take a minute fetching them. I don't mind waiting at all.'

He stared out at her from under the mackintosh hat, which he'd pulled down for some reason so that it hid his eyebrows. 'I shan't be able to remember the seat. You come too, Gloria. Please.'

After a lot more finger-clicking inside they found the row. In the beam of the usherette's torch Gloria saw that their seats were already occupied. Even more slowly than before, Mr Huws-Evans began shuffling sidelong away from her; there was some disturbance. Gloria, waiting in the aisle, turned and looked at the screen. The man with the profile was dancing with the star now and all the other people had gone back to their tables and were watching them. Gloria watched them too, and had forgotten where she was when a moderate uproar slowly broke out and slowly moved towards her. It was Mr Huws-Evans with the crisps, which were rustling and crunch-ing like mad. Men's voices were denouncing him, some of them loudly and one of the loud ones using words Gloria didn't like, in fact one word was the word she called 'that word'. Her cheeks went hot. Mr Huws-Evans was saying things like 'Very sorry, old boy' and 'Hurts me as much as it hurts you,' and every so often he laughed cheerily. Everywhere people were calling 'Ssshh.' Gloria couldn't think of anything to do to help.

A long time later they were outside again. It was clear at once that the rain had stopped holding off hours ago. Mr Huws-Evans took her arm and said they'd better run for it, and that was what they did. They ran a long way for it, and fast too, so that the high heels were doing some terrible slipping and skidding. Opposite Woolworth's Gloria nearly did the splits, but Mr Huws-Evans prevented that, and was just as effective when she started a kind of sliding football tackle towards a lady in bifocal glasses carrying a little boy. That was just outside Bevan & Bevan's, and Gloria didn't mind it much because she'd guessed by now that they were going to Dalessio's, a fairly flash Italian restaurant frequented by the car-owning classes – unless, of course, they were making for Cwmbwrla or Portardulais on foot.

There was a queue in Dalessio's and Gloria panted out the news that she was going to the cloakroom, where there was another, but shorter, queue. While she waited her turn she felt her hair, which must have been looking dreadful, and wondered about her face, to which she'd applied some of the new liquid make-up everyone was talking about. She was glad to find, in due time, that she hadn't been looking too bad. Touching up with the liquid stuff didn't quite provide the amazing matt finish the advertisements described, in fact she wondered if she didn't look a bit like one of the waxworks she'd seen that time in Cardiff, but there was no time to re-do it and it must surely wear off a little after a bit. She gazed longingly at the ear-rings in her bag, and at the new mascara kit, but these must certainly wait. Taking a last peep at herself, she reflected gratefully, as her father had often exhorted her to do, that she was very lucky to be quite pretty and have all that naturally curly naturally blonde hair.

Mr Huws-Evans had a table for two when she joined him.

He took the bag of crisps off her chair and laid them reverently at his side. Gloria thought he seemed very attached to them. What did he want them for, and so many of them too? It was a puzzle. Perhaps he guessed her curiosity, because he said: 'They're for the party. They said I was to get them.'

'Oh, I see. Who'll be there? At the party? You did tell me when you asked me, but I'm afraid I've forgotten.'

'Not many people you'll know, I'm afraid. There'll be Mr Pugh, of course, from Allowances, and his wife, and Miss Harry from Repayments, and my brother – you've met him, haven't you? – and my dentist and his, er, and his friend, and two or three of my brother's friends. About a dozen altogether.'

'It sounds lovely,' Gloria said. A little tremor of excitement ran through her; then she remembered about poise. She arranged herself at the table like one of the models who showed off jewellery on TV, and purposely took a long while deciding what to have when the waitress came, though she'd known ever since passing Bevan & Bevan's that she was going to have mixed grill, with French fried potatoes. She was soon so lost in thoughts of the party and in enjoying eating that it was like a voice in a dream when Mr Huws-Evans said:

'Of course, the real difficulties come when we have to decide whether something's income or capital.'

Gloria looked up, trying not to seem startled. 'Oh yes.'

'For instance,' Mr Huws-Evans went on, drawing a long fishbone from his mouth, 'take the case of a man who buys a house, lives in it for a bit and then sells it. Any profit he might make wouldn't be assessable. It's capital, not income.'

'So he wouldn't have to pay tax on it, is that right?'

'Now for goodness' sake don't go and get that mixed up with the tax on the property itself, the Schedule A tax.'

'Oh yes, I've heard of that. There were some figures I –'

'That still has to be paid.' He leaned forward in an emphatic way. 'Unless the man is exempt of course.'

'Oh yes.'

'Now it'd be much easier, as you can imagine, to catch him on the sale of several houses. But even then we'd need to show that there was a trade. If the chap buys them as investments, just to get the rents, well then you couldn't catch him if he sold out later at a profit. There'd be no trade, you see.'

'No.' Gloria swallowed a mushroom-stalk whole. 'No trade.'

'That's right.' He nodded and seemed pleased, then changed his tone to nonchalant indulgence. 'Mind you, even the profit on an isolated transaction could be an income profit. There was the case of three chaps who bought some South African brandy, had it shipped over here and blended with French brandy, and sold it at a profit. But the Court still said there was a trade. They'd set up a selling organization.'

'Ah, I get it.'

'You'll be perfectly all right just so long as you remember that income tax is a tax on income.'

Gloria felt a little dashed when Mr Huws-Evans found nothing to add to his last maxim. She hadn't spoken up enough and shown she was taking an interest. He couldn't just go on talking, with nobody helping to make it a proper conversation. And yet – what could she have said? It was so hard to think of things.

Mr Huws-Evans launched off again soon and she cheered up. He questioned her about herself and her parents and friends and what she did in the evenings. He watched her with his big brown eyes and tended to raise his eyebrows slowly when she got near the end of each bit she said. Then, before asking his next question, he'd let his eyes go vacant, and drop his jaw without opening his mouth at all, and nod slightly, as if each reply of hers was tying up, rather disturbingly, with some fantastic theory about her he'd originally made up for fun: that she was a Communist spy, say, or a goblin in human form. During all this he dismantled, cleaned, reassembled, filled and lit his pipe, finally tamping down the tobacco with his thumb and burning himself slightly.

At last it was time to go. In the street Gloria said: 'Well, thank you very much, Mr Huws-Evans, I enjoyed the food ever so much,' but he wasn't listening; he was rubbing his chin hard with some of his fingers, and beginning to say:

'Shave. Got to have a shave before the party. That blade this morning.'

They boarded a bus and went a long way on it. Mr Huws-Evans explained, quoting figures, that a taxi wasn't worthwhile and that he personally was damned if he was going to lay out all that cash on a car simply to make a splash and impress a few snobs. He paid the conductor with coins from a leather purse that did up with two poppers. This purse, Gloria thought, was somehow rather like the mackintosh hat and the string bag with the crisps. After doing up the purse and putting it safely away Mr Huws-Evans said that his digs, where the shave was going to happen, were quite near Mr Pugh's house, which was where the party was going to happen. He added that this would give them just nice time.

They got off the bus and walked for a few minutes. The rain had stopped and the sun was out. Gloria cheered up again, and didn't notice at first when Mr Huws-Evans suddenly stopped in the middle of the pavement. He was looking about in rather the same way as he'd done in the foyer of the Odeon. He said: 'Funny. I could have sworn.'

'What's the matter, then?'

'Can't seem to remember the right house. Ridiculous of me, isn't it? Just can't seem to remember at all.'

'Not your digs it isn't, where you can't remember, is it?'

'Well yes, my digs. This is it. No, there's no T.V. aerial.'

'Never mind, what's the number?'

'That's the silly part. I don't know the number.'

'Oh, but you must. How ever do you manage with letters and things? Come on, you must know. Try and think, now.'

'No good. I've never known it.'

'What?'

'Well, you see, the landlady's got one of those stamp things to stamp the address at the top of the notepaper and I always use that. And then when I get a letter I just see it's for me and that's all I bother about, see?' He said most of this over his shoulder in the intervals of trying to see through some lace curtains. Then he shook his head and walked on, only to bend forward slightly with hands on knees, like a swimmer waiting for the starting-pistol, and stare at a photograph of a terrier which someone had arranged, thoughtfully turned outward, on a windowsill. 'The number's got a three in it, I do know that,' he said then. 'At least I think so.'

'How do you manage as a rule?'

'I know the house, you see.'

Mr Huws-Evans now entered a front garden and put his eye to a gap in the curtains. Quite soon a man in shirtsleeves holding a newspaper twitched the curtain aside and stood looking at him. He was a big man with hair growing up round the base of his neck, and you could guess that he worked at some job where strength was important. Mr Huws-Evans came out of the garden, latching its gate behind him. 'I don't think that's the one,' he said.

'Come on, why not just knock somewhere and ask?'

'Can't do that. They'd think I was barmy.'

Eventually Mr Huws-Evans recognized his house by its bright red door. 'Eighty-seven,' he murmured, studying the number as he went in. 'I must remember that.'

Gloria sat in the sitting-room, which had more books in it than she'd ever seen in a private house before, and looked at the book Mr Huws-Evans had dropped into her lap before going up to have his shave. It was called *Income Taxes in the Commonwealth*, and he'd said it would probably interest her.

She found it didn't do that and had gone to see if there were any interesting books in the bookcase when the door opened and an old lady looked in. She and Gloria stared at each other for about half a minute, and Gloria's cheeks felt hot again. The old lady's top lip had vertical furrows and there was something distrustful about her. She gave a few grunts with a puff of breath at the beginning of each one, and went out. Gloria didn't like to touch the bookcase now and told herself that the party would make everything worthwhile.

When Mr Huws-Evans came back he had a big red patch on his neck. 'These razor-blade firms,' he said bitterly, but made no objection when Gloria asked if she could go and wash her hands. He even came to the foot of the stairs to show her the right door.

The liquid make-up looked fine, the mascara went on like distemper on a wall and the ear-rings were just right now. She only hoped her white blouse and rust cocktail-length skirt, the only clothes she had that were at all evening, were evening enough. When she came out the old lady was there, about thirty inches away. This time she gave more puffing grunts than before and started giving them sooner. She was still giving them when Gloria went downstairs. But then Mr Huws-Evans, as soon as he saw her, jumped up and said: 'You look absolutely stunning, Gloria,' so that part was worthwhile.

After they'd left, what Gloria had been half-expecting all along happened, though not in the way she'd half-expected. It now appeared that they were much too early, and Mr Huws-Evans took her into a park for a sit-down. Before long he said: 'You know, Gloria, it means a lot to me, you coming out with me today.'

This was hard to answer, so she just nodded.

'I think you're the prettiest girl I've ever been out with.'

'Well, thank you very much, Mr Huws-Evans.'

'Won't you call me Waldo? I wish you would.'

'Oh no, I don't think I could, really.'

'Why not?'

'I . . . I don't think I know you well enough.'

He stared at her with the large brown eyes she'd often admired in the office, but which she now thought looked soft. Sadly, he said: 'If only you knew what I feel about you, Gloria, and how much you mean to me. Funny, isn't it? I couldn't have guessed what you were going to do to me, make me feel, I mean, when I first saw you.' He lurched suddenly towards her, but drew back at the last minute. 'If only you could feel for me just a tiny bit of what I feel for you, you've no idea what it would mean to me.'

An approach of this kind was new to Gloria and it flustered her. If, instead of all this daft talk, Mr Huws-Evans had tried to kiss her, she'd probably have let him, even in this park place; she could have handled that. But all he'd done was make her feel foolish and awkward. Abruptly, she stood up. 'I think we ought to be going.'

'Oh, not yet. Please. Please don't be offended.'

'I'm not offended, honest.'

He got up too and stood in front of her. 'I'd give anything in the world to think that you didn't think too hardly of me. I feel such a worm.'

'Now you're not to talk so silly.'

When it was much too late, Mr Huws-Evans did try to kiss her, saying as he did so: 'Oh, my darling.'

Gloria side-stepped him. 'I'm not your darling,' she said decisively.

After that neither spoke until they arrived at the house where the party was. Mr Huws-Evans's daft talk, Gloria thought, was to be expected from the owner of that mackintosh hat – which he still wore.

When Mr Huws-Evans's brother caught sight of her their eyes met for a long moment. It was because of him – she'd seen him once or twice when he called in at the office – that she'd accepted Mr Huws-Evans's invitation. Originally she'd intended just to look at him across the room while she let Mr Huws-Evans talk to her, but after what had happened she left Mr Huws-Evans to unpack his crisps and put them in bowls while the brother (it was funny to think that he was Mr Huws-Evans too, in a way) took her across the room, sat her on a sofa and started talking about interesting things.

企鹅丛书

英国短篇小说精选（二）

克里斯托弗·多利 编

*

外文出版社出版
（北京百万庄路24号）
世界知识印刷厂印刷
中国国际图书贸易总公司发行
1989年（36开）英文第一版（中国版）
ISBN 7-119-00885-4/I·142（外）
10-E-2408
00400